Martine Oborne li
spent most of her
she was a director of Rothschilds. She
daughters and two sons.

She is the author of *Mother Love* and *Baby Love*,
also published by Piatkus.

Praise for Martine Oborne:

'sharply observed, engaging and, best of all,
a satisfying old-fashioned denouement'
Daily Mail

'A lively novel that takes a light-hearted look
at the pitfalls of working mothers'
Woman's Own

'A sparkling novel that's touching, credible
and relevant'
Publishing News

Also by Martine Oborne:

Mother Love
Baby Love

Children's Books

Princess Lullaby & the Magic Word
Juice the Pig
I Love You More
One Gorgeous Baby

Getting Even

MARTINE OBORNE

PIATKUS

ᕼᕼ   Visit the Piatkus website!   ᕼᕼ

Piatkus publishes a wide range of exciting fiction and non-
fiction, including books on health, mind body & spirit, sex,
self-help, cookery, biography and the paranormal. If you want to:

- read descriptions of our popular titles
- buy our books over the internet
- take advantage of our special offers
- enter our monthly competition
- learn more about your favourite Piatkus authors

visit our website at:

www.piatkus.co.uk

All the characters in this book are fictitious and any resemblance to
real persons, living or dead, is entirely coincidental.

Copyright © 2002 by Martine Oborne

First published in Great Britain in 2002 by
Judy Piatkus (Publishers) Ltd of
5 Windmill Street, London W1T 2JA
email: info@piatkus.co.uk

The moral right of the author has been asserted

A catalogue record for this book is available from the British Library

ISBN 0 7499 3289 9

Set in Palatino by Palimpsest Book Production Limited,
Polmont, Stirlingshire
Printed and bound in Great Britain by
Mackays of Chatham plc, Chatham, Kent

To my sister

PART I

Twenty-four – fat, single and spitting blood

Chapter One

Of course, she should have seen it coming a mile away, thought Polly. It was classic Adele, absolutely A1 fucking classic Adele.

She stood up and saw that she had been sitting on a big lump of black tar. She rubbed at the stain it had left on the seat of her jeans but it just smeared and made her fingers all sticky.

No one else would have believed Adele could do such a thing but *she* should have known. Of all people, surely Polly had learnt by now what Adele was capable of. After all, they were twin sisters.

Polly plodded further down the beach. It was deserted except for a small boy at the water's edge. She stopped and watched him for a few minutes as he played, crouched with his back towards her. Most of time he was stationary but, every now and then, he would scuttle crab-like a few yards further along the shore.

Polly had no great interest in working out what he was doing and lifted her eyes to the bleak horizon where grey sea met grey sky. She had walked the length of the beach a dozen times at least going over and over what had happened but she still came to the same conclusion. It was unforgivable. She would never forgive Adele and she would never rest until she got her own back.

She stumbled on a rock and fell heavily on one side. It had been such a rush packing for Ned's house that she had forgotten to bring any sensible shoes. Polly took off her high-heeled boots and turned up her jeans. She knew that subtracting four inches from her height made her look dumpier than ever but why should she care? What did it matter any more? There was no one there to see her. Or no one that she cared about. The only man she wanted was miles away, hundreds of miles away, and Polly shuddered to think what he might be doing.

She stood up and walked on. The sand was cold and wet and the wind froze her face and ears but the pain was almost welcome as a distraction from her thoughts.

Polly noticed that the boy was moving in the same direction as she was but he was oblivious to her presence. He seemed to be making rows and rows of tiny sandcastles. The ones he had made perhaps only fifteen or twenty minutes earlier were already being swept away by the incoming tide.

It reminded Polly of the bucket and spade holidays she had had with her parents as a kid. They had often gone to beaches like this one but not in Yorkshire, always Devon. Her mother seemed to have a thing about Devon. Most of the neighbours went to the Costa Brava but Mum said that Spain was for the riff-raff – Devon was a much *nicer* place for a holiday. Polly smiled as she remembered how sometimes they had arrived on the sand dressed as though they were embarking on a polar expedition. Even in pouring rain and howling wind, they had still gone to the beach every day.

Polly and Adele had not minded much. There was nothing else to do in Devon and, of course, they had both loved the ponies. Every morning, Polly's dad would give them enough money for two rides each. Adele would take both of hers at once but Polly liked to save the second one until just before it was time to go back to the guesthouse. It gave her something to look forward to all day.

The ponies were small and for children only. When Polly was riding, she loved the rough warm solidity of the pony's back and sides against the flesh of her legs. She loved to stroke its matted oily mane and feel the strong curve of its neck. Until one day when everything was spoiled.

She and Adele must have been about ten or eleven at the time. It was the first day of the holiday and, as soon as they got their money, the girls ran off as usual towards the place where the pony rides started. Adele had always been really good at running and got there first. Polly had been plump even then and found it hard to keep up. Adele was already seated on her ride when Polly came panting up to join her.

'Sorry love,' said the pony ride man, grasping Polly by the shoulder. 'You're too old for the ponies.'

'I'm not,' Polly replied, wriggling free and running up to a beautiful white pony with a long shaggy mane. She patted the animal's neck. 'You let my sister on and she's my twin. Aren't you, Adele?'

Polly remembered Adele giggling, or sniggering perhaps, and suddenly feeling afraid that her sister would deny this. But it didn't matter. The man had

5

made up his mind and came over and took the pony's reins from Polly's hands.

'Sorry love,' he repeated. 'I should have said, "You're too big." Your sister's much lighter than you are. I'm afraid that you are just too heavy.' He emphasised the last two words as he led Polly's pony towards another child and Polly had slunk away feeling mortified.

But it was true. She had always been bigger than Adele and still was. Adele was probably a size eight or ten while Polly was a good size sixteen and at least three inches shorter than her sister.

Even the euphoria of going out with Charles for the past year had done nothing to help Polly lose weight. Other women seemed miraculously to shed pounds when they fell in love. But not Polly. She wondered now whether it would have made a difference to the way things had turned out if she had been a stone or two lighter. Charles had always said he liked her the way she was, that he found her curves sexy.

Polly put her hand inside her coat and pinched the roll of fat that overhung the top of her jeans. Sexy. She almost laughed. She was about as sexy as the Michelin man's mother, she thought to herself, recalling a nickname Adele had once given her.

Polly's mother, Sue, had rarely criticised Adele when she teased her sister about her weight but Polly's father always came to her defence. 'She's a strapping young woman,' he would say. 'Built like her old man is our Pamela.' Polly remembered how he would accompany these remarks with a friendly slap on some amply covered area of her body. (He always insisted on calling Polly by her real name, no matter how much she begged him not to.)

Polly wandered on down the beach. Adele had always been the slimmer and prettier twin. She even had a more beautiful name. Polly often wondered how her parents came to select Adele and Pamela as names for their twin daughters. One name was classy and sophisticated, the other was drab and conjured up images of spinsters and Sunday School teachers. It was as though from the word go Polly had been destined to stay forever in her sister's shadow. And, to top it all, Adele was also far cleverer than Polly.

John Taylor used to read to his daughters from a big history book every night. He had left school without taking a single public examination but Polly's father had an innate patriotism and loved British history – it was quite amazing the things he knew and he was constantly urged by his friends to put his name forward for TV quiz shows.

Polly remembered the big history book still. It had a frayed blue-grey cover and gold curly writing on the spine. It had been called *Our Island Story* or something like that and Polly's heart would sink as she watched her father lift it off the shelf. Before he started reading, John would test her and Adele on what they had listened to the night before. Adele remembered everything whereas Polly was useless. On one occasion, her father had asked who had been conquered by the Vikings and Polly had replied the Anglo-Sexuals. Adele had teased her mercilessly for months.

Then Polly remembered their first day at school. They had only been five years old but she could still see the headmaster in her mind now, proudly showing them the pictures hanging on his study wall.

'I bet you don't know who that is,' he said, pointing to one particular portrait.

Polly had shaken her head but Adele stood on her tiptoes and piped up immediately.

'It's Nelson,' she said.

'Quite right, quite right. And do you know who Nelson was?' asked the headmaster, clearly poised to give them a lecture on the subject.

'I know nearly all about Nelson,' said Adele. 'I'll tell you as much as I can.' She paused and took a deep breath. 'Well, he fought in the Battle of Trafalgar and his name was Horatio and he died in eighteen hundred and five and was buried in brandy.'

The headmaster and Polly both stared at Adele as though she had suddenly grown antennae or something. Eventually, the headmaster found the words to congratulate Adele on her knowledge and from that day on she was considered the most intelligent child in the school by every member of staff. Polly, by comparison, was a dullard.

Things did not improve as the girls had grown older. Polly was so outshone by Adele that she generally avoided going out with her sister. Needless to say, Polly was the one who managed to develop both acute acne and myopia. She remembered going to a party with Adele once when she was fourteen and refusing to wear her thick-lensed spectacles. It was so dark at the party that Polly could hardly see a thing. The food was all on a big table and when she went to get something she found herself standing next to a boy she really liked. She took some pâté and spread it over a cracker. The boy couldn't take his eyes off her as she did this. It was only when Polly put the

8

cracker to her lips and tasted chocolate truffle that she realised why. The boy burst out laughing and Adele said it served her right for being so vain and not wearing her glasses.

After that, Polly begged her father to get her some contact lenses. Her mother said it was a waste of money as Polly would never be a beauty but her father got the lenses.

Polly rubbed her eyes as she continued her walk. The wind was getting stronger and sand blew in her face and made her eyes stream. Or was she crying? She rubbed the tears from her face and blew her nose.

But it wasn't really sad, thought Polly, so much as pathetic. In fact, she had been pathetic all her life when it came to Adele. She had never stood up to her sister.

She thought back with a shudder to the Gotta Gotta game they had played as kids. It worked like this. When you really wanted something badly, when you had just *gotta* have it, you said 'Gotta Gotta' and had to pay a forfeit. If Polly wanted to play with one of Adele's toys, Adele might ask her sister to stand on one leg for ten minutes. If Adele wanted to watch one of Polly's videos, Polly might ask her sister to cluck like a chicken all around the garden. If it was something really big, the ultimate Gotta Gotta forfeit might be applied – this was to run to the corner of the street, touch the postbox and run back. Stark naked except for pants.

As they grew up, Polly's mother started to buy Adele really fantastic clothes. She didn't like to waste too much money on Polly but Adele had been blessed with good looks, said Sue, and she really ought to make the best of them. So, as a teenager, Polly was often desperate to borrow her sister's clothes – at least, the ones she could squeeze into. For this, Adele always sought to extract the ultimate Gotta Gotta forfeit. At first it was not too bad. The Taylors lived in a quiet street and their house was only two from the corner. If you made a good recce before you set off, you were more than likely to get to the postbox and back without anyone spotting you.

But Polly's figure was developing fast. In her early teens, Adele's chest was still flat as a board while Polly was in a C cup. 'I think we should revise the ultimate Gotta Gotta forfeit to allow pants *and* a top,' Polly had suggested but Adele would not hear of it.

One day, Polly simply had to borrow Adele's new shoulder-padded dress and decided to take on the ultimate Gotta Gotta challenge. She stood at the gate in her dressing gown and looked nervously up and down the street. There was no one about and so she took a deep breath, dropped the gown and ran. It could have taken no more than ten seconds before she was back inside the gate and reclothed in her dressing gown. But then she heard a sharp tapping sound and looked up to a bedroom window, the window of her parents' room, and realised her mistake. Polly had forgotten to check where her mother was and Sue had clearly been watching from the window and had seen everything. Adele thought it was a huge joke and later pretended to know nothing about the Gotta Gotta game when Polly tried to explain.

Which was classic Adele, thought Polly. She remembered sitting at home in her room that night fuming with rage. Polly no longer had need of the shoulder-padded dress since she had not, of course, been allowed to go out with her friends as a punishment for her appalling behaviour. Sue had been beside herself with shock and outrage. 'It was disgusting, John. She's almost a grown woman – her breasts were bouncing about all over the place. Can you imagine what the neighbours must think?' She had then turned to Polly. 'And then you make up a whole pack of lies to try to get poor Adele into trouble too.'

'I'm sorry,' Adele had said to Polly later. 'But if I'd told them the truth they might not have let me go out either.' Classic Adele.

Back on Filey beach, over ten years later, Polly shivered. All in all, it was surprising that it had taken her so long to really hate her sister as she did now, she thought, pulling her coat more tightly around her. But it was not too late.

She picked up a large green stone streaked with red and pounded it into the palm of her other hand. She would get her own back on Adele or die.

There must have been a murderous look on her face as Polly thought this because, the next thing she knew, Ned had grabbed her from behind and was screaming, 'Help! Police! I've found a crazed psychopath on the beach.'

Polly spun round and she had to admit it was a comfort to see Ned's big warm smile.

'What on earth have you done to your face?' he cried.

Polly rubbed her cheeks with her hand.

'No,' laughed Ned. 'That's only making it worse. You've got black marks everywhere.'

11

'It must be the tar,' said Polly.

'You look like you're on the warpath.' Ned wiped Polly's face with the sleeve of his sweater. 'What's this lethal weapon?' he added, taking the stone from Polly's hand.

'I found it on the beach.'

Ned examined it closely. 'It looks like a bloodstone.'

'Most appropriate. The perfect murder weapon – it already looks as though it's covered in blood.'

They laughed.

'You'd better throw it away,' said Ned but Polly took the stone and slid it inside her pocket.

They had stopped walking and Ned was watching the boy on the beach.

'I came down to pick up Frankie,' he said.

'Is that Frank on the beach?' Polly looked at the boy who was still crouched over his work.

'Yes,' said Ned. 'He loves it here, thank heavens. He's a complete brat at home and always in trouble at school.'

'What's he doing?'

'He sort of carves pictures out of the sand. Come down and have a look – they're quite good actually.'

Ned slipped an arm round Polly's shoulder and they walked towards the water.

'Does it help, getting away – being here for a few days?' he asked.

'Oh yes, it helps enormously. I think, if you hadn't whisked me away, I really might have committed murder.'

They sat down a few metres from Frank and watched the boy as he worked. Ned started to make a castle in the sand with his hands.

'It must have been a horrible shock,' he said. 'Do you want to talk about it?'

'Not much.' Polly started building her own little castle. Ned's was tall and straight but hers was squat and wonky. 'It's just that – well, for the first time in my life I had everything I wanted. Charles was so special. I no longer felt second to Adele or jealous of her.'

'You don't need to feel second to Adele.'

'I do. I'm short, fat and ugly and stupid – when you put me beside my sister. There's no denying it.'

Ned looked at her and smiled but did not attempt to contradict the remark, Polly noticed miserably.

'There are lots of good things going for you, Polly,' he said. Polly glared.

'There's your new job at the *Daily Globe*, for a start. You must be pleased about that.'

'I suppose,' said Polly. She poked windows in the walls of her castle and a little crooked door. Ned was right. She had been looking forward to starting her new job. She had been really excited but now it did not seem to matter so much. 'You don't understand. My career is never going to be that important to me. The only thing I really want is to find the right man and settle down.' She smacked the sand from her fingers and rubbed tears from her eyes. 'I never thought I would find someone as wonderful as Charles—'

'Christ, Polly,' interrupted Ned. 'You're only, what, twenty-four? You'll find someone else. Perhaps someone better.'

Polly's nose was running. She wiped it and buried her face in her scarf. 'No, Charles was the one. There'll never be anyone else.'

'Well, it's not so bad being single,' said Ned. Polly

13

watched him build his tower taller and taller. It looked like a scale model of the Empire State Building. 'I plan to stay that way my whole life. The only thing I really want is to make a success of my work, my writing. I can't stand it when my girlfriends start getting all needy and want the C-word.'

'The C-word?'

'You must know the C-word. It's what all women want.'

Polly shook her head.

'Cadbury's chocolate,' said Ned.

Polly laughed. A box of Milk Tray had certainly been her answer to many a dark day.

'Only joking. The C-word is commitment, of course.' Ned frowned at his tower in the sand. 'I don't want kids and caravans and Christmas bloody pudding. I want to stay free.'

'We couldn't be more different,' said Polly, forcing a smile.

Ned stood up. 'You need to make a break when you get back to London. Find somewhere else to live and stay away from Adele for a while. I'll help you look around, if you like. I might even know someone looking for a flatshare.'

'Thanks,' said Polly. 'You're right. I suppose I can't go on living in Adele's house.'

'You suppose? Aren't you certain?'

'Well, yes, of course. But I'll miss Minty.'

'Minty is Adele's responsibility and it's about time she realised it.' Ned bent down to smooth the sides of his castle.

'But I love her so much. In fact, it feels now like she's the only person I've got.'

As Polly said this, Ned looked down at her and held out his hand. 'Come on,' he said. 'Get up and we'll stamp on them.'

'What?'

'The sandcastles. It will help get rid of all that negative energy.' Ned jumped on his tower. He kicked and stamped until it was completely flat.

'Now your turn,' he said.

Polly jumped on her sandcastle and was amazed to find how exhilarating it was. She jumped and jumped until it was totally smashed.

'Does that feel better?'

Polly's face was quite flushed. She had to admit that she did feel a bit better and she could not help a genuine smile. Ned had been so sweet and yet she hardly knew him. He had just happened to call on the day it had all happened, when her whole world had come crashing down. Poor bloke, thought Polly, it was probably the last thing he wanted but he had been kind to her. He had picked up the pieces and suggested that she escaped for a few days to his parents' house in Yorkshire. He was probably itching to get back to London and his work.

'Let's drag Frank away,' said Ned, 'and then I know somewhere we can get a really good cup of hot chocolate.'

Polly picked up her boots and they trudged over to Frank who was putting the finishing touches to an enormous seagull that he had sculpted into the sand. Polly looked back at the line of works along the beach he had already completed. There were dogs and dinosaurs, spiders and crabs and other creatures that could not be readily identified.

'Don't you mind when the sea comes up and washes them all away?' asked Polly.

Frank stood up and stared at her. 'Not really. Anyway, I don't much like hanging on to things once they're done. I like starting again.'

Then they turned and walked, all three of them, back up the beach towards the street.

Frank was right, Polly acknowledged to herself. There was no point in hanging on to things – things that were over and finished – but, on the other hand, she could not bear to let go. She would never let go.

As the cold sea wind bit into her face, Polly squeezed the bloodstone in her pocket and resolved that one day she would get even with her sister. She would play Adele at her own game and win back Charles whatever way she could.

Chapter Two

Ned's mum, Margaret, was waiting for them when they got back.

'You poor love, I've never seen such a red nose,' she said. Frank grinned and started humming 'Rudolf the Red-Nosed Reindeer.' Margaret scowled at her younger son and took Polly by the arm. 'I put the kettle on the minute I saw you coming up the path. A nice cup of tea will soon warm you up.'

Ned went upstairs to his room and Frank followed Margaret and Polly to the kitchen.

'Be off with you, you mischief,' cried Margaret as Frank went straight to the fridge in search of something to eat. 'You'll be having your tea in half an hour and you can get your things ready for school tomorrow while you're waiting.'

'But I'm starving, Mum,' said Frank, extracting a chocolate biscuit and looking appealingly at his mother.

'Oh, go on then – but no more, mind,' said Margaret taking the tin of biscuits from Frank and putting it on the table. Frank scooted out of the room and Margaret smiled at Polly.

'Kids,' she said as she poured the water into the teapot and set it beside the biscuit tin in front of Polly.

17

'I'd better go and find a clean shirt for him or there'll be chaos in the morning.' She poured milk in a cup and gave it to Polly. 'You make yourself at home. Do you want me to call Ned down?'

'No, I'm fine, Mrs Butler.'

'Margaret,' insisted Margaret, taking the lid off the biscuit tin. 'I'll be back in a few minutes.'

Polly clasped her mug of tea and raised it to her lips. Ned's family had made her very welcome but she did feel rather an intruder. The Butlers' house was a small, modern semi on the outskirts of Scarborough. Somehow, when Ned had invited her to spend a few days at his parents' house in Yorkshire, she had expected something different. A big house and garden. She had not expected Ned to have to move into his kid brother's room while she slept in his bed.

Semi-consciously she took a chocolate biscuit from the tin. It was interesting that she had presumed Ned was rich just because he had been at Cambridge with Adele. In fact, Polly had spent a whole year sharing a flat with Ned and Adele at Cambridge but she had learnt next to nothing about him in those days. He would get up early to go rowing and was usually home late. When he did stay in, he spent most of his time in his room reading.

Polly took another biscuit. She now knew that Ned had gone to a big comprehensive in Scarborough and won a place to read English at Downing. His mother had been so proud of him, Ned had told Polly, that she had literally danced for joy when they received the news. Polly thought of a similar occasion when her own mother had heard that Adele had won her place to read history at Jesus. Sue had been delighted, of course, but she had said that she always knew that Adele would do it. Polly was the one who had gone running around the house like a lunatic crying, 'She's done it. She's done it. She's done it!' It had somehow seemed to compensate for her own disappointing A level results: a B grade in English and an F in French. There was no point in Polly trying to find a university, let alone Cambridge.

'Fish'n'chips,' said Ned as he came into the room. Polly wiped biscuit crumbs from her lips and looked in horror at the empty tin. 'If you're still hungry, that is.'

'Sorry,' said Polly. 'All that fresh air must have given me an appetite.'

Ned perched on the table and poured himself some tea. He was a big man and the kitchen was quite small so that he seemed to fill it almost entirely. He had rowed for Goldie, the Cambridge B boat, and still had a strong, broad physique. 'Well, you can't come to Yorkshire and not sample the world's best fish'n'chips.'

As he spoke Margaret came back into the room and Polly quickly picked up the lid of the biscuit tin but it was too late.

'Has Frank been in here? How many biscuits did that little monkey take?' she cried, pushing Ned off the table. Ned stood up and gave his mum a hug. She was short and very fat but he almost lifted her off the floor.

'It wasn't Frank,' he said.

'You!' laughed Margaret. 'This boy eats like a horse. He should be as fat as I am.' She smiled at Polly and bustled out of the room again.

'Thanks,' said Polly to Ned.

*

19

Polly got changed in Ned's room. It was small and untidy. Most of the space was occupied by a huge drum kit and there were books everywhere. One had a dried-up ham sandwich in the middle of it.

Polly rummaged in her bag for her new black leather jeans. Charles had bought them for her only three weeks ago, as a Christmas present, and she remembered him telling her how sexy she looked in them. And she had felt good in them. They were a change from the usual stretch denims that she wore.

Now it was a struggle to get the zip done up. They had been tight before Christmas but now they were a nightmare. Polly lay down on the floor and pulled in her stomach.

There was a tap at the door and Margaret's face appeared. Polly sat up abruptly, fat bulging over the top of her trousers.

'Sorry dear. I forgot to give you a message.'

'It's OK,' said Polly. 'Come in.' She got to her feet and pulled her shirt down over her jeans to hide the gaping zip.

'Do you need a hand there?'

'I think it's a hopeless case.'

'Would you like to borrow one of my girdles? They're very good.' Polly shook her head but Margaret had already disappeared. Polly wriggled out of the jeans and looked again in her bag. She had packed in a hurry and not brought any appropriate clothes. There was nothing else to do, she concluded, but to put her old denims on again with the tar stains all over the backside.

'Here, give it a try.' Margaret had returned and gave her what looked like an enormous pair of shiny cream cycling shorts. Polly did not want to offend Ned's mum and so she heaved the contraption up over her thighs and was amazed to find that the thing really was a miracle. Although the surplus flesh was now pushed up around her midriff and down around her knees, her stomach was completely flat. She squeezed back into the leather jeans. The zip did up effortlessly and when she pulled down her shirt, the bulge above her tummy did not show a bit.

'You look fantastic,' said Margaret.

'Thanks.'

Margaret smiled and turned to go. 'Oh, I almost forgot again. Your sister phoned while you were at the beach.'

'Adele?'

'Yes, I think that was the name.'

Polly's expression froze. She could hardly believe that her sister had the nerve to call her.

'You can use the phone by my bed,' said Margaret. 'It's a bit quieter there than in the hall where Frank is practising headers.'

'Thanks.'

Polly brushed her hair and tidied up her make-up. She had forgotten her blusher but that was no problem as her cheeks were burning at the thought of Adele daring to ring her. What on earth did she want to say? What on earth was there to say? For once, sorry was not going to be good enough.

Polly had no face powder and her nose was still shining horribly. She found a bottle of Lily of the Valley talcum powder in the bathroom and applied that. Her face was soon white with two bright red spots on each cheek, like the face of a character in a children's picture book.

It was then that she thought of Minty again and suddenly there was the sound of breaking glass downstairs, followed by Margaret ordering Frank out of the house. Perhaps something had happened to Minty? Adele was so selfish and irresponsible, it would not be that surprising if there had been an accident—

The thought filled her with dread. Polly had hardly spent a day away from Adele's daughter since she was born. She remembered the day that her mother had broken the news. 'If it had been you, Polly, I would not have been so surprised,' Sue had said. Polly's mum had always considered Polly something of a slut ever since the day she had come in unusually early from work and found Polly making out with a boy on the sofa. Polly had been sixteen and they had not really been doing much but her shirt had been undone to the waist and her bra was up around her neck. Her mum had been horrified.

'What's happened?' Polly had asked and her mother told her the whole story about Adele. Polly knew that her sister had been seeing one of her tutors at Cambridge and that their friendship was becoming something more serious. Oliver Bunk, Head of the History faculty at Jesus, was a married man and had a reputation for coming on to his students.

'She says he is going to leave his wife and they will get married before the baby is born,' said Sue. Polly put her arm around her mother.

'I suppose that will be all right,' continued Sue brightening up a little. 'I mean, I suppose he's really quite a catch – being a university don and every-thing.'

But Oliver Bunk did not leave his wife and, by the time Adele acepted that he was never going to, it was too late to have an abortion. Adele was nineteen years old and in the middle of her degree course.

'Having this baby will ruin her life,' said Sue. 'How will she cope looking after it?' It was the long Easter weekend, Polly remembered. She had been sitting with her parents, watching *The Sound of Music* on TV and nibbling her way through a whole chocolate egg, when the solution suddenly seemed obvious.

'I'll look after the baby for her,' she said.

'You?'

'Why not? I've got this dead-end job on the *Dulwich Observer* which is going nowhere. The baby's due in August and, by that time, Adele will only have one more year until she finishes her degree. I could go up to Cambridge, share her flat and look after the baby—'

'But Pamela,' broke in her father as the credits to the film started to roll. 'You are not Julie bloody Andrews. That's too much of a sacrifice. I think Adele has got herself into this situation and she must deal with it.'

'It wasn't entirely her fault,' said Sue.

'Look, don't argue,' said Polly. 'I wouldn't offer if I didn't want to do it. You know that I like kids. I'd really enjoy looking after a baby for a year.'

And so that was how Polly got to Cambridge. It was difficult, at first, being surrounded by all those clever and eccentric people. She had found it intimidating and had taken refuge in her role as Minty's nanny. Adele was working hard and there were all kinds of things she said she had to do in her free time, so Polly spent most of her days and evenings in the flat with her sister's baby.

At first, she was useless. She hadn't realised how much work it was looking after a small child. She remembered being up all night once with Minty crying. She couldn't work out what was wrong until the following morning when she changed the baby and found that her mascara wand had got stuck inside the baby's vest. It must have been horribly itchy for the poor child.

But somehow Polly and Minty got by and it was not long before Polly realised that she had fallen in love with little Minty.

'Her name is Araminta,' Adele would often say but to Polly she was Minty and always would be, thought Polly now, as she picked up the phone by Margaret Butler's bed.

Her heart was pounding as she punched out the numbers and she was relieved to find that the answerphone was on. Polly was in the middle of leaving a message when Adele picked up the phone. Her voice was breathless.

'Sorry, Poll,' she said. 'I was a bit tied up.'

'Why did you call me?' asked Polly. She just needed to check that all was well with Minty and then she would slam down the receiver.

'Well, I was just wondering how you are, er, and everything?' Adele was still breathing heavily.

'How do you think I am?'

'Sorry, I—'

'Don't bother,' said Polly. 'Just tell me that Minty is OK?'

'Well, actually, that's why I was ringing—'

'What? What's happened?' It had been troubling Polly ever since she had left London. Adele had become so dependent on her as Minty's nanny that now she was probably incapable of looking after her daughter by herself.

'Nothing serious,' said Adele. 'I mean she's quite well *physically*. It's just, well, she's very upset, of course, that you suddenly disappeared without even saying goodbye. She makes me read your note to her over and over and she cries all the time.'

Polly swallowed hard. She hated to think that she had hurt Minty. Dear Minty. It wasn't her fault that her mother was a bitch from hell.

'She keeps asking me when you are coming back.'

'I'm not,' said Polly. 'I can't. I can't go on living in your house after—'

'I know,' said Adele. 'It's just—'

Adele paused but Polly could hear her heavy breathing. She still had not quite recovered her breath.

'Perhaps you would just come back and explain things to her,' said Adele eventually. 'I'll keep out of your way.'

'Explain things?' Polly felt disgust. 'You want me to tell her the real reason why I left?'

'Well, no,' stammered Adele. 'I mean, it's just that I've never seen her in such a state. She cried herself to sleep tonight.'

Polly said nothing but a huge lump had formed in her throat. It was horrible to think that Minty was so upset and she longed to comfort her.

'I'll call her tomorrow in the morning and I'll come and see her as soon as I'm back in London.'

'Thanks,' said Adele.

'In the meantime,' Polly swallowed hard, 'tell her that I love her.'

She put down the phone quickly before she started to cry. Then she lay back on Margaret's bed and began to piece things together.

The answerphone had been on and Adele's phone was right beside her bed. Adele had been quite breathless when she answered, which was unusual. Adele was normally so cool and in control.

There could be no other explanation, thought Polly, except that she had called while Adele and Charles were having sex. Adele must have been desperate to speak to her to interrupt things and pick up the phone.

The thought of her sister having sex with Charles made Polly want to retch. It just wasn't fair. Charles had been the only lover Polly had really enjoyed. Sex with Charles had been incredible. She buried her head in Margaret's pillow and the only thing she could think of was Charles's penis. It had surprised Polly when she had first seen it and held it – in fact, it had amazed her. It was not that it was particularly long but it was fat, very fat. It was the fattest one Polly had ever seen in her life – not that she had seen that many. It was so fat, thought Polly, that her fingers did not meet when she put her hand round it.

Polly looked up as Ned suddenly appeared at the door.

'Coming?' he said.

Precisely, thought Polly, as she sat up, wiped her eyes and got back on her feet. Charles had the kind of penis that would even make an ice queen like Adele come. It was bad enough that her sister had stolen her man but the thought that she had got her hands on the most fantastic penis in the world as well was the final straw.

Chapter Three

Ned's dad insisted on giving them a lift into town.

'It's OK,' laughed Ned. 'We are old enough to get the bus on our own and I can just about remember my kerb drill.'

Keith said nothing but he took the car keys from his wife's outstretched hand and nodded towards the door.

'I'll pop your dinner back in the oven,' called Margaret, as Keith led the way to a small two-door car parked on the drive outside.

Polly told Ned to sit in the front passenger seat since he was much taller than she was and then she squeezed into the back. There was an ominous ripping sound which, once Polly was seated, she was relieved to find was only the zip of her jeans giving way a few ratchets.

As they drove, Ned flicked through a paperback he had brought with him.

'I can't find where I was,' he muttered. 'I know I left something marking my place in this book but someone must have taken it out.'

Polly glanced at the book and recognised it as the one that had contained the ham sandwich. She said nothing and they continued the journey in silence.

'Do you want me to pick you up later?' asked Keith when they pulled up outside the restaurant. It was called Generous George's.

'No thanks,' said Ned. 'After Polly's put away one of George's suppers, we'll never squeeze her back in the car again.'

'Thanks a lot,' said Polly, as Ned slammed the door shut and waved goodbye to his father.

'Only joking. But that car is ridiculously small – you should see it when all four us go on holiday in it.'

'Do you still go on holiday with your family?'

'If they'll let me,' said Ned as he opened the restaurant door. 'I'm usually so broke, it's the only option.'

'I think I'd rather stay at home than go away with my mum and dad.'

The room was loud with conversation and laughter and the air was thick and warm with the smell of fried food and crowded tables.

Ned led the way to a small table against the far wall. Polly took off her jacket and hung it on the back of her chair. On the wall there were framed photos of all the celebrities who had eaten in the restaurant. Most of the pictures included a large swarthy man, presumably the eponymous proprietor of Generous George's.

'That's Kevin Stanick,' said Ned, pointing to a photograph of a bearded, bespectacled little man who hardly came up to the proprietor's ample waistline. 'My hero. I always like to sit at this table next to him, if I can.'

Polly hesitated. She was used to Adele's friends talking about things and people she had never heard of. They were all so much cleverer than she was and she did not like to display her ignorance.

In normal circumstances she would have just smiled, changed the subject and let Ned's remark pass. But Ned was different. Polly felt far more relaxed with him and was sure that he would not make her feel stupid.

'Sorry,' she said. 'Who is Kevin Stanick?'

Ned opened his eyes wide and stared at Polly. 'Kevin Stanick? You mean you've never heard of Kevin Stanick?'

Polly blushed. Perhaps she had been wrong about Ned after all, she wondered, as she noticed the faces at nearby tables turning to stare at her.

'Of course you've never heard of Kevin Stanick,' continued Ned. 'I don't suppose there's a single person here tonight who's heard of Kevin Stanick.' He glowered at the couple sitting at the next table and they looked down at their plates but, by this time, it seemed that half the people in the restaurant had stopped eating and were looking at Ned and Polly.

'What about you?' said Ned, getting to his feet and going over to a black man wearing a red knitted beret. 'Do you know who Kevin Stanick is?' The man shrugged and his girlfriend, sitting opposite, burst into giggles.

'And you?' asked Ned, turning to the girl. The girlfriend stopped giggling and shook her head.

'I'll pay the bill of anyone here tonight,' said Ned, looking around him, 'anyone who can tell me who Kevin Stanick is.'

There was a buzz of interest in the restaurant at Ned's offer.

'Isn't he a striker for Aston Villa?' called a woman, sitting behind Polly.

'Don't be ridiculous,' said a man, probably her husband.

'An actor. Wasn't he in that film about a psychopathic driving instructor?' asked another man.

'No, that was Kevin Stanford,' corrected his partner.

'One of those TV chefs?'

'No,' interrupted a woman. 'Isn't he that ice skater – the one who skates with his labrador?'

Ned shook his head.

'That one-legged astronaut?' asked a man.

'I've got it,' cried the girlfriend of the man in the red beret. 'Remember that funny story in the papers about the bloke whose wife chopped off his balls and cooked them in a stew? That was him, wasn't it?' The girl's partner stared at her.

'That wasn't a funny story,' he said.

'And it isn't the right answer either,' said Ned.

Suddenly Generous George, the proprietor, who had been watching the scene from the other side of the counter, came round it into the room and manoeuvred his huge bulk surprisingly gracefully through the tables and over to Ned. He squinted at the picture and put his head on one side.

'I'll be blowed if I can remember myself,' he said. 'It must be at least ten years since that photo was taken – I look so slim.'

'Give up everyone?' asked Ned. There was a general murmur of resignation and defeat.

'Kevin Stanick is a screenwriter. One of the most successful screenwriters of all time.' Ned went on to list all the films that Stanick had written. There was a rising crescendo of comment among the audience as he went on. These were all films that they knew well and loved and yet no one had known who had written the screenplays.

Ned sat back down in his chair and turned to Polly. 'Sorry about that. It's just that people remember the director and the actors of a good film but never the poor bastard who wrote the script.'

'You seem to feel strongly about it,' said Polly.

'I do. Since my greatest ambition is to be a screenwriter myself. Of course, I can't hope to be in the Stanick league but I've always loved films and would love to write one and see it produced.'

'That would be fantastic.' Polly was amazed that Ned could have such a big ambition. Was it really possible that people, ordinary people, could just go out and be screenwriters? To her, Los Angeles and multi-million-dollar film contracts might as well exist on a different planet.

'It's a dream,' said Ned. 'But dreams do sometimes come true.'

They ordered fish and chips and tea and after a short while the food arrived at the table. It was only then that Polly realised how hungry she was again. It was about thirty hours since the whole dreadful thing with Charles and Adele had happened. The experience might have caused another woman to lose her appetite but, for Polly, it had had the contrary effect. It felt as though there was a gaping void inside her that, no matter how much she ate, could not be filled.

When they had almost finished eating, Polly realised that she had been so deeply absorbed in her own thoughts that she had not said a word during the whole meal. Ned must think she was unbelievably dull and rude and, after he had been so kind, she really should have made more of an effort to be sociable.

'Your parents are very nice,' she blurted out at random.

'Yes, they are,' said Ned.

'I haven't heard a cross word between them all the time I've been up here.'

'Well you've only been here one day.' Ned laughed as he put down his empty cup and poured more tea from the pot.

'My parents argue all the time,' said Polly. 'Always have.'

'All married people do.'

'Not like my parents. Dad's not so bad but Mum is dreadful. She finds fault with nearly everything that my father does. I think he embarrasses her.'

'All husbands embarrass their wives. And all wives embarrass their husbands.'

'God, you are so cynical about marriage, Ned.' Polly nearly added that she would never have been embarrassed by Charles but decided to let it go.

'Sorry,' said Ned.

'It's a class thing with Mum and Dad, I suppose,' said Polly. 'Mum works as a secretary at a local private school and all the mums there are very middle class. Her dad was a teacher and her mum was a midwife.'

'And your father – what does he do?'

Polly smiled. 'He's a film maker.'

'A film maker?' Ned almost choked on his tea.

'Yes. He makes CCTV films of people's drainage systems. He's a plumber.'

Ned laughed.

'Dad left school at fifteen and worked on a building

site. After a while, he got apprenticed to a plumber and learnt the trade. He set up his own business. It specialises in doing these CCTV films – often for big clients and Dad's done well with it. We've never really been short of money.'

'But your mother isn't happy?'

'No. Sometimes she seems very bitter towards Dad. It's not just the class thing, it's almost as though he has done something she can't forgive.'

'Does she talk about it?'

'God, never! Well, at least not to me. Perhaps she talks more to Adele – Adele has always been her favourite.' A frown set on Polly's face as she thought of her sister again.

'It's not all Adele's fault,' said Ned.

'Isn't it?'

'Well, I know it's painful but it was Charles's fault too, wasn't it?'

'Charles's fault?' asked Polly in a puzzled voice. It had not really occurred to her that she should blame Charles as well. But, perhaps, Ned was right. After all, Charles could easily, and should have, said no.

'But Adele always gets what she wants,' Polly heard herself say.

'She's an ambitious woman and a successful one, I'll grant you that,' said Ned. 'Out of all the crowd we went around with at Cambridge, Adele must be earning as much or more than the rest of us put together.'

'I don't care about her job or her money. Why did she have to take Charles, the only person I ever wanted?'

'It seems very cruel. But if Charles and Adele have

34

a thing for each other it's surely better to find out sooner—'

'Rather than later – after we were married,' Polly finished for him, her eyes filling with tears.

Ned reached across the table and took her hand. 'You poor thing. It was dreadful how it happened.' The tears poured down Polly's hot cheeks. 'After the way you'd helped Adele with Minty and everything, it's scarcely believable.'

A shadow fell over the table and Ned and Polly looked up to see Generous George beaming down at them. Polly quickly wiped her face and George started to collect their plates.

'Fancy me forgetting Kevin Stanick,' he said as he stacked Ned's plate with its last few remaining chips on top of Polly's empty one. 'Who would have thought it? And *Phantom Warrior* is one of my favourite movies.'

'I hope, if I ever get to be a screenwriter, you'll have a picture taken with me and you'll remember who I am.'

'Of course, of course, lad. A picture right here next to Stanick,' said Generous George, grinning at Polly, 'and with your missus in it too, if you like.'

Ned laughed. 'Now that's one thing I can be sure of. As Stanick once said: "If you want to be a success with your work, it's better to stay single."'

'You'd better not tell that to my old lady,' laughed George. 'She says I'd be nothing without her.'

Ned asked for the bill but Generous George lived up to his name and insisted it was on the house.

Polly pulled on her jacket and followed Ned out into the cold dark street.

'I thought tomorrow, we'd go to Scarborough's famous sweet factory?' said Ned. 'It's a really tacky place where they make huge sticks of shiny pink rock. The sort of stuff that makes your teeth ache just to look at it. And the smell is unbelievable – it's like wading through thick liquorice soup.'

'It sounds fun but don't you need to get back to London?'

'Not really. Do you?'

'My new job doesn't start until next Monday.'

'That's good.'

'But what about *your* work?' asked Polly. 'I don't want to be accused of putting the great career on hold.'

Ned laughed. 'Piss off. So long as you don't start demanding the C-word, I think I can spare a few days for a friend in need.'

'Thanks. In that case, I'd love to go to the sweet factory.'

'I thought so. But we'd better stop off somewhere and get you some bigger jeans first.' Ned glanced down at Polly's stomach and she looked down as well. To her horror, Polly saw that the zip of her jeans had now burst wide open and a huge dome of luminescent cream girdle protruded like a giant wart.

Chapter Four

A week later, Polly was back in London and wore a straight black skirt for her first day at the *Daily Globe*. It was a size fourteen and extremely tight. She was late and, as she ran as fast as she could along Holborn Viaduct and down into Snow Hill, she could not help worrying that the skirt would split.

She had not intended to stay at Adele's but Minty had been missing her so much that, when Polly arrived back on the Sunday evening and Minty was already asleep, she decided to stay over and see her niece before she went to nursery school the following morning.

Inevitably, Polly had ended up agreeing to drop Minty off at school and now she was running late. Minty had got a Sugar Puff wedged into one ear and it had taken precious minutes to dislodge. Then Polly had caught the wrong bus up from Minty's nursery and had had to walk – or run – much further than she expected. By the time Polly arrived at the front desk of the *Daily Globe*, she was panting for breath.

'Hello, I'm Polly Taylor,' she said, clasping her over-full bag to her chest like a shield. 'I'm starting work on the Features Desk today.'

Before the receptionist had time to reply, Polly felt a hefty slap on her back.

'Who on earth is this?' cried a voice. The slap and the exclamation took Polly by surprise and her bag spilled almost its entire contents over the receptionist's desk. As she struggled to reload it, Polly turned to see who was behind her. It was a short fat man, at least forty years old, wearing an extremely loud and dirty tie.

'Careful,' she said.

'Do I know you?' asked the man.

Polly glared at the insolent man and shovelled stuff into her bag. There were pens, lipsticks, a tub of hot chocolate powder, a pocket camera, a pair of Minty's pants, a few bills, keys and a roll of loo paper. He had not even apologised for making her upset her things, she fumed to herself. She was certainly not going to introduce herself first.

'First, tell me who *you* are.'

'I am Den Christie,' said the man.

Polly stopped what she was doing and gaped. 'Den Christie?'

The man nodded and Polly gulped. Den Christie was the editor, the editor of the whole damned paper.

'Sorry,' she said. 'I'm Polly. Polly Taylor. I'm starting today on Features.' She put out her hand but Christie grunted and waved it away.

'I saw that thing sticking out of your bag as soon as I walked through the door,' he said. 'What the hell do you think you're doing bringing it in here?'

Polly followed the direction of the editor's angry stare. He seemed to be looking at a roll of magazines and a newspaper that stuck out of her bag.

Christie grabbed at the newspaper. It was the *Telegraph* and, as he took it, it somehow seemed to bite him in the hand.

Christie screamed and Polly could hardly believe her eyes as Minty's pet miniature rabbit, Bobbin, flew through the air and scooted under the receptionist's desk. The receptionist screamed and leapt on to her chair. The editor sucked at his hand and Polly saw blood trickling on to the cuff of his shirt.

'Oh my God, I'm so sorry,' said Polly. 'He's got very long teeth. I don't know how—'

'Just catch the bugger.'

It took some time for this to be achieved. In fact, it was Christie himself who eventually cornered the creature and stuck a wastepaper bin on top of it.

'I'm sorry,' said Polly again and started backing away from Christie as soon as order had been restored.

'No, wait,' said the editor. 'You didn't answer my question.'

'What question?'

'Why you brought that thing in here?'

'The rabbit? I'm sorry. It was a mistake. You see—'

'No, not the rabbit, you fool,' thundered Christie. 'Anyone can see that the rabbit was a mistake – unless you're a complete lunatic. I meant that newspaper.'

'The *Telegraph*?'

'Exactly.'

'I don't know. I never read it myself. My sister takes it. I think my niece must have put it in the bag to, well, catch any mess that Bobbin made. I mean it is the most absorbent newsprint you can get.'

Christie laughed. 'Well, I don't mind anyone shitting on the *Telegraph*. In fact, that's to be encouraged.' Polly

39

nodded. 'I just thought for a moment,' continued Christie, 'that you were one of those snotty-nosed new graduates that we get in here who think they're too bloody smart to read the tabloids.'

'I'm not a graduate,' said Polly.

'Good.'

'Excuse me, sir,' interrupted the receptionist. 'Shall I get Security to remove the, the rabbit?' She pointed to the wastepaper basket which was now beginning to propel itself around the floor.

'Put it in a box and get it taken to the kitchens,' said Christie. 'I haven't eaten rabbit pie for years.'

Polly paled.

'And tell them to marinade it in red wine first,' added Christie as he stormed off towards the lifts.

Polly looked at the receptionist in horror.

'You'll get used to the boss,' said the receptionist. 'He's a big joker.'

'Was he joking?'

'Of course. I'll get Security to keep the rabbit for you in their office but please make sure you take it home with you tonight.'

'Thanks,' smiled Polly. 'I will.'

When Polly eventually arrived in Features she was almost an hour late, but no one seemed to notice.

The head of Features, a man called Bernard Carslip who had interviewed Polly and given her the job, was busy bawling someone out about a piece they had written in the Saturday paper.

A thin woman with spiky, bright red hair sat in a chair opposite Carslip's desk saying nothing, just soaking up the abuse.

'Who the fuck gives a fuck about flowers?' he yelled. 'Why on earth would our readers want a Guide to the Perfect Polyanthus?'

'I showed you my copy before I filed,' said the woman.

Carslip grunted and waved the woman away. He watched her go, looking rather satisfied with the performance he had produced. Then he strode across the room towards Polly and Polly wondered whether his behaviour, his display of power, had been partly for her benefit. Some sort of warning.

'Ah, Polly, sweetheart, I'd quite forgotten you were starting today.' Carslip smiled and Polly could not help thinking how much his face resembled that of a trout. Even when he smiled, his thin scaly lips turned down at both ends. She hoped that Carslip would not make a habit of calling her sweetheart.

But before Carslip could say another word, the door swung open and Christie burst in on the scene.

'I want you all upstairs in my office in five minutes,' he yelled and then disappeared.

Carslip took a deep breath and wiped his oily face. 'OK, guys and dolls. Get your stuff together and up to the steakhouse.' But the instructions were superfluous. Everyone in the office was already busy collecting their papers and scurrying for the door.

'Den hates people being late,' Carslip told her as he himself left his desk. Polly looked around her. She was soon going to be the only person left in the room.

'Hang on a minute,' she said. 'Where is the steakhouse?'

'Den's office – top floor,' said Carslip over his shoulder.

'Why is it called the steakhouse?' she asked as she ran after Carslip and managed to squeeze into the lift with him and the rest of the team who were already crammed inside. Everyone burst out laughing.

'You'll soon find out,' someone said.

The steakhouse was a big office. There was a huge desk and an enormous table for meetings. Everyone clustered down the far end of the table and Christie, of course, sat at the head. He was smiling which everyone, apart from Polly, knew was a very bad sign.

'I want to congratulate you,' he said. Carslip realised he was in dangerous waters but he could not help taking the bait and put on his broad trout grin.

'Yes, well done Carslip,' continued Christie. 'Saturday's features pages were a triumph.' He paused, for effect, and then continued. 'A story about how Bencombe Abbey, one of the most elite and blue-stockinged girls' schools in the country is organising *lesbian* as well as heterosexual "socials" for its pupils. It's a cracking good story. In fact, it's a fucking stupendous, splashable story.'

There was another pause. Christie had risen to his feet while he had been speaking. He had both hands, palm down, on the table and was leaning his full weight on them. He stared at Carslip like a hungry predator. Everyone waited for the 'but' to fall and it did.

'But.' Carslip visibly retreated as far back into his chair as he could. Polly could not help being reminded of the way the red-haired journalist had been squirming in her chair before Carslip only minutes earlier.

'But,' repeated Christie. 'Whose idea was it to conclude at the end of the article that this is a good idea? "Laudable", I think, was the word you used.' Carslip wriggled and a trickle of sweat ran down one side of his face. '"Ludicrous" would have been more like it,' Christie added with a snort of contempt.

Carslip said nothing. Neither did any of his colleagues.

Christie kept up his grilling, without a single interruption, for a full five minutes, which Polly thought quite impressive. Eventually he had had enough fun with his prey and told them to go.

'Oh, Carslip,' he added as they all got to their feet. 'Is your extension 5755?'

'Yes,' said Carslip.

'Have the telephone engineers spoken to you this morning?'

'No.'

'There's a wiring fault in the system they're trying to fix,' said Christie. 'I don't think any extension ending 55 should be used after two p.m.'

'What?' said Carslip. 'But—'

'Oh, Carslip, stop fussing like a little girl,' yelled Christie. 'Can't you use someone else's fucking phone for a few hours?'

'OK.'

'And, by the way, Olga – I really liked the polyanthus piece. No kidding,' Christie said to the red-haired woman.

It was the final straw for Carslip and his face looked more troutlike than ever.

The meeting broke up and the team clattered down the back stairs to the fourth floor. Carslip's face was as red as if he had been in an oven and it was clear to Polly why Christie's office was dubbed the steakhouse.

'Bad luck,' said one of his colleagues but Carslip just grunted and disappeared into the Gents.

'Would you say that was "*au point*" or "well done"?' someone asked Olga, who was walking next to Polly.

'Definitely on the pink side,' said Olga. Then she looked at Polly. 'When it comes to Den's roastings, honey, you ain't seen nothin' yet.'

Carslip remained tender for the rest of the day. He found a desk for Polly by clearing a table which had been piled high with papers and books and gave her a phone to plug in. And that was it. He went back to his desk without a further word. Everyone seemed very busy and Polly sat at her table for some time before summoning the courage to ask what she should do.

Carslip was sitting at his desk, head down and supported in his hands.

'You want to know what to do?' he echoed rather absently.

Polly nodded but Carslip could not see this.

There was a pause and then Polly continued, 'Yes. I'm sorry to bother you but what should I do?'

Carslip looked up and stared blankly at Polly. Then suddenly he scowled and slipped back into gear.

'Write a fucking feature, of course,' he barked.

It seemed to Polly that, when Christie was not around, Carslip did the best he could to imitate his boss's style.

Polly took a step back and was about to retreat to her desk but she still did not have an answer to her question. It was all very well to say write a feature but a feature about *what*? Didn't he care? Polly decided it would be better to persist with her questioning now and risk annoying Carslip than to come back again in five minutes and drive him completely mad.

'About what?'

'It doesn't matter,' said Carslip, an expression of affected amusement on his face. 'We won't publish anything you write for a few weeks yet. New recruits always write like shit – we have to *teach* you how to write before we unleash you on our readers. Write something like you did for that magazine you used to work for.'

'The baby magazine?'

'Yes, that will do.'

'I could do something about the posh private nurseries that are springing up in the City. My niece has just started at one. My sister says she likes to have her daughter at a school near to her office. But then her job is so demanding and she has to leave so early and come home so late that she's never able to take Minty or collect her—'

The phone on Carslip's desk started to ring. Polly waited while he took the call.

'Yes, yes,' he said. 'Christie said something about it . . . All right, I'll try to keep off the phone after two . . . What was that? You say it could be dangerous to use the phone after two?'

Carslip waved Polly away as though she were an irritating fly.

'Don't be ridiculous – what do you mean it might give the engineer a dangerous shock on the other end of the line?'

It was clear that Carslip did not want to discuss her article further so Polly went back to her desk.

She was pleased to discover that, in her absence, someone had conjured up a PC for her and she felt a shiver of excitement as she sat down in front of her screen. Adele might have stolen Charles but Ned was right. Her job at the *Globe* was certainly going to be interesting.

Polly wrote all morning. Even if there was no chance of her article being published, she knew that her first piece of work needed to be good. Carslip had not said how many words he wanted but Olga said she should aim at about 1500.

By the time she had finished, Polly was pleased with what she had done. She read it through once more, made a few small amendments then printed it out and took it over to Carslip's desk.

Carslip was not there. In fact, Polly suddenly noticed that hardly anyone was in the office at all. She glanced at the clock, saw that it was one thirty and immediately realised that she was starving hungry. She left her piece in the centre of Carslip's desk and decided to go out and get a sandwich. Christie had referred to the kitchens so there was a good chance that there was a staff canteen but no one had told her where it was and, anyway, Polly felt like getting some fresh air.

It was very cold outside but the sun was shining and there were tiny snowflakes falling. They were so tiny that they drifted both upwards and down as they blew in the wind.

Polly began to feel herself relax. She had dreaded going into Adele's flat the night before but she had spoken to Minty three times during the week and each time the little girl had burst into tears and begged Polly to come and see her as soon as she was back.

Polly and Ned had returned to London by train and arrived at Euston in the early evening. Polly thanked Ned for everything and was on the point of going to the tube station when Ned had suggested a quick drink.

The quick drink had turned into a number of drinks and, by the time Ned bundled her into a taxi, it was late and Polly was so pissed that she was almost looking forward to seeing Adele and giving her a piece of her mind.

The house was dark and quiet as Polly let herself in. It was a large maisonette on the ground and first floors of a terraced house in one of the most beautiful Georgian streets of Islington. A very desirable residence except for the fact it was directly below the flat in which the artist, Oliver Johnson, was murdered years ago. This former resident's time at the house was commemorated by a blue plaque on the wall but Polly would never have chosen to live in a place where something so dreadful had happened. Adele said Polly was being stupid and irrational and that lightning never strikes twice in the same place. The maisonette was simply perfect, pronounced Adele, and so she had gone ahead and bought it. Only two years later, the property market in Islington had boomed and the maisonette was now worth a fortune.

It was classic Adele, thought Polly, as she queued for her sandwich at the deli next door to the *Daily Globe*. Adele was always right.

She thought back to the previous evening again. Polly had let herself in with her own key and, as

47

soon as she had closed the door behind her, she went up to Minty's room and peeped in at her little niece. Minty was lying on top of her duvet, her head and one chubby arm dangling awkwardly over the side of the bed.

Polly regretted not getting back early enough to see Minty before she went to sleep. She crept into the room and gently rearranged the child so that she was warm and comfortable. Then she kissed Minty on the cheek and stroked her dark curls.

Ned was right, thought Polly, as she ordered a ham on ciabatta with lots of mustard. It had been wonderful to see Minty again – Polly had really missed her while she was in Yorkshire – but there was no way that she could go on living with Adele after what had happened. She would have to get a flatshare with someone or rent a room.

But leaving Minty would be horrible, she thought, as she waited for the sandwich to be made. For the third time her mind drifted back to the night before. She had left Minty's room as quietly as she could and then gone along to her own room. Opposite Polly's bedroom door another door led to Adele's room. She recalled the last time she had been in there and what she had done. She could not help feeling ashamed but, at the same time, she knew that it was the least Adele deserved.

Polly had been about to turn and go into her own room when Adele's door had suddenly opened and her sister appeared. Polly jumped at the horror of seeing Adele again. It was the first time since that dreadful day.

'What do you want?' asked Polly.

48

'I heard you come in.'

Polly said nothing. She wanted to spit or scream or say something savage but was suddenly frozen.

'I'm glad you're back,' said Adele.

'I'm not back,' said Polly. 'I just came to see Minty. I'll stay over tonight, if that's OK, and move out tomorrow.' She glanced over Adele's shoulder at the darkness inside her sister's room. Her heart beat furiously as she wondered whether he was there.

Adele shook her head. 'He's not here, if that's what you're thinking.'

Polly glared at Adele. 'You disgust me.'

'I'm sorry,' said Adele. 'It—'

'Don't bother.'

'Araminta is heartbroken about you moving out.'

'You should have thought about that before you started shagging my boyfriend.'

Adele gave a slight shrug and took a step back inside her room.

'I'm really sorry,' she said. But Polly knew, of course, that she wasn't.

'Is that all you wanted to say?' she asked.

Adele hesitated. 'Well, I was just wondering whether you might drop Araminta off at nursery in the morning. I know she would love it, if you would.'

'And it might just save you the trouble of doing it yourself?'

'I admit it's been a nightmare without you, Poll. I've been late to work every day.'

It was dark in the hallway but Polly got the full force of that pathetic pleading look that her sister always conjured up when she was asking a favour. Of course, Polly's first instinct had been to tell Adele

49

to go to hell but then she thought of Minty. Dear, beautiful, *innocent* Minty. Minty was only four and it really wasn't her fault that her mother was the biggest shit in the world.

'Look, Adele, the thought of doing you a favour makes me vomit,' Polly said at last. 'But I want to be with Minty so I'll do it.'

'Thanks,' said Adele. 'Now that you're moving out, I'll be getting an au pair but these things take time.'

'Just for tomorrow, mind, and then I'm leaving. Much as I love Minty, she is your daughter.'

'Thanks,' said Adele, looking relieved. 'I think on Mondays she has gym and she needs to take—'

'I know all that.'

'Of course,' said Adele and the two sisters had turned their backs on each other and gone to bed.

Polly took her sandwich, Coke and crisps from the young Italian who passed them across the counter and stuffed them into one of the snack bar's tiny carrier bags. How could Adele have done it? How could Adele have ruined everything with her selfishness? The pain flooded back. Being away with Ned had helped, of course, but now she was back to reality and the full horror of what had happened rose up again like a huge wave of nausea. She sat on a bench, opened her sandwich and ate quickly. Not only the thought of Adele was making her feel sick but, after all that drinking with Ned, she had woken up with a bad hangover.

The first sound she remembered had been the shower in the bathroom next door to her room. Adele always got up at six if she could and went for a run. She then came back home and showered before getting ready to go to work. Polly had calculated that it must be around seven o'clock. As she groped on her bedside table for her watch, a tub of Nivea, a loo roll and a bottle of perfume all crashed to the floor. She stared down at the bottle, which had spilled nearly all its contents. It had been another Christmas present from Charles and she'd worn it on *that* occasion too because he had said how much he liked it. She reached down to pick up the bottle but the door had burst open and Minty ran in and got to it first.

'Oh Polly, your lovely perfume. Your favourite perfume,' cried the little girl, trying to sweep the fast-evaporating liquid back into the bottle.

'Don't worry,' Polly had said. 'Leave it and jump up here and give me a hug.'

The little girl climbed into bed beside her aunt. She was carrying her favourite teddy, a ragged old bear that she had christened PissEyes and Adele was always trying to chuck out.

'Oh, Polly, Polly, Polly,' cried Minty. 'I thought you were *never* coming back.' They snuggled together under the blankets and hugged each other.

It felt like old times, their old routine. Minty would get into bed with Polly while Adele got ready for work. They would wait until Adele had left, usually no later than seven fifteen, then they would get up and make eggs or pancakes for breakfast, read stories, play games. Minty did not need to be at school until nine and so there was no rush except that the time would pass so quickly that they always ended up being late.

'I missed you so much,' Minty said, putting her arms round her aunt's neck and holding her tight. 'I love you, Polly. Don't go away again, promise?'

'I missed you too,' said Polly. 'Tell me what you've been up to.'

'Nothing, it's been horrid.'

'Hasn't it been nice having Mummy look after you?' Polly had not been able to resist asking this question.

'No, it's been horrid. She says she's going to get rid of Bobbin. She says there's not enough room for him in the house and he smells.'

At that moment, Adele stuck her head round the door. Her shiny black hair was neat and well conditioned. She was wearing a fitted red suit and carried a large black briefcase.

'I'll pick you up later, darling,' said Adele coming over and depositing a kiss on the back of Minty's head. Minty wriggled further under the blankets but, as her mother backed off again towards the door, she resurfaced.

'Can't Aunt Polly pick me up?' she asked.

Adele shook her head. 'I told you, sweetheart. Aunt Polly has an important new job. Things have to change and we are going to find a really fun lady to look after you from now on.'

'I don't want a fun lady,' said Minty, projecting her bottom lip and scowling. 'I want Polly.'

Polly squeezed the little girl tight. 'Don't worry, sweetheart. I'll pick you up from nursery.' Then Polly glanced across at Adele and added, 'Just tonight.'

Later, in the kitchen, Polly had poured herself a large glass of water. She knew that drinking fluids was supposed to rehydrate the body but it just seemed to make the alcohol swim round her system that much quicker. Her head was spinning as she went into the bathroom to brush her teeth.

She remembered thinking that it was her first day at the *Daily Globe* and she looked a wreck. The recent glimpse of Adele's clear, clean complexion, her bright eyes and glossy hair had made her feel even worse. Of course, Adele had virtually given up drinking years ago and was always advising Polly to do the same. Ever since that night with Oliver Bunk, thought Polly, although they never talked about it. Her mother had told her. Sue said that it happened at a party, a Christmas party. Adele had had too much to drink and her notorious tutor had taken advantage of her. As a result, Adele rarely drank these days.

Adele was in control of her life, Polly thought, as she filled the basin with cold water and splashed her face. She knew what she wanted in life. Stratton Walsh, the big investment bank in the City where Adele worked, only hired a handful of graduates each year out of many hundreds of applicants. Adele had studied assiduously before her interviews, reading the *Financial Times* and the *Economist*, going to lectures on finance and investment. She probably knew more than the people asking the questions.

But Adele had never shown much interest in men. Well, not after the Bunk affair, thought Polly. So why Charles? Why, given that most men fell at her feet, did she need to choose Charles of all people? Polly had been asking herself these questions over and over again when suddenly she heard Minty scream that something was stuck in her ear and she had gone deaf. Polly had immediately rushed back downstairs to the kitchen.

*

By the time Polly got to her desk after her brief sandwich lunch, everyone else was back and the place was buzzing. Carslip looked at his watch.

'Pretty late for a new girl?' he sneered.

'Sorry,' said Polly. She was about to add that she had gone to lunch late but Carslip was already talking again.

'I read your piece and I must say I found it highly entertaining.' Not even the flicker of a smile showed on his thin trout lips. 'You weren't around to discuss it so I sent it straight upstairs to Den so that he could have a good laugh at it too.' Polly shifted her weight uncomfortably from one foot to the other. 'You've got a lot to learn, sweetheart. We're not writing nursery stories now.'

Then he disappeared and Olga came over and sat down on Polly's desk.

'Don't worry about him,' she said. 'It's just his damned inferiority complex. When he's been grilled like a kipper by Den, he always takes it out on one of us.'

Polly was about to reply when Olga suddenly leapt to her feet. Christie had just torn into the room.

'Who wrote this?' he yelled at Carslip, flapping a few sheets of A4 in his face. Carslip sniggered and nodded towards Polly. Christie marched back across the room to Polly's desk. Olga had slunk away and Polly cringed as far back in her chair as she could.

Christie threw the papers on to her desk and Polly saw to her horror that they were covered in marks and deletions made with a thick blue pencil. Her work had been decimated.

'It's brilliant. It's fucking brilliant,' cried Christie. 'I haven't read such an interesting and genuinely *funny* piece of work for a long time. A lot of you guys,' he glanced around him, 'could learn a thing or two from this kid. Like me, she may not have gone to university but she has real talent.'

Polly felt her face going blood red. She wanted to ask about all the changes Christie had made. It did not look to her that much of the original was left but she said nothing.

'Of course, I made one or two changes, cut it down to about eight hundred,' continued Christie. 'But I want it in Thursday's Section Two with *her* byline, OK?'

'But we never—' stammered Carslip. 'I mean she only joined today.'

'You heard what I said,' yelled Christie, storming out of the room.

Everyone stared awkwardly at Carslip then suddenly the phone on his desk started to ring and he took refuge in answering it.

As he did so, there was a blood-curdling scream from Carslip's receiver. Everyone in the office heard it and froze.

'Oh fuck. The telephone engineer.' Carslip's face went white as he dropped the phone but the agonised screaming continued. 'I've electrocuted the fucking telephone engineer. Christie will kill me.'

'What about the poor engineer?' said Olga, picking up the receiver which was eerily silent now.

'Fuck,' said Carslip. 'Fuck.' He grabbed the receiver, listened to the silence for himself and then replaced it and sat down behind his desk.

There was a ghastly pause as everyone stared blankly

at each other and then suddenly Christie came back into the room roaring with laughter.

Carslip stared at him for a moment and then understood and rose to his feet.

'You bastard.'

Christie was weeping with laughter. It took a while before he could speak.

'Get a sense of humour, man,' he said in the end but Carslip's face was like that of a hooked fish.

Christie made for the door again but then stopped in his tracks. He turned and walked over to Polly's desk. He stood there looking at her for a moment as though he was weighing something up in his mind. Then suddenly he said, 'Yes. Why not? I think I've got a job for you.'

'What job?' stammered Polly.

'It's not really a job for Features,' continued Christie. 'But it requires some rather unique talents. She's a bit of a looker, wouldn't you say, Carslip? I reckon she's in with a better chance than anyone else we've got.'

Christie waved Carslip over. 'Come on. I want you and Polly to come upstairs with me. I've got a special assignment that I think Polly might want to cut her teeth on. I'll take you both through it.'

Carslip flashed Polly a look of sheer hatred as they followed Christie through the swing doors to the lifts. It was as though Carslip had decided that she was the one who would suffer as a result of the horrible prank Christie had played on him.

Polly followed the two men up the stairs in silence. She felt certain that Carslip would never call her sweetheart again.

Chapter Five

'Watch out,' a cyclist yelled as he swerved to miss her but Polly was already on the bus. She had had to run less than a hundred metres to catch it but she was completely out of breath. She glanced at her watch. It was 5.45 p.m. – she had fifteen minutes to get to Finsbury Square, if she was not to be late picking up Minty from her nursery school.

She fished her mobile out of her bag and rang Adele's office again. Adele's line was still switching directly to voicemail and Polly had already left messages both on the voicemail and with Adele's secretary. She sighed and phoned another number.

'Ned? Sorry, are you busy?' The background noise on Ned's mobile was so loud and chaotic Polly could hardly hear his voice at all.

'No, I've just got one more drop and then I'm done.' Polly was confused at first but then she remembered Ned's part-time job as a motorbike courier in the City.

'Great,' she said. 'I don't suppose you're free later are you?' Poor Ned, she thought, he must have had enough of her all the week before. She was probably the last person he wanted to see but who else could she ask?

'Why?'

'Well, I'm afraid I was going to ask you another favour.' There was a screech of brakes.

'Bloody lunatic,' said Ned. 'Some woman running to catch a bus nearly got herself killed. I can see why they call guys like me dispatch riders.'

'Are you OK?'

'Fine. What was it you were saying?'

'Well,' continued Polly. 'I wouldn't ask you if I could think of anyone else to ask.'

'Thanks very much.'

'No,' laughed Polly. 'It's just that, well, Ned, do you think you could get me some cannabis?'

'Cannabis? You mean grass, pot, dope, that kind of cannabis?'

'Yes I need some. Urgently,' whispered Polly, covering her mouth as she spoke. A boy of about eleven was sitting beside her and was clearly trying to listen to every word she said.

'Without wanting to sound like your mother, I think it's a mistake.'

'I'm desperate – really. Can you get me some?'

'I suppose.'

'Fantastic,' cried Polly. 'You are a lifesaver. Can you bring it to Adele's flat tonight?'

'I thought you were moving out?'

'I am,' said Polly. 'But I promised to pick up Minty and now I've got to do this cannabis thing tonight.'

'What cannabis thing?'

'I'll explain later. What time can you get to me?'

'Is eight thirty OK?'

'Fine, perfect. Oh, and don't forget all the other stuff as well.'

'What stuff?'

'Well, you know. The papers or whatever you use to roll it up in.' The schoolboy sniggered and Polly bit her lip. 'Look, Ned, sorry. I don't think I can say any more. I'll see you later. And thanks.'

'See you later,' said Ned.

The boy was still staring as Polly put her phone back in her bag. His face suddenly broke into a wide cheeky grin.

'I can get you some of that,' he said.

'What? I don't know what you mean,' said Polly, looking out of the window. It was already dark and the traffic was moving slowly.

'Yes, you do. You were asking your bloke to get you some dope.'

'Shhh,' hissed Polly, glancing around her. 'Little boys like you should not be out alone at this time of the night. School must have finished ages ago.'

'I've been in detention,' said the boy proudly.

'Surprise, surprise,' said Polly as she got up and squeezed past him. 'I'm sorry not to be able to chat more but this is my stop.'

'Don't get stoned,' he yelled after her.

Polly ran across the grass square towards the huge office block that housed Minty's nursery. The boy on the bus had brought back memories of her own school days. She was often in detention, usually for not having done her homework or for not concentrating in class. She had met her first boyfriend in detention, the one that her mother had caught her snogging on the sofa. He had been the first of a series of short, squalid and unsatisfactory relationships. Polly fairly swiftly reached the conclusion that her boyfriends were only after one thing and that that thing was not particularly rewarding. She had begun to think that she would never enjoy sex. Until she met Charles, of course, and Charles had changed everything.

Charles had been a wonderful lover. He was slow and considerate and seemed to do all the right things. Polly had experienced her first orgasm ever with Charles and she was amazed by the sensation. To start with, she had assumed that Charles was a very practised lover but he told her that he had been working so hard at his job for months before he met her that he had become almost celibate. Making love to Polly was the most special thing ever to happen to him. Polly had been happy to believe this and furthermore she still believed it. Adele might appear more of a trophy girlfriend – she was undeniably prettier and classier than Polly – but surely she could not match her in bed? Surely Adele, who was always so neat and tidy and so shiny and clean, could not do the things for Charles that Polly had done, the things Charles had loved so much?

'Sorry,' said a voice. It was a man in a brown coat with the collar turned up. 'Are you picking someone up?'

'What?'

'From the nursery?'

'Oh, yes, of course,' said Polly.

'You're a bit late,' said the man. 'I've already locked the front door – you'll have to go in at the side.' He pointed down the street and Polly set off in the direction indicated.

When she eventually arrived in Minty's classroom,

Minty was sitting silently beside her teacher. She was pale and close to tears.

'I thought you weren't coming. I thought you'd forgotten me,' she said as she jumped up at the sight of her aunt. Polly lifted Minty into her arms and hugged her.

'Sorry, poppet. My boss made me stay late.'

'You sound like Mummy,' said Minty. 'Mummy always arrives late when she's picking me up but I didn't think—'

'Sorry,' said Polly again. Being compared to Adele, even by a four-year-old child, was unbearable. 'Come on, let's stop at McDonald's on the way home.' Minty's little face lit up at the suggestion.

'Thanks. But don't tell Mummy. She says burgers make you fat and give you spots.'

'She's right. But I'm already fat and spotty so it doesn't matter.'

'You're not,' said Minty. 'When I grow up I want to look exactly like you.'

Polly smiled. It was one of the nicest compliments she had received in her life.

'One Happy Meal with chicken nuggets and Seven Up and one Grown Up Cheeseburger meal with a Diet Coke, please.'

Polly looked across at Minty who was sitting at a table in the corner of the restaurant, her chubby little legs swinging back and forth as she waited for her food. From a distance, she was beginning to look quite a big girl. And yet, thought Polly, it seemed only a short time ago that she had still been a toddler. Minty and Polly had been able to spend almost every

61

long summer afternoon in the park since Polly's job as a columnist on *New Baby* magazine had meant she could squeeze most of her work into the evenings.

Minty had loved the swings but she preferred to be the pusher rather than the swinger and Polly had had to suffer the indignity of wedging herself into the tiny swing seats. 'I'll be the mummy,' Minty would say emphatically, 'and you be the little girl.'

As Polly picked up the loaded tray of McFood, her mobile started to ring. She dashed across the restaurant upsetting the Diet Coke and soaking her cheeseburger in the process. But she managed to answer the phone before it rang off.

'Adele?' Polly gave Minty her Happy Meal and set about salvaging her own food.

'No, everything's fine,' she continued into the phone. 'Minty and I are at—'

'McDonald's, I suppose,' cut in Adele.

'Don't worry, she's not eating beefburgers,' said Polly. She felt like cutting her sister off but she really needed to speak to her. 'Look Adele, something's come up and I must go out tonight. I wanted to make sure you're back in good time.'

'Will you put me to bed?' asked Minty, holding out the longest chip she could find for her aunt. 'And read me stories?' Polly took the chip and nodded.

'I'll be back by eight,' said Adele. 'Nine at the latest.'

'OK,' said Polly. 'But nine at the latest. And, if it's all right, I'll stay over tonight and move out of my room tomorrow.' She found her own longest chip and gave that to Minty.

'Fine. Stay as long as you like,' said Adele. 'What's the big date?'

'It's not a date. Just my boss.'

'Your boss? That was quick work.'

Polly was not amused. Adele seemed to presume that she was already over Charles, that she could substitute another man for him without a moment's hesitation. But there was no point trying to explain; Adele had no understanding of how real human beings felt. Polly said goodbye, put the phone away and turned her attention back to Minty.

'What toy did you get?'

Minty held up an ugly little action figure.

'Oh sorry, did I get a *boy*'s Happy Meal?'

'Its OK,' said Minty. 'I'll give it to Harry at school.' She thought for a moment and then added, 'Harry will like it – he's just a boy.'

Polly smiled and ate her burger. It tasted a bit strange after its dousing in Diet Coke but she was too hungry to care.

Minty's words had made her think back to Carslip. Although he looked more like a fish, he was just a boy. He could not have been older than thirty but he was clearly determined to assert his authority over her. He had been absolutely livid when Den Christie had told Polly what he wanted her to do.

'She's far too inexperienced,' he had cried. 'She'll make a complete mess of it. We could end up being sued.'

Which was certainly true, thought Polly. The last thing she wanted to do was this assignment. It was almost certain to end in disaster and she felt uncomfortable about the ethics of the whole idea. She had tried to object but Den was having none of it. He had set his heart on the project and she would have been risking her job to have refused to do it.

Den seemed to enjoy baiting Carslip, who was still furious about the telephone engineer stunt. The final straw was when Den asked Polly to join him for a drink so that he could brief her about the assignment more fully. Unfortunately Carslip had stormed out of the room before he had the chance to hear Polly say no.

Den was surprised and irritated to have his invitation refused and Polly felt quite proud of herself for having got one up on him.

She hurried back to her desk and put her things together. She was getting very late for picking up Minty.

'Oh, quick, quick,' sneered Carslip. 'Mustn't keep lover boy waiting.'

Polly rushed out of the door without bothering to reply. Carslip could think what he liked.

Minty insisted on bringing home the remains of their meal for Bobbin, although Polly explained that rabbits were not big McDonald's fans.

'He has unusual tastes,' insisted Minty as she force-fed the creature who, much to Polly's amazement, bolted everything down with apparent enthusiasm.

Suddenly Adele appeared. She took in the scene in an instant, strode across the room and snatched Bobbin out of Minty's hands.

'Good God, Polly,' she said. 'You'll kill the creature.'

Bobbin glared angrily at Adele and then vomited up the entire contents of his stomach, all over the front of her jacket. It was hard not to laugh and Polly made no attempt to restrain herself.

Adele gave the rabbit back to Minty and took off her jacket.

'It can't be time for Aunt Polly to go out already,' said Minty.

'No, I managed to get home early,' said Adele, scowling at the jacket. 'It's probably ruined. But I'll try taking it to the dry cleaner's in the morning.'

'But I want Aunt Polly to put me to bed,' said Minty as Adele folded the jacket and put it in a plastic bag. She went over to Minty and put her arms round the little girl's shoulders.

'Poor Mummy,' said Adele. 'Don't you want me to put you to bed?'

Poor Mummy, my arse, thought Polly, turning away. 'I'll have a quick shower, if that's OK?' she said. Minty peered over her mother's shoulder and looked appealingly at Polly. 'And then I'll put Minty to bed before I go out, if you like.'

'Thanks,' said Adele without turning her face to look at her sister. Ned was right, thought Polly again. Even though she loved being with Minty, it was unbearable living under the same roof as Adele. She would have to find somewhere else.

Ned arrived after Minty was asleep and, although Adele was in her room working on a report and the rest of the flat was free, Polly insisted on taking Ned into her own room.

'I have to smoke it *now*,' said Polly. 'And, if Adele gets even a whiff of it, she'll chuck us both out.'

'Why? What's happened?' asked Ned putting down his bag and a six-pack of bottled beer. 'I didn't know you smoked cannabis.'

'I don't. That's the whole point. I've never even smoked a cigarette properly in my life so I need to start practising.'

'Why?' Ned looked bewildered and so Polly explained about her assignment.

'It's for work,' she said, passing Ned a bottle opener for the beer. 'My boss has fixed up for me to go to this party. Apparently the Home Secretary's son will be there. You know, Jane Whitehouse, the minister who wants a big crackdown on drugs.'

'The one who wants to lock you up for even looking at a joint?'

'Yes,' said Polly. 'Den thinks it would be a great scoop if her son were to be seen at a party where people were doing drugs.'

'That sounds a bit cheap,' said Ned, handing Polly a bottle of beer.

'Thanks. Yes,' said Polly. 'I really don't want to do it but it's hard to argue with Den Christie and it was my first day.'

'And you've never smoked a joint before?'

Polly shook her head. 'I tried smoking cigarettes once but they made me violently sick and I've never touched them since.'

'Blimey. When's the party?'

'Tonight.'

'Tonight?'

'Yes, I have to meet Den's son in some bar on the King's Road at ten thirty. He's going to introduce me to his friend – the one who's invited to the party and then the idea is that we go on with the friend as well as the friend's friends.'

'How old are these kids?'

66

'I don't know, I didn't ask.'

'Well, I know Whitehouse's son came down from Cambridge recently. He was at Downing, my college.'

'That must make him about twenty-one or twenty-two,' said Polly.

Ned took a sip of beer. 'Why didn't you tell Den you'd never smoked?'

'I couldn't. I know it's pathetic but I decided, well, he'd think I was an idiot if I said I couldn't smoke. He had been so complimentary about some article I'd written and overruled my boss, the head of Features, who thought it was trash. He told Carslip to put it in the paper straight away. I couldn't really say no to the assignment.'

'Well, I suppose it's simple enough so long as you don't inhale too much or you probably will start throwing up. I'll make up a few joints and you can try a few puffs now.'

Polly watched and drank her beer while Ned cleared some space on her table and set out his things. By the time that Adele stuck her head round the door an hour later, the room was heavy with smoke and Polly and Ned were both lying on the floor staring at the ceiling. There were empty beer bottles scattered about the floor.

'What on earth is going on here?' asked Adele. 'I thought I could smell a strange smell.'

Polly and Ned sat up like a pair of naughty children.

'Sorry, Adele,' said Ned. 'It was my idea. I should have asked you first.'

'Yes, you should have,' said Adele. 'I thought you'd left all that crap behind you in Cambridge – I certainly did. I wouldn't touch the stuff these days. It fuddles your brain. I'm trying to write a complex piece of analysis on the US Diet and Supplements market and it's really not helpful being half-stoned with passive smoking from the room next door.'

'Well, I must go to my party,' said Polly, getting unsteadily to her feet.

Adele looked at her watch. 'Yes. It's nearly ten o'clock. Come on, Buttons,' she added to Ned. 'We'd better let Cinders get on her way before she turns into a pumpkin. She looks about the colour of one already.'

Polly said nothing. She knew that Adele would love to know where she was going. Until she had met Charles, Polly had hardly gone out in the evenings at all. She was usually babysitting for Adele, which actually made up for the rent that she had never been able to afford to pay.

Adele waved her hand in front of her face and walked across the room to open the window. Ned put on his coat, picked up his things from the bedside table and helped Polly to put them into her bag.

'Just don't bring that stuff into my house again,' said Adele as Ned and Polly opened the front door, 'or I'll—' But they were already down the steps and out of ear shot before Adele finished speaking.

'Or what?' said Polly. 'Do you think she might give us a detention?' It was not very funny but Polly could not stop giggling. Perhaps it was nerves.

'Are you OK?' asked Ned. 'Look, Polly, I really don't think you're up to this job tonight. Why don't you call your boss and tell him you can't make it.'

'What? He'd go berserk. I'd get something worse than a detention if I did that.' She giggled again but then stopped suddenly. The cold air was making her head swim and she felt a small ripple of nausea sweep through her stomach.

They walked up to the Angel. Polly had planned to go by tube but Ned insisted she took a cab.

'Get your boss to reimburse you – it's the least he can do,' he said.

Polly clambered inside the taxi and then Ned was gone and she was all alone. Oh my God, she thought, what on earth was she doing?

The cab driver shut the little dividing glass door with a thud. Perhaps he could smell the dope, she mused, as she settled back in her seat and closed her eyes.

Only ten days ago her life had been totally different. Polly had had her dull but satisfactory job writing a column for *New Baby*. She wrote funny pieces about the trials and tribulations of new motherhood. She wondered whether any of her readers suspected that she had never had a child, that she was just a surrogate mum for her niece.

The column had not been well paid and Polly had often needed to supplement it with odd jobs but it had enabled her to be around for Minty while she was a toddler. And, of course, it had been through *New Baby* and one particular odd job that she had met Charles.

It was the Christmas before last. Polly, particularly strapped for cash, had seen the ad in a local paper. *PART-TIME SANTA required for department store.* She hesitated at first then picked up the phone. It turned out that the hours they wanted were perfect and the pay was good too. She decided to give it a go.

Polly had expected it to be hell but was surprised

to find that she enjoyed the job. The children were so sweet and innocent and excited. The little ones did not seem to notice that her face, although well obscured with white whiskers and beard, was hardly that of an old man and the older ones were too polite or too smart to say anything – perhaps they really thought they might not get their toys on the way out if they upset Santa.

The only problem was the heat. Wearing a thick Santa suit for hours at a time in a hot department store was suffocating. She did a four-hour stint in the middle of which she was given a ten-minute break. She got a big bottle of water, locked the grotto door and then sat down and dropped her cloak around her waist. She sat there in her bra, sipping her water and letting as much heat escape from her body as possible.

She had only just started the job, when she met Charles. She had to interview him for *New Baby*. Charles worked for a baby food manufacturer called Green Baby which specialised in natural and organic recipes. The company had just received an industry award for one of its best-selling products, Top Banana, and *New Baby* wanted to run a piece on it.

Polly had arrived late at Charles's office. She had been late dropping Minty off with the childminder she used when she needed help looking after Minty during the day and she and Charles sat looking at each other for several seconds before she recovered her breath.

'Mr Goodwood,' she managed eventually.

'Before we start,' Charles had interrupted immediately. He leant across the table towards her and reached out to touch her face. 'Perhaps I might remove that sticker on your cheek unless it's supposed to be there?' Polly blushed and her hand shot to her face. She removed the sticker, which she saw was the one of the Fat Controller from Minty's Thomas the Tank Engine collection. Minty liked to play doctors with her stickers and pretend they were plasters.

'Er, sorry,' she said. 'My niece.'

'How old?' Charles had asked.

'Three and a half,' replied Polly. 'She lives with me – and my sister, her mother, of course.'

'How nice. A friend of mine has a little girl of about that age. They live in Scotland but they've come down to stay with me for a few days. I was wondering what the little girl might enjoy doing.'

Polly and Charles chatted and Polly ended up suggesting that he took her to see Father Christmas at her store. After all, the grotto was really rather good with moving Santa's helpers and reindeers that sang. She did not, of course, mention her own personal role.

'A good idea,' said Charles and it must have been at least half an hour before they got on to the subject of Top Banana.

What a really charming man, Polly had thought, as she left Charles's office. He had seemed so interested in children, which was unusual for most of the men she knew. She could not think of any boyfriend of hers who had liked children much. Even her girlfriends were not that interested in kids. Most of them wanted to delay motherhood until their thirties and took great comfort from the fact that many women did not start their families until their forties.

But Polly's number-one ambition had always been to settle down and have loads of kids with someone who loved children as much as she did. Someone, perhaps, like Charles, she could not help wondering. But that was ridiculous, she had told herself, as she raced to the department store and hurried to her changing room. She would probably never see him again.

And Charles did not visit the grotto that day or the next. It was Friday and she had almost given up hope that he would come. She was halfway through her morning stint and on her break when the door burst open.

'Oh my God,' cried Polly. 'Didn't I lock it?' She was face to face with Charles again, completely topless, apart from her bra, with a long white beard hanging down between her breasts.

'Sorry,' said Charles, blushing slightly and pulling the little girl at his side out of the grotto. 'I don't think Santa is quite ready to see us yet.'

They laughed about it heartily later that day over a drink but Polly had felt mortified at the time. First the Fat Controller sticker and now this, she thought. The man will think I'm a complete lunatic.

But Charles had been intrigued and he could not help telling her how erotic he had found it discovering her half-naked in the middle of the department store.

'It's just as well Victoria was chaperoning me,' he said. 'Or who knows what might have happened in Santa's grotto?' And that was how it had all begun, the start of a whole year of sheer bliss. She and Charles had been almost inseparable and the sex, well, the sex had been magnificent. She did not like to admit it but Polly really did miss Charles's penis, that big, fat, stupendous instrument. It had been hers entirely but now was only hers in her dreams.

*

'OK, love. Wakey, wakey.' The glass door slid back with a thump and the cab came to a halt. Polly opened her eyes and rummaged for the only twenty-pound note in her purse.

'Can I have a receipt please?' she asked, wondering whether she should ask Ned for a receipt for the cannabis as well. It was turning into a very expensive evening.

She paid off the cab and turned to face the pub. It was seething inside but a small boy touched her arm as she made her way towards the door. He was about fourteen, she guessed.

'Are you Polly Taylor?' he asked.

'Yes,' replied Polly hesitantly.

'I'm Ed Christie.'

Polly was unsure what to do next. She stared, in horror, at another boy who stood some distance apart who looked even smaller still.

'Is that—?' she stammered.

'My friend, Warren,' said Ed, nodding. 'We would have waited inside,' he added. 'But they wouldn't let us buy a drink. The bloke behind the bar is a real dickhead – he insisted on seeing ID.'

'I'm not surprised. How old are you?'

'I'm fifteen but don't worry. Warren turned sixteen last weekend.'

'What do you mean "Don't worry"?' asked Polly. Ed did not reply and Polly did not really want to hear the answer.

'I can't go to a party with you two,' continued Polly. 'I look old enough to be your mother.' But Ed ignored her.

'Come on,' he said, pushing her towards his friend. 'It's getting late.'

Polly stared at the minuscule Warren. She was not sure whether to shake hands or to pat him on the head.

'The party is just around the corner. Let's go.'

Polly and her two charges, neither of whom quite reached the height of her shoulder, set off. The effects of the cannabis were beginning to wear off and Polly was feeling very apprehensive. Just don't get yourself arrested, she said to herself, as Warren slipped his hand through her arm.

Chapter Six

The room was full but, from a quick scan, Polly could see that no one looked over the age of eighteen.

'Are you sure Richard is supposed to here?' she asked Warren.

'Richard?' he looked at her blankly.

'Yes, Richard Whitehouse. You know, the Home Secretary's son.' Polly wondered what Ed had told Warren and felt she should be careful about saying too much.

'Oh, you mean Nicholas. Would you like me to introduce you to him?'

'Nicholas?'

'Richard's younger brother.'

'Christ. How old is he?'

'Fifteen.'

'Fifteen?'

'Same age as me,' put in Ed.

'Sorry,' said Polly. She felt really out of her depth. The prospect of a party with twenty-one-year-olds had seemed bad enough but kids of fifteen?

'Would you like a drink?' asked Warren.

'Yes, several,' she replied.

They made their way towards a table and Ed gave

Polly a bottle of beer. It did not taste good but Polly gulped it down nonetheless. It was helping to steady her nerves. She would stay for half an hour or so, she decided, and then make some excuse to leave. How would Den ever know what had really been going on that night at the party? She might even bribe Ed to tell his father that the Whitehouse kid had not turned up.

'Nicholas.' Warren suddenly reappeared at her side with a tall fair-haired boy. 'This is Polly.'

Polly blushed and smiled and Nicholas smiled back. He had a lovely smile and was quite handsome but he was clearly absurdly young.

'Good to meet you,' said Polly. 'How's—' She had to check herself from asking how was school. She clutched her bag. There was no way she could offer this child a joint. Den had to be crazy even to consider this stunt.

'How's things?' she said.

Nicholas talked a bit about all the media fuss there had been over his mother's most recent political outbursts.

The air was thick and dry with smoke and Polly drank her beer. Although the alcohol was making her feel more relaxed, it was also making her very drowsy. Perhaps it was the combination of beer and the cannabis she had smoked earlier?

'I think I'd better sit down for a while,' said Polly, lurching towards a sofa. Nicholas quickly shifted a few coats and they sat down.

He then continued to drone on about politics. It was clear, thought Polly, that the boy took after his mother. She upended her bottle and drained the last few drops.

'I'll get you another,' said Nicholas, jumping to his feet and disappearing into the crowded room.

Polly leant her head back on the sofa, relieved to have a few moments to herself. She was feeling so tired that she could hardly keep her eyes open and, within seconds, she had fallen fast asleep.

By the time she came to, things had changed considerably in the room. There were now definitely a few older people. As she staggered to her feet, Polly was amazed to come face to face with Adele. Adele was wearing pink knitted hot pants which would have looked disgusting on anyone but Adele. She still managed to look sensational as she stood there grinning down at Polly.

'What on earth happened to your shirt?' asked Adele. 'Looks like Cinders decided to come to the ball with or without the aid of her fairy godmother.'

Polly looked down and saw, to her surprise, that she was wearing *that* shirt, the beautiful white silk shirt that Charles had bought her. She could have sworn she had arrived wearing something else.

It was the shirt that she had intended to wear that Saturday, that terrible day when Charles had come to lunch at Adele's flat, but – like an ill omen – when she had taken it out of the dryer, she had found it covered in green smears. Minty had somehow managed to slip half an avocado in the machine while the shirt was drying.

There were still horrible green smears all over the front and sleeves and Polly could not imagine how she found herself wearing the shirt now. She had no recollection of changing and Adele was right. It looked awful.

'Perhaps your trusty friend Buttons will come to your rescue and clean it up for you,' laughed Adele, turning on her heel. Buttons, thought Polly. Her trusty friend? Perhaps she meant Ned. Oh what a relief it would be if Ned had decided to follow her to the party. She cast her eyes around the room in search of him but was surprised to come face to face with Charles.

'Hello, Polly,' he said, smiling that beautiful smile. 'Why did you never tell me your sister was Adele Taylor, *the* Adele Taylor?'

Polly felt numb and confused. Charles knew the answer to that question well enough. She had been careful to keep Charles away from Adele throughout their relationship. Had she always feared that her sister might steal him away? Perhaps, she thought. Or, at least, she had not wanted to run the risk. Charles had been suspicious that Polly never invited him back to her place, unless she was sure that Adele would be out, but it became harder and harder to keep the two of them apart.

In the end Charles and Adele met, but not through Polly. They met independently, as if by fate. Adele's firm, Stratton Walsh, was acting for a big US food company that was doing a survey of the UK food industry. Adele had been asked to prepare a report on a number of fast-growing food companies, including Green Baby, Charles's company. Charles had been very impressed by Adele's professionalism and efficiency. Also, a lot of other things, thought Polly, like her endlessly long thin legs and perfect skin and drop dead gorgeous cheekbones.

She wanted to find something cutting to say in reply

to Charles's question but both Charles and Adele had disappeared.

Polly glanced about her and was amazed to find Minty.

'Minty, darling,' she cried. 'What on earth are you doing here?' Minty was wearing a black leather jacket and her hair had been dyed bright pink.

'Mummy is always too busy to come to my parties so I thought I'd start going to hers.' Polly was shocked. She had to get Minty home as quickly as possible. She remembered Minty's last birthday party. It was true – Adele had been too busy at work to take the time off. She had asked Polly to take charge and they had hired a clown called Professor Potty. The professor had asked Minty to help with some of his tricks and, at the end of the show, he asked her what she wanted to be when she grew up. Minty had replied at once.

'I want to be one of those mummies who stays at home and looks after her children.'

Polly had been glad at the time that Adele had not been there to hear her daughter's words.

But, before Polly could take hold of Minty now, she too had disappeared and Polly's mother and father were standing in front of her.

'I can't understand this,' she said. 'This party is like a dream, a nightmare.'

'So nice to see Charles and Adele,' said Sue, glancing across the room. Polly could just make out Charles and Adele in the corner talking to *Carslip*. This was unbelievable, thought Polly. Curiously, above all the noise, she could even hear what they were saying.

'Of course Polly was fun,' said Charles. 'Quite sexy

in an untidy way, if you know what I mean.' Carslip's trout lips were quivering as he laughed.

'It's for the best really,' said Sue. 'I mean, Minty really needs a father and Adele needs a husband.'

'Husband?' asked Polly.

'Oh sorry, darling, didn't Adele tell you that Charles has proposed?' No, thought Polly, this really had to be a nightmare. 'You have to admit Adele Goodwood sounds nice – better than Polly Goodwood. That doesn't sound right at all.'

'Pamela Goodwood,' corrected her father. Pamela, thought Polly. How was it that she had ended up with that dreadful name? Her mother had explained to her once. Since they had twin girls, it had been decided that Sue would name one and John the other.

'It was my mother's name,' John said to Polly.

But Polly could take no more. She rushed out of the room into the hall and somehow found her way to the bathroom. When she looked in the mirror and saw herself, she nearly died. She was wearing nothing more than her white Father Christmas beard and Ned's mum's shiny cream girdle.

Polly fell to the floor and screamed.

'Are you all right? Are you all right?'

Polly opened her eyes and came face to face with a young man who looked familiar but whom she did not at once recognise. She was not lying in the bathroom but on a sofa. There were people swimming about the room but she no longer saw any of her family.

'I'm sorry, I must have fallen asleep and had a bad dream.' She tried to sit up and realised that she could not. She was lying underneath the young man and his hand was inside her shirt. She pushed his hand away and wriggled out from under him.

'I'm sorry, I'm not sure what I've been doing. I must have had too much to drink. Was I molesting you?' The boy laughed and shook his long fair hair out of his eyes. Polly noticed that he was naked from the waist up.

'No,' said the boy. 'I've been trying my best to molest *you* for the last half an hour but you were fast asleep and kept ranting on about people I've never heard of. I thought I'd never wake you up.'

'Sorry,' said Polly, checking herself all over. At least her shirt was still on and her jeans were done up. Fortunately, they were such a tight fit that it was like wearing a chastity belt. There was no way that anyone could remove them without considerable conscious assistance from herself.

The boy was smiling at her and looked very familiar but still Polly could not place him. She was beginning to feel nauseous. The ripple that she had experienced earlier in the evening came back and was fast building itself into a wave.

'Can I get you a glass of water?' asked the boy perceptively. But it was too late. Polly could not stop herself. The wave suddenly rose up inside her and, like the incident with Bobbin, it exploded all over the nearest person.

There was a sudden blinding flash and Polly turned to see Ed holding a camera and Warren grinning at his side. She turned back to look at the boy. His face, his hair and his chest were all covered in vomit but, at last, she recognised him. Nicholas Whitehouse, the Home Secretary's son, of course.

81

'Yessss. Classic one, Nick. Thanks Polly,' said Ed. 'Dad will kiss my arse for this.' Warren tossed a handful of paper napkins at Nicholas and then the two boys were out of the room in a shot.

Chapter Seven

Polly swore she would never drink or smoke again in her life. The following morning at her desk she still felt ill and, to make things worse, some of the bad dream she had experienced at the party was already starting to come true.

'I met your sister last night,' said Carslip. He had not yet asked her how the assignment had gone. Perhaps he could tell all he needed to know from the colour of her face.

'Adele?' Polly looked up and the pain in her head went shooting through her eyes as she stared at Carslip.

'Yes. She's younger than you, isn't she?'

'She's my twin.'

'Sor-ry.'

'How did you meet?'

'Well, Den was invited to dinner by Hubert Good-wood. He's a prospective Tory candidate at the next election. Poor bugger doesn't stand a chance, of course – the Tories are going to be completely shafted – and there was no way Den could be bothered to see him. So he sent me along.'

Hubert, thought Polly. Charles had often talked

about his brother but she had never met him. Hubert was a lawyer who lived somewhere out beyond the North Circular in Colingate, where his prospective constituency was, and he was always tied up either with his work or politics.

'It was a bloody good dinner,' continued Carslip.

'How did you meet Adele?'

'Oh, she just happened to be in the restaurant at the same time with her boyfriend, Hubert's brother. Charles, I think his name was.'

Polly gritted her teeth. She could not bear to hear Charles described as Adele's boyfriend.

'What was the restaurant?' she asked.

'Le Caprice.'

'Le Caprice?'

Charles had never taken Polly to Le Caprice. He had been generous and taken her to lots of nice restaurants. But not Le Caprice.

'Hubert insisted that they join us and we had a most interesting conversation,' said Carslip. He had clearly learnt something he wanted to tease her about and obviously intended making the most of it.

'Really,' said Polly.

'Yes, she told me all about you, *Pamela*.'

Polly scowled. 'How fascinating that must have been.'

'It was, believe me, Pussy. You'll find out soon enough how fascinating it was.'

Pussy, thought Polly. *Pussy?*

'Isn't that what Adele's little girl used to call you when she was a baby?' Carslip grinned his big trout grin.

Polly said nothing.

'Very suitable, I'm sure,' he added. 'But I'll have to ask Den about that.'

Polly opened her mouth to reply but, at that moment, Den himself stormed into the room and made straight towards them. Carslip leapt off Polly's desk and Polly, despite her whole body aching, managed to sit up straight.

'Fantastic, absolutely fucking fantastic,' cried Den, throwing a photograph on to the desk. Eddie had done a brilliant job. The picture could not have been better – or worse, depending how you looked at it – even if it had been stage-managed.

'We're going to splash on it tomorrow,' he said, 'with the headline SPLASH. Do you think, Polly, you could write a few lines of copy to go with it?' Carslip stared at the photograph, his jaw hanging open. Polly wondered whether he was going to be sick himself.

'Who is it?' he stammered.

'The Whitehouse kid, of course,' said Den.

'I thought – I mean, I thought the idea was—'

'The drugs angle? No, that was a lousy idea, Carslip. Tacky as hell. I don't know why you didn't tell me that last night.'

'I, well—'

'Polly tried to tell me but, since I wouldn't let her get a word in, she just went ahead and did her thing.'

'So I can see,' said Carslip, picking up the photo for a closer look. 'Disgusting.'

'Fucking brilliant,' said Den. 'This girl is a real star. Right on fucking target,' he added. 'She's wasted on Features – I should really have her on the news desk.'

Carslip sneered at Polly. 'What happened? Did you mix the poor bastard's drinks?'

Polly shrugged her shoulders. 'I'm not sure what happened. It was a sort of accident.'

'It was sheer fucking genius,' said Den. 'I'm going to buy you champagne after work tonight. Six o'clock, OK?'

Polly felt her stomach heave. 'Sorry, Den. Perhaps another night.'

Den raised an eyebrow. It was the second time the woman had snubbed him, he thought, but what the hell? He would get to her in the end.

He bent towards her and touched her under the chin. His breath was stale with cigarette smoke and Polly had to turn away to stop herself from throwing up again.

'Keep it going,' he said. 'Keep it going like this and you'll have old Arse-lick's job here in no time.'

Carslip looked as though he was going to explode with indignation but he said nothing until Den had left. Then he leant over Polly's desk and hissed, 'I'll get you for this, Pussy. Your dear sister has given me all the ammunition I need.'

Polly had been a bit wary at first about getting on the back of a motorbike but now that they were off, she was beginning to feel better. The cold night air was clearing her head at last.

'What a nightmare,' she said, clinging on to Ned and closing her eyes.

'It sounds as though the assignment couldn't have gone better,' Ned pointed out.

'But Carslip, my immediate boss, is livid – there's no telling what he might do to get his own back. I wonder what Adele told him.'

'He's probably just winding you up. Where do you want to try first?'

They went to see the rooms in Muswell Hill and Crouch End first. They were considerably cheaper than the one they were planning to look at in Highbury but the rooms were both very small and the Crouch End one smelt horribly of fried food.

'That was revolting,' said Polly as she climbed back on the bike. 'I thought I was going to be ill again.'

'Let's do the one by the Arsenal and then go to the pub?'

'OK,' she agreed.

The room near the Arsenal was in a small Victorian house owned by a woman in her thirties. She had frizzy brown hair, gold-rimmed spectacles and an American accent.

'I want a quiet, non-smoking woman,' she said, showing Polly the room.

It was perfect. A plain double bed, pine dressing table and a wooden floor. The curtains and rug looked clean.

'I don't smoke,' said Polly. 'And I lead a very quiet life.' She hoped that the woman was not telepathic and could not see the image that Polly was conjuring up of herself the night before.

'My name is Zeta,' said the woman. 'Scorpio?' she added suddenly and Polly jumped.

'Sorry?'

'No. Cancer, perhaps.'

Polly stared at Zeta.

'Your star sign, my dear,' she explained. 'I need to know. When is your birthday?'

'Er, July. The ninth of July.'

'Exactly,' said Zeta, 'as I thought. Cancer. Cancer is fine.'

'Thanks,' said Polly, glancing at Ned.

'It's important to ensure that the household is astrologically balanced,' said Zeta.

'Of course,' replied Ned.

'I'll think it over and give you a call in the morning,' continued Zeta and she smiled warmly at Polly as she took down her number.

'Of course she'll offer you the room,' said Ned as he placed a bottle of Coke in front of Polly and took a swig of Bud.

'I do hope so,' said Polly. 'It will be such a relief to move out of Adele's.'

'I can imagine.'

'I can't understand why I ever trusted her. You know, she was the first person I told when I started having suspicions about Charles.'

'Suspicions?'

'There was nothing obvious,' continued Polly. 'Charles had always been generous. But when he started showering me with presents, I couldn't help wondering if he was feeling guilty about something. I found out later that he'd already taken Adele out to dinner twice on evenings when he told me that he was working.'

'The bloke's a bastard – you're well shot of him.'

'Well, he *was* working, of course. He was doing that food project with Adele but Adele clearly had other projects in mind. To think she even had the nerve to ask me to babysit for her while she was out with my boyfriend. Can you believe it?'

Ned shook his head. 'Especially after all you did for her in Cambridge.'

'I know, when I think how worried I was about her having a baby in the middle of her degree course,' said Polly. 'I must have been crazy.'

'It was a very generous thing to do.'

'I suppose if my own career had not been so, well, non-existent at the time, I wouldn't have done it. I had this dreadful clerical job at a local paper in Dulwich and I couldn't bear the thought of someone as clever as Adele messing up her chances of getting a degree.'

'You're right. She would never have coped if you hadn't come up and looked after Minty.'

'Don't you think so?'

'No,' said Ned. 'She should be eternally grateful to you – it was a big sacrifice.'

'I suppose,' said Polly. 'But it was a good experience for me in the end. I really enjoyed looking after Minty and – although I hate the thought of having helped Adele – I can't say, even now, that I regret doing it.'

Ned smiled and listened.

'And I guess it was how my writing career got started,' added Polly. 'It was in Cambridge that I started writing articles on babycare.'

'Was that how you got the job with *New Baby*?'

'More or less.' Polly picked up her Coke.

'If you get the room with Zodiac Zeta, do you need me to help you move your things?' asked Ned. 'I could borrow a mate's van on Saturday.'

'That would be brilliant.'

'I'd let you stay with me in the meantime but there's really no room.'

'That's OK.'

'Is there nowhere else you can stay?'

'I think I can bear it for another couple of days,' said Polly. 'I try to stay out of Adele's way. But, if Zeta doesn't come through, a girl at work says I can sleep on her floor for a while.'

'OK. But let me know as soon as the Mystic American calls.'

'Thanks.'

Ned drained his beer and got up to buy another round but Polly wanted to go. She had hardly slept at all the night before and felt exhausted.

'I'll give you lift,' said Ned.

And he did, thought Polly, in more ways than one. She wondered how she might have survived the last couple of weeks if Ned had not been around to give her a lift.

Chapter Eight

The nightmare was always the same but the worst thing was that every morning she would wake up and know it was all absolutely true. She relived that dreadful day she had lost Charles to Adele every night in her dreams.

It had started out as a perfectly normal Saturday morning and Polly could never have guessed that it would end up being the worst day of her whole life.

She had got up late and skimmed through the papers while Minty sat at her feet and drew elaborate 'tattoos' on Polly's legs with a red felt-tip pen.

As usual, Polly planned to go over to Charles's flat in Kensington where she would stay until the following night.

'Leave the water in the bath,' she called to Adele, who was in the bathroom, and then added, 'I'll get it,' as the phone began to ring.

'Hello, darling,' he said.

Polly was always thrilled to hear his voice. 'Hello.'

'Look,' said Charles. 'The builders have completely gutted the kitchen and this place is a wreck. I can hardly breathe for the dust – I don't think we can stay at my place this weekend.'

'What do you mean?' asked Polly.

'Well, why don't I come over to you?'

Polly glanced around her. She could still hear a faint ripple of water as Adele soaked in the bath. 'I'll have to ask Adele. I've told you how depressed she is, how she hates me having people to stay. I'm sure I told you all about my sister.'

'Yes. But not the truth,' said Charles.

Polly froze. 'What do you mean?'

'I met Adele recently. I asked how her depression was and whether she was up to having visitors at home yet.'

Polly said nothing.

'Once we'd sorted out the little misunderstanding,' continued Charles, 'we both thought it was very funny. Why on earth have you been trying to hide me from your sister?'

'Why didn't you tell me you'd met Adele?' said Polly. 'When did you meet her?'

'There's no need to be so defensive. But why don't you answer my question first? Why have you been keeping Adele such a secret?'

Polly was not sure what to say. The truthful answer was too embarrassing to admit.

'I don't know,' she mumbled. 'I thought Adele might be uncomfortable having to explain about Minty and everything.' Polly felt an idiot as she said this. It made her sound ridiculous and self-righteous.

'That's crazy,' laughed Charles. 'It's nearly the twenty-first century, Poll. I'm hardly likely to condemn some-one for having a baby out of wedlock, am I?'

'I suppose not.'

'Look, why don't I come over and we can all have

lunch together and a good laugh about it? What do you say?'

'I don't know. I think Adele has other plans.'

'*Moi*?' said Adele coming into the room in a trailing white bathrobe. 'What are you saying about me now?' she added.

Polly covered the phone. 'Why didn't you tell me you'd met Charles?' she hissed.

'Christ, I don't know. I didn't want to upset you, I suppose. You'd tried to hard to keep us apart for so long.'

Polly sighed. 'Look Adele, Charles wants to come over here for lunch but *you're going out*, aren't you?'

'Not that I'm aware of,' said Adele quite loudly and then added in an even louder voice, 'I should love to have lunch with you and Charles. How sweet of you to suggest it.'

Polly scowled and went back to Charles.

'Did you hear that?' she asked.

'Sounds brilliant. When do you want me?'

'Any time,' said Polly. It was true that she wanted Charles any time and all the time – but she did not want to share him with her sister.

'I'll be over by one,' said Charles and rang off.

Polly and Minty walked to Sainsbury's to buy things for lunch.

'Can I help you cook?' she asked. 'Can we make a cake? Is it a special occasion?'

Polly smiled. 'Not really,' she said. But she could not help feeling excited about seeing Charles. She was always excited to see Charles.

It had been stupid, she told herself, that she had

been so paranoid about Charles and Adele meeting and, since Charles had now proposed, it would only have been a matter of time before she had to tell him the truth about her sister, that she was not the manic depressive she had portrayed.

Perhaps it was as well that it had all come out into the open. Perhaps Charles was right and they could all have a good laugh about it.

Polly bought a chicken to roast and some ginger to rub over it – she had read somewhere that it was a good alternative to boring old lemon. She had a list of ingredients to make the sticky chocolate pudding that she knew Charles loved.

'Can I lick out the bowl?' asked Minty.

'Of course,' smiled Polly. She was beginning to enjoy the prospect of the lunch and put a half-bottle of vodka and two bottles of white wine in the trolley.

'Can we get Coke as well?' asked Minty. So they got a six-pack of cans and checked out.

Polly and Adele drank the vodka as they prepared lunch and Polly had to admit she was starting to relax.

'God, I never realised you were such a good cook,' said Adele. 'Why do you seem to exist solely on Pot Noodles and takeaway pizza, if you can do all this?'

'I can never be bothered to cook just for myself,' said Polly. 'Keep stirring the chocolate or it will go all crumbly and disgusting.'

Adele stirred and sipped at her drink. Minty sat on the floor licking a chocolate-covered spoon and getting chocolate all over her face and clothes.

'So what do you make of him?' Polly found herself asking.

'Charles?'

'Of course. Do you like him?'

'He seems very nice. Bloody good catch, Poll.'

'He's perfect,' said Polly. 'Faultless.'

'Easy.' Adele took another swig of her drink. 'I wouldn't say that about any man.' Polly topped up Adele's glass.

'I thought you'd given up drinking?'

'I have,' said Adele. 'I just felt in the mood for a drink today. I suppose the prospect of being with you two lovebirds is too much for lonely old me.'

'Lonely old you,' laughed Polly. 'You could have any man you wanted.'

'Do you think so? Any man?'

'Yes, of course, you know it.'

Charles arrived early carrying two bottles of ice-cold champagne.

'What's this for?' said Polly. 'We're all going to be pissed as newts at this rate.'

'Well, I suddenly realised we haven't celebrated the good news yet,' said Charles.

'Good news?' Although Charles had not yet bought her a ring, Polly wondered whether he was referring to their recent engagement.

But he was not.

'Your job,' smiled Charles. 'Your new job on the *Globe*. I think we should drink a toast to your future Fleet Street career.'

'Yes, I think we'd better do it quickly,' laughed Polly. 'The editor was not around when I had my interviews but apparently he's hell. The life expectancy of a new recruit at the *Globe* is about a week, I'm told.'

'You'll be brilliant,' said Charles as he popped open a bottle of champagne. Polly pulled the table out into the middle of the kitchen and Minty helped her to lay it.

The lunch was a success. They drank and ate and laughed and talked but, even after two helpings of sticky chocolate pudding, Polly was still feeling a bit pissed. She was not used to drinking so much, particularly in the middle of the day.

'Can I go and watch TV now?' asked Minty.

'Yes, of course,' said Polly.

'She's a sweet girl,' said Charles.

'Do you really think so?' said Adele. Her cheeks were flushed and she was slouched across the table but still managed to look superbly elegant.

'Yes,' said Charles. 'And it's amazing how you've coped with your job, Adele, and looked after Araminta as well.'

It was an open opportunity for Adele to tell Charles everything Polly had done for her but she said nothing.

'I don't know how you've managed it,' continued Charles. 'You're an amazing person.'

'Thank you,' said Adele, looking directly into Charles's eyes.

Polly wanted to break in and say something about what she had done for Minty but it would only sound churlish, she thought. Charles poured the remains of the wine into his own and Adele's glasses. He seemed to have forgotten Polly's existence. Polly touched his hand with her glass.

'Oh, sorry, Poll,' he said and emptied half of his own glass into hers.

'How is the baby food report going?' he asked Adele. The conversation moved on to the project that Charles and Adele were working on and totally excluded Polly. She listened to the discussion all about the organic foods sector, its growth prospects and economics. But there seemed to be a subtext to the conversation that Polly could not fail to pick up.

God, don't you think you've got the wrong sister? she felt Adele asking as she maintained eye contact with Charles.

Polly told herself that she was being ridiculous but, nevertheless, she felt desperate to break the mood and struggled to her feet.

'I suppose we'd better start to clear up.'

'Oh leave all that, Polly,' said Charles but Adele was sitting up straight now.

'I must go up to the bathroom,' she said, slowly taking her eyes off Charles as she stood and left the room.

'Polly! Polly! The video's got stuck,' a voice came from the next room. 'Can you help me?'

Polly went into the sitting room to help Minty and when she came back the kitchen was empty. She could just hear the sound of Charles's footsteps disappearing up the stairs.

He must need to use the loo as well, thought Polly, her heart beating fast. She sat back down at the table and drank the rest of her wine. She waited and then drank the remains of her sister's wine. There was still no sign of either Adele or Charles. She looked at her watch. They had both been up there for ten minutes at least, she thought, as she drained Charles's glass too.

She waited another ten minutes and was not sure what to do. Should she go up and investigate? What on earth could they be up to, she thought, but only one possibility came to mind.

How could they be so crass and insensitive to sneak off upstairs together while she was still in the house? It was scarcely credible.

Polly got to her feet and started to clear the table. She made as much noise as possible. Perhaps if they heard her banging around downstairs, doing all the tidying up, perhaps then they would realise that they had to come down.

But there was nothing. She waited an eternity for another ten minutes to pass but still there was neither sight nor sound of them. Polly took a deep breath and started up the stairs. She could see the bathroom door was open and no one was in there. The door to Adele's bedroom was closed, however, and Polly could not bear to listen for noises. She rushed back downstairs and paced up and down the kitchen. How could she? How could Adele do this to her, she cried. It was everything she had always feared might happen but worse. Far worse. How could Adele be so cruel?

She knew that they had both had a lot to drink. She could imagine that Adele might have come on to Charles upstairs but to take him into her bedroom while his girlfriend, her sister, was still sitting at the table downstairs. It was inhuman.

Polly looked at her watch again and again. She thought about storming into the bedroom and demanding what was going on. But the predictability of the scene that would confront her was too dreadful to contemplate.

Then suddenly she heard someone go to the bathroom.

'Down in a sec, Poll,' called Adele. 'I've just been showing Charles a few papers.' Polly thought she heard a smothered giggle as Adele said the last words.

It was unbearable. Polly turned towards the stairs but, as she did so, little Minty appeared.

'Is something wrong?' asked the little girl.

Polly stopped dead in her tracks. Was it fair to let Minty watch Polly tear her mother to shreds? How could she have a horrible scene in front of this innocent child?

'Can we go out to the park?' asked Minty.

The last thing Polly wanted to do was to take her niece to the park. She wanted to gouge Adele's eyes out and tear off her long skinny limbs.

'Please,' said Minty.

'OK,' she said. Polly scribbled a note on the table. *Gone to the fucking park so you can get on with your fucking fucking in peace. OK?*

Polly slammed the door behind her and let Minty lead her down the street.

'Come on,' said Minty. 'It will be getting dark soon.' Polly walked beside Minty like a zombie. Somehow they got to the park and did all the things they usually did there. Polly was on total autopilot – her mind was back at the house in Noel Road committing unspeakable acts of violence on her sister. But Minty seemed oblivious of this, as she diligently built her sandcastles and then smashed them down again with her spade.

Of course, Polly was angry with Charles too but

she was already telling herself that it was not really Charles's fault. Adele knew that when she turned the charm on to full power, no man could resist her. Polly had seen her seduce men on previous occasions but not her own sister's boyfriend. Under her own eyes. It was unbearable.

When they got back to the house, Charles and Adele were not there. Polly's note was still on the table but it had been turned over and on the reverse side Adele had written *Sorry Poll. I'll be back soon and let's talk.*

Polly crumpled up the note and threw it on the floor. Talk. Talk! She wanted to scream, not talk. She would never speak to her sister again, she vowed, as she slammed a tray of fish fingers in the oven for Minty's tea.

She would get her own back on Adele, she swore, as she rubbed Minty dry after her bath.

Then she got into bed with Minty and read stories. They must have read at least a dozen but Polly was not thinking about the words she was saying. Her mind kept on playing and replaying the dreadful ordeal. It still hardly seemed real.

'And they all lived happily ever after,' were the words she said as she put down the book and switched out Minty's light. But, to herself, she was saying again and again that she would never rest until she had got even with Adele. Adele would pay for this and pay dearly, she resolved to herself bitterly.

When Minty was asleep, Polly went to her own room. She was lying awake in her bed still fully clothed when, some time later, she heard the sound she had been waiting for, the front door opening. She listened to the familiar sounds of Adele checking that all the electrics were switched off and bolting the door and then her tread on the stairs.

Polly wanted to rush from her room like a mad woman and bludgeon her sister to death but she stayed still, merely clenching her fists and breathing faster and faster. There would be other ways, other opportunities, she said to herself.

Half an hour later, all was quiet but Polly was still awake. It was impossible to sleep and she had been pacing up and down her room like a caged beast. She knew that she must see Adele. She could not believe that Adele had not, at least, had the decency to come and apologise.

She opened the door and crept along to her sister's room. Adele's door was ajar and Polly went into the room. Adele was fast asleep, her beautiful face in profile on the pillow, her naked shoulder and arm visible. Polly stood over her and watched. She looked like an angel but she was really the devil incarnate. On a chair by the bed, Adele had made a neat pile of her clothes. Is that how they had looked, wondered Polly, when she had removed them for Charles in the same room only hours earlier? Had she made him wait while she folded them up and stacked them neatly on the chair?

The bitch, thought Polly, as she glanced around the room. There was a large pair of scissors on top of Adele's desk. Polly picked them up and felt the blades. They were very sharp. Perfect, she thought, as she returned to Adele's bed and stared again at the flawless white skin. She held the scissors tightly in her right hand and then picked up the clothes. It took a long time but she cut all of them into tiny shreds.

On the way back to her room, Polly jumped in fright. The phone had started ringing and the sudden noise, following straight on the heels of her crime, startled her.

Her first thought was that it might be Charles. She would be angry of course, she thought, as she picked up the phone. She would be furious. But she knew already that she would forgive him. She had to forgive him.

'Hello?'

'Is Adele there?' The voice that answered was not Charles's but it was vaguely familiar.

'She's asleep,' said Polly. She wanted to say, *She's asleep – the bitch, the bitch, the cold-hearted bitch* but just managed to restrain herself.

'Oh, I'm sorry,' said the caller. 'I hadn't realised how late it was.'

'Is it?' said Polly numbly. She had lost track of the time.

'It's nearly midnight. Can you leave her a message?'

I never want to speak to the bitch again in my life, thought Polly, but she said, 'Yes.'

'Tell her Ned called.'

'Ned? Is that Ned-from-Cambridge Ned?'

'Yes. Is that Polly?'

'Yes.'

'Wow, long time no speak. How are you?'

Polly paused for a moment. What was the right answer to Ned's question? *Fine, fine* or *Shit, absolute shit – I feel like killing myself.* She opted for the former but Ned was not convinced.

'You don't sound too well,' he said. 'Are you sure you're OK?'

Ned's voice was kind. He hardly knew Polly and could have no desire to hear her problems but, at least, he sounded as though he cared. Polly burst into tears. She cried for a long time before she could form any coherent words but Ned stayed on the line. Eventually, she managed to sob out an abridged version of what had happened.

'That sounds terrible. I can't believe Adele could do such a thing.'

He paused. 'Look,' he added. 'I'm going up to Yorkshire to visit my old mum and dad tomorrow. Perhaps you'd like to come with me? Escape for a few days?'

Polly said no, she was OK. She did not want to trouble Ned but both she and Ned knew that she was not OK and being around Adele would only make things worse.

'Come with me,' said Ned.

'Are you sure?'

'Absolutely. I'll meet you at Euston Station – ten o'clock tomorrow morning.'

'Where will you be?'

'Oh, I don't know – how about outside that shop that sells all those fancy knickers and things?'

'OK,' said Polly. 'Outside the knicker shop. Thanks.' She put down the phone and lay back on her pillow. It felt almost like the hand of God – having Ned ring up like that and provide her with an escape, before she did something really crazy. It would be better to go away, to recover her strength.

Polly closed her eyes but still could not sleep. What

Adele had done was truly unforgivable, she repeated to herself, and she vowed never to rest until she had got her own back on her sister. Until she had won back Charles.

Chapter Nine

Dear Polly.

Charles stared at the empty page before him. It was not an easy letter to write. Of course, he should have called Polly days ago but it was now too late for the phone.

It had been a relief when Adele told him that Polly had gone away to stay with a friend for a few days. He hated to face the music but the guilt would not go away. He knew he had behaved appallingly and Polly had really loved him, perhaps still did. On the other hand, she might now hate him and that was an unbearable thought.

I can't think what to say, wrote Charles truthfully. *I don't know what came over me.* But that was not true. Charles knew exactly what had come over him. It had been lust, pure unadulterated lust. He had never been able to resist a woman like Adele. She was beautiful, confident and intelligent and the first couple of times he had met her she had given the impression of being totally indifferent towards him, as though she had barely noticed him.

He had been a bit pissed and had followed her up the stairs just in hope of a snog – not with the intention of taking her to bed. Or had he? He felt his penis start to harden as he thought back to that day.

Adele had not locked the bathroom door and was doing something to her face in the mirror when he had gone in. For a split second, he had thought of apologising, backing out of the room and waiting outside but, before he knew what had happened, she was in his arms. Her tongue was in his mouth and her hands running up the sides of his back.

'God, I want you,' he remembered muttering, or something like that. If it had not been for all the booze, of course, they might have waited. They would have waited. Neither of them had wanted to put Polly through hell but it had just been unstoppable. By the time they were in Adele's room and doing what they had to do, there was no going back. It had been Adele's idea to say they had been looking at some paperwork for the babyfood project in her room but Charles knew that no excuse would do. Polly was not a total idiot. And now she must hate him.

Charles threw down his pen and stood up. It was ten o'clock and he should have been at work but he had stayed late to see the plumber. The builders had pulled out the old kitchen but there was a problem with resiting the sink where Charles wanted it. It would mean a new manhole, a double seal, they told him the night before. The plumber would be round in the morning to have a look.

Charles wandered out to the kitchen. There were two men. They had only arrived a few minutes earlier but they were already having a break. One was crouched and leaning against a wall. He was reading the back page of a tabloid and sipping his tea. The other, a man Charles had not seen before, was staring at a hole in the floor.

'How's it going?' asked Charles.

'Fine,' said the man staring into the hole. The plumber, presumed Charles. He was a big man with a curly brown ponytail. 'Of course, we'll have to get consent from Building Control for the manhole but that shouldn't be a problem.' The other man stood up and all three of them stared into the hole. There was not much to see – just a dirty waste pipe with a hole in its side and water seeping out. It was making a bit of a stink though, thought Charles.

'How long will it take?'

'Depends on the council,' said the plumber. 'But we'll get the notice in tomorrow and I'll tape some cardboard over the hole for you.' Charles nodded. 'Perhaps, you should avoid overloading the system though.'

'You mean, go to the pub for a shit?'

'Exactly.' The men went back to work and Charles picked up the newspaper that had been left on the table. It was the one that Polly had just started to work for.

Charles could not help wondering how she was getting on and then, to his amazement, he noticed her byline on the front page. It seemed that she was responsible for the vomit story about the Home Secretary's son.

Impressive, he thought. And it certainly implied that she was not wasting her time pining over him. Charles felt his stomach lurch. He had assumed Polly would be heartbroken about the business with Adele. He had been convinced that she was passionately in love with him. In fact, the power of her love had been beginning to get on his nerves. Perhaps that had also driven him into the arms of Adele.

He went back to his room, closed the door and picked up his pen again.

I tried calling but couldn't get you. I have been thinking about you all the time. He wanted to go on and say that it had been pure madness, drunkenness, that he wanted her back, he wanted her to forgive him. But did he really want that? In fact, if he were honest for a few moments, he knew that he had felt an enormous relief when he had blown his relationship with Polly apart. He had already been regretting the proposal.

He had asked Polly to marry him one evening, once again after he had had a bit too much to drink. Actually, he was not aware that he had *asked* her precisely. They had talked about marriage and he had said how much he would like to get married some day and have kids. Polly had made the jump from the general to the specific.

'Oh, Charles, really?' she had said. 'I would so love to marry you and I so want to have children too.' He should have put her right, there and then. He should have explained that he had been talking generally – you know, at the right time when the right woman came along. But he could not bear to do it. Polly's face was beaming with happiness and how could it hurt if she thought Charles wanted to marry her? He had just resolved to be more careful in the future and avoid setting a date for the wedding.

It was a shame about Polly, he thought. He had really enjoyed having sex with her. She was probably the best lay he had ever had, even though she seemed to have an absurdly low opinion of her body. She was sensational. Just the right amount of flesh and all those wonderful curves. He wished that the builders were not there as he suddenly fancied disappearing into the shower for a wank.

But Polly had had to spoil it all by being so damned needy. It had become a routine. Every time, after the sex but before she let him fall asleep, she would ask the same question.

'Charles, do you love me?' The words almost made his hair stand on end.

'Don't ask silly questions,' he would answer but she always did.

And that, of course, was the wonderful thing about Adele. Adele was not an emotional cripple, like Polly and all the rest of his past girlfriends. Adele was different. She knew who and what she was and she was proud of it. She didn't need a man to keep telling her all the time how brilliant she was, how much he loved her. They had spent almost all of the last ten days fucking insatiably but never once had Adele raised the 'love' word. It was a funny thought, laughed Charles, but he almost *loved* her for that.

Adele's self-possession was a challenge. She seemed unique in being the only woman in the world who did not want to tie him down. There was no way he could give up Adele and go back to Polly now, thought Charles. He needed to win Adele, he needed to control her. He wanted to tame her, to bring her to her knees so that she too would beg him to tell her he loved her.

It was not a scene that was easy to imagine. Adele was so cool and proud. He realised that he was beginning to worship the ground on which she stood. Charles Goodwood was becoming needy himself. He wanted to have Adele all for himself. It was a curious feeling, one that he had never experienced before. Perhaps, after all, he was falling in love?

Charles went back to the letter. The important thing now though was to apologise so that Polly did not write him off as a total shit and – what else? Of course to keep her dangling. Charles liked to keep all his exes dangling, dangling on bits of string that he could pull in whenever he wanted. There were countless occasions when he had been between girlfriends and had needed a fuck. It had always been easy to make the phone call, make the date. The ex always thought this was her big chance, Charles was coming back to her at last, and in many cases he might have done. But they were all so bloody needy.

Except Adele.

My poor darling, I'm so sorry, he wrote and left it at that. He signed, sealed and dropped the letter into the postbox on his way to the tube. And then it was off his mind at last, he thought with relief.

Polly opened the letter the following evening. It was Friday, her last night at Adele's. Zeta had got back to Polly that morning and offered her the room and Ned had agreed to help her move in the following day.

Polly had just made herself a toasted cheese sandwich and was about to go to her room to carry on with her packing when Adele came into the kitchen with a handful of letters.

'The only one for you,' she said, holding out the

letter and watching Polly as she recognised the handwriting on the envelope. It was from Charles. And Adele was right; Charles was the only one for her and always would be.

Polly glared at her sister, picked up her supper and went upstairs to her room.

Polly's room, as usual, was in a terrible state but this time because she had, for once, been tidying up. She was trying to pack everything into boxes so it was easier for Ned to get it all in the van the following morning.

She put her sandwich on the floor and made some space on the bed to sit down and read the letter. She read it at least a dozen times until she knew every word by heart.

Dear Polly. Was it significant that he said 'dear'? Was she still dear to him or was that just an expression he had used automatically, a formality? Almost certainly the latter, she had to admit to herself but still she could not resist imagining Charles saying those words – *dear Polly*.

She stood up and immediately put her foot in the toasted sandwich but Polly still picked it up and took a huge bite. Reading the letter was making her dreadfully hungry.

I can't think what to say. He was embarrassed, sorry, thought Polly. Of course he was, wouldn't anyone be? Yes, perhaps, but not everyone would admit it, she told herself.

I don't know what came over me. I do, Polly screamed to herself. It was that bitch, Adele. She was all over you like the bloody measles. It must have been like trying to escape the embrace of a boa constrictor. Polly tried to picture Adele coiled round Charles and mercilessly dragging him into her room but the more pragmatic side of her mind was already casting doubt on this scene. Surely a grown man, over six feet tall, could have extricated himself if he had really tried? It was undeniable, Polly had to concede. But then perhaps Adele had a kind of hypnotic effect on men. Charles might have been genuinely paralysed.

I tried calling you but couldn't get you. Now that was certainly true, thought Polly. Adele was hardly likely to tell Polly that Charles had been trying to get hold of her and she would never have passed on Ned's number in Yorkshire. Nonetheless, said a nagging voice within her, Charles had known that Polly was starting at the *Daily Globe* that Monday and it was not difficult to find the paper's number. There had been five whole days when he might have called her, when she had been dying for him to call her. But it was probably too late by then, said a more positive voice. As time had passed since that dreadful Saturday, it would have been harder and harder to pick up the phone and Charles had probably decided it would be better to write.

I have been thinking about you all the time. This was the sentence that did the most. It made Polly's heart beat twice as fast and her face flush. She took another huge bite of her sandwich. What else could it mean? Charles was not only sorry but he regretted what had happened between him and Adele. Why, otherwise, would he have been thinking about her all the time?

The letter was signed *'yours ever, Charles'* not *'love, Charles'*. But wasn't that better? Wasn't that what she always wanted to be? To be his, forever.

Polly put the remains of her sandwich down on the floor, folded the letter and put it safely in her bag. She looked around her at the mess and set about her packing with renewed vigour.

She would get out of Adele's house and start thinking about herself for a change. She would go on a diet again and really stick to it this time. She would get a haircut – she could not remember the last time she had been to the hairdresser's – and get her highlights redone. She would make sure that the next time she saw Charles he was in no doubt about what he was missing.

It was ridiculous that she had been prepared to give in so easily, she thought to herself. Just because poor Charles had fallen temporarily under Adele's spell, it did not mean that he would be blind forever. Already he was sorry and Polly would forgive him: in time. In no time, she thought, if she were honest. But, no, it would be a mistake to go running after him at once, immediately after receiving this letter. She would let him sweat it out a bit. She would get herself looking as fantastic as she possibly could and then she would make her move.

Polly heard Adele laughing on the phone downstairs. That's right, she thought, you enjoy yourself while you can – but the last laugh will be on you, my dearly beloved sister. I swear it. She wanted to let out an absurd cackle to endorse this thought but she just kicked the half-eaten cheese sandwich under the bed. It might be weeks before Adele discovered it there and in the meantime it would become putrid and disgusting and make the most terrible smell.

Chapter Ten

'One of us simply has to go. It's either Bobbin or me.'

Ned heard Polly laugh on the other end of the phone. She always enjoyed his impersonations of Adele.

'I thought Minty was going to choose Bobbin, at first,' said Ned.

'Poor Minty, she must be very upset.'

'I said you were really excited about the idea of looking after him and Minty could visit whenever she likes.'

'Yes. It's very kind of Zeta to agree – she doesn't usually allow her lodgers to have pets. But she says rabbit chi is OK.'

'Rabbit cheese?'

'Chi,' said Polly. 'You know, energy or whatever. According to Zeta, rabbit chi is calming and therapeutic.'

'Not according to Adele,' laughed Ned. *'He does his ghastly little poos everywhere. There's a terrible stink in the house and he is always giving the nanny asthma attacks,'* he continued, doing his Adele impersonation again and Polly had to laugh.

'How were things at Noel Road?' she asked. 'Other than the Bobbin crisis.'

'Well, the new nanny was just leaving with her boyfriend when I arrived. She said something about Adele having already made them miss the start of the film they were going to. I don't think she will last long.'

'What about Minty? Is she OK?'

'I can't really say,' said Ned. 'She insisted on getting Bobbin out of his cage one last time before I took him away and the creature hopped straight off to the bathroom where it went completely bonkers. I'm dreadful with animals and, by the time I'd got hold of the brute, he'd upset a huge jar of face powder and made a terrible mess. *He's used up £50 worth of my new Factor Whatever face cream*, screamed Adele – although I could only see a tiny speck of something on the poor creature's nose.'

'Adele does spend a fortune on make-up,' said Polly. 'Good old Bobbin.'

'That's not what I was thinking. Especially when he nipped me in the finger as I shoved him in the cage. I never realised that rabbits had such sharp teeth.'

'Poor you. Thanks so much for going to get him.'

'I'll tie the little bastard on the back of my bike and drive him over to you later, if you like?'

'Is that safe?'

'Only joking. I'll walk him over.'

'Thanks, Ned. I'm sorry to be such a nuisance. I would have gone to collect him myself but I really didn't feel up to seeing Adele again – even after all this time.'

'How long is it now since you moved out?'

'Two months,' said Polly.

'You miss her, don't you?'

'Adele?'

'No, you twerp. Minty.'

'Yes I do. Badly.'

'Look, I'll ring up Adele and suggest that you and I take Minty out for the day next Saturday. I'll pick her up and drop her back, if you like.'

'Oh Ned, that would be fantastic.'

'So long as I promise not to let Minty anywhere near the bike, I expect Adele will agree. The nanny doesn't work weekends and I think your sister is already feeling the weight of her increased maternal responsibilities. She must, at last, be realising how much she took you for granted.'

'I doubt it. But are you sure, Ned, about Saturday?'

'Of course.'

'I mean, I don't want to be a pain. I thought you liked to spend Saturdays working?'

I do, I do, thought Ned. With the courier job that he really needed for the cash, he only got the chance to do his writing in the evenings and at weekends. So why the hell was he offering to spend a whole day with someone else's kid? The truth was, he had to admit, that he had hardly been able to write at all for the last couple of months. Something had broken his concentration and, for the first time in his life, he was finding it hard to come up with ideas.

'I'll do extra on Sunday,' he said.

'Thanks,' said Polly.

Ned put down the phone. He sat for a few minutes in front of his friend's PC. It was bloody decent of David to let him use it but he had been sitting there in front of the screen for an hour hardly writing a thing. The words just would not come. His thoughts kept drifting away to other matters.

Perhaps a break would do him some good, he thought. It was possible that he had been overdoing things, trying too hard. He wandered into the sitting room. David was out and so Ned looked for a CD to put on. There was nothing apart from classical and a lot of choral stuff – not really Ned's taste at all. He was surprised that it was David's.

David had been in the same college as Ned at Cambridge. They had both rowed in the University's B boat, Goldie, and had enjoyed many good nights out together with lots of beer and loud music, nothing fancy like this stuff. But then Ned remembered David's girlfriend, Katriona. Wasn't she always dragging him off to concerts these days? They must be her CDs. She had probably chucked out all David's stuff, poor bastard. That's what women did to you, thought Ned. They tried to take you over, to change you. Oh, it was usually quite slow and subtle to start with and you were so gagging for them that they could make you do anything they wanted. But, before you knew where you were, you were tied down, hand and foot: listening to their music, eating their food, doing all *their* bloody stuff all the time.

He felt hungry and wandered into the kitchen. He crouched down in front of the fridge and had a good root around. There were all kinds of girlie things, like taramasalata and live natural yoghurt and cream cheese and masses of rabbit food. Dear old Bobbin would have a field day in here. But also, thank God, he found milk, eggs, bacon and bread. Poor David had not been totally emasculated yet.

Ned got out the frying pan and made himself a fried egg and bacon sandwich. It was delicious. He wolfed it down, then picked up Bobbin in his cage, left a note for David and let himself out of the flat.

It was seven o'clock on a Thursday evening and Ned had nothing much to do until he met up with Polly later, so he decided to go home for a nap. He walked and it took a good twenty minutes from David's to his own place, if that's what you could call it. Ned was literally living in a broom cupboard in Cornwall Mansions, a converted Victorian almshouse in Rosebery Avenue. The cupboard was on the main stairs and had come with a flat that another Cambridge friend of his was renting on the next floor up. It had separate access and the friend didn't need it so Ned asked to use it.

'You can't live in a bloody broom cupboard,' said his friend. But Ned had assured him that he could. It was only temporary until he found something else, he had said, but he had been there for nearly six months now.

The rent was cheap – he gave his friend twenty pounds a week – but there was only just enough room to squeeze in a mattress. You could forget about swinging cats or even rabbits. Anything else that went in had to go on top of the mattress and there was no window – just a vent in the door. Hardly surprisingly, Ned had never invited anyone back to 'his place'.

It was a dreadful way to live but it was one up on the street, he thought, as he passed some poor bastard huddled under a dirty blanket in a doorway. And, after all, he was quite happy on his own, wasn't he? He had never felt the attraction of dinner parties and

118

all that cosy middle-class materialism. A mattress in a cupboard and the use of a friend's PC were good enough for him.

Polly was now well settled in her new room. Zeta lived a quiet life, rarely going out. But, on Thursday evenings, she had people round for a 'meeting' and that evening she had invited Polly to join in. Polly watched Zeta's guests arrive from her bedroom window. Some were elderly and some looked like teenagers. Some arrived in expensive cars and others looked as if they might have been sleeping rough on the streets. Polly wished she had asked what the meeting was about and almost regretted declining Zeta's offer.

Since moving out of Adele's, she had been leading almost as quiet a life as Zeta's. Of course, her new job was absorbing and she was really enjoying it but, when she got home in the evening, there was nothing. Except her memories, of course.

Memories of nights out with Charles. The way he had laughed when she had struggled with the menus of the smart restaurants he used to take her to. The night he had persuaded her to try her first oyster. The night they had first gone to bed together. His penis.

But no, she thought. Enough of that. She picked up a magazine and tried to read an article about 'sex substitution'. Apparently stroking pets was a big help. Poor Bobbin, thought Polly, I hope he can cope with the extra attention.

She looked at her watch. Ned and Bobbin would be there any minute. Ned had been so kind. It was hard to believe that she had lived under the same roof as Ned for almost a year in Cambridge but had never got to know him. He had always kept himself to himself. She wished she could be more like him, that she could just focus on her work and blank out everything else.

But Charles *was* everything else. Charles was everything she had always wanted. He was the future husband, future father of her children. He was the man with whom she would buy a house and start a family and get on with the things in life that were really important. Being a wife, a mother, a homemaker. Creating the family life that, perhaps, she had never had. A happy home.

Ned said there would be other men but Polly was not so sure. She examined her face in the mirror after she had brushed her hair. The lines between her nose and mouth were already beginning to deepen and she had to remember to hold her head up straight or she had a bit of a double chin. She had tried to stick to her diet but it had been so hard.

For a week she had skipped lunch every day and was actually starting to feel really slim. Her trousers felt looser and she had managed to squeeze into a skirt she had not worn in years.

But Carslip was giving her a hard time at work and eventually she had taken refuge, as she always had done, in King Size Mars bars and quickly the pounds had crept back on.

The long evenings were the most difficult times to avoid temptation. Evenings that could only be filled with tubes of Pringles, packets of chocolate digestive biscuits and cans of fizzy drinks.

But, at least, it wasn't booze, she thought, like her mum. She had watched Sue progress from having the odd glass of wine when Dad took them all out to dinner to regularly downing at least half a bottle of vodka every night. Her hair was thin, her face quite lined but Sue wore lots of make-up and this usually made her look younger than her true age. Nonetheless, she was a sad case, thought Polly, as she got to her feet.

The doorbell had been ringing on and off for the past half an hour but Polly had recognised a particularly loud blast. A confident, masculine blast.

'Ned,' she thought and soon she heard a heavy tread on the stairs approaching her room.

She opened her door and looked out. She could hardly believe her eyes.

'What did he say?' asked Ned.

'Oh, I can hardly talk about it,' said Polly. It was over an hour later and still her heart was racing. 'I hope you didn't mind me calling you and rearranging to meet in the pub,' she added. They were sitting at a table in the Highbury Tavern with Bobbin in his cage on the table between them.

'Not at all.' Ned had bought Bobbin a carrot and was trying to wedge it through the bars.

'It's just that we needed to talk,' said Polly. 'You know – on our own.'

'I understand.'

There was silence for a while and Polly watched Ned as he fed Bobbin.

'Do you want to tell me about it?' asked Ned. The words immediately made Polly's eyes fill with tears. Ned was so kind, too kind, she thought.

'Do you mind? It must be dreadfully boring for you.'

'I don't mind,' said Ned, stuffing the carrot further into the cage as Bobbin continued to gnaw hungrily.

'He said he just needed to see me. I was so surprised. I know I looked a state and the room was a complete mess. All the time we were talking I was trying to kick things under the bed.'

'He just needed to see you?'

'He said that he wanted to say how sorry he was and to check I was OK. It was so embarrassing.'

'What? Seeing him again?'

'No – when he discovered a half-eaten family size pack of cheese and onion Hula Hoops under my pillow.'

'It might have been kinder to have stayed away.'

'Oh, do you think so?' said Polly. 'That's what I thought at first. But then I started wondering again and I realised that was exactly the point.'

'What was the point?'

'Well, if Charles really had not wanted to see me again, he would not have gone to the trouble of finding out where I was staying and turning up like that, would he?'

'So?'

'It must mean that he misses me. Ned, I'm sure that, if Adele gave him up, he would come back to me at once.'

'Probably,' said Ned. 'Unless he's crazy. Which, by definition, I suppose he must be – for choosing Adele over you in the first place.'

Polly blushed. 'Do you think Charles is crazy?'

Ned grinned. 'Like the bloke who went to the doctor's wrapped in clingfilm?' he asked.

'What?'

'The doctor said, "I can see you're nuts."'

They both laughed.

'That is a really terrible joke,' said Polly.

'But it did the trick.'

'What trick?'

'It made you laugh,' said Ned, touching Polly's hand. 'You were looking so serious. You know, you've really got to put the Charles thing behind you.'

'But I can't,' said Polly. 'I can't give up and let her win.'

'Adele?'

'Yes, I have to get even. I have to win back Charles.'

'Polly, that's ridiculous. Forget it. Forget all about them and get on with your *own* life.'

Polly said nothing for a moment but stared at Bobbin, who was contorting himself to reach a shred of carrot that was dangling outside the bars of the cage.

'He asked to kiss me,' she said.

'Did you let him?'

'I couldn't resist. I tried to at first. But he held my arms and forced his mouth on to mine.'

'You should have told him to fuck off.'

'I know and I did try to push him away but then I just let go. I just gave in and let him kiss me, really kiss me. It was incredible – I can't describe what it was like.'

Ned sipped his beer and looked away.

'Sorry,' said Polly.

'No, go on,' said Ned. 'What happened then?'

'Well, he wanted to—'

'Make love to you?'

'Yes.'

'Did you?'

'No.'

'Why not?'

'I don't know. I just couldn't. I wanted to and he clearly wanted to.'

'So?'

'I don't know. At first, I thought, why not? Perhaps, if we went to bed together again, he would remember how good the s—, how good things used to be.' Ned picked up the remains of Bobbin's carrot and took a bite.

'I'm sorry,' said Polly. 'You don't want to hear all this.'

'I do,' said Ned, looking up. 'I'm interested, really.'

'Well, he was all over me. He told me how much he'd missed me in bed and he was kissing me like he wanted me so much.' Polly shivered as she thought about it. 'But I said we had to talk first. I asked him if he was leaving Adele.'

'What did he say?'

'He just said, "Oh, let's not talk about Adele," but I insisted.'

'And?'

'He said he couldn't leave her.'

'Why not?'

'I don't know. By that time, the mood had changed and he said he was sorry and he really ought to go. The minute I closed the door behind him, I realised what an idiot I'd been.'

'Why?'

'Oh Ned, don't you see? He was crying out for me to take him back and I just had to make it difficult. I am such a fool.'

'Maybe.' Ned had finished his beer and went back to the bar for another.

Polly watched him go. He was tall and broad-shouldered with dark untidy hair. He wore a scruffy jacket and faded jeans and Polly could not remember a time when she had seen him in any other clothes. Poor Ned, she thought. He probably had enough problems of his own without listening to hers all the time.

'So what are you going to do now?' asked Ned when he returned.

'What do you mean?'

'Are you going to call him?'

'Well, perhaps I should wait a couple of days. What do you think?'

Ned frowned. He had spilt some of his beer on Bobbin.

'You're not going to give up on him, are you?'

Polly shook her head and she watched the rabbit wriggle as he tried to lick the beer off his ear. 'He's the only one,' she said.

'Then I think you should give it your best shot.'

Chapter Eleven

The following morning Polly skipped breakfast and squeezed into her black leather jeans. When she appeared at the newspaper in them, Carslip almost had a heart attack.

'Did you put those on for Den, Pussy dear?' he sniped.

Polly said nothing. She had called Charles at his office before she had left for work. She knew how he liked to get to work early.

'Polly?' His voice had sounded a bit alarmed. But, no, not alarm thought Polly – just surprise. A pleasant surprise, she hoped.

'I must see you for lunch,' said Polly. 'I'm sorry about last night.'

'Don't—' Charles had started to say. Don't what? she wondered now. Don't be sorry? Don't meet me for lunch? But Polly would never know.

'There's a bar across the street from your office called the Green Goblin. I'll be there at twelve,' she had said and she quickly put the phone down. Why had she done that? Why had she not waited to hear Charles's response? Had she not heard the faintest 'but' before the line went dead. But what? But there's no point,

Polly? But I can't make it? She did not want to hear those words. Polly clung to her memory of the night before. He had held her in his arms again. He had tried to make love to her. He would be hers again, she was certain of it. Perhaps even that night . . .

'A pity Den's not in today,' said Carslip and Polly stopped dreaming. She had already booked to have her hair done at half past ten and hoped she would be able to come up with a good enough excuse to escape the office for her appointment. But she did not need to worry for long. Carslip came to her aid.

'There's been a big flood down in Kent somewhere,' he told her. 'Loads of people up to their necks in mud. I want you to get down there, Pussy. Find a few people to interview and write a really good, colour piece on it for us. Sort of brown, turd colour, I suggest?'

Polly got to her feet. 'OK,' she said.

'I do hope the trousers don't get ruined,' he added with mock concern. 'I'll get a snapper to go with you.'

'Don't bother,' said Polly. 'I can arrange that myself.'

She asked the photographer to meet her downstairs in the lobby at two. The timing would be tight but she could just about make it before darkness started to fall. It was risky and Carslip would love it if she messed up but, at the end of the day, Charles was more important than her job. Far more important.

Polly was the only customer in the Green Goblin. She sat on a stainless steel stool by the window and sipped a glass of champagne. Why had she ordered champagne, she wondered. Was she really so certain that there would be something to celebrate?

A procession of three women arrived and sat down at the bar, bearing gifts like the three wise men, thought Polly. They were obviously waiting for someone else, someone special – perhaps a friend, whose birthday it was.

Polly listened to their conversation.

'God, I never thought Higgins would let us all out of the office *together*.'

'Anyone would think our bosses were incapable of picking up a phone.'

'Men,' laughed the black woman.

'That bitch you work for is as bad,' said an older woman, looking at the third, a thin pale girl. The older woman could easily have been her mother.

'Women bosses are the worst,' said the girl.

Polly checked her watch and took another sip of champagne.

The door swung open again and she looked up but it was not Charles. It was the woman that the other three had been waiting for.

'Nibbles!' A cry of recognition went up.

'Over here,' called the black girl quite unnecessarily since the bar was empty apart from Polly.

The woman called Nibbles made her way across the room. She was short, despite wearing very high heels, and wore a tight skirt that exaggerated her wide hips. Her hair was blond and rather obviously permed and, as she smiled, Polly saw that she had bright white incisors that jutted over her lower lip. She reminded Polly of Bobbin. Perhaps the nickname Nibbles had something to do with those teeth?

'Sorry,' said Nibbles. 'Charles asked me to go and get him a sandwich before I left.' Polly felt her blood go cold at the sound of his name. Charles? Was it *her* Charles, she wondered as she felt her ears straining, almost twitching, to hear more.

'You're so lucky,' said the older woman.

'What do you mean?' asked Nibbles. Her three companions giggled.

'You know,' said the black girl. 'To work for Charles Goodwood – he's so gorgeous.'

· There could be no mistaking now, thought Polly. Charles Goodwood. So gorgeous. There could not be the slightest doubt as to the identity of Nibbles's boss. Polly strained to hear more.

'He said it was no problem if I wanted to go out for lunch, especially since it's my birthday,' said Nibbles. Polly felt her cheeks flush. She wondered whether Charles had tried to call her at the *Globe*. She had not been able to go back to the office after her hair appointment as she wanted Carslip to think she had already gone off on his assignment. She could easily have missed Charles's call.

'He's so sweet,' purred the thin pale girl. It was kind of him to let his secretary go out, thought Polly, but it was also clear that he was not going to turn up for lunch with her. He had asked Nibbles to get him a sandwich.

Polly should really have left at once but she wanted to eavesdrop a little more, so she bought herself another glass of champagne and sat down slightly closer to the group of women.

Nibbles opened her presents and said all the right things. One of the presents was a black push-up bra and Nibbles's friends made her try it on over her shirt.

'Charles will certainly notice you in that,' laughed the black girl.

'He touched my face yesterday,' said Nibbles in a soft voice. 'He said I had a newspaper smudge on my cheek but I think it was an excuse.' Polly thought immediately of the day she had met Charles, the day he had removed the Fat Controller sticker from her cheek.

'Oh, poor Nibs,' said the older woman, putting an arm round her friend's shoulder. 'She's never gotten over that grope at the office Christmas party.'

Grope? Office Christmas party? Polly could hardly believe her ears.

'That was years ago, wasn't it?' said the pale thin girl, who drained her glass and sat back in her chair. Years ago. Thank God for that, thought Polly. She had feared for a moment that Charles might have been seeing this woman, Nibbles, while he had been going out with her.

'Must be three years ago,' said the older woman. 'He was one of the new graduates who started that year.' Three years, thought Polly, that was well before she had ever met Charles. Just because he had been ensnared so treacherously by Adele, there was no reason to think that Charles was some kind of philanderer. Polly breathed an audible sigh of relief and Nibbles glanced across at her.

'It was more than a grope,' said Nibbles. 'I saw him for several months after that party.'

Polly could not help being surprised at this revelation. Nibbles was not an unattractive woman. In fact, thought Polly, as she watched Nibbles cross her short plump legs and expose a considerable amount of

130

dimpled thigh, she could imagine a lot of men thinking her quite sexy. But she was certainly not in the same league as Adele. Perhaps Charles was not really that fussy about the women he went to bed with, said a voice in Polly's head. But that was ridiculous, Polly told herself at once. Nibbles probably had a fantastic personality and it was a good thing that Charles could appreciate that in a woman as well as the length of her legs.

'Charles was the only one for me. No one else will ever be the same,' added Nibbles. Polly heard the words and shivered. Isn't that exactly what she, Polly, had said – Charles was the only one?

As Nibbles's friends rallied round – 'Come on, cheer up. It is your birthday', someone said – Polly drained the second glass of champagne and got to her feet.

She had not drunk much but, having missed breakfast and lunch, the alcohol had gone straight to her head.

She must see him, Polly thought to herself, as she made her way to the bar and stumbled over the older woman's huge handbag. The waiter caught Polly's arm and steadied her. Then she quickly paid her bill and left.

Outside in the street, she looked up at the black and white office block that towered above her like a giant Liquorice Allsort. She had no idea which window was closest to Charles's desk but she imagined him looking out of it, seeing her there and rushing down the stairs. Then she told herself that was absurd and she slipped inside the revolving glass entrance door.

'I've come to see Charles Goodwood,' she informed the receptionist as she arrived unsteadily at the front desk. The receptionist looked hard at Polly as if to say *not again* but that was crazy, thought Polly – she had never set foot in the place in her life.

She waited while the receptionist tapped out a number and heard her say in a bored voice, 'There's a visitor here in reception for you, Charles.'

The receptionist listened before turning to Polly. 'What's the name?' she asked.

'Polly. Polly Taylor,' she said, reddening slightly. For God's sake, Charles must have guessed who it was. She played with a small display of Top Banana yoghurt pots that sat on the counter.

The receptionist was listening on the phone again. A slight frown flitted across her brow but then she turned to Polly and smiled.

'I'm afraid he's just about to go into a meeting. He says he will call you later.'

'Later?' said Polly, the yoghurt pots tumbling down. 'No, I need to see him now.' She grabbed the phone out of the receptionist's hand, the young woman sighed and began to reassemble the yoghurt display.

'Charles?' Polly cried into the phone. 'Charles? It's me, Polly. Look, I really have to see you – it will only take a minute.'

Without a moment's hesitation, Charles said he would be right down. Polly gave the phone back to the receptionist with a triumphant flourish. Why had she felt in such a panic? What was it that she needed to do? Why was it so urgent that she should see Charles at once?

A few minutes later, Charles appeared and Polly

was taken aback. She knew that he was good-looking but it always surprised her just how gorgeous he really was.

He was wearing a dark grey suit and pale blue tie. His eyes were blue and his hair long, blond and silky. He smiled and Polly felt her heart leap into her mouth. It was beating so fast that she wondered if she would be able to speak.

'What on earth are you doing here? Has something happened?' asked Charles, taking Polly's hand and guiding her across the lobby to some low black leather seats. Black leather on black leather, Polly's jeans creaked as she sat down.

'It was just last night, I—'

'I'm sorry about that,' interrupted Charles.

'No, I—'

'Listen,' said Charles. 'You're a beautiful woman, Polly, and you're sexy as hell but . . .'

'But?'

Charles shook his head and looked away. 'It's no good,' he said.

'What do you mean, it's no good? Do you mean Adele? Do you think I can't forgive you after Adele?'

'Polly' said Charles but Polly did not want to be interrupted.

'I love you, Charles. You know I've always loved you. We can go back to how we were. We can forget everything that's happened over the last couple of months.' Polly could feel the receptionist staring at her but she did not care.

'We can't,' whispered Charles and he looked away.

'Why not?'

Charles turned back to face her. He was the most

handsome man Polly had ever seen. She wanted to wake up beside him every morning, she wanted—

'Adele and I are engaged.'

Polly wanted to die.

'The mud is everywhere,' said the woman, a baby in one arm and a toddler on the opposite hip.

'It's awful,' said Polly. The snapper snapped. The water was up to their thighs but Polly didn't care. She wouldn't have minded if it had been over her head.

'Do you want to see upstairs?' asked the woman with the children. 'I had to put the animals upstairs.'

Polly started to shake her head but the snapper said, 'Go on. A cute picture of the family huddled together in the bedroom with cats and dogs might be good.'

They followed the woman upstairs and found themselves squashed into a bedroom with about thirty pigs. They were huge, the size of cows.

'Christ,' said Polly, opening the door again to escape.

'Careful,' said the woman, slamming the door shut. 'They're large Gloucester Whites – don't frighten them.'

The snapper was delighted. He pushed Polly and the woman in among the pigs and started to take his pictures.

'You look dreadful,' laughed Carslip when he saw the photographs the following morning. 'Look where that great pork chop is putting his snout. He must have been turned on by those leather jeans you were wearing, Pussy.'

Polly said nothing.

'I think they're brilliant,' said Den. 'Well done, Polly.'

Carslip pulled a face. 'Bitch,' he muttered under his breath. 'Yes, it looks like yesterday was your lucky day again.'

Lucky? thought Polly. It had been one of the worst days of her entire life.

Chapter Twelve

'Get me a drink, for heaven's sake. A stiff one.'

'Sea breeze?'

'Perfect,' said Sue. It had been good of Joyce to meet her at short notice. She had been dying to tell her news to someone all day. Of course, she had told John but that didn't count. All he had done was grunt and say, 'I thought that Charles was Pamela's fella.' Sue had told him weeks ago that Charles had dropped Polly for Adele but her husband never seemed to listen to a word she said.

'Men,' she sighed as she took a gulp of her vodka and cranberry. 'John drives me crazy.'

'What's the bastard done now?' asked Joyce, re-arranging herself on the bench opposite Sue. She was shovelling huge handfuls of kettle crisps into her mouth. Sue would hate to be fat like Joyce. In fact, she was only half a stone heavier now than the day she got married and she intended to stay that way.

'Well, I spent all afternoon buying stuff to cook a genuine authentic Thai supper for him – I got that recipe off the telly, that programme – *Eva Eats*.'

'She clearly doesn't, of course,' said Joyce.

'What?'

'Eat. There's not an ounce of flesh on the poor love. Except for her boobs and they can't possibly be natural.'

'How can you tell?'

'Well, it's obvious,' laughed Joyce. 'That woman has the arms and legs of a stick insect and breasts bigger than mine. It doesn't make sense. And she never wears a bra.'

'I suppose the TV producers like all that,' said Sue, blushing slightly and pulling her jacket around her tightly. She had never admitted to Joyce that she had had a boob job herself a couple of years earlier but she was sure that her friend suspected – she was always dropping hints.

'The cameramen certainly like it. The other night, when she leant over that bowl of noodles, I thought we were going to see two big meatballs pop out on top of them.' Joyce roared with laughter and Sue laughed too. Joyce was crude but she had been a good friend to Sue over the last few years.

'Anyway, he wouldn't touch Eva's Thai supper,' said Sue, frowning at a crack in the varnish of her long blue fingernails. 'He went down to the chippy and got himself some fish and chips.'

'Ungrateful. They all are. My Kev was the same.'

Sue had never met Joyce's Kev but she had heard so much about him that she felt she knew him as well as her own husband. She listened as Joyce retold the story about the time when she had taken Kev to a restaurant and he had shown her up by insisting on eating his peas with his spoon.

'Uncouth and ungrateful is what I said,' she finished emphatically.

'My mother warned me about marrying beneath myself,' said Sue. 'I had a good job as a secretary in a bank – I could have married a man in a suit. But I'd been seeing John since I was fifteen and just couldn't give him up.'

'It's never too late,' said Joyce. Sue laughed and took another drink.

'Once a plumber's wife, forever down the drain,' she said.

'Come on. John's done well with his business.'

'I suppose,' conceded Sue. John had thought it unnecessary for her to have her boobs done but he had not made a fuss, he had happily stumped up the cash.

'A self-employed plumber is better than a bloody school caretaker. My Kev didn't have an ounce of ambition in his body – except in one place, of course,' laughed Joyce. 'They're always ambitious in that department.'

Sue smiled. She and John had not had sex for months. She didn't miss it at all. It was a relief to be honest but she did wonder what had happened. John used to have such a high sex drive.

Joyce finished her crisps and popped each fat finger into her mouth in turn to suck off the salt.

'Ugh,' she cried. 'I still have that bloody head lice stuff all over me.'

'Who is it this time?' asked Sue. Joyce had four children, all still at school, and there was never a time when at least one of them didn't have head lice.

'Darren. And Billy too, probably. I did the pair of them to be sure.'

'Good idea.'

'And then I had to do Kylie's verruca and give Zoe another worm tablet. They're worse than bloody pets – I can't wait until they're grown up. Tell me it's better when they're grown up.'

Sue smiled. She had had some difficult times with her girls. There was no denying that she had been devastated when Adele told her she was pregnant. The prospect of Adele repeating history, getting pregnant – as she herself had done – before she was married or at least settled with a proper partner had been terrifying. But now, of course, things were different.

'Adele's getting married,' she said.

'Really?' said Joyce. 'I knew Polly was but—'

'No that's off. I don't think it was ever serious with Polly. Poor Polly always gets over-excited and starts imagining things. I'm not sure that there was ever a real proposal.'

'But Adele? Tell me all about it. Who is he?'

'Well,' said Sue. She could not bring herself to tell Joyce that Charles was actually Polly's ex-boyfriend, certainly not that Polly considered him to be her ex-fiancé. 'He's called Charles.'

'Charles? That's a coincidence,' said Joyce. 'Wasn't that the name of Polly's chap? You never told me much about him.'

Sue blushed and sipped her drink. Joyce had an amazingly good memory.

'Polly never tells me anything about her boyfriends but Adele is different.'

'So, does this new Charles have a job?'

'He's an executive in one of the fastest-growing food companies in the country.'

'Food?'

'He works in the head office, something in the accounts department, I think.'

'Accounts?'

'Yes, I mean – he doesn't actually make the food, just sort of organises loans and things for the company.'

'I see,' said Joyce vaguely. 'And what does he look like?'

Sue grinned. 'He's very good-looking. He has long blond wavy hair.'

'Sounds a cherub.'

'He's very tall and slim.'

'What's the catch?'

'That's it – he is the catch, the catch of a lifetime. His father is a "Sir".'

'Ooh,' said Joyce.

'His father is the boss of some Oxford college. I think they call him a "bursar" or something.'

'Wow. Money?'

'I presume so.' Sue realised that she had not thought much about the money. Charles Goodwood, with his good looks and his good job and being the son of Sir Thomas and Lady Viola, was enough for her.

'Adele's always been the lucky one out of the two,' observed Joyce.

'Not lucky,' said Sue. 'It's just that Adele makes more of an effort, always has done. She takes care of how she looks, what she wears. She works hard. If Polly had followed her sister's example, she wouldn't be the shambles that she is. She only has herself to blame.'

Of course, thought Sue, if it had been Polly who had called her and told her that she was up the spout, then she would have understood. It was what she had expected of Polly ever since she found her rolling around on top of that poor schoolboy that afternoon. The poor child had looked as though he was being suffocated. It was just as well Sue had arrived home early or Polly might have smothered him to death.

'I saw your Polly's name in the paper the other day,' said Joyce.

'Really?' John took the *Globe* but Sue rarely bothered to read it – too many tits and bums all over it, she would complain.

'Yes, something about pigs. She seems to be doing well. I remember that front-page story she did about Jane Whitehouse's son getting plastered and throwing up all over himself. There was a disgusting picture of the boy – stark naked and covered in vomit.'

'Sounds the sort of thing that Polly would get involved in,' said Sue. She remembered the day she had seen Polly streak down to the corner of the road topless. She knew then that there was something wrong with the girl. John stuck up for her, of course, as he always did but Sue knew: she would come to no good.

Both Sue's and Joyce's glasses were empty and Sue offered to get another round.

'Thank you very much,' said Joyce. 'I think we should celebrate Adele's news. Has she set a date?'

'September the sixth,' said Sue. 'Adele wants a big bash.'

'What does John say about that? I don't suppose I'll get a penny out of Kev when Kylie and Zoe get married, if they ever do.'

'He likes a good party – probably too much – he'll almost certainly do something embarrassing and show us all up. But he's relaxed about the money.'

'He's not such a bastard after all, then?'

No, thought Sue, picking up the empties and making her way to the bar. In fact, John had been sweet. He had said he would treat her and the girls to a day at Beaumonts, a really upmarket health and beauty place, just before the wedding so that they could pamper themselves as much as they wanted.

So why was it that he annoyed her so much?

Sue knew the answer to that question but it was yet another secret. Another thing she had never told Joyce. The fact remained that John had done something unforgivable. Totally unforgivable. And Sue had no intention of ever letting him forget it.

Ned arrived with Minty at half past ten. They went to see a puppet show at the Little Angel Theatre and then to lunch at Pizza Express. It was now two o'clock and there were still four hours to fill before Minty was due back at Adele's.

Ned said that Adele had asked him not to bring Minty back before six as she was going shopping. She had made a point of adding that she was going to look at wedding dresses but Ned spared Polly this information.

Polly settled the bill while Minty was still scraping out her bowl of ice cream. Polly had not seen her niece for over two months and she really seemed to have grown in that time.

'Let's go back to my place,' said Polly. 'Would you like to see where I am living?'

'Oh, yes please,' said Minty. 'I can't wait to see Bobbin.'

'He's very excited too.'

'And do you still have all your treasure?' asked Minty.

'Sounds interesting,' said Ned.

'She means the worthless clutter that litters my bedside table and just about every other horizontal surface in my room,' laughed Polly. Minty had always loved exploring in her room; she had called it Aunt Polly's treasure cave but Adele had said it was more like a rubbish tip.

They got the bus up towards Arsenal and stopped to buy cakes for tea at the baker's shop in Highbury Barn.

'Aunt Polly and I used to buy cakes every day on the way home from school,' Minty told Ned. 'Mummy says it's a bad habit.'

Polly laughed. 'That says it all. Why your mummy is slim and I'll always be so fat that I'm bursting out of my clothes.' Since her meeting with Charles, Polly had completely lost control of her diet. She did not think she would get the black leather jeans on again even if she were wearing one of Ned's mum's girdles.

'I think you're lovely, Aunt Polly,' said Minty. 'I'm going to look just like Aunt Polly when I grow up,' she added to Ned.

Polly laughed again but Ned smiled at Minty and said, 'A brilliant ambition.'

Minty chose her cakes and asked whether she could carry them home. Then they walked hand in hand down the hill to Zeta's house.

It was quite a squeeze once they were all inside Polly's room. Polly and Minty sat on the bed and Ned on the floor. Polly had a few picture books which she read to Minty and then Ned made some stories up.

They were really good, thought Polly. Ned had an amazing imagination.

'Tell me the one about the bear called Hug again and how he got his name,' said Minty. Polly lay back on her pillow as she listened. It was an idyllic scene, she realised. They were like a happy family: mum, dad and little girl. Except, of course, it was nothing like that. Minty would be gone in a couple of hours and Ned, although he was a natural with kids, said he had no interest in producing children of his own.

Charles had been different. He had often told her how much he would like to settle down with the right woman and start a family. They were so compatible and, if it had not been for Adele, it would have been her, Polly, going shopping for a wedding dress that afternoon. The thought made her burn with hatred for her sister.

'Mummy is going to be a bride,' said Minty, suddenly sitting up.

'Yes,' said Polly, although she still refused to accept it. Perhaps Charles had proposed in a fit of pique just because she had refused to go to bed with him the night he had come round to see her. Oh, how she regretted her behaviour now. If only they had had sex, Charles would have realised what a mistake he had made.

'I'm going to be a bridesmaid, a beautiful bridesmaid.'

'I'm sure you are,' agreed Polly, giving Minty a hug.

'Mummy says the wedding is in September.'

'Are you sure?'

'Yes, I heard Mummy telling Granny and Granny

said it was the same day as her birthday.' The sixth of September – they had set a date too, thought Polly. It was typical of Adele. As soon as Charles had proposed, she had to get everything organised to the last detail.

'When is September?' asked Minty. She had eaten the icing off all six of the cupcakes they had bought and left the sponge bits but Polly did not care.

'Well, it's nearly the beginning of April now. So, May, June, July, August, September.' She counted the months on her fingers and held them up to Minty.

'Five,' said the little girl.

'Yes, just over five months.'

'That's a long time,' said Minty, licking her sticky fingers. 'I can't wait that long.'

But I can, thought Polly. I could wait forever.

'What's this?' The child had picked up a large stone that was on top of some papers on Polly's table. 'Is that real blood?' she asked, pointing at the thick red streaks.

Polly took it in her hand and shook her head.

'Remember this?' She showed it to Ned.

Ned frowned.

'It's from Filey beach,' continued Polly. 'I kept it as a memento of those dark days back in January when you saved me from total despair.'

'Oh yes, the bloodstone,' laughed Ned. 'I thought you were going to brain me with it, at first.'

'I like it,' said Minty. 'Can I have it?'

'Sorry, darling,' said Polly. 'I want to keep it – for luck. But, if I go to that beach again, I'll find one just the same for you, OK?'

'Thanks. Can we watch some TV now?'

'OK,' said Ned. He helped Minty with the TV controls and the two sat together and watched a kids' programme about an animal hospital.

Polly held the bloodstone in both hands and closed her eyes. Just over five months, she calculated. That was about twenty weeks. Twenty weeks to get herself in shape and win back Charles before he was lost to Adele forever. She picked up a piece of sponge cake and was about to pop it in her mouth but stopped and threw it in the bin. She was determined that this time she would really do it.

Chapter Thirteen

Four months later and still refined sugar had not crossed her lips. Polly was wearing a short skirt and was aware how good her legs were looking as she strode across the office to her desk.

'Sorry, Bernard,' she said. 'I have to be off now.'

'Off? It's half past three, Pussy,' said Carslip, his trout lips flopping open. 'And you spent over an hour at the gym this lunchtime. A bit of a short day, even for Den's Pussy, isn't it?'

'I am not Den's Pussy.' Polly scowled at Carslip and continued to put her things together. 'And, if you must know, it's my niece's birthday party and I really want to get to it on time.'

'Oh, your niece's birthday party. That explains everything. Hold the front page – it's Polly's niece's birthday party. Why didn't you say so straight away?'

'Stop taking the piss.'

'Sor-ry. I was forgetting how important a niece's birthday party is. Silly me.'

'Well, it is important to me,' said Polly.

Carslip sneered. He was about to say something further when Den appeared. Polly immediately stopped packing up her bag and sat back down behind her desk.

'What's going on here?' asked Den, immediately noticing the tension between Polly and her boss.

'Pussy here has a kids' tea party she has to go to. Hurry up, princess, we don't want you to be late,' said Carslip.

'A tea party!' exclaimed Den.

'I'm sorry,' said Polly. 'It's a very special thing for me. I'll make the time up tomorrow, I promise.'

Den stared at Polly. 'You're an odd one. But I've noticed how hard you've been working since you joined. It must be six months now and you're doing a great job.'

'Thank you,' said Polly.

'You don't seem to have much of a social life though, do you? I thought it was personal when you turned me down for that drink but I've noticed how you stay here until late almost every night.'

Carslip sniffed.

'And the only time you ask for time off is to go to a kid's tea party,' continued Den, sitting down on the corner of Polly's desk.

'It's not any kid. She's very special to me.'

Den smiled. 'I understand,' he said although Polly doubted that he did.

Then Den suddenly got up and turned on Carslip. 'Let her have the fucking afternoon off, Arse-lick, you bastard.'

And so it was sorted. Polly ran down the stairs and hailed a cab. She could not really afford it but she did not want to disappoint Minty by arriving late. It was only as the cab turned into Noel Road that Polly started to feel nervous.

It was a long time since she had seen Adele, since she had stepped through that door, and she wondered how she would be received. As she checked her make-up in her mirror and pulled down her skirt, she wondered whether Charles would be there.

She had called him a few times since their last dreadful meeting in the lobby of Green Baby but he refused to meet her. Perhaps he did not *dare* to see her, wondered Polly. Perhaps he already regretted getting engaged to Adele and was afraid that if he saw Polly—

She told herself to stop being ridiculous but she could not help grasping at straws. Her heart pounded as she rang the bell.

The door was opened by Minty and a big gang of friends.

'Aunt Polly!' cried the little girl, launching herself into her aunt's arms. 'I was so afraid you wouldn't come.'

'Silly,' said Polly. 'Happy birthday, darling.'

Minty was back on her feet and pulling Polly into the party room.

'We have cake and jelly, sausages and ice cream and a conjurer,' she said.

'Sounds great,' said Polly, spotting Charles immediately. He was blowing up balloons and let one go shooting off around the room as he recognised her. The children squealed with delight and chased after the balloon.

'Polly.' Charles came over to her at once and kissed her on both cheeks. 'You look, er, fantastic. Have you

149

lost weight or something?' Polly blushed but, before she had a chance to answer, Adele had appeared at Charles's side.

'Oh Polly, I'm so glad you made it,' she said. 'Minty has been talking about seeing you for days – weeks actually. It's been driving me mad.'

Polly said nothing. She could still feel Charles gazing at her. She felt his eyes trace slowly over her face, down her neck and shoulders, around her waist and over her thighs. It was a hot day and she was wearing a low-cut T-shirt.

'You look fantastic,' he repeated. Adele sniffed.

'Charles, look. It's nearly four thirty. That entertainer, Mrs Doodah, is already half an hour late. Would you be an angel and call her?' Charles backed away and Polly and Adele were left alone.

'You do look well,' said Adele. 'Is everything OK?'

Polly glared at Adele. Of course things were not OK. Things would never be OK, she wanted to yell, but instead she let Minty take her hand. 'I'll play some games with the kids,' she said.

'Thanks,' said Adele.

Polly arranged musical bumps. Charles came back into the room and offered to do the music as Minty wanted Polly to join in the game herself. Polly bounced up and down with the little girls and she felt Charles watching her every movement. She wished she had worn a bra and that her skirt was not so short but then, catching a glimpse of Charles's face, she changed her mind. She was sure that she was dressed perfectly.

So it was amazing but not surprising when he called her the next day.

They met for a drink after work in a bar they had gone to when they had been together. But things had changed. There was new management and a very noisy band was playing in a corner of the room.

'Thanks for coming,' yelled Charles.

Polly smiled.

'I had to see you. No chance to talk at the party yesterday.'

'What?'

'No time to talk,' yelled Charles.

'What?' said Polly again. She could hear him but she wanted to go outside.

There was a small pub garden and they took their drinks out there.

'It's great to see you.' Charles started again.

'You too,' said Polly. They sipped the cold beer. Charles asked about her job and Polly asked about his. They chatted for a while but still Charles did not bring up the subject, the only subject, that Polly really wanted to discuss.

So, as soon as there was a pause in the conversation, Polly launched in.

'How are the wedding plans?'

Charles looked startled.

'Fine,' he said. There was another silence and then he added, 'No, not fine really. Not fine at all.'

Polly said nothing. Her heart was beating fast but she waited for Charles to continue.

'That's why I had to see you,' he went on. 'Seeing you yesterday, well, just confirmed my doubts.'

'Doubts?'

'Yes.'

'About what?'

'Adele, of course.'

'You mean – getting married?'

'Yes, obviously. I mean, I thought I was ready for it but now it's getting so close I'm not so sure.'

'Have you told Adele how you feel?'

'No. Why on earth would I do that?'

'It might help.'

'It would only upset her and then, if we do go ahead with the wedding, it would have spoilt everything.'

Polly said nothing. She wanted to reach across the table and take Charles's hand but she resisted. That would be too presumptuous.

'Seeing you yesterday made me realise—' Charles continued and then suddenly paused.

'What?' prompted Polly.

'Well, I don't know. How much I still fancy you I suppose. I mean, I shouldn't have those feelings any more.'

Polly felt like jumping into his arms at once. Yes, yes, she wanted to cry, that's right. You don't love Adele. You really want *me*, Charles. This whole thing has been a terrible mistake. She started in her seat.

'Of course, I know Adele is the right choice,' said Charles and Polly sat back down again. 'She's beautiful and intelligent. She will be a perfect wife and I will be very proud of her. Araminta is a sweet girl and I look forward to being a proper father to her.'

We could have our own kids, Polly wanted to yell but instead she said, 'Do you love her?'

'Love her?'

'Yes. Adele – do you love her?'

'Well, of course, I suppose. I don't know. She's never asked me that question.'

'And you've never told her?'

'No.'

'Don't you think it's important?' asked Polly.

'Do you?'

'Yes.'

Charles said nothing for a while. He just stared rather morosely at his drink like a sad and confused child. Polly wanted to scoop him up in her arms and tell him not to worry, that it would all be all right in the end.

'I'll have to go through with it,' he said at last.

'Why?'

'I can't pull out at this late stage.'

'Why not?'

'Oh, it wouldn't be fair and, anyway, I'd probably regret it. I mean, where am I going to find someone as good as Adele?'

Polly's face fell and Charles realised his mistake at once.

'I'm sorry,' said Charles. 'You know how fond I am of you, Polly, but I have to be serious. Adele is just the kind of wife I need.'

'Need?'

'Yes. I mean, sex and everything was so much better with you, of course, but—'

'But what?'

'But nothing,' said Charles. 'It's too late now.'

Polly sighed.

'You're making a big mistake,' she said. 'You have to marry the person you *love*.'

'I wish it was as simple as that for me.'

'Otherwise, you shouldn't marry at all.'

'I suppose not.'

'Why not delay? Ask for a bit more time?'

'Adele would go crazy. She would call the whole thing off at once.'

'Would that be such a bad thing?'

Charles paused as he seemed to weigh Polly's suggestion in his mind.

'I don't know.'

'I mean, if it was Adele who called the wedding off, how would you feel then?'

'Well, I suppose I wouldn't try that hard to change her mind,' said Charles.

Polly smiled. That was all she needed to hear.

'It says here that the package includes a facial, steam treatments, a massage and a manicure. There is a nutritionally balanced organic four course lunch,' read Sue.

'I hope they don't make us eat prunes,' said Adele.

'I hope they allow us to have a drink,' said Sue, as Adele turned off the M11.

Polly said nothing. She sat in the back and lacked the energy to try to participate in her mother's and sister's conversation.

'I only hope we'll be able to get away by five – I really must get back into the office tonight,' said Adele.

'That's crazy,' said Sue. 'Can't whatever it is wait until tomorrow?'

'I shouldn't tell you – it's strictly confidential – but I'm working on a bid for Charles's company. Charles has got some share options and, if it goes through, he should make quite a bit of money out of the deal. Not to mention the bonus that I will get at Stratton for the transaction.'

'That will be nice.'

'Yes. The bloke who lives in the flat above me is thinking of selling.'

'The Johnson flat?' asked Polly. 'Where that artist was murdered?'

'Yes,' said Adele. 'Charles and I thought we might buy it and reconvert the building to how it originally was. One big house.'

'You can't buy a flat where someone has been murdered,' said Polly. But Adele ignored her.

'I suppose it will give you a lot more space, which will be useful when you have more children,' said Sue.

'Mum!' laughed Adele. 'You know I don't want any more children.'

Didn't she? thought Polly. Did Charles know that?

'Araminta is gorgeous but she's quite enough. I'd never be able to work the way I do, if we had more kids.'

'You work too hard,' said Sue. She glanced around the soft tan leather interior of Adele's car and smiled. 'I must say though, your firm certainly appreciates you. This car is beautiful.'

Adele smiled. Polly had been amazed when Adele had indicated the gleaming new Mercedes parked outside her house. Apparently it was standard issue for all newly appointed managers.

They drove on and soon saw a sign to Beaumonts. It had started to rain and Adele switched on the windscreen wipers.

'Do you think they have sun beds?' asked Sue.

'I'm sure they do,' said Adele.

'I had hoped to get a decent tan before the wedding,' continued Sue, 'but this summer has been a complete washout.'

Has it? wondered Polly. She had been so busy at work that she had hardly noticed it was summer at all. Things were still as bad as ever with Carslip and there seemed nothing Polly could do to get him back on side. He seemed determined to hold a grudge against her forever.

She had told him that she was taking the day off to go to a health and beauty place with her mother and sister and he had teased her mercilessly.

'Don't forget to have your whiskers curled, Pussy,' he taunted when she had left the office the night before. Polly ignored him.

'Have a great time,' said Olga kindly and Polly thanked her. She could not have explained how much she was dreading the event. The prospect of a whole day in the company of the most hateful and irritating women in the world was bleak but she had accepted so that her father would not think her ungrateful and it had been really generous of him to pay for the trip. In addition, of course, she knew it might be her last opportunity to win back Charles. Her last opportunity to speak with Adele, to persuade her that marrying Charles would be a mistake. Could she do it, she wondered. She was certainly going to have a bloody good try.

When they arrived at Beaumont House, an elderly ginger-haired man offered to park Adele's car. Then they went into the house, checked in and, after a brief introduction to their programme, were given individual appointments with 'Sister'.

'We like to give you a quick medical check on arrival,' explained the receptionist. 'Just so that we

156

know what you hope to achieve during your stay with us.' Polly smiled. She doubted that Sister would be able to help with her particular ambitions.

'Ms P. Taylor?'

Polly's name was the first to be called and she got up and went into Sister's room.

The nurse was a reed-thin woman of about thirty-five. She looked as though she had once been heavier as the skin on her cadaverous face was deeply folded and wrinkled.

Polly responded politely to Sister's enquiries about her diet.

'And what about your exercise regime, Ms Taylor?'

'I sometimes run for the bus,' she said with a smile. Sister said nothing.

'Just joking,' added Polly. But Sister was not amused.

'Would you stand up, Ms Taylor, and take off your robe?'

Polly did as she was told and suffered the indignity of Sister casting a critical eye over every inch of her body. Then Sister opened a drawer in her desk and extracted a large pair of stainless steel calipers with which she pinched at Polly's flesh. The calipers were cold and Polly flinched when they touched her.

Eventually Sister seemed to have completed her examination. She weighed Polly and told her to put her robe back on.

'As I thought,' Sister remarked when she was reseated behind her desk and Polly was dressed and sitting down again. 'Quite a high fat quotient for a woman of your age.'

'What?' said Polly. 'But I've just lost nearly a stone.'

Sister smiled. 'Another of your little jokes, Ms Taylor?'

Polly scowled. It was quite outrageous that this woman should imply that she was fat when she was feeling slimmer than ever before in her life.

'I think you should keep a food diary while you are here,' said Sister. 'Then we can check what percentage of your daily intake is fat.'

Polly had had enough of this woman and got to her feet. 'And then you will tell me to give up chips and just eat cabbage and lettuce leaves.'

'Possibly.'

'Well,' said Polly. 'Let me tell you, Sister – not everyone wants to eat rabbit food all day.' She wanted to add that she would not want to look like a dried-up old stick like Sister anyway but she managed to hold her temper.

Sister smiled. 'Have you ever tried *looking* at your food?'

'Looking?'

'Yes, I find it helps to spend at least fifteen minutes looking at your food before you pick up your knife and fork. It helps you appreciate what you are about to eat.'

'Doesn't the food end up getting cold?' asked Polly.

'I'm being serious, Ms Taylor.'

So am I, thought Polly, but she said nothing. Sister wrote something on a card and said that she hoped Polly enjoyed her stay.

'Hand this to the receptionist outside,' said Sister. Polly took the card. In the top right hand corner were the initials FLC.

Sister saw Polly puzzling over the letters.

'It stands for Fitness Level C,' she explained but Polly was convinced it was really for Fat Lazy Cow.

*

Fifteen minutes later Polly sat dripping with sweat in her personal steam cabinet. Adele was seated in a similar contraption beside her.

The cabinets looked rather like large fridges but they were as hot as ovens inside. There was a hole in the top of each cabinet through which one's head stuck out but the rest of the body felt as though it was in the equatorial jungle.

The therapist had put two timers on the table between Adele's and Polly's cabinets. There were ten minutes more to survive.

'Are you OK?' asked Adele.

'No,' said Polly. The room was dimly lit and there were only the two of them there plus an abundance of potted palm trees and yucca plants. It would be a good moment, perhaps the only chance she would get, to speak privately with Adele.

'I saw Charles the other day,' she said.

'Really?' Either Adele was relaxed about this information or she gave a very good impression that she was. But Polly's heart was pounding, both with the heat and apprehension.

'Are you sure you're doing the right thing, Adele?' she blurted out.

'What do you mean?'

'You know, marrying Charles?'

Adele looked witheringly at Polly.

'Forget it,' she said.

'What do you mean?'

'I've decided. I'm going to marry him and why shouldn't I?'

'But do you love him? And does he love you?'

'What business is that of yours?' asked Adele. Her

face was red now and Polly doubted it was only the steam that was getting to her.

'You know very well what it means to me,' said Polly.

'I do not.'

'I love him, Adele. I really love him and I want him back. It's not too late to—'

The timer closest to Adele started to buzz loudly and the therapist, a plump young woman in a tight white uniform, appeared out of nowhere. She opened the door of Adele's cabinet and Polly watched her slim naked sister step out and into the large white towel the therapist held up for her.

It was the first time that Polly had seen her sister naked in years and it made her think back to the days when they had played the Gotta Gotta game. Of course, the Gotta Gotta game. If you really wanted something badly enough, you paid the ultimate forfeit and then the other person couldn't refuse. It was a matter of principle.

'Hang on a second,' called Polly as Adele and the therapist disappeared. 'I need to get out too.' Polly glanced at her own timer and realised, to her horror, that the needle was still on ten minutes – it must be stuck.

'Help,' she cried. 'Help!'

Sue and Adele were waiting in the dining room. It was a large peaceful room with a high ceiling and enormous windows looking over the grounds. All the diners were mooching about in nothing but their huge white Beaumonts bathrobes and slippers, picking at salads and pieces of fruit.

It was hardly surprising that many people turned to stare as Polly came bursting into the room, hot and breathless. She stormed over to the table where her mother and sister sat. She just caught the end of their conversation. Sue was saying something about having just had a massage by a woman who had once massaged Cilla Black.

'Just wait until I tell Joyce,' she said.

Adele did not reply. She could see Polly steaming towards them and knew that something was up.

'Where on earth have you been?' she asked – as if she didn't know, thought Polly.

Still standing, Polly poured herself a glass of water and downed it in one.

'I was stuck in that jungle box for half a bloody hour before that therapist came back again. I think I've sweated out every ounce of fluid in my body.' She poured another glass and downed that one too.

'Are you OK?' asked Sue, looking at Polly nervously.

'No, I'm not OK,' said Polly. Then she turned to Adele and suddenly dropped her bathrobe to the ground.

It was only for a second, maybe two, that she stood there totally naked and then she picked up the robe and put it back on. There were gasps and murmurings all around the room.

'Polly, what on earth are you doing?' asked Sue.

Polly continued to stare at Adele. 'She knows,' said Polly. Sue looked from Polly to Adele.

'I don't know what you're talking about,' said Adele. 'Sit down, Polly, for God's sake, and stop creating scenes all over the place.'

Polly did not sit down.

'Gotta, gotta,' she said and Sue stared at her as though she was completely mad.

'Sorry?' said Adele.

'You remember. Gotta, gotta. I've got to have him, Adele – so will you please, please back off? I'm begging you.'

Polly was about to drop the robe again but Adele stood up and forced her into her chair.

'Sit down,' she said. 'And we'll talk about it.'

Polly stayed in her chair.

'Look, Polly,' said Adele. 'You can run round this place a hundred times stark bollock naked, if you like, but I won't give in. I won't give him up.'

'Why not?'

'Because I want to get married. Araminta needs a father and I need a husband. I don't think you have any idea what it's like to be a single mum.'

Oh yes I do, thought Polly, but she said nothing.

'Charles is a good man and he cares. Why shouldn't I marry him? Why shouldn't we be happy together? It's not as though he was ever in love with you anyway.'

'Did he say that?'

'No,' said Adele. 'But I can tell. I mean, how could he have done what he did to you, if he cared about you?'

'How could you?' yelled Polly.

'I'm sorry. It was a mistake. But it was just one of those things. I'd had too much to drink and we got carried away.'

'How could you?' repeated Polly.

'Look. It was bad how it happened, but it was inevitable. It was going to happen sometime anyway.'

'Why?'

'The attraction between us was irresistible.'

'But I'm your sister. How could you steal your own sister's boyfriend?'

'Any normal sister would be happy for me,' said Adele. 'Instead of harping on about the past.'

'You are unbelievable,' said Polly, rising to her feet again. 'You are fucking unbelievable.'

'Please, Polly, please,' said Sue looking alarmed. A pencil-thin waitress was making her way directly towards their table.

'Would madam like the melon or the sea grass salad?' she asked Polly.

Polly glared at her.

'I'm going out to lunch,' she said, suddenly feeling ravenously hungry. 'There's a fish and chip shop down the road. You might like to try it one day before your ears start growing and you get a bobble tail.'

Chapter Fourteen

The morning after the wedding, Polly woke up in Charles's bed.

She stared up at the same familiar ceiling, the same cracks and the same heavily over-painted cornice work running around the perimeter. She cast her eyes down the facing wall. There was the same print of an enormous yellow express train making straight for the foot of the bed.

It was nearly a year since she had slept there but nothing had changed except, of course, the face and body of the person who slept beside her.

Polly stared at the man who snored gently on her right. Who was he? And what on earth were they both doing here?

As consciousness slowly returned so did vague memories of the night before, the day before. The day of Charles and Adele's wedding.

Polly almost groaned but checked herself. She did not want to wake up her companion – at least, not until she could remember who he was.

Again she stared at his face. The profile was curiously similar to that of Charles but bigger in every dimension. This was a much heavier and older man.

His hair was thinner and receding. He had heavy bags under his eyes.

Polly inched away from him as he turned over in his sleep. She could now see the whole of his face. It was fat and scrunched up as he leant into his pillow. But he had the same golden eyelashes as Charles and the same earlobes. These little resemblances were uncanny.

But then, suddenly, Polly gasped and the man opened one eye. At last, she remembered who he was.

'Hubert,' she cried.

Hubert smiled.

'What? How?' Polly sat up in bed and realised she was naked except for her pants. 'Oh God,' she said. 'What happened?'

'Don't you remember?' asked Hubert, pulling a face. 'My very best performance – and you don't remember a thing?'

Polly felt sick. She knew that she had had a lot to drink but she still could not remember going to Charles's flat or what had happened then, although that now appeared self-evident.

'Did you? I mean, did we?'

Hubert laughed. 'Oh Polly,' he said. 'I can't torture you any longer. No, we didn't. I mean no, I didn't since you were probably up for it.'

'Oh God,' said Polly. 'How embarrassing. I must have been so drunk.'

'We both were, fortunately. If I had been capable of performance I might have been less altruistic.'

'What happened, Hubert? Can you remember?'

'More or less.'

'Tell me. Tell me every gory detail – I have to know.'

165

'OK,' said Hubert. 'But let's get dressed first. We'll walk down the road to Langham's and get a decent breakfast inside us at the same time, don't you think?'

'That would be great,' said Polly.

Hubert ordered smoked salmon and scrambled eggs for them both, and cappuccinos.

Polly tucked in greedily. She had kept her weight down for the wedding but what was the point in worrying now? She had almost killed herself trying to look as sensational as she possibly could for the bloody occasion. But it had not made any difference. There had been no last-minute drama. The ceremony had gone ahead totally to plan and now Charles and Adele were married.

The thought made her feel suddenly nauseous; she put down her knife and fork and watched Hubert eat.

'What happened to your finger?' she asked, noticing that the tip of Hubert's right index finger was missing.

'Oh, an accident years ago,' said Hubert. 'When I was a kid I got into a fight with a waste disposal unit.'

'Gruesome,' said Polly. 'Poor you.'

'I've always been rather accident prone,' smiled Hubert. 'Is the food OK?'

'Fantastic. I was just thinking back to yesterday.'

'Ah, is your memory coming back?'

'Well, I can remember the wedding OK.' Polly could remember seeing Adele looking absolutely stunning in a beautiful white silk dress and Charles at her side looking so proud and yes, God damn it, so happy too.

'Charles has done well,' said Hubert. 'Your sister is beautiful.'

'Yes.' But it's only skin deep, thought Polly. She's a ruthless, ugly monster underneath, as Charles would eventually find out.

'Little Araminta looked very sweet too.'

Yes, Minty had looked beautiful. She had worn a pale blue dress and had a circlet of sweet peas in her hair which made her look totally angelic.

'I want to be a bridesmaid for you too one day, Aunt Polly,' she had said at the reception. Polly had laughed. There seemed little hope of that, she had told herself, as she knocked back another glass of champagne.

Hubert got up and found some newspapers. He handed Polly the *Globe*. 'This is your paper, isn't it?' he asked.

'Yes,' said Polly, noting that Carslip had the splash – yet another sleaze story about a Tory minister who had been caught with his pants down. Hubert glanced at the story over her shoulder.

'We're going to get annihilated at the next election,' he said.

'What, the Tories?'

'Yes. Evans is holding off to the last minute to call the election but it's no good. They'll never recover their popularity in time.'

'Aren't you standing for election?'

'Yes. I'm the Tory candidate for Colingate.'

'Of course. I think I knew that. Is Colingate a good seat?'

'Not for a Tory. I don't have a chance of winning it but, if I do well enough, I might be given a safe seat for the next election.'

Polly started to eat again.

'Are you staying in London for long?' she asked.

'Charles wants me to stay at the flat for a while. As you know, he's trying to sell it now that he and Adele are buying the rest of the house in Islington.'

Polly shuddered. Adele had suggested that Minty might want the room, that room, where Johnson was killed. Polly had had a big row with her about it and even Sue had been forced to agree with Polly. Adele had eventually backed down and agreed to use it as her study.

'It's a big improvement,' said Hubert.

'What?'

'Living in Kensington as opposed to commuting from Colingate. I wouldn't mind buying the flat off Charles myself and I could probably afford it. But then, if I ever do get elected to Westminster, I'll have to take a big cut in salary.'

'What do you do?'

'I'm a lawyer. I specialise in libel caes.'

'We have our fair share of those at the *Globe*.' Polly told him with a smile, thinking back to the week before when Den had given Carslip another roasting. Apparently some TV star was suing because he wrote a piece saying her boobs were not flat, they were actually concave. Her lawyers had enclosed a photo which they claimed proved her point – or *points*, thought Polly. Carslip had insisted she must have had implants but Den told him to shut up and just get her paid off.

'I thought I was boring you rigid with stories about my work last night but it's clear you were not listening to a word I said.' Hubert smiled and licked cappuccino froth from his lips.

'I'm sorry,' said Polly. 'Did I behave appallingly?'

'Well,' said Hubert. 'You looked great. Everyone was saying how slim and wonderful you were looking.'

'Were they? Who?' Polly still could not help hoping that Charles had noticed her. She had made such an effort to starve herself for days before the wedding. She had spent a fortune on her hair and her dress. She had even done sit-ups.

'Oh, I don't know,' said Hubert. 'Everyone.'

'So, what happened?' asked Polly. 'Was I behaving like a complete piss artist?'

'Not at all. You were very elegant. I don't think anyone had noticed how drunk you were. Well, not at first, not until—'

Polly held her breath. What on earth had she done?

'Are you sure you want to hear all this?' asked Hubert.

'Yes.'

'Well, there was this ball pond thing. Do you remember the ball pond thing?' Polly remembered the ball pond thing. With horror.

'I think it had been set up for the kids,' said Hubert, 'and there was this chute – a sort of great pipe like a water slide – which you could slip down into the ball pond.'

'I didn't?'

Hubert laughed. 'Don't worry. It was really a magnificent sight. Your skirt went whooshing up over your head. You know you've got fantastic legs.'

Although Polly had never received a compliment about her legs in her life before, she still looked horrified.

169

'Those red suspenders were quite—'

'Oh no,' said Polly. She had forgotten all about wearing the red suspenders and stockings.

'Everyone thought it was very funny and I have to say, well, it livened things up a bit,' continued Hubert, taking a large bite of toast.

'What happened after that?'

'I offered to take you home.'

'Thank goodness.'

'The only trouble was that you refused to come.'

'Oh no.'

'You insisted on having one dance with the bridegroom.'

'Oh my God.'

Hubert touched Polly's hand. 'Are you really sure you want to hear this? Everything?'

Polly nodded.

'Well, Charles took you in his arms. I thought you were going to faint or throw up.'

'Did I?'

'No.'

'Thank heavens. So what happened?'

'You started snogging him.'

'What?'

'You were all over him.'

Polly put her hand over her mouth.

'Of course, Charles backed off and I don't think many people noticed the incident.'

'He backed off?'

'I have to say Adele took it very well.'

'What? The snog?'

'Yes,' said Hubert. 'But I wasn't thinking about *that* particular snog.'

'What do you mean? Was there another snog?'

Hubert smiled.

'Later on at the party, Charles went missing and Adele asked me to help look for him. I didn't like to tell her that you had gone missing too.'

'Go on,' said Polly.

'We found you in the garden, lying side by side in the bouncy castle,' continued Hubert. 'As soon as you saw me and Adele approaching, you grabbed Charles, rolled on top of him and started snogging him again.'

'We had to climb on to the bloody bouncy castle to drag you off him,' said Hubert. 'It was a nightmare. It still makes me feel sick to think about it. I was bouncing about all over the place and I'd also had a lot to drink. Adele was almost pissing herself laughing. She thought it was so funny – which was pretty good of her in the circumstances.'

'Christ, how embarrassing,' said Polly.

There was a pause as they both sipped their coffee.

'So, is that it?' asked Polly.

'Not quite,' replied Hubert. 'When I tried to pull you off Charles, you seemed to have got your hand stuck inside his pants.'

'Oh my God. Did Adele notice?'

'Definitely. You should have seen the expression on her face.'

Polly shook her head. 'I can hardly believe it.' She didn't care that she had upset Adele but it was clearly a shameful way to have behaved.

'After that, I took you back to the flat.'

'Thanks,' said Polly. 'It sounds terrible. Did anyone else see what happened?'

'Fortunately not.'

'Thank God for that.'

'Yes. I know you were pissed but it was a dreadful thing to do to your sister on her wedding day,' said Hubert.

'Dreadful,' repeated Polly. But she could not help thinking how dreadful it was that she could not remember a thing about the incident.

She had been snogging Charles. She had even, it seemed, had her hands down his trousers and she could not remember a thing. Perhaps, worst of all, she had missed seeing that expression on Adele's face.

'It was disgusting. I've never been so embarrassed in all my life.' Sue slammed the frying pan on to the hob.

'Not so loud, love,' said John.

'You were almost as bad,' continued Sue.

'Why?' John looked up from his newspaper defensively.

'Your speech,' said Sue, cracking an egg on the side of the pan and plopping it into the sizzling hot oil.

'What was wrong with my speech?'

'Well, fancy saying that Adele used to drive you round the U bend when she was a kid. I mean, do we have to broadcast to the whole world that you're a plumber?'

'What's wrong with being a plumber?' said John. 'Even Sir Thomas and Lady Viola need someone to unplug the john every once in a while.'

Sue put two slices of bread in the toaster.

'You are so crude – just like your daughter Polly.

Fancy going down that chute and exposing herself like that.'

'*Our* daughter. And she was wearing underwear.' John had seen the snogging incident on the dance floor but Sue had missed it and he had not told her about it.

Sue sniffed.

'She's always been an exhibitionist. Poor Adele. It must have been so embarrassing for her.'

'Most people saw the funny side of it,' said John. 'And then Charles's brother was very helpful.'

'Yes, thank heavens he kept an eye on her and eventually took her away. I saw him helping her into his car. She was making a scene even then, calling Adele a bitch or something, saying Adele deserved to be hurt. I think she must be mad.'

'I think she must still be in love with Charles,' said John.

'But that's ridiculous,' said Sue, jiggling the eggs a little in the pan.

'You can't just switch love on and off like a tap.'

'You seem to know a lot about the subject.'

John went back to his paper. Sue stood with the frying pan behind his back. She had loved him once, she knew that. She had loved him with all her heart and, perhaps, she still did. But things would never be the same and he only had himself to blame.

'How was it for you?' asked Ned. Polly smiled. It was a relief to see Ned again. It had been months since they had last met up and she realised now how much she had missed him.

'Hell,' said Polly. 'I don't remember a lot but, apparently, I behaved really disgracefully.'

173

'What a pity I wasn't there. It sounds more exciting than my parents' silver wedding anniversary.'

'I can't bear to talk about it,' said Polly. 'You might get the full unexpurgated version of events from Adele.'

Ned handed Polly a slice of pizza. They were having a takeaway supper in Polly's room and watching the TV.

'Well, at least it's all over now. You can put it behind you and get on with the rest of your life.'

Can I? thought Polly. She had got some sort of revenge by making the scene at the wedding but Adele had won the war. She had won Charles.

Two weeks had passed but still Polly thought of nothing else. If anything, she felt worse than that day on Filey beach. It now seemed so much more hopeless and final. Back then, there had been a chance that Charles might realise his mistake and they might get back together again. But now he had actually *married* Adele.

'How's the job?' asked Ned.

'Oh fine,' said Polly. 'I really love it, although my immediate boss hates me. I think he thinks I'm after his job.'

'You have been producing some good stuff. Your articles are really funny.'

'Do you think so?'

'Yes. In fact, I'm writing a script for a stand-up comedy thing I'm doing at the Asp and Ashes in a few weeks' time. I wondered whether you might have a look at it for me.'

'I'd be delighted. But, Ned, you're a Cambridge English graduate – I didn't even go to university. You don't need my advice.'

'I'd really appreciate it.'

'OK,' said Polly and Ned got the papers out of his bag.

They sat up to the small hours of the morning working on the script, adding things and cutting others and howling with laughter at the jokes, particularly the really bad ones.

It had been very therapeutic, thought Polly, when she eventually said goodnight to Ned. Charles would find out soon enough what a dreadful error he had made and, in the meantime, she would bide her time and, like Ned, think only about her work. But, one day, sooner or later, she felt sure there would be another opportunity to win back Charles and she would not let Hubert or anyone else drag her away. One day, she would get even with Adele.

PART II

Twenty-six – fat, single and giving up hope

Chapter Fifteen

Polly had been living at Zeta's for nearly two years and had been attending the Thursday evening meetings for some time.

The meetings were part transcendental meditation and part study of religious texts from the Bible to the Koran and Buddhist scripts. If Carslip or Adele knew what she was doing, thought Polly, as she flicked through the New Testament in search of Luke Chapter 15, they would tease her dreadfully. But she really enjoyed the meetings.

It was certainly better than sitting in her room watching TV or reading magazines. Zeta was sweet and the people in the group were all very nice.

They had finished the first meditation session and it was time to listen to the reading.

'I'm sure you're all familiar with this passage,' said Zeta. 'It's the Parable of the Lost Son – the Prodigal Son.'

They read the verses and discussed the story.

'Who do you most identify with?' asked Zeta. 'The younger brother, who went off and wasted all his money and was then welcomed back into the arms of his father? Or the elder son, who always did the right thing and was resentful when his father celebrated his brother's return?'

Polly wasn't sure. It was true that she was the useless daughter. The one who had failed to make much of her life, who walked in the shadow of her brighter, more successful sister. But, on the other hand, she was the one who had been most loyal to her family. It was over a year now since Adele's wedding and her mother told her that Adele and Charles had not visited once.

'Poor Adele – she works so hard,' Sue had said the last time Polly had spoken to her mother and Polly had indeed felt resentful. She worked hard too and yet never failed to remember her parents' birthdays. She went down to Dulwich regularly once a month. Was it right to resent the fact that her parents loved her sister and that, no matter what Adele did, they would always go on loving her?

Another ten minutes of meditation followed and then the meeting was over. After a short while, Zeta and Polly were alone.

'Have another glass of wine,' said Zeta.

'Thanks,' said Polly.

'You were very quiet this evening,' said Zeta. 'I always enjoy hearing your views – you have such forthright opinions.'

'Do I?' Polly held out her glass to Zeta.

'Yes. You're so intelligent – it's a real bonus having you in the group.'

'Thanks,' said Polly. 'But I'm not intelligent. I messed up my A levels.'

'Why was that?'

'Oh, I don't know. I think I was worrying about my sister.'

'Your sister? I didn't know you had a sister, Polly.'

'Yes. I can hardly bear to talk about her.'

'Why? What happened to her? Is she ill?'

Polly laughed at Zeta's question. Of course Adele was ill but not in the way her friend was thinking.

'We fell out – some time ago. It's a long story.'

'You mean you haven't made things up yet?'

'No. I don't suppose we ever will.'

Zeta shook her head and took Polly's hand. 'That's very sad.' Polly could sense that Zeta wanted to say more but was holding back.

'She did something unforgivable,' explained Polly. But Zeta said nothing and neither did Polly. After all, there was really nothing more to say.

'It's the obvious solution,' laughed Charles. 'We'll have to get you married off.'

'I'm such a walking disaster, I don't think I'll ever find anyone brave enough to take the plunge with me,' laughed Hubert as he heaved his plaster-clad leg on to the sofa. Araminta, who was sitting there, shifted along into the far corner. She was reading a book and hardly looked up at the arrival of her stepfather and uncle.

'Hi there,' said Hubert.

'Hi,' said Araminta, continuing to read.

Charles kissed the little girl on the top of her head and shrugged.

'Harry Potter,' he said to Hubert.

Hubert winced a little as he rearranged his leg.

'If you'd only taken my advice about avoiding those flats,' said Charles. Hubert grimaced. Charles had certainly been right about the flats.

Hubert thought back to the evening before. There

was a campaign in Colingate against a new motorway proposal and, as prospective Tory candidate for the constituency, he thought he should do his bit to help the locals protest about it. He had a huge leaflet drop to do and he had managed to persuade Charles to help him for one night.

They had been working for over two hours and were almost finished when Charles had suggested skipping the last block of council flats and going for a drink. 'There's hardly a Tory in the whole constituency and you're unlikely to find any votes in those flats whether you get the motorway scotched or not,' he had said. But Hubert insisted.

'These people are just as important as anyone else,' he had said. 'But we won't knock, we'll just stuff the leaflets through the letter box.'

They were on the top floor and almost finished when suddenly disaster struck. As Hubert stuffed a leaflet through a letter box, there was a terrible growling and snarling and he got a glimpse of some very sharp teeth snapping at his fingers. Hubert quickly withdrew his hand but the dog had ripped his leaflet in two. Charles burst out laughing.

'That was a close shave,' he said and leant against the door as he laughed. But suddenly the door swung open and Charles fell into the flat. The door had clearly not been closed securely and a huge Alsatian leapt over Charles and jumped straight at Hubert's throat. The two men wrestled with the dog for minutes that seemed like hours until an elderly lady appeared.

'Sweetpea! Sweetpea, come here this instant.' The ferocious dog submitted meekly to his mistress's voice and retreated to her side.

'He was just trying to be friendly,' she explained to Hubert and Charles who were both on their knees checking themselves over for damage. Charles had a bite on his wrist and Hubert had a few scratches on his face but there was nothing more serious than a lot of dear Sweetpea's saliva everywhere.

Hubert mopped at his face with his blue rosette. 'Of course, of course, just being friendly,' he said, getting back on his feet. Then, addressing the woman, he added, 'Here's a leaflet on the motorway protest.' The woman smiled and took the paper but Sweetpea snarled.

'And I hope that, when the election comes, I can count on your vote, madam, as well as the enthusiastic support of your dog.'

'The election?'

'It will probably be in May,' said Hubert.

'May? That's a long time. I might be dead by then.' She laughed. 'Anyway, I haven't made my mind up yet – I'm what you might call a floating voter.'

'Well, let's hope you float in my direction,' suggested Hubert, trying to smile at the woman without taking his eyes off Sweetpea who still looked capable of unilaterally calling off the ceasefire at any moment.

'I'm floating between the Monster Raving Loonies and the Anything But the Tories party.'

'Great,' said Charles as he and Hubert eventually legged it down the stairs. The woman and her dog were safely behind a closed door. They were free and Charles could not think of a time when he had looked forward to a pint of beer so much. But somehow Hubert, possibly as a result of the recent confrontation with Sweetpea, managed to slip. He fell heavily down a whole flight of stairs and succeeded in breaking his leg. They had spent the rest of the evening in the local A&E.

'Of course, if I had a wife,' said Hubert, who seemed now to be reflecting on his brother's latest advice, 'I'd certainly have a better chance of getting a safe seat next time around.'

'Hello Hubert,' said Adele. She swept into the room carrying a large bag of groceries and some flowers. 'So sorry about the leg.'

'Thanks,' said Hubert. 'Pour me a Scotch, Charles, will you?' he added.

Charles fixed the drinks and Adele set about making some supper.

'I was saying to Hubert,' said Charles as he gave Adele a glass of fizzy water. 'We need to find him a wife.'

'A nanny more like it,' said Adele putting a cushion behind Hubert's back. 'Are you comfortable?' she asked.

The invalid smiled and nodded. But, just as Adele was about to disappear back into the kitchen, he added, 'You wouldn't be an angel and pass that paper to me, would you?'

Adele gave Hubert the paper. It was the *Daily Globe*.

Hubert flicked through it and suddenly burst out laughing. 'That sister of yours is a total nightmare.'

'Tell me about it. What has she done now?'

'Oh, she's done an interview with Teddy Gifford. You know, that minister who resigned last year when it was revealed he owned a lap dancing bar in Soho. It's very funny.'

'Why?'

'She says he had a large ginger cat sitting on his lap while she was conducting the interview. Her first question is,' Hubert picked up the paper and read. '"Tell me, Mr Gifford, do you always need to have a pussy in your lap?" Apparently Gifford gave a start at the question, the cat leapt up and clawed him in the balls. It's hilarious.'

Adele smiled. 'Of course, Polly is a candidate.'

'What? A candidate in the election?'

'No, you dodo. A matrimonial candidate.'

'Me and your sister?' laughed Hubert. 'It would be a marriage made in hospital.'

'I thought you got on rather well with her. You took her back to Charles's flat with you after her appalling exhibition at our wedding, didn't you?'

'I told Charles not to tell a soul about that,' said Hubert. 'It just goes to show that you should never trust your brother.'

'Or your sister,' said Adele. 'I know she was pissed but—'

'She was so drunk that she didn't know what she was doing. She didn't remember a thing about it when I told her what she'd done the following morning. She was horrified.'

'Well, anyway. You did spend the night with her, didn't you?'

'Technically yes.' Hubert smiled. 'But nothing happened. We were both totally comatose.'

Hubert smiled as he thought back to that night. He had enjoyed taking Polly back to Charles's flat, undressing her and getting her into bed. But, although he had said he was too pissed to perform, he had

185

not wanted to make love to her. He found women attractive, very attractive, but he often found it hard to get turned on sexually. Seeing Polly lying semi-naked on the bed had just made him feel paternal towards her, as though he wanted to protect her.

'She's a nice girl,' he said. 'And clever. Probably far too nice and clever to saddle herself with a lunatic like me.'

'I wouldn't be so sure,' said Adele. 'At least it would get her off the shelf. I can't believe that she is still sulking about me and Charles after all this time.'

'Yes. I don't know all the background but she does seem very bitter towards you.'

'She doesn't seem to realise that her relationship with Charles would never have worked, that I have really saved her from a lot of unnecessary misery. I mean, Charles would never have married me, if he'd really wanted Polly, would he?'

At that moment, Charles came back into the room. He had a small bowl of green olives that he put down in front of Hubert.

'What's this about Polly?' he asked.

'We were just discussing her undying love for you,' said Hubert.

Charles blushed. 'Don't be ridiculous.'

'No. Actually, I was thinking of proposing to her,' said Hubert.

'What?' cried Charles, almost choking on an olive.

'Steady on,' said Hubert.

'You can't be serious,' said Charles as Adele thumped him on the back. 'I mean, there's no way that Polly—'

'Your wife seemed to think she might consider the idea.'

186

'But Polly – I mean, Polly would never marry *you*,' continued Charles.

'Thanks very much.'

'I mean, she believes in love and everything. She'd never marry anyone but—' He stopped himself from saying more.

'It might be worth a try,' said Hubert. 'She wants to settle down and have kids. I'm not exactly John Travolta—'

'I think she goes more for the Russell Crowe type,' interrupted Adele.

'Who?' said Hubert.

'It doesn't matter.'

'Well,' continued Hubert. 'I don't suppose I'm exactly like this Crab fellow either but I think I could be a good husband. Perhaps, with a bit of luck, a good father.'

Charles stared at Hubert. 'I can't believe this,' he laughed. 'You must be joking.'

'Why?'

'Look, Hubert,' said Charles. 'I thought you never wanted kids. You always said you never wanted them.'

'Perhaps I've changed my mind,' said Hubert. It was true that he had often said to Charles that he would never have children. But, perhaps, that was largely because he was worried he might have trouble making them. The idea of being a father was, on the other hand, quite appealing. He was genuinely fond of kids.

Charles shook his head.

'We can all change our minds, can't we?' continued Hubert. 'I mean, you always said that you wanted loads of kids.'

187

Charles's face paled at these words and he shot a glance at Adele.

'We have Araminta,' she said, looking across at her daughter who was still curled up with her book in the corner of the sofa.

'Yes,' said Charles. 'We have a child already.' He put out a hand and touched Araminta on the shoulder but she shrugged it off and wriggled out of reach.

'Anyway,' said Hubert. 'Don't take it too seriously. It's only a thought, an idea. A proposal, perhaps?'

Charles laughed at last. 'If you didn't have a broken leg, Hobbit, I'd give you a good kicking,' he said and the subject was put to rest.

But the subject did not rest for long. It arose frequently in Hubert's mind over the following weeks and refused to go away. Why shouldn't he ask Polly out?

'Mr Goodwood?' Polly's voice stammered over the name.

'Yes, some bloke called Goodwood on my line,' said Carslip. 'Wants to speak to you, Pussy – I'll transfer him.'

Polly went back to her desk to take the call. Her heart was beating fast. It was months since she had spoken to Charles. She wondered what he wanted. Perhaps he was unhappy and wanted to confide in her? Perhaps he had, at last, discovered the great error he had made in marrying Adele?

'Hello, Polly. I wondered whether you are doing anything for supper tonight?' The voice was faintly familiar but it was not Charles's.

'Who is that?' she asked.

'Oh sorry,' said Hubert. 'It's Hubert. Hubert Goodwood – Charles's brother.'

Of course, thought Polly. It was Hubert. The man
who had rescued her from trying to rape a bridegroom
in a bouncy castle. She had not seen him since the
morning when they had woken up in bed together in
Charles's flat.

'At least it would be a first for me,' said Polly.

'What?'

'Going out on a first date with a man I have already
been to bed with.' Hubert laughed and Polly noticed
Carslip's eyebrows rise a fraction as he listened to her
conversation.

'What do you say then?' enquired Hubert. There
was no need to consult her diary; Polly never went
out in the evenings. Then she realised it was a Thursday.

'Sorry,' she said. 'I'm busy tonight.'

'Something exciting?'

What the hell, thought Polly.

'A meditation and Bible study class,' she said, glancing
at Carslip whose eyebrows had shot to the top of
his head.

'A what?' asked Hubert.

'The theme tonight is "Love Thine Enemies", said
Polly, staring pointedly at Carslip. 'I don't think that's
a subject I should miss.'

'What about tomorrow?'

'That would be nice.' Would it? Polly wondered.
Did she really want to spend an evening with Hubert?
But she knew that she did. Not only was it likely that
Hubert would take her to a good restaurant but they
would almost certainly talk about Charles. And, if she

couldn't be with Charles, then the next best thing was to talk about him with someone.

'I'm still at Charles's flat,' said Hubert.

'Really?' said Polly. 'You haven't found a buyer after all this time?'

'Charles thinks I'm not showing them round properly. But it's only fair to point out that patch on the beam that looks so much like dry rot, don't you think? I mean, a woman like yourself, with such high ethical standards, would underst—'

'Piss off, Hubert,' laughed Polly.

'OK. But tomorrow night. How about I book a table at the Bluebird in the Kings Road and we meet there at seven thirty?'

'Fine, thanks,' said Polly. 'Oh, and don't forget to get a good story for my paper as well.'

'Oh please,' protested Hubert in mock despair. 'And I thought you had accepted just because you were after my body.'

Polly laughed. 'Nothing personal. But, if you bring me a story, we can claim the bill on my expenses.' Carslip was still listening. He was signalling now for her to get off the phone. She still had another thousand words to write for the next day's pages.

'I'll try not to disappoint you,' said Hubert.

'It's great to see you,' said Polly.

Ned smiled. They sat in a greasy spoon cafe round the corner from Polly's office and drank tea. Ned had been making a delivery nearby and had called on the off chance that Polly had time for a break.

'How's the job going?' he asked.

'Very well,' said Polly. It was true. She had been

working hard and everyone, apart from Carslip, thought she was doing brilliantly. Den had just given her a big pay rise.

'What about you? Are you writing?'

Ned pulled a face. 'I keep trying but nothing seems to be working right at the moment. I used to be so focused but lately I'm distracted by, well, anything.'

'Does this distraction have a name?' asked Polly.

Ned laughed. 'Yes, you're right. She does.' He paused for a moment and continued. 'She has a number of names, in fact. I seem to have run through at least half a dozen women over the last year.'

'But no one special?'

'That's the whole point,' said Ned. 'I don't want anyone special. I make quite an effort to pick the girls who only seem to want a good time. But it's still somehow boring.'

'Quite the opposite problem for me,' sighed Polly, pushing away the jam doughnut that Ned had bought for her. 'I've hardly been out with anyone since—' She paused.

'Since?'

'Since Charles.'

'Charles?' Ned took a big bite of doughnut which left sugar all round his lips. 'You're not still pining away for *him*, are you?'

Polly looked defensive. 'You don't understand,' she said. 'No one does. I'll never get over Charles.'

'Not if you're so determined not to,' said Ned, licking jam off his fingers.

'I'm sorry. You're right. I suppose I am being pathetic but, really, it does still hurt.'

'You should get out more.'

'Yes.'

'What are you doing tonight?'

Polly shook her head. 'Busy,' she said.

'Tomorrow?'

'Busy.'

'Saturday?'

'I'm having dinner with my editor, Den Christie,' said Polly, pulling a face.

'Well, it looks as though you're already on the case,' laughed Ned. 'You don't need any help from me.'

'Thanks anyway,' said Polly.

Ned kissed her when they said goodbye. It was a tiny kiss but Ned missed her cheek and it landed on her lips.

As she watched Ned climb back on his bike, Polly licked off the sugar that Ned's kiss had left behind. He was really a very sweet man.

Chapter Sixteen

Polly licked her lips again. She had just eaten a second bag of crisps and really should have had nothing at all since she was going out to dinner with Hubert that evening. She stared at herself in the mirror. She was twenty-six years old but already had the start of a double chin and the hips of a mother of four. She had thrown away her scales over a year ago, straight after Charles and Adele's wedding, and now she had no idea what her weight was – except, of course, that it was heavier. Probably heavier than it had been at any other time in her life.

In a few years' time, she said to herself, she would be fat and thirty and well and truly on the shelf.

She took the same tired old black dress off her rail, the one she wore so often now as so many of her other clothes had got too tight. She wondered why Hubert had suddenly invited her out. It was probably something to do with the election that was coming up. Hubert must think that she might be able to influence the *Globe*'s political coverage. Some chance, Polly laughed to herself. Den called all the political shots and woe betide the political editor if he failed to stick to Den's line.

The Tories were being crucified by the press. Den had supported them for a long time but there had been one sleaze scandal after another and Den relished every salacious detail. The *Globe* had now become the leading paper for digging up ever more Tory dirt.

Polly brushed her thick, dark blond hair. At least that was still looking in good nick, she thought. She put on some lipstick and grinned at her reflection. She had the sort of plump but nice girl-next-door looks that would suit a High Street cafe, not the gaunt, sophisticated looks of the women who frequented the restaurants that Hubert went to. The restaurants that Charles and Adele went to. If Charles were to see her now, wondered Polly, would he be glad that he had chosen Adele? Almost certainly. There was no way that Adele would ever let herself go the way that Polly had. Adele would probably still have a size eight figure even when she was a grandmother.

Polly screwed up the bags of crisps, grabbed her coat and vowed to eat the bare minimum at dinner.

'Go on, have another chocolate,' said Hubert. He had already insisted on three substantial courses and now there were gorgeous Belgian truffles with the coffee. Polly popped one in her mouth. She had the willpower of a gnat, she told herself, but she would skip breakfast the following morning.

'So how are Charles and Adele?' said Polly. She had spent the whole evening hoping that Hubert would start talking about Charles and she could wait no longer.

'I think the builders are driving them crazy. The reconversion of the flat upstairs should have been completed ages ago but it looks like it's going to take at least a couple of months more.'

'But they're happy?'

'Happy?'

'Well, yes, of course they're happy,' said Polly. 'Silly question. They've only been married just over a year. Hardly time for the seven year itch?'

Polly laughed but Hubert said nothing.

'And Minty?' continued Polly, feeling embarrassed by her previous questions. What had she expected Hubert to say? That they were already filing for a divorce?

'She's really growing up,' said Hubert. 'She always seems to have her head in a book when I go round there. But Adele said she's been having some problems at school.'

'What sort of problems?'

'Oh, some kind of bullying. Girls being bitchy – you know the sort of thing. You women never grow out of it, do you?'

And I never will, thought Polly, if you're referring to my dearest, darling bitch of a sister.

'Minty was always so popular at school,' she said.

'And then, of course, they keep changing nannies.'

'Is that Aussie girl still there?'

'No. She was really nice. But I think Adele got a bit jealous of her.'

'What do you mean?'

'Well, you know, Adele didn't like the way she would put on short skirts in the evening and sit on the sofa right next to Charles.'

'I can imagine,' said Polly. She would never have hired an attractive young au pair if she had been married to Charles. But Polly was surprised to hear that Adele was bothered. It was so unlike Adele to be jealous; she was generally so self-confident.

The waiter came over to the table and gave Hubert back his credit card. Hubert gave Polly the bill in case she might find an excuse to use it although they had not spent much time talking about politics. It was still not clear to Polly why Hubert had invited her out.

'Shall we go back to the flat for a nightcap?' he asked as they stepped into the street.

'OK,' said Polly, 'if you're not expecting me to end up in the same predicament as last time.' Hubert pulled a face.

'Am I so resistible?' he asked and slipped his arm round Polly's shoulder.

Polly was surprised. Perhaps it had been a straight-forward date after all. Perhaps Hubert was just a slow operator and it had taken him over a year to pluck up the courage to invite her out. Not altogether incredible, thought Polly, given her behaviour that first time they had met.

But her and Hubert – was that really feasible? Hubert was a bit of a twit and physically was not very attractive. He was considerably overweight and almost bald but he had a kind face and he was a kind man. A voice inside her suggested to Polly that she might do worse. But that was ridiculous, she told herself at once.

Nonetheless she did not ask Hubert to remove his arm.

When they got to Charles's flat, they had difficulty getting in the front door. There were two huge mahogany wardrobes standing in the hallway and three more in the small sitting room.

'I'm afraid there's another one in the bathroom and two more in the bedroom,' said Hubert.

'Why? Where have they come from?' asked Polly, sitting on a chair sandwiched between two of the massive pieces of furniture.

'I went to an auction to buy a wardrobe and found one I really liked. They are rather splendid, aren't they?'

'But was it necessary to buy so many?'

'Well, I started bidding and thought I'd got the thing for a really good price,' said Hubert. 'But the following day when it was delivered, I realised that I'd bought a job lot of eight identical wardrobes.'

'Hubert,' laughed Polly. 'You are an idiot.'

'Yes, and to think I had been quite willing to pay eight times the going rate. It's so embarrassing.'

Hubert put a glass of brandy in Polly's hand and sat down on the floor opposite her. There was nowhere else to sit where they could see each other. Polly felt Hubert looking at her legs.

'Why did you ask me out?' she asked.

'Isn't it obvious? You're a stunningly attractive woman and I wanted to ask you to marry me.' Polly spluttered into her glass but before she could reply, Hubert continued.

'Only joking,' he said. 'I wanted to flog you a wardrobe, of course.'

They both laughed and Polly felt the relief of laughing, really laughing until the tears rolled down her face. Whatever Hubert wanted, she was glad he had got in touch.

The following night Polly went out again. After months of complete social vacuum, she was suddenly busy.

This time she was seeing Den.

As she had suspected from the beginning, Den was not the kind of man who would take no for an answer. He had invited her out relentlessly. He was short, ugly, twice divorced and almost twice her age but he was her editor and so, in the end, she had agreed. There could not be much harm in just having dinner with the man, she told herself.

They went to the Met Bar for a drink first. It was noisy and crowded but Den thought it was the kind of place that would impress Polly and he was right, although she could not help feeling how out of place she and Den looked. They were simply not glamorous enough.

They went on to eat at Nobu and Polly hated to think what the bill must have come to. She felt sure that Den would be looking for a return on his investment.

'No thanks, I'm exhausted,' said Polly when inevitably he invited her back to his flat. Hubert could be trusted to behave properly but Den was quite another case. He would certainly try something on and Polly already knew that he did not understand the word no.

Polly expected Den to hassle her but he gave in unusually graciously.

'I'll drive you home then,' he said and Polly accepted the offer.

When they arrived at Den's car Polly was not surprised to find a sports car. It was a rather elderly Porsche but Den was very proud of it.

'Careful,' said Den as Polly clambered awkwardly inside. She was glad she had worn trousers.

As they drove, they talked about work.

'Why does Arse-lick call you Pussy?' asked Den.

'My niece used to call me Aunt Pussy when she was little,' said Polly. 'My sister told Carslip once and he has teased me ever since.'

'The man's a bastard.'

'Well, Adele also told him that my real name is Pamela. So, I suppose it could be worse. I think being called Pamela is even worse than being called Pussy.'

'What a bastard,' repeated Den indignantly. Polly almost laughed. It was true that Carslip was a bastard but most people thought Den was an even bigger one.

'It's lousy when you have a crap name but Polly is nice,' said Den. 'Not like Den.'

Polly could not think what to say in response to this. 'Den is nice too' was a lie and would almost certainly be misconstrued.

'I'll tell you a secret,' Den went on putting his hand on Polly's knee. Polly shifted her leg and Den put his hand back on the steering wheel. 'My name isn't really Den.'

'Really? What is it?'

'You must swear never to tell a soul. No one knows this except my family.'

'Girl Guides' honour,' said Polly.

'OK,' laughed Den. 'It's Devlin. Devlin. Can you believe that?'

'It's not great,' said Polly. But she was not sure that Den was any better.

'It's bloody awful,' said Den. 'Right up there in the Pamela league.' They drew up outside Polly's house. 'Well,' said Den leaning over towards Polly. 'I'm glad we've got something in common – even if it's just dreadful names.' He tried to kiss her lips but she managed to turn her head in time so that he kissed her on the cheek. Nonetheless Polly was overwhelmed by stale fumes of cigarette smoke and alcohol. She coughed and thanked him for dinner.

Den laughed. 'I didn't think they made girls like you any more,' he said as she opened her door.

'What do you mean?'

'Well, you're not a slapper. I mean, I suppose I'm going to have to propose in order to get my fucking leg over?'

Polly laughed as well. 'Dream on, Den. I'll see you on Monday.'

The Porsche squealed away from the kerb and Polly burst out laughing. Den could be crude and foul-mannered but he was a good man. She could well believe that he was not used to having his amorous advances spurned.

The following night was Sunday and she had another date but, this time, it was only Ned.

'God, what a weekend,' said Polly as Ned passed her a beer.

'How did the hot dates go?'

'Hotter than I'd expected. Two out of two.'

'What do you mean?'

'Both of them proposed to me.'

'You're joking,' said Ned, spilling his beer.

'And why should you be so surprised that men are falling over themselves to marry me?'

'I'm not. But two proposals from two first dates – that's pretty impressive.'

'Well, neither of them were serious,' said Polly. 'They were both conditional offers.'

'Conditional on what?'

'Well, one wanted to offload eight Victorian wardrobes and the other just wanted a shag.'

'Very romantic. I'm sure you must have been tempted.'

Polly laughed and shook her head.

'Back to waiting at home for Bonnie Prince Charlie, then?'

Polly frowned. 'No, you were right. It was good to go out. It was fun and I had a really good time but . . .'

'But?'

'But you're also right. Compared to Charles, both of these guys are nothing.'

'Maybe. But Charles is gone. History. You've got to forget him.'

Polly sipped her beer. 'What about you?' she asked. 'Exciting weekend?'

'Not bad,' said Ned, smiling. 'I've been working non-stop and I really feel I'm on to something at last.'

'That's brilliant news. What is it?'

'A film script. I know it's a bit ambitious but it's what I really want to do.'

'Fantastic.'

'When it's done I think I might get myself to LA somehow or other and show it around,' said Ned.

'Someone told me you really need to go out there personally and get your face known – spend six months or a year there. What do you think?'

Why not, thought Polly, but curiously she did not like the idea at all. She would miss Ned if he went away.

Chapter Seventeen

Polly had bought some new clothes.

This was partly because she had been on another crash diet and lost over half a stone, partly because she had absolutely nothing to wear and partly because she had come into some money. It wasn't exactly a fortune but it had cleared her overdraft and meant that she could enjoy building it back up again to the limit.

Would you approve, Aunt Julia? she wondered as she examined herself in the mirror. She was wearing a tight white T-shirt with a sugar pink row of hearts down one shoulder and jeans that barely covered her hips. There was a considerable expanse of flesh between the two items of clothing but Polly had also been going to the gym regularly for the last couple of months and so she felt just about brave enough to bare it.

'She didn't leave a penny to Adele,' Sue had said resentfully. Polly had been surprised to hear this. She had not been aware of being her aunt's favourite and wondered what on earth she had done to become a beneficiary of her will. 'I suppose she felt sorry for you,' Sue added.

It was amazing that Aunt Julia had left anything to anyone in Sue's family, thought Polly. Her mother and her sister had not been close and Polly had only seen Aunt Julia occasionally at weddings and funerals.

Polly brushed her hair and reapplied her lipstick. She had been surprised to receive an invitation to Adele's party. It had been casually delivered the night before, rather as an afterthought. Polly had called to speak with Minty and Adele had answered the phone.

'You're home early,' said Polly. It was only five o'clock and she had not left her own office yet.

'I needed to get a few things organised for tomorrow,' said Adele.

'Tomorrow?'

'Oh, the party – you know.'

Polly said nothing.

'Sorry, didn't I send you an invitation?' continued Adele. 'The building work is finished at last and Charles and I thought we might celebrate now that the house is all back in one piece.'

'I see.'

'Would you like to come over?' asked Adele. 'If you've nothing else to do.' It was definitely an afterthought but Adele still might easily not have asked her. She probably wanted to show off the new house, thought Polly.

She hesitated. The temptation to refuse was enormous. Of course, she had something else to do. Doing anything out of the company of her sister had to be better than watching Adele swank about at her own party. But, on the other hand, she had not seen Charles for months and the thought of seeing him again still sent a rush of adrenalin through her veins.

'I don't know,' she said. But she was already thinking about what clothes she might squeeze into, if she starved herself for the next twenty-four hours.

'Hubert is coming,' said Adele.

'What's that supposed to mean?'

Adele laughed. 'You're so touchy. We all know about you and Hobbit.'

Polly felt her face burn with anger. It was true that she had been seeing Hubert a bit over the past few months but they were hardly an item.

'There is no such thing as "me and Hubert". You know that.'

'Well, I'm not sure he would be happy to hear you say that.'

'Really?' Polly was in no mood to allow Adele to tease her but the comment made her stop and think. Was Hubert indeed becoming fond of her? Was it right, in that case, that she should lead him on and keep him hoping?

'Well, you decide,' said Adele. 'If you come, you'll be very welcome.'

'Let me speak, let me speak,' Polly heard a small voice in the background.

'OK,' said Adele. 'I'll hand you over to Araminta.'

'Aunt Polly, please come to the party,' said Minty. 'I'm staying up really late and Mummy's bought me some new flared jeans.'

'They sound great,' said Polly.

'Daddy will be at the party too. And you really like Daddy, don't you?' It was the first time that Polly had heard Minty refer to Charles as Daddy. She did not like it. It seemed to complete the circle, the tight family circle of Minty, Adele and Charles, leaving her firmly on the outside.

'There will be lots of really good things to eat. Mummy has hired *caterers*.'

'Wow,' said Polly.

'And you can see Bobbin. It's great now that we have more space and Mummy says we can try having Bobbin at home again. I was so glad when Ned brought him over.'

'Yes, I do rather miss him.'

'Please come, Aunt Polly,' pleaded Minty. 'I'll have no one to talk to if you don't come.' Polly smiled to herself. A picture of her spending the evening with seven-year-old Minty on her lap, while everyone else chatted and partied, flashed through her head.

'OK,' she said. 'If you promise to look after me.'

'I will,' said Minty. 'I promise.'

Polly arrived late but the party was still in its early stages. Minty jumped into her arms the moment Polly stepped through the door.

'I'm so glad you're here. There's an emergency and Mummy and Daddy are too busy to help. They won't listen to a word I say.'

'Why? What's the matter?' said Polly, wriggling out of her jacket and balancing it on top of the huge mountain of coats that were piled on the banister.

'It's Bobbin. Come quickly. I think he may be dying.'

Minty took Polly up to her room, a room she hardly recognised. Gone were all the trains and fire engines that they had spent so many hours playing with only a year or so earlier and, in their place, were pots of glittery make-up and nail varnish. On the wall were posters of pop stars and the dolls' house had been dismantled and shoved under the bed to make room for Minty's new CD player.

The rabbit was in the far corner of his cage, huddled into a tight ball.

'Perhaps he doesn't like the noise?' suggested Polly. The beat from downstairs was literally throbbing through the floorboards.

'He's got blood on his nose,' said Minty, opening the cage door and pulling the creature out. 'Look.'

Polly tried to look but Bobbin was uncooperative and refused to be examined.

'Need a hand?'

Polly turned to see Hubert standing in the doorway.

'Uncle Hobbit,' cried Minty. 'Uncle Hobbit will help.'

Polly passed the rabbit to Hubert.

'I thought I'd find you up here,' he said.

'How did you know I had arrived?' asked Polly. 'I was hardly through the door when I was whisked up here to "Casualty".'

'I saw your jacket on the stairs. And also Minty had disappeared so it did not require too much sleuthing to arrive at the appropriate conclusion.'

'The other end. It's his nose,' said Minty, watching Hubert carefully examine Bobbin's backside.

Hubert turned the creature around but Bobbin was still tightly curled up.

'I'm good with pets,' said Hubert.

'Uncle Hobbit has a cat called Pom Pom,' said Minty.

'When it comes to animals you just need to be firm,' said Hubert, grasping Bobbin under the chin and gently holding back his ears.

'Can you see the blood?' asked Minty.

Whether Hubert saw any blood on Bobbin's nose Polly would never know but she could soon see a lot of blood on Hubert's nose.

'Aargh,' he cried, dropping the rabbit on to the bed. 'He bit me.' Hubert struggled to recapture Bobbin but slipped and hit his face on Minty's dressing table. When he stood up he had a streaming nosebleed and Bobbin was still on the loose.

Minty dived under the bed to look for her rabbit and Polly grabbed a cloth to help Hubert mop up his nose. He dabbed at his face with what, on closer inspection, turned out to be a pair of Minty's knickers.

'Don't dab. Just hold it tight,' said Polly, pressing the knickers over Hubert's face.

'I think you must have frightened him,' said Minty from underneath the bed. 'That's why he bit you.'

'He's got bloody sharp teeth,' muttered Hubert.

'He only uses them when he's upset,' said Minty, re-emerging with the trembling animal cradled in her hands.

'It doesn't take much to wind the Bobbin up, does it?' said Hubert.

'Poor Bobbin, he's in shock.'

'Me too,' said Hubert, sitting down on the side of the bed. He removed the knickers from his nose but the blood continued to pour around his mouth and chin.

'I'll get a wet cloth to clean you up,' said Polly.

She stepped outside the room and looked across to the bathroom, just in time to see Charles and Adele going in there. Her stomach lurched as she thought back to that dreadful day, the day when Charles and Adele had disappeared together after lunch. Of course you could say that Polly had behaved or, at least, had attempted to behave equally badly at Adele's wedding. But that had been different. Not only had she been blind drunk but she had also been seeking to exact her revenge. There was no way that she would have done what Adele had done in the first place. It was important to remember who had started the whole thing.

As Polly reasoned with herself she was taken by surprise when Charles suddenly opened the bathroom door.

'Ah, Polly,' he said. 'I didn't know you were waiting. There is another loo downstairs.'

Polly blushed and said something about needing to clean up Hubert.

'What on earth has he done now?' asked Adele, appearing at Charles's side. Polly noticed that her sister was doing up the buttons of her shirt.

'He has a nosebleed,' said Polly.

It was quite clear that Charles had been making love to Adele in the bathroom. Maybe they had not actually had sex, maybe he had just been fondling her breasts or had slipped his hand up that short black leather skirt. Whatever, thought Polly, it all meant the same thing. That Charles still fancied Adele, that their marriage was working, that there was no hope for Polly.

'He got into a fight with Bobbin in Minty's room,' she added.

'That man is a disaster,' said Adele, opening a

bathroom cupboard and pulling out a white flannel which she ran under the tap.

'Thanks.' Polly took the flannel from Adele.

'I hope that comes out,' said Adele, staring at Polly's chest.

'What?'

Adele pointed and Polly looked down to see that she had Hubert's blood splattered all over her brand-new top.

'The little beast scared the life out of me,' said Hubert when Polly got back downstairs and joined the circle of people clustered around him. He was lying back in a chair with an ice bag balanced on his forehead and was clearly enjoying the attention he was attracting. 'Polly was magnificent,' he continued, pointing to the bloodstains on Polly's chest. 'Totally fearless, as you can see. If I'd seen a creature attack someone so viciously, I'd like to think I'd have stood my ground like Polly and come to the rescue.'

Polly smiled. 'Don't be ridiculous. It was a rabbit, Hubert, not a velociraptor.'

'You could have fooled me,' said Hubert. 'I suppose I'm lucky it didn't go for the eyes – or somewhere else equally painful.'

They laughed.

When Hubert had recovered sufficiently, he introduced Polly to some people at the party but she was not enjoying herself. She kept looking around for Charles and was dismayed to see him stick close to Adele's side.

'Shall we go on somewhere else?' suggested Hubert.

'OK,' said Polly. There was no point in staying. In

fact, she could no longer see what had been the point in coming. What had she hoped to achieve? Had she expected Charles to take her into his arms, abandon Adele and run away with her? She was living in cloud cuckoo land, as her mother would say. She let Hubert put his arm round her and lead her out into the street.

They got a cab straight away and Polly did not object when Hubert gave the driver his home address.

Back in Charles's flat – no, Hubert's flat, Polly corrected herself – they drank brandy and sat close together on the sofa.

'Sorry about your shirt,' said Hubert, gently touching the blood spots on Polly's left breast. 'Will it come out?'

Polly shrugged.

'Shall we try rubbing cold water into it?' asked Hubert. Polly laughed.

'I'd like to do that,' said Hubert, continuing to rub Polly's breast and, to her surprise, Polly felt her nipple harden at his touch.

She looked up and it was clear that Hubert was moving in to kiss her. She could have said no. Hubert was not the sort of man to force himself on a woman but she didn't want to.

She let Hubert kiss her and she kissed him back. She let him lift up her T-shirt and she helped him pull it over her head. He unzipped her jeans and she helped him to pull them off.

They were soon naked together on the sofa kissing and caressing each other. It was the first time Polly had done this since Charles but why not? Why had she been keeping herself celibate? What was the point in waiting for a man she could never have?

Hubert had a very different body to his brother's. He was much heavier and, despite the lack of hair on his head, his body was much hairier. Polly let him climb on top of her. She was willing to have sex with him. But nothing happened.

'What's wrong?' she asked as Hubert rolled off her and sat up on the side of the sofa.

'I'm sorry, Polly. I don't know what it is. I find you very attractive but, somehow, I can't seem to . . .'

'Don't worry. Let's just sleep together.'

They went through to the bedroom and cuddled up in bed. It was warm and comforting being with Hubert and Polly was not disappointed about the lack of sex. It was enough just to be held by a man again, to feel loved. She suddenly realised how much her body had missed being hugged.

'Perhaps in the morning,' said Hubert, propping himself up on one elbow.

'Don't worry about it,' said Polly. 'Just hold me.'

So Hubert took her in his arms again and they fell asleep.

Chapter Eighteen

There were, of course, many advantages to being Hubert Goodwood's girlfriend other than the one that kept returning to Polly's mind.

For a start, Hubert was a nice man, a very nice man, and Polly enjoyed being really looked after for the first time in her life.

Secondly, although she had not given up her room at Zeta's, Polly was now living in Kensington for much of the time and the shops and bars were so much nicer there. They were more expensive too but Hubert was generous and seemed to enjoy treating her.

Also, it helped to keep Den at bay. Now that he realised Polly had a proper boyfriend, he harassed her less often.

And, above all, there was room at Hubert's flat for Minty to stay and the three of them often spent the weekend together, like a proper family. Minty loved Pom Pom, Hubert's hugely fat, spotlessly white cat, and they would all sit on the sofa together on Sunday afternoons with Hubert reading the papers while Polly, Minty and Pom Pom just snuggled up together and watched TV.

Polly should have been happy through and through

but the other good thing about being Hubert's girlfriend made her uneasy.

'How do you know he's jealous?' asked Ned.

'Look, ever since I've been with Hubert, he's called me almost every week,' said Polly. 'At first, we would just chat on the phone but then he asked me to lunch—'

'And you couldn't say no.'

'Well, yes, I know I should have.' Polly sipped her beer. 'But what's wrong with having lunch with someone?'

Ned crossed his legs and surveyed the crowded bar. 'It's not just someone, as we both know. Don't you think you're messing Hubert around a bit?' he asked. 'Not to mention Adele.'

'I'm not messing Hubert around. I only had lunch with him and I didn't try to force-snog him, I swear.'

But Ned did not laugh.

'Oh, Polly, you of all people should know. You may end up hurting Hubert – just because you are enjoying making his brother jealous. Doesn't that sound cruel?'

'Well, yes,' said Polly, putting down her bottle, 'if you put it like that, it does. I would hate to hurt Hubert – he has been so kind to me and he is such a sweet man.'

'But?'

'But I am not misleading Hubert. I enjoy going out with Hubert but it's not serious. I mean, I've never told him that I love him.'

'Still waiting for Charles to give up on Adele?'

'Not really. I mean, I'm not trying to break up their marriage or anything.'

214

Ned sighed. 'Did Charles ever tell you that he loved you?'

Polly said nothing. She stared blankly at the table.

'In which case, you can't say that Charles ever misled you, that he was ever serious when he was going out with you.'

'It was different between me and Charles,' protested Polly. 'If Adele hadn't interfered—'

'Really, Polly, it's pathetic,' said Ned. 'You are pathetic.'

The words hurt as they were intended to and Polly felt tears start in her eyes. She hated to think that Ned disapproved of her. Ned was her friend, the friend who had always supported her, who had always *liked* her.

'Really, Ned, I am not trying to break up Charles and Adele's marriage. For a start, I would hate to upset Minty. I am sure she has got very fond of Charles now as her stepfather.'

'How considerate you are of other people's feelings,' said Ned with heavy sarcasm.

'And I do care about Hubert's feelings,' continued Polly. 'I am very fond of Hubert. He does make me feel, well, comfortable. Really comfortable.'

Polly thought back to that morning. Hubert had woken with a slight erection and, with a little difficulty, he had managed to maintain it while they had sex. She loved sleeping with Hubert but was it really satisfactory that they so rarely did more?

Ned suddenly grabbed her arm. 'Look Polly, that's not enough. If you're going to go on seeing Hubert you've got to make a proper commitment to him—'

'Commitment? I thought that word was an anathema to you?'

215

Ned looked angrier than Polly ever remembered seeing him. 'When I first met you, you wanted more than just comfort. So much more. You wanted love and passion. You thought I was stupid not to see that personal relationships are all that really matter.'

'I know I did,' said Polly, fighting back tears. 'But that means winning back Charles, don't you see? And you're the one who's always telling me to forget that.'

Ned let go of her arm and turned away.

Polly got to her feet.

'I'm sorry I even discussed it with you,' she said. 'I'm leaving.'

'Fine,' said Ned. He stayed in his chair and watched Polly make her way to the door. It was a warm summer's evening and only a short distance lay between the pub and the tube station.

But it was a long slow walk for Polly as she thought over her conversation with Ned. Why had he been so angry? Did he really understand her so little? Was he really so concerned for Hubert's feelings?

It did not seem to add up. She had always been able to confide in Ned. She had almost seen him as her accomplice in trying to win back Charles and get her own back on Adele. So why was he behaving so oddly?

When she got to her room, there was a message from Hubert on the answerphone.

Hello my dearest darling girl. I'll call you again later. Polly deleted the message. Perhaps Ned was right, she thought. Perhaps Hubert really did love her. What then?

But the thought was not wholly unwelcome. Hubert

was not Charles. He was not a great lover, not the man she really wanted, but he was kind and good and he might even love her. And Polly needed to be loved. Her mother had never loved her as much as Adele. Her father loved her but was always kept at bay by Sue. And then Adele. Adele had shown just how much she loved her sister that Saturday afternoon over two years ago now. Whatever Ned said, Polly would never forgive her for that. How could she?

'So will the Tories ever come back from this defeat?' the interviewer asked Hubert.

'Of course,' said Hubert. 'It will take time but we'll get there.'

'How?'

'One step at a time.'

Polly was listening in bed in her room at Zeta's house. She had a streaming cold and Hubert had come over to look after her.

'I have to give this interview on the radio,' he said. 'But they're sending over a broadcasting van and I can do it in that.'

Although the Tories had been massacred in the election, Hubert had done amazingly well in his seat. He had not won but he had more than halved the enormous Labour majority that he had faced.

'So, after your personal performance in Colingate,' said the interviewer, 'will you get a safe seat in the next election?'

'I hope I am selected,' said Hubert.

'What sort of person do Tory party members go for these days?'

'Well,' laughed Hubert. 'They are, of course, very

tolerant and open-minded people and would always choose the candidate who they think will do the best job for their constituency. But I suppose, all things being equal, they would prefer someone fairly young, happily married with a useful professional life.'

'Like yourself?' asked the interviewer.

'Not quite. But I'm working on it.'

Sue and John were also listening to the radio. They were driving back from a visit to Charles and Adele's house. It had been Araminta's birthday and they had taken her to see a film.

'Listen. That's Charles's brother,' said Sue.

'Hubert?' asked John. 'The one our Pamela is seeing?'

Sue sniffed. 'I can't see that lasting.'

'Why not?'

'He's far too clever for Polly. I mean, he's going to be an *MP*.'

'What's so clever about that?' asked John. 'Half these MPs couldn't fix a piss-up in a brewery.'

'Listen.' Sue turned up the volume but the interview with Hubert was already over. 'We missed it,' she said, switching the radio off.

They were driving south over Blackfriars Bridge and Sue felt tired. She checked her reflection in the sunshield mirror.

'Do you think I should have the bags under my eyes done?' she asked.

John glanced across at her. 'You can't make yourself twenty years younger, if that's what you want to do. Face it. We're getting older, Susan. We're grandparents.'

'It's OK for you,' said Sue. 'But for women, it's different.'

'Why?'

'I was always proud of my looks – like Adele.'

'That girl thinks of herself too much, if you ask me,' said John, slowing down at the lights.

'I think she's incredible the way she juggles her job and looks after Araminta and still looks a million dollars.'

'I'm worried about that little girl,' said John.

'Araminta? Why? She's a perfect child.'

'The way Adele lets her dress. All those crop tops or whatever they are, and platform soles. I mean, she's only just seven. She's a child, not a bloody Spice Girl.'

'I'm sure Adele knows what she's doing.'

John shifted gear and the car surged forward.

'Araminta told me that no one went to her Sports Day at the end of term.'

'Really?' said Sue. 'I didn't know about that.'

'Her school is ten minutes' walk from Adele's office but Adele was too busy to go.'

'And Charles was too busy as well?'

'I suppose so,' said John. 'But, anyway, she's not his kid – you can't expect him to feel the same way.'

Sue glared at John. 'I don't remember you going to many Sports Days.'

'That's because you went,' said John. 'It's a mother's job – first and foremost.'

'Times have changed.'

'Well, Araminta was upset. She said she asked if she could invite Pamela but Adele refused.'

'Polly interferes too much with that child,' said Sue.

'I can understand how it must upset Adele. It, well, *undermines* her authority.'

'I don't think the girl has been happy since the day Pamela left Noel Road,' said John. 'I think she's still pining for her after all this time.'

They drove in silence until they reached their house in Dulwich. Sue was really irritated by what John had said. She hated it when he criticised Adele. What right did he think he had to find fault with her? She was the one member of the family they could all be proud of. She had worked hard and got into Cambridge. She had a fantastic job and was earning lots of money. And there was her father, slagging her off. What had he done with his life, asked Sue. He'd left school without any qualifications and had one of the dirtiest jobs in the world. A plumber. What right had a plumber to criticise his investment banker daughter?

John pulled into the drive. 'Open the garage for me, love,' he said.

Sue got out of the car and slammed the door. Garage, garage, garage, she said to herself. Not *garridge*, the way John had pronounced it.

It was no good, she thought, as she tugged open the garage doors. He would never change. She had married into the gutter and there she was destined to stay. But Adele was a different matter. Adele had the opportunity to be everything and have everything she had ever wanted.

'What on earth happened?' asked Polly as Hubert staggered through the door. He was doubled over in pain and blood dripped from his mouth. Polly leapt out of bed and helped him to lie down. He was coughing and clutching his ribs.

'Just a beating, just a bit of a beating,' he managed to say.

'Who did it? Shall I call the police? An ambulance?'

'No, no,' said Hubert, lying still and breathing heavily. 'I'll be all right in a minute.'

When Polly was convinced that Hubert was not badly injured, she went downstairs to make him a cup of tea.

By the time she got back, he was sitting up in bed, his face dirty and bloodied but smiling. Polly sat down beside him and took his hand. She did care. She did really care about Hubert, she thought to herself.

'I came out of the van and there were two men waiting. They set about me almost at once,' said Hubert.

'Oh my God. Why?'

'It was all a stupid mistake. They just didn't give me time to explain.'

'What happened?'

'Well, it was the radio van,' said Hubert, suddenly snorting with laughter and then wincing with the pain that this caused to his bruised mouth. 'They saw that bloody great aerial thing on top and thought it was one of those TV licence detectors. They called me an effing snoop and laid into me.'

'How dreadful, Hubert,' said Polly. 'Didn't the man in the radio van hear what was going on?'

Hubert shrugged. 'I called out but he just drove off. Either he didn't hear me or he just didn't want to get involved.'

'Poor you,' said Polly. She sat carefully beside

Hubert on the bed and put her arms around him as though he were a child.

'That feels nice,' he said. Polly kissed him on his sweaty balding head and hugged him tight. She cared for Hubert but she would always love him the way she might love a child, the way she loved Minty.

She rubbed her face against his head, willing herself to feel more. Why could she not feel passion for Hubert in the same way she had experienced it for Charles? She did not like to see Hubert hurt.

'Is there anything I can do for you?' she asked.

Hubert looked up into her face and tried to smile. 'Yes. Marry me.'

Chapter Nineteen

'Congratulations,' said Den.

'Thanks,' said Olga. Her appointment to head of Features had been announced that day. 'But don't forget Polly,' she added, running her fingers through her flame-red hair so that it stood up on end. 'The youngest number two on the Features desk that the *Globe* has ever had. That's quite an achievement in two and a half years.'

'Absolutely,' added Den. 'I knew she had the makings of a star when she arrived on her first day with that rabbit who liked shitting on the *Daily Telegraph*.'

'Congratulations Pussy,' said Carslip, although the words seemed to stick in his throat.

'Thanks,' said Polly as everyone round the table raised their glasses.

'It's such luck that an opportunity arose for you to move on to the political desk,' said Den to Carslip. 'He's always been keen on politics,' he added to Polly and Olga, 'but, being a bit of a leftie, he was never much good to us while the Tories were in power.'

Carslip said nothing.

'Carslip has fantastic connections on the Labour

front bench,' continued Den. 'He must be glad to leave Features to you girls.'

Polly and Olga exchanged a smile. Polly knew that Olga hated being referred to as a 'girl' and it showed how pleased she was with her promotion that she just let the remark go.

Carslip stared down at the table. He seemed to be muttering something under his breath, thought Polly. He was obviously livid about being shunted into politics and he seemed to think that Polly had somehow brought the whole thing about. He had never liked her and now he would bear an even bigger grudge.

Polly emptied her glass and allowed Den to fill it up again. She had, in fact, only heard about the promotions that day. She had gone up to see Den to remind him that she was out the whole of the following week on holiday and expected him to be in a filthy mood. He never seemed to take time off himself.

But, although he had forgotten all about Polly's holiday, he seemed delighted.

'Good, perfect timing,' he had said. 'It's important to take a break before you start a new job.' At first, Polly thought that he was going to sack her but then he started saying how Carslip was letting the features pages get a bit dull. He was worried about losing Olga and Polly and wanted to see what they could do without Carslip bossing them around all the time. Polly was both delighted and horrified by the news.

'Does Bernard know about all this?' she asked.

'Carslip? Oh no, I haven't told him yet. You'd better ask him to come up and see me,' said Den.

'I think it might be better if you called him yourself,' said Polly.

'OK, but don't worry about Carslip. It's a dog eat dog world in newspapers and everyone has to move on at some stage. We can shunt Carslip off to Westminster and see how he gets on there.'

Den told Polly what her new salary would be and said she should speak to someone in Admin about her car.

'My car?' Polly could hardly believe her ears. She was earning a good salary and being offered a company car. A few years ago, when she was in the back office of the *Dulwich Observer*, she would never have thought it possible.

'Yes,' said Den. 'The job comes with a car. Not exactly a Bentley but it should have four wheels. Any objections?'

'Er, no, of course not.' Just as Polly had found it hard to admit she had never smoked cannabis, she did not like to say that she could not drive. But Den had already guessed.

'The extra salary should more than cover the cost of a few driving lessons. And, if you like, I could take you out for a bit of practice.'

Polly laughed. 'No, Den, thanks. I'll manage.'

'Great,' said Den. He was really quite charming, thought Polly, on the rare occasions when he tried.

'Oh and one last thing,' said Den as she turned to go.

'Yes?'

'I insist on buying you and the rest of the gang downstairs a drink after work. There's a bar round the corner called the Toad. We'll meet there at six, OK?'

'OK. And thanks again, Den.'

'You earned the job,' said Den. 'I might still want to get my leg over but I'm not going to fuck the *Globe* in the process.'

Polly laughed. Den was not such a bastard after all.

'Of course she's shagging the old goat,' said Carslip, licking his greasy trout lips.

'I don't believe it,' said Olga, glancing across at Den who was ordering another bottle at the bar.

'Den is besotted and she knows it. She's creaming him for all he's worth but she'll be out on her pretty little arse in the end.'

'Sssh,' said Olga. 'Here she comes.'

Polly returned from the Ladies and sat back down at the table. Everyone from the office had left now except for Den, Carslip and Olga.

'I really should be off,' said Polly.

'I suppose Tory Boy will be waiting for his little Pussy to get home,' said Carslip.

Den plonked another bottle on the table and sat back down next to Polly.

'One last drink before you go,' he said, picking up the bottle and topping up Polly's glass.

'Actually, I'm not seeing Hubert tonight,' said Polly.

'Ooooh,' said Carslip with affected alarm. 'I hope there hasn't been a lovers' tiff.'

Polly ignored this remark. 'In fact, I'm surprised none of you has asked me what I'm doing on my week off.'

'Oh sorry, Polly,' said Olga. 'I forgot all about you going on hols.'

'Where are you going?' asked Den.

'I don't know,' said Polly. 'Hubert's arranging it – it's a surprise.'

'How romantic,' said Olga. 'But why aren't you seeing him tonight?'

'Well,' said Polly, suddenly blushing. 'You see, we're getting married tomorrow and it's, well, traditional not to see—'

'You're getting married?' Den nearly fell off his chair. 'Tomorrow?'

Polly nodded.

'Good God, Polly,' cried Olga. 'Why didn't you tell anyone? We would have got you—'

'Exactly,' said Polly. 'I didn't want any fuss.' But was that really the reason, she wondered. Why had she been so reluctant to tell anyone that she was marrying Hubert? Was it because she was never that confident that she would actually go through with it?

'I can't fucking believe it,' said Den.

'Why not?' asked Polly.

'I mean, it's an important decision. You've only been going out with the bloke for a couple of months.'

'Five actually.'

'Still, that's no time at all. I certainly wish I'd thought more carefully before I took the plunge.'

'Plunges,' corrected Carslip.

'Yeah,' said Den, draining the last of the champagne into his glass. 'They were the biggest and most expensive mistakes of my life.' Carslip and Olga nodded sympathetically.

'Crikey,' said Polly. 'This is encouraging.'

'Sorry, Polly,' said Olga. 'But it was a bit of a shock.'

'Let's get another bottle,' said Den.

'Oh no, I really have to go,' said Polly.

'Why, what are you doing?'

'Well, nothing. I thought, perhaps, I'd get an early night.'

'An early night?' cried Den. 'You'll have plenty of time for cups of Horlicks and early nights when you're stuck at home drafting old Hubert's party political broadcasts for him.'

'Not quite the portrait of married life I had in mind.'

'Never mind. We're taking you out tonight for a night to remember and I will not take no for an answer.'

Polly laughed and Den got the champagne.

An hour later, they left the bar. Olga was meeting some friends and set off for the tube station. Carslip, although he hated to leave Den and Polly alone, realised that playing gooseberry was not going to endear him to his boss.

'See you then,' he said. 'And congratulations, double congratulations, to you, Pussy.'

'Polly,' roared Den. 'Unless you want me to call you Arse-lick *every* time I see you.'

'Sorry. *Polly*,' said Carslip, flashing a look of pure hatred at Polly.

'That guy is such a git,' said Den as Carslip strolled away down Snow Hill.

'He's jealous,' said Polly.

'OK, a jealous git then,' laughed Den, hailing a taxi.

Poor Carslip, thought Polly. If he wasn't such a git,

as Den put it, she would actually have felt sorry for him. Being so full of hatred and resentment made him a real loser.

Den gave directions to a restaurant Polly had never heard of and then helped Polly inside the cab.

They drank and ate and drank and talked. Polly knew that she should get home. She knew that she would have a terrible hangover the next day, the day of her wedding. But the truth was that she was enjoying being with Den. Why shouldn't she celebrate her last night as a single girl?

Den ordered another glass of wine each with the bill and, by the time they were ready to leave, Polly could hardly get to her feet.

'I don't feel too well,' she said.

'Let's get outside,' said Den.

A few minutes later, they were walking along the Embankment. Polly's head was still swimming but Den's arm was almost holding her up.

'Sorry,' she said. 'I'm very heavy – I must be killing you.'

'Not at all,' said Den. He pulled her round to face him and kissed her.

His breath had its usual tired stale taste but she did not push him away at once. His arms were strong and held her tight around her back. One hand moved down and grasped her buttock. It was only then that she came to her senses.

'For God's sake, Den,' she said.

'Sorry, it's just that you're so sexy, Polly.'

'Me? You must be joking.' But Polly enjoyed the compliment. Hubert often told her that she was attractive, beautiful, and that he loved her. But did he find her sexy? Not really, thought Polly sadly. Hubert still found it difficult to make love to her.

'Why don't you marry *me*?' asked Den.

'What – another plunge? Don't you remember what you said about marriage earlier?'

'Third time lucky,' grinned Den.

'Don't be ridiculous. Anyway, I've already agreed to marry Hubert. I have already pledged my troth, as they say.'

'Not yet,' said Den. 'There's still time to change your mind.'

'Why should I change my mind?'

'Well, do you love him? Do you really love Hubert?' There it was again, thought Polly, that same damned question. First Ned and now Den. Why did people keep asking her it?

'Why would I marry him if I didn't love him?'

'I don't know.' said Den. 'People get married for the strangest reasons sometimes – money, power – revenge?'

Polly leant over the stone wall and looked down at the river. Den was running his hand up and down her back. She did not even *like* Den, she told herself, but she did find his touch deeply erotic. It had not seemed important, the sex thing, or the lack of sex thing, with Hubert but now suddenly she felt full of desire.

Den let his hand drift down to rest just under her buttocks. It felt nice there and Polly did not ask him to move it. She could easily imagine herself in bed with Den, having sex with him. Perhaps having good sex with him. But that was crazy. She was going to marry Hubert. She had made up her mind and, after all, she did love him. Really.

'You're a fantastic-looking girl,' said Den. 'You could have any man you wanted.'

Polly laughed. 'That's not true. I can't have *any* man.' In fact she couldn't have the one and only man she wanted. Wasn't that what it was really all about? Was she truly marrying Hubert only to get back at Adele and Charles – to show them that she would not sit meekly on the shelf, that she could get on with her life and win a man, a good man? Was it, after all, just a subconscious effort to make Charles jealous?

She shivered and Den held her tighter.

'You can have me,' said Den. He turned Polly round and pulled her towards him. Through her jacket and trousers she could feel his rock-hard penis pressing against her. God, she thought, she had not realised how much she had been missing sex.

Polly cried all the way home in the taxi. It was two in the morning and she knew that she would look a wreck for the wedding.

She had not had sex with Den but that was hardly thanks to herself. She couldn't think what had come over her. Why had she let him take her home? Why had she let him pour even more booze down her throat?

It sickened her now as she realised that she had been more than willing to take off her shirt for him. She had loved the way he had sucked and played with her breasts. Hubert hardly seemed to be aware they existed. All the time she was telling herself that it was just fooling around, that she did not need to go any further if she didn't want to.

But it had been Den, in the end, who had put a stop to things.

'I don't think we should,' he said, suddenly sitting up.

'What?'

'Believe me, Polly, I want to fuck you stupid.'

'So?' Was it the drink or her nerves about the wedding? But Polly had never wanted sex so much, so urgently, in all her life. Had she secretly hoped that Den would force himself upon her? Would she have convinced herself afterwards that she had been pressured into it?

'We'll regret it,' said Den. 'You'll come into the office in a week's time, having married dear old Hubert, and you just won't be able to look me in the eye.'

He was right, of course, thought Polly. It was appalling that she had been on the point of betraying Hubert the night before their wedding. She wondered whether she would have come to her senses before it had been too late. It was humiliating that Den had been the one to call a halt first.

Polly watched Den as he straightened out his clothes. Then he sat down beside Polly on the bed and pulled the bedclothes up over her breasts. He almost reminded her of her dad tucking her up in bed and saying goodnight.

'Thanks,' she said, suddenly feeling very embarrassed. 'I'm sorry.'

'Don't worry about it,' said Den. 'I'm the one who will be sorry – tomorrow morning when I realise what I missed out on.'

'You must think I'm such a bitch, to be in your bed the night before I marry Hubert.'

'Perfectly traditional to spend your last night of freedom having a one-night stand. I don't think you're exactly breaking new ground here.'

'I feel so ashamed. Why do I behave so badly sometimes?'

'God, how many times do I have to tell you?' cried Den. 'You're a really nice girl, Polly. We all make mistakes and getting married is a stressful thing.'

'I suppose.' Polly felt on the brink of tears.

'Look, Polly. I'm genuinely very fond of you and I hope Hubert makes you very happy. He's a lucky bloke. A very lucky bloke. And I hope he bloody appreciates you.'

The tears rolled down Polly's cheeks. Den was being far too nice to her, far nicer than she deserved.

'Do you want to sleep it off here or shall I call a cab?' he asked.

She lay in bed. She had stopped crying now but still she could not sleep. It was less than nine hours until the ceremony and Polly had never felt in such a mess, so confused. If only she could talk to someone, someone who would understand.

She stared at the telephone. There was no point calling her mother or father. Certainly there was no point calling Adele. She would rather die than confide in Adele about anything.

Then suddenly she gasped. Of course.

She picked up the phone. It was three o'clock in the morning but she had no qualms about making the call.

'Ned? Ned, is that you?'

'Hello?' The voice was very sleepy.

'Ned, listen. It's me, Polly.'

'Hello?'

'Ned, I'm in trouble. I need to see you, quickly. Can you meet me?'

There was silence then, 'Who is that?'

'It's me. Polly,' repeated Polly.

'Polly?' said the voice. 'Oh sorry, you must want Ned.'

God, thought Polly, who on earth had she been speaking to?

'It's Frankie,' said the voice. 'Ned's brother, remember?'

Frankie. Of course, thought Polly, the kid who made sand sculptures on the beach. He must be about fifteen by now.

'Can I speak with Ned?' asked Polly.

'Ned has given me his phone,' said Frankie. 'It's got really good games.'

'Great. Can I speak with him?'

'Sorry. He's not here.'

'When will he be back?'

'Not sure.'

'Well, where is he?' There was still a hope that he was somewhere that Polly could reach him. Ned would listen and know what to do. Ned would help – he was the only person that Polly wanted to talk to.

'LA,' said Frankie.

'LA?'

'Yeah. You know, Los Angeles. I don't know where he's staying but he calls quite often. I could give him a message next time.'

'Don't worry,' said Polly. That would be too late.

Chapter Twenty

Polly slept restlessly but when she awoke everything seemed much clearer. It made total sense to marry Hubert and there was no need to discuss it with Ned.

Hubert was a kind man with a great sense of humour and she did love him. She felt terrible when she thought back to her behaviour the night before and what might have happened. She resolved that she would be a good and loyal wife to Hubert, that she would take her marriage seriously and make it work. She would show Charles and her oh-so-successful sister that she was not going to sit on the shelf pining for the rest of her life.

Polly looked in the mirror. Her eyes were puffy and a bit bloodshot. She stood on the bathroom scales and could hardly believe that she seemed to have put on nearly half a stone overnight.

The sad truth was, she thought as she rummaged in the bathroom cupboard for the Optrex, that she was fat and nearly thirty. It was unlikely she would find a more attractive proposal than Hubert's. The one man she had wanted had been stolen from her and, for all Den's saintliness the night before, she really did not want to be the third Mrs Christie.

But why marry at all, she asked her reflection. Perhaps it would be better to stay single?

Polly shook her head at herself. It had been her lifelong ambition to get married and have children and she did not relish the prospect of being a single mum. She saw herself in her late thirties, her biological clock ticking away like a time bomb, and being forced to hunt down a man, any man, to get her pregnant. She had read in the papers about a woman who had had sex with her son's best friend, hoping that he would get her pregnant and then want nothing to do with the pregnancy or the child. Commentators had been outraged and had called the woman's behaviour exploitative but Polly thought she understood what the woman might be going through. She could easily imagine herself in a similar predicament.

No, she did not want to get that desperate, she thought, as she got into the shower and let the warm water pour over her head. Hubert was a great catch by any standards. They had good times together. They laughed a lot. He was always courteous and generous to her. It was only the sex thing that was a bit unsatisfactory – but perhaps that would improve in time.

They loved each other – maybe not with as much passion as Polly might have wished – but it was a sound, secure kind of love. An enduring love, she told herself, as she washed the cigarette smoke out of her hair. It was time for a new life, a new start. There was probably as good a chance as any that her marriage to Hubert would work. As good as the chance that Charles and Adele's marriage would continue to work? asked a little voice inside her head but she switched the shower on to cold. She might never forgive Adele for what she had done but she would stop obsessing about it. She would start thinking about herself. And Hubert.

The water was icy cold and, although Polly fiddled desperately with the controls, she could not get it back to hot and had to finish rinsing her hair in the freezing water.

Zeta was waiting with a cup of hot chocolate when Polly eventually emerged in the kitchen in her dressing gown and slippers.

'Excited?' asked Zeta. 'You look as though you're shivering.'

'I made a balls-up in the shower. Those temperature controls have always been a bit sticky,' said Polly as she sipped her drink. 'I suppose I feel more apprehensive than excited.' She certainly had a strange churning feeling in her stomach but that was more likely to be due to the excesses of the night before.

'That's understandable. To be expected really,' said Zeta. 'It's a big step.'

'Have you ever been married?' asked Polly, suddenly realising how little she knew about Zeta. Zeta was always so selfless; she was always concerned about what was happening in Polly's life and rarely talked about herself.

Zeta shook her head. 'I've not found the right man – yet.'

Exactly, thought Polly. But who does? Actually, she had once found the right man but she had lost him or, more accurately, had him stolen from right under her nose. But no, she told herself, there was no point going down that track again.

'Do you think there is only "one", Zeta? I mean, don't you think that there might be at least two or three who might not be absolutely perfect but would be, well, good enough?'

Zeta laughed. 'You are funny. I hope you've not had second thoughts.'

Polly shook her head. She had not had second thoughts. She had not even had third or fourth thoughts, she had had *nth* thoughts where n is a very large number as her school maths teacher would have put it.

'Do you need any help getting dressed and everything?'

'No,' said Polly. 'I've got a very simple dress and jacket. I didn't think a tiara and train would look quite right in a register office.'

'I remember dreaming about having a big white wedding when I was a little girl,' said Zeta.

'I think every little girl does,' said Polly. And most big ones too, she thought to herself as Zeta went to collect the post. That had been the kind of wedding that Polly had envisaged having with Charles. The dream had come true for him but the bride had been Adele.

For God's sake, pack it in, she snapped at herself. She was doing it again: thinking of Charles and Adele.

When Polly arrived at the register office, Charles was waiting for her outside. It was a windy day and he had to raise his voice for her to hear.

'Hubert's not here,' he shouted.

Polly's heart leapt into her throat. Could it be that Hubert had changed his mind? She had been so pre-occupied about her own doubts that it had not occurred to her that poor Hubert might be feeling the same way.

'What's happened?'

'Don't worry,' said Charles, moving closer so that he did not need to shout. 'He'll be along soon but there was an accident at the flat last night.'

'What? Is he all right?'

'Yes, he's fine. But he's a lucky bastard – and not just because he's marrying you.'

Polly stared at Charles in disbelief. She was minutes away from getting married and he was flirting with her. Was he really inviting her to change her mind or was she being ridiculous?

'He nearly killed himself,' said Charles.

'Good God. What happened?'

'Well, the fridge in the flat has been a bit temperamental for years. I always thought we should chuck it out but Hubert fiddled around with it once when it broke down and got it working. After that, he had a kind of personal attachment to the damned thing, as though he was the only person who understood it.'

'Is he OK?' said Polly. She was holding tight to her hat which was in constant danger of being blown away down the street.

'Yes, fine. Don't worry.'

'But what happened?'

'Well, the fridge must have caught fire in the middle of the night. Fortunately, the old Hobbit had stuffed it full of Bollinger for the party today and the bottles all exploded and woke him up.'

'Poor Hubert. Are you sure he's OK? He wasn't burned or anything?'

'He's fine,' said Charles. 'Not a blister. But he's a

bit upset about the Bolly, of course. He said it was an expensive way of putting out a fire.'

Polly could not resist laughing. 'Poor, dear, Hubert,' she said, wiping her eyes.

'I think it's a sign,' said Charles.

'How do you mean?'

'A sort of warning to you, Polly, about what you're letting yourself in for – by marrying this lunatic.'

'Why? Do you think I shouldn't?' asked Polly as a taxi drew up at speed beside them.

Charles turned to look at the cab. 'It's Hubert. Thank goodness you're here, at last,' he cried as Hubert jumped out of the cab. 'Your bride is beginning to get cold feet.' The two men laughed and Polly smiled. It was clear that Charles had no intention of trying to change her mind.

The ceremony proceeded without further catastrophe and they all returned to Charles and Adele's house since Hubert's flat was still filthy with smoke.

More champagne was acquired and the guests drank the health of the bride and groom.

John made a short speech, very similar to the one he had produced at Adele's wedding. Sue scowled at him from beneath the brim of her hat.

'Where on earth did she get that thing?' Adele asked Polly. 'It looks like a giant marshmallow.'

Polly said nothing. She was feeling rather hot and asked Charles to open a window.

Hubert made a speech. It was funny and everyone laughed heartily, particularly when he recounted his nearly fatal encounter with the fridge. Polly looked around her and felt oddly disembodied. It was as though she were watching the scene from outside her body, as though she were a guest at her own wedding. It was hard to believe that she had really done it. She had really married Hubert.

When the speeches were over, Polly joined her parents who were talking with Sir Thomas Goodwood, Charles and Hubert's father.

'How's business in the plumbing trade then?' asked Sir Thomas.

'John does specialist CCTV services and sleeving.'

'Sleeving?' asked Sir Thomas.

'It's a type of relining that works well for drains that are difficult to access,' said John. 'You put this enormous rubber thing down one end and then blow it up. It's a bit like a giant condom.' Both men laughed but Sue scowled.

'It's the latest technology,' she said.

Polly left them to it. She had spotted Minty in a corner of the room, curled up in an armchair and reading a book.

Polly sat down beside her niece and gave her a hug.

'Hello, sweetheart – I've been so busy I've hardly had a chance to speak with you. Are you OK? Did you enjoy the wedding?'

Minty looked up, smiled and nodded and then went back to her book.

'What are you reading?'

'It's called *How to be a Genius Vet*.'

'Is that what you want to be when you grow up?'

Minty nodded.

'I think you'll make a genius vet,' said Polly. 'You are always so good with animals.'

'How is Bobbin?' asked Minty.

'Fine.'

It was really sad that Adele had decided Bobbin was still too smelly to keep in the house and had asked Polly to take him back.

'Who will look after him while you are on honeymoon?' asked the little girl.

'Zeta. She's very fond of him. She says he has good karma.'

'I'm sure Bobbin will never forgive me for sending him away again.'

'Oh sweetheart,' said Polly, putting her arm round Minty. 'I'm sure he understands and loves you.'

'Who understands and loves you?' asked Charles, suddenly joining them and seating himself on the arm of Minty's chair.

'You wouldn't understand,' said Minty, going back to her book.

'Precocious adolescence,' laughed Charles. 'She's only seven but still likes to give her parents a really hard time.'

Polly smiled but it was the first time she began to feel worried about Minty.

'So, how does it feel to be Mrs Goodwood?'

Polly stared at Charles. Was he trying to make a joke?

'I wasn't sure you'd go through with it,' he added.

I so nearly didn't, thought Polly. In fact, she could not help thinking back to her conversation outside the church and wondering whether, if Charles had given her a bit more encouragement, the slightest hope that he regretted marrying Adele, then— But that was ridiculous, she told herself.

'Quick, catch that bird,' cried someone.

The room was suddenly swept into chaos as people tried to capture a pigeon that had flown in through the window. The poor creature was terrified. It landed for a few seconds on top of Sue's marshmallow hat and Sue screamed hysterically.

'No, no, Granny, you're frightening it,' cried Minty, jumping to her feet.

'Don't worry,' said Hubert. 'I'll get it.' He made a lunge for the bird, tripped over the book Minty had dropped on the floor and crashed heavily to the ground, taking his new mother-in-law with him.

Chapter Twenty-One

John drove slowly round the car park looking for a space. It was a Saturday morning and crowded. He was glad that Pamela had come with him. She had just arrived and was staying the night as Hubert had gone down to Bournemouth for the Tory party conference.

'How is he?' asked John.

'Over there,' said Polly. 'That woman is just going.'

John pulled up beside the forthcoming space and waited for the woman to strap in her children and take her trolley back to the trolley park.

'Hubert?' Polly went on. 'He's fine. The neckbrace came off last week.'

'I felt so sorry for him. He took such a nasty fall at the wedding trying to catch that bloody pigeon. It must have been hell having to wear a neckbrace all through the honeymoon.'

Polly blushed. She did not want to discuss the honeymoon. Hubert had taken her to Venice and it had been beautiful, stunning, and very romantic but things had been a disaster in the bedroom. It had been such an effort to help Hubert perform. Poor Hubert, he had been really upset, but Polly could not help feeling disappointed.

John parked the car and they got out. There was a strong wind and dry curls of leaves were swept into their faces.

'How's Mum?' asked Polly. She wanted to change the subject and she had sensed that something was wrong between her parents the minute she had walked through the door.

'She's not talking to me,' said John, disentangling a trolley from the long snake of them beside the supermarket door.

'She's very moody these days. She didn't seem that happy at the wedding.'

'No. She gave me a bollocking for embarrassing her in front of Sir Thomas and Lady Viola.'

'What did you do?'

'Oh, I don't know. Spent too long talking about plumbing and horses, I suppose – the only things I know anything about.'

'Rubbish,' laughed Polly. 'You know lots of things. Do you remember that old history book you used to read to me and Adele? I think you must have known it off by heart.'

John smiled. 'Yes, those were good days.'

'Anyway, Tom really likes you,' said Polly. 'He's got a share in a horse running at Sandown next week. He told me to tell you it might be worth a small each-way bet.'

'What's it called?'

'Second Chance.'

'Good name. I'll put a tenner on it,' said John. 'To win.'

They worked their way up and down the aisles without much further conversation. John seemed a bit preoccupied and, just as they were about to pay, he dashed off and returned with three bottles of vodka which he plonked on the checkout counter.

'I suppose the least I can do, before I go, is to buy her some booze,' he said.

'Go? What do you mean? Go where?'

'I'm leaving her. I've made up my mind.'

'What? What on earth happened?' asked Polly. Her parents' relationship had never been great but it had been the same for as long as she could remember. She had always assumed they were both resigned to it.

'I suppose I've given up,' said John, starting to load the bags of groceries back into the trolley. 'It's never going to work now. She hates me.'

'I don't think so. I think she really loves you but, for some reason, refuses to show it.'

'Maybe.' John paid the checkout boy and steered the trolley towards the door. 'But it's too late. I've made up my mind to go.'

Polly helped her mum put the shopping away. She had done this job so many times that she knew Sue's system, the way she liked to make separate piles on the kitchen table for the fridge, the freezer, the cupboard. Once things were sorted into their piles, they were stored.

The two women worked silently. John was in the next room watching TV. He was watching the horse racing, as usual. Polly had been unable to get her father to tell her why he had suddenly decided to leave and it was an ideal opportunity to discuss the matter with her mother. But Sue was tight-lipped and silent as she worked. She had never confided in Polly.

'Have you seen Minty?' said Polly eventually, trying to break the ice.

'I went up and babysat for Adele last weekened,' said Sue. Polly noticed tears welling in her mother's eyes. 'I stayed over on Saturday night,' Sue continued, her voice breaking slightly.

'What is it? What's wrong, Mum?'

Sue stopped. She put a large pack of noodles over her face and sat down at the table. Polly took the noodles and gave her mother a tissue. There were tears streaming down her cheeks.

'What is it? What's the matter?' She sat down beside Sue and put her arm round her mother's shoulder.

'It's him,' she said, nodding in the direction of the sitting room. 'That was when it all happened.'

'What?'

'The night I was away. I suppose he had it all worked out. As soon as my back was turned, he must have called her and got her over.'

'Who?'

'Some woman. Rosie, she's called. Well, she wasn't very rosy when I'd finished with her.'

'Tell me what happened,' said Polly.

'I came back early. I'd told John I would stay at Adele's for lunch but then I changed my mind. Charles's mother was coming over and, you know, I never feel comfortable with that woman so I decided I'd just go home.'

'And?' Polly asked the question although she had a horrible feeling she could guess the rest.

'I caught them,' said Sue.

'You mean, they were—'

'Not exactly. He said that she was a Jehovah's Witness

and he had felt sorry for her and invited her in for a chat. Can you believe that?'

Polly said nothing.

'They were both drinking coffee in the kitchen,' continued Sue, 'but I could tell from their faces what they had been up to. And John never drinks coffee – he always has tea.' The tears poured down Sue's face as the scene came back to her.

'I went straight up to the bedroom,' said Sue. 'The bed was made but I could still tell. The place was just too tidy. There's no way that John would have gone to the trouble of making the bed so nicely and tidying the room.'

Polly squeezed her mother's arm.

'And then there was her bag in the hall. I made her empty it out. John was yelling and going on, of course, saying she had just been trying to spread the good news or something.'

'What was in the bag?'

'Nothing.'

'Nothing?'

'Well, you know, the usual things, a lipstick, her purse, some keys.' Sue paused then added, 'And a copy of St John's gospel.'

'A copy of St John's gospel? Are you sure she wasn't really a Jehovah's Witness?'

Sue glared at Polly through her tears. 'It's not a joke,' she said.

'Sorry,' said Polly. 'But how can you be so sure?'

Sue didn't answer.

'I mean, Dad might have been a bit lonely and just invited her in for a cup of coffee.'

Sue shook her head.

'How can you be so sure?' repeated Polly.

Sue looked up at her daughter. 'It isn't the first time he's betrayed me,' she said. 'And I told him I had to know the truth.'

'What did he say?'

Sue wiped her eyes. 'He admitted it. The fool – he had to go and admit it.'

Polly had planned to stay the night with her mother and father since Hubert would not be back from the conference until the following Wednesday but the atmosphere was unbearable. She stayed for supper. Sue cooked John's favourite meal of steak and chips but they ate in silence.

Then Sue gave Polly a lift to the station.

'How are the driving lessons going?' she asked.

'I've only had one so far and that was a disaster. The sun was blinding me and I managed to veer off the road down some cul de sac. We came to a sudden dead end and I had to slam on the brakes. The instructor hit his head on the windscreen.'

'Why didn't he use his dual control?' said Sue.

'I think he had been too busy combing his hair and generally preening himself,' said Polly. 'He's a complete creep.'

'Typical man.'

'Oh Mum. Don't be too hasty. Why don't you give Dad another chance? I'm sure he doesn't really want to leave.'

'You don't understand,' said Sue as she pulled up outside Herne Hill station.

Polly kissed her mother goodbye and got out of the car.

249

'I'll call,' she said.

Then she ran up the steps and over the bridge but the train had already left the station.

'Damn,' said Polly as she searched in her bag for the mobile phone that had started to ring. It was Hubert.

'Hi darling,' he said. 'I've just run into a friend of yours here in Bournemouth.'

'Really?'

'Carslip, I think was the name. He looked rather like your new driving instructor.'

'Yes, they must have come out of the same mould.'

'You sound a bit down,' said Hubert.

'It's just my parents,' said Polly. 'Dad's thinking of running off with a Jehovah's Witness.'

'Sounds desperate.'

'I think he is.'

'Well, my parents just called,' said Hubert. 'They want us to spend Christmas with them at Banbury.'

'That would be nice.'

'Yes, it will be a really good family get-together.'

Something that would clearly not be on offer at her own parents' house, thought Polly.

'Charles and Adele are going too.'

'What?' said Polly. The next train was arriving and people were jostling to get on to it.

'Charles and Adele,' repeated Hubert. 'It should be fun.'

'Won't it be too much trouble for your parents to have us all?'

'No, they love entertaining. They insist we stay from Christmas Eve right through to the New Year.'

'OK,' said Polly. 'It will certainly be a nice break.' Then she said goodbye and squeezed into a seat. A whole week under the same roof as the woman she hated most in the world and the man she still, if she was honest, loved more than any other.

Oh, why was love so damned perverse, she wondered as they pulled out of the station. Her father should love her mother, she should love Hubert and Adele . . . Well, Adele should go to hell.

Chapter Twenty-Two

Lady Viola Goodwood was half-naked as she pummelled the cranberries in a large bowl but her son was used to finding her this way.

'It gets so hot in the kitchen that I always end up doing a striptease,' she said, pulling a moth-eaten green cardigan over her huge well-worn bra and kissing Adele on both cheeks.

Charles kissed his mother and heaved a case of champagne on to the kitchen table.

'Wow, your father will be pleased with that,' said Viola. 'I'll put a couple of bottles in the fridge straight away.'

'Anything we can do to help?' asked Adele in a tone that implied she would far rather get out of the steamy kitchen as fast as she could.

'No, nothing at all,' replied Viola. 'Just take your things upstairs and make yourselves comfortable.'

'Thanks,' said Charles. 'Where's Araminta?'

Araminta and the nanny, Karen, had been staying with his parents for nearly a week already. Charles thought, at first, he would enjoy a break from the mess that Araminta made around the house but he had really missed the little girl.

'They've taken the dogs for a walk,' said Viola. 'They'll be back soon.'

'I'll unpack the huge sack of presents we've got stashed in the car then,' said Charles.

'Yes, you'd better hide them before she gets back,' said Viola. 'Araminta is very excited.'

Charles and Adele left the room but Viola ran after them.

'Oh, Charlie,' she said. 'I thought you and Adele might have the twin room next to us this time. It's only fair to let the newlyweds have the big double room in the wing.'

'Twin beds,' said Charles pulling a face as they unloaded their stuff into the room. 'For a whole week. How long does the old girl think *we* have been married?' He pulled Adele towards him and kissed her. She pushed him away.

'Not now. I just heard your father come in.'

'So?'

'So – he'll be suspicious if we're stuck up here for too long.'

'I know a time when you were not so worried about things like that,' said Charles.

Adele smiled. 'That was before you were mine.'

Charles closed the door and flung himself on to one of the beds. He clasped his hands behind his neck and watched Adele unpack the charger for her mobile phone. She had a fantastic arse, he thought, as his wife bent over to plug the charger into the wall.

'Did you have to bring that thing with you over Christmas?' he asked.

'After the bid I did for Green Baby,' said Adele,

'they moved me on to the transaction side of corporate finance and have now given me the MPC account to work on.'

'The big US magazine company?'

'Yes, they're looking at acquisitions in the UK.'

'Not over Christmas though.'

'I don't know,' said Adele. 'This is the perfect time of the year to launch a bid – if you're going hostile.'

'Come over here,' said Charles. 'I'm thinking of going hostile right now.'

Adele laughed and went over to Charles. She sat astride him and Charles felt his penis go hard as Adele bent forward to kiss him on the lips. When they had made love and were resting under the sheets, Charles held Adele close.

'That was good,' he said. 'Do you think we might have done it this time?'

'Done what?'

'You know. Made a baby?'

Adele grinned. 'You are silly.'

'Can you feel anything funny going on inside?' asked Charles.

'Of course not.'

'It felt special for me, that time.'

'Doesn't it always?'

'I'm sure it must be more special when you are making a baby, a new life.'

'You are almost as sentimental as my poor sister,' laughed Adele.

Charles frowned. 'Don't you want a baby?' he asked.

'Of course I do.' But, even then, Charles suspected that she was lying.

*

Polly got away from work late. Den had been worrying about the shortage of staff there would be between Christmas and the New Year and was horrified when he realised that Polly would not be in either.

'Can't you get in for a couple of days?' he said.

'Sorry, I'm off to my in-laws,' said Polly.

'The toffs up in Oxford?'

'They're not that smart. From the way he dresses you'd think Sir Thomas only shopped at Oxfam,' Polly gave Den a sheet of paper.

'This is a rota of all the people in Features coming in over the break. And I've put my phone number down too. For emergencies only, OK?'

'Thanks,' said Den. Polly suddenly felt sorry for her boss.

'Aren't you taking any time off?' she asked.

'No, I always come in over Christmas. I prefer it.'

'Prefer it to what?' Polly knew very little about the two ex-Mrs Christies but she knew there were children. Both divorces had been acrimonious and Den never talked about his family.

'Being on my own,' said Den. Then he laughed. 'Of course, if you'd chosen me rather than dear Hubert, we would be flying off to Barbados now.'

Polly grinned. 'I think with an offer like that you might find someone to take my place.'

Den shrugged and went back to his office. Polly realised she had said to Den precisely the thing that people had said so often to her about Charles.

She packed her bag and got a taxi home.

'Great,' said Hubert when she arrived at the flat. 'If we leave in half an hour, we should arrive in time for dinner. Mother always cooks a goose on

Christmas Eve and potatoes roasted in goose fat are the best.'

Polly smiled. Hubert was like a child when it came to food.

There was a slow crawl out of London on the M40 and it gave them plenty of time to talk.

'I haven't seen Charles and Adele since our wedding,' said Hubert.

'Me neither,' said Polly.

'They've been married for over two years now.'

'Two years and three months.'

'They seem happy. Don't you think?'

'Yes, it seems so.'

They drove on in silence. Hubert had accidentally put a tape in the cassette player the wrong way round and could not get it out again so they could not listen to music and there was nothing on the radio.

'Do you think Adele will have another baby?' asked Hubert.

'Adele?' said Polly. 'I doubt that she would want to.'

'Why not?'

'Well, Minty is more than she can handle as it is.'

Hubert changed lanes.

'Charles always wanted a big family,' he said.

'I know.'

'What about you?'

'You mean us?' asked Polly. She suddenly realised that she had no idea whether Hubert wanted children or not. It was one of the most important things in her life and, somehow, she had married Hubert without knowing what he thought about it.

'Yes,' said Hubert. 'Do you want to have kids?'

'Yes, I do.' Polly wondered why Hubert had brought the subject up. Did he want to start a family or did he want to give up on sex altogether? 'But, perhaps, we should wait a few years,' she said.

They drove on and Polly could not help wondering whether that was the answer she would have given Charles, had they married.

'OK,' said Hubert. 'Just let me know when you're ready.'

'Thanks.' Polly put her hand on Hubert's thigh and gave it a squeeze. He would make a wonderful father, she felt sure.

'Have you remembered your stockings?' asked Minty as soon as Polly and Hubert arrived.

'Our stockings?'

Hubert grinned. 'Sounds exciting.'

'Your Christmas stockings,' said Minty.

Polly laughed. She put a large tin of mince pies on the side in the kitchen. She had made them herself and was rather proud of them.

'I think Father Christmas struck me off his list years ago,' she said.

'Well, I've got you a present anyway,' said Minty. 'I bought it with my own pocket money. Guess what it is?'

'Something to eat?' asked Polly.

'No.'

'Something to wear?'

'No.'

'Something to play with?'

'Maybe,' said Minty.

'Well, don't tell me any more,' said Polly. 'I want a surprise.'

After Polly and Hubert had said hello to everyone, Minty showed them up to their room.

'Granny says that you and Uncle Hobbit must have the best room because you've just got married,' said Minty. 'Why is that?'

'I don't know,' said Polly. 'But it's very kind of her.'

'Mummy is a bit pissed off about it,' said Minty. 'She and Daddy have got to sleep in separate beds. What's wrong with that?'

'Nothing, but it's nice to cuddle someone sometimes.'

Minty climbed on to Polly's lap and gave her aunt a big cuddle.

'I'd like to sleep with you,' she said, looking up at Hubert. 'Uncle Hobbit can have my bed. There's table football in my room and a fridge and my room is right next door to yours.'

'Tempting but no thanks,' said Hubert.

'I don't know why grown-ups like sleeping together. I think it's disgusting. When I went to a sleepover with my friend Charlotte I had to share a bed with her and she *wet* herself and I had to sleep in the damp bit.'

Hubert laughed.

'Grown-ups don't wet themselves,' said Polly and decided to change the subject. 'Did you write and tell Father Christmas what you want?'

Minty nodded excitedly. 'And I've already hung up my stocking. Come and see.'

The stocking was a long thin woolly shooting sock

and was hanging from the bedpost of Minty's bed. There was a note attached to it.

'I've told Father Christmas that if he doesn't have enough room in the stocking, he can leave things on the bottom of my bed. Do you think that sounds greedy?'

'No, very sensible and practical,' laughed Polly. 'Would you like me to put my present to you on the end of your bed too?'

'Yes please. But don't let Father Christmas see you. You might frighten him away.'

'Does Araminta still believe in Father Christmas?' asked Sir Thomas, topping up his wife's glass. They had finished dinner and were drinking brandy in the drawing room.

'Absolutely,' said Charles. 'Although she's seven and a half, having no older brothers and sisters makes it easier to keep the secret.'

'I suppose it's the last year that she will really believe,' said Polly. 'Someone at school is bound to tell her.' She still remembered the horror she had felt when Adele had told her that Father Christmas did not exist. She had gone sobbing to her mother demanding that she tell Adele, at once, that she was wrong. Sue had only turned to Adele and said, 'It was mean to tell your sister, Adele. It would have been years before she worked it out for herself.'

'How are your parents?' asked Viola, suddenly turning to Adele.

'Fine,' said Adele. Polly nodded. She did not feel like explaining that her father had moved out a week ago, being unable to bear the prospect of spending

Christmas with a wife who had not spoken to him for two months.

'Let's drink a toast to absent friends,' said Thomas. They raised their glasses and, as Polly sipped the brandy, she suddenly thought of Ned.

'Absent friends,' boomed Hubert and everyone else repeated the words.

'Have you seen Ned?' Polly asked Adele.

'I got a Christmas card.'

Polly took another sip of brandy. Why was it that *she* had not received a Christmas card? Perhaps Ned had sent one to her old address, to Zeta's house? Did he know that she was now married to Hubert and living in Kensington? Had anyone told him?

'Is he still in LA?' asked Polly.

'Yes,' said Adele. 'He seems to like it there but he says he's flat broke, living on the beach or something.'

'Sounds like Ned,' smiled Polly. She drained her glass and shivered. How good it would be to be like Ned, she thought. To be so focused on your work that you don't need anything or anyone else. Her own job had been going really well since her promotion and everyone said that she must be in line for Olga's position as head of Features in a few years' time. But it did not seem that important to Polly. Not compared to other things.

'Merry Christmas, darling.' Hubert poured her another drink and smiled at her warmly. She had got what she wanted, hadn't she? A good husband and the prospect of having a family. It was enough. It had to be enough.

*

Hubert was propped up in bed reading the double Christmas edition of the *Spectator*. Polly was flicking through a big pile of *Home and Garden* magazines that were stacked on the bedside table.

'Is this the only mag your mum buys?' asked Polly.

'I bought a subscription for her a few years ago but I think she just puts them directly on this table.'

'She probably would have preferred *Vogue* or something.'

'Or even the *Beano*,' laughed Hubert, turning out the light.

Polly snuggled down beside her husband and then suddenly sat bolt upright again. 'Hell. I forgot to put Minty's present on her bed.'

'Give it to her at breakfast.'

'No, I promised,' said Polly, getting out of bed. 'It's in the car.'

'I'll get it,' said Hubert.

'No, don't worry, I'll go. I need a glass of water too after all that brandy.'

Polly pulled on Hubert's dressing gown and her socks and made her way downstairs. All the lights were out and she crept about so that she would not disturb anyone.

She went out of the front door, ran across the drive to her car and found the present. It was a tiny parcel containing a little silver necklace and so it took a while to locate in the numerous bags of presents that still filled the boot. Polly was shivering as she ran back to the house but she noticed a light on in the kitchen. She could easily have got her glass of water from the bathroom next to her room but she decided to go to the kitchen. She wondered who was still up.

As she approached the kitchen door she heard voices and there was no mistaking who it was. Charles and Adele. But they weren't exactly talking, Polly realised as she stood behind the door.

'Not here, Charles,' said Adele. 'Supposing someone comes down and catches us?'

'I want to, I have to have you now,' said Charles. 'It makes it more exciting, knowing that someone might catch us.'

'You're crazy.'

'You are irresistible.'

The door was open a crack and Polly could see Adele standing in front of the Aga, Charles holding her in his arms.

'Be quick then,' said Adele.

Charles's trousers slipped down to his knees and he had already taken off his shirt. Adele had her red satin skirt pulled up around her waist. Polly could hardly believe her eyes but they were doing it, standing up, against the Aga.

'Careful,' said Adele. 'My bum is burning.'

Charles said nothing and Polly looked at his beautiful back and the muscular buttocks that worked savagely away at Adele. Her sister was wearing those hold-up stockings that looked so sexy on her but, whenever Polly wore them, they just made huge unsightly bulges.

Polly backed away from the door, suddenly afraid she was going to throw up. There was a huge crash and Polly glanced back inside the kitchen. Adele had knocked over a tin, the tin of mince pies that Polly had brought for Viola. They were scattered all over the floor.

Charles hesitated but Adele encircled his waist with her legs. 'No, no. Don't stop,' she said. 'We'll chuck them in the bin and no one will even notice.'

Back upstairs, Polly went to Minty's room and put her present at the foot of her niece's bed. The stocking was still empty and Polly wondered whether Father Christmas would have the energy to fill it after he had been attending to the stockings downstairs.

Minty slept with her face on her hand and Polly swept the hair from her cheek.

'My angel,' she said and kissed her lightly.

By the time she got back to her own bed, Hubert had fallen asleep. It was a relief, thought Polly, as the sight of Charles and Adele making love had made her feel wretched.

She thought again of Charles's penis and recalled the wonderful sex they had once had. Hubert was gentle and very affectionate but she wanted the raw passion that Charles had provided. She and Hubert rarely made love and when they did it was over in a few seconds.

Hubert grunted in his sleep and turned over. Polly cuddled up behind him. Would she ever love Hubert enough that the sex would not really matter?

She listened to the sound of Charles and Adele making their way noisily upstairs. There was silence for a while and then she heard someone approaching. The door opened and Polly sat up to see Charles framed in the doorway, naked except for a Santa's hat. He was holding a large bag.

'Sorry,' he said. 'Wrong room.' He closed the door and was gone.

The following morning Charles apologised again.

Everyone was getting ready to go to church and Charles and Polly were alone for a few minutes in the kitchen.

'I must have given you a fright,' he said.

'Not really,' said Polly, playing with the little beanie baby frog that Minty had given her over breakfast.

'It reminded me of that time I burst in on you in the grotto in that department store. When you were sitting there in your bra.'

Polly blushed. The thought had occurred to her too. In fact, she had stayed awake half the night thinking about it.

'We had some good times, Polly,' said Charles, touching her arm.

'Yes,' said Polly. 'But they're over now. You are married and so am I.' They were standing right beside the Aga in the same spot where Charles had stood with Adele the night before.

Although she despised herself as soon as it happened, Polly felt her whole body suddenly ache for Charles to take hold of her. But she knew that was crazy. It wasn't just that they were both married but Charles was clearly happily married to Adele. And she was happily married too.

'I must get ready,' she said. 'Hubert hates to be late.'

Charles stood back and she left the room. Sod him, she thought. Sod him, sod him, sod him. Why the hell couldn't she get him out of her head – not to mention her body?

On her way upstairs Polly bumped straight into Adele, who made no comment about the tears burning down Polly's cheeks. Adele just turned a blind eye to

264

anything she had no wish to see. That was, of course, classic Adele, thought Polly, as her sister gave her a perfunctory smile.

'Merry Christmas, Polly,' she said.

PART III

Twenty-nine – thin, married and still not happy

Chapter Twenty-Three

'Happy New Year,' said Ned as he sat down at the table next to Polly. They were in a crowded pizza bar in Holborn and it was two years since the Christmas Polly had spent with Charles and Adele at the Goodwoods.

'Ned Butler – a fugitive polygamist. I still can't take that in.'

'Once you've taken the plunge the first time, the next is easier,' laughed Ned.

'You sound like my boss although he would not agree it gets easier.' Polly put down her menu. 'But why all Beryls?'

'Why not? I thought about Pamelas originally but decided Beryls were better – or worse, whichever way you look at it.'

'The audience loved it,' said Polly. Ned had done a stand-up comedy show at the pub in which he played the character of a bigamist on the run from both the law and his ex-wives, all of whom were called Beryl. It had been very funny.

'Thanks.' Ned waved to attract the waitress's attention. 'But, six years after university and jobless, apart from odd bits of work like this, it's hardly impressive.'

'You haven't told me about LA,' said Polly. 'You were out there a long time.'

'Yes. It's nice to be back though. I really enjoyed spending Christmas with Mum and Dad and Frankie.'

'How are they all?'

'Same as ever. Mum still thinks I'm a genius although she must be disappointed. Frank has just started at an art school in Manchester. He really is a genius although he's been causing my parents a lot of grief recently.'

'Why?'

'Oh, he got arrested doing some pop art stunt the other day.'

'What was it?'

'Somersaults in Trafalgar Square.'

'That doesn't sound too outrageous.'

'He was naked and accompanied by a giant blow-up doll that he simulated indecent acts with in the fountain.'

Polly laughed. 'I don't remember hearing about that.'

'He hadn't organised any press,' said Ned. 'Which just goes to show how innocent and naive he still is. It was luck – good or bad, I'm not sure – that one of the red tops' photographers just happened to be there and got a few shots that were splashed all over the papers the next day.'

'How funny.'

Ned smiled. 'It took Dad a while to see the funny side – but Mum was very good about it.'

'Ready?' The waitress stood beside their table, her weight thrown casually on one leg, her pen poised in mid-air.

'Just a regular margarita,' said Polly. 'And a bottle of Becks.'

'Same for me – but make my pizza a large one,' said Ned without even looking at the menu.

'I'm thinking about doing a teacher training course,' he went on when the waitress had gone. Polly did not know what to say to this. They were scarcely the words of the ambitious, confident friend she had once known.

'I suppose you could get a lot of writing done in the holidays.'

Ned looked hard at Polly. 'Remember that day on Filey beach?'

Polly nodded her head. 'Of course.'

'I knew exactly what I wanted then and so did you.'

'Did I?'

'Yes,' said Ned. 'Remember that bloodstone? You wanted to smash it into Adele's head.'

Polly laughed. 'I've still got the stone on my bedside table. So, it's still possible.'

Ned shook his head. 'No, you've got what you wanted.'

'Have I?' asked Polly.

'Yes. You're married to a great bloke and no doubt you'll have kids soon enough. That's what you wanted wasn't it?'

'Yes,' said Polly. 'I really wanted to find Mr Right.'

'Isn't Hubert Mr Right?'

Polly hesitated. 'Yes, of course. Hubert is a lovely man, a wonderful husband. In fact, if anything, he's too nice. I'm very fond of him.' Polly wondered what she was trying to say.

'But you're not sure that he's really "the one"?'

'No. I am,' said Polly. 'It's just, well—' She did not know why she was saying these things to Ned. The truth was that she and Hubert were very happy. They hardly ever had sex but their marriage was a success. They got on so well together.

'What then?'

'I suppose, it's just that the way I feel about Hubert. I love him but, well, it's not the same way that I felt for—'

'Don't say it,' cried Ned. 'I can't believe that you're still pining for his brother.'

Polly shifted in her chair and looked around the restaurant. 'Of course I'm not. I gave up on that ages ago. Adele won hands down, as usual.'

The beers arrived and they drank.

'I'm staying with Dave at the moment,' said Ned. 'You remember the bloke who used to let me work on his PC? I lost the broom cupboard.'

'You sound disappointed. Even Dave's spare room has to be better than a broom cupboard,' laughed Polly.

'I'm not so sure. The poor bastard is married now and his wife is worse than a sergeant major for making sure the place is kept tip-top tidy all the time.'

'At least your views on marriage haven't changed.'

Ned grunted. 'Are you still in Kensington?' he asked.

Polly shook her head. 'Hubert's got a safe Tory seat for the next election in Kidbury. It's near where his parents live so we've moved out there. We commute in every day but it's not too bad. Forty minutes to Paddington.'

'Sounds very comfy and suburban,' said Ned. 'And how's the job?'

'Good. I really enjoy it, particularly since my old boss Carslip was moved off to politics.'

Ned said nothing and Polly decided to go to the loo before the food arrived.

When she returned to the table, Ned had got out a paperback and was reading. As she arrived he took a paper napkin and stuffed it between the pages as a bookmark.

'At least, that's an improvement on the old ham sandwich you used to use,' said Polly. They both laughed.

Ned hadn't really changed at all, thought Polly. In fact, quite literally. She suspected that he was still wearing exactly the same clothes she had seen him in the last time they had met, over two years ago.

'You still haven't told me about LA,' she said.

'What is there to say? I gave it my best shot but it wasn't to be. I wrote two scripts while I was out there and found a good agent but he couldn't get even a nibble of interest. There seems no point in going back.'

'Well, I shan't be sorry about that. It's really good to see you, Ned. I'll never forget how kind you were to me when—'

'Don't mention it.'

'When I heard your voice on the phone at work today, I thought I was dreaming. I hadn't realised how much I've really missed you. Why didn't you call me before you went away?'

The pizzas arrived and Ned seemed to need the pause in the conversation. In the end, he answered Polly's question with a question of his own.

'What would have been the point?'

'To say goodbye.'

Ned cut a slice of his pizza.

'Adele told me that you were marrying Hubert,' he said. 'It was a bit of a shock at first.'

'It all happened very quickly.'

'Yes.'

'I tried to call you the night before the wedding,' said Polly.

'Why?'

'I don't know. Last-minute nerves, I suppose.'

'I don't suppose I'd have been much help. I mean, marriage is hardly a subject I know much about.'

Polly ate her pizza.

'Anyway,' said Ned. 'You went ahead and took the plunge.'

'Yes.' Polly put down her knife and fork. 'I was a bit worried it was my last chance. I couldn't bear the thought of being a fat, single thirtysomething.'

Ned shook his head. 'I've never understood you, Polly,' he said. 'Why do you have this absurdly low opinion of yourself?'

'Do I?' laughed Polly. 'I think it's just called being realistic.'

'Don't be silly. Why do you always put yourself down?'

'I don't know, I suppose it's Adele. I've always compared myself to Adele.'

'What?' laughed Ned. 'You're far nicer than Adele and prettier too.'

Polly blushed. It was true that she had lost a lot of weight since she got married and she felt and looked better than she had ever done in her life. She wondered why that was. Perhaps it was because she wasn't trying so hard any more.

'You could have had any man you wanted. Still could.'

'Rubbish.'

'OK – except for fucking Charles,' said Ned, glaring at her and wolfing down the rest of his food. Polly had already eaten as much as she wanted.

'Come on,' he said when he had finished. 'I'll walk you to the tube station. Thanks so much for coming to watch me.'

Ned paid the bill and they went. It was still quite early in the evening and Polly was surprised that Ned suddenly seemed in a rush.

They walked side by side in silence down Chancery Lane. Ned seemed deeply preoccupied and Polly slipped her hand through his arm. She felt him flinch but he did not push her hand away.

When they got to the station they stopped and faced each other.

'It was so good to see you,' said Polly.

Ned stared at her but said nothing.

'I think you should keep on with the writing. You must.'

Ned still said nothing and Polly was worried that she had upset him.

'You mustn't give up hope – your dreams,' she said.

Suddenly Ned took her in his arms and kissed her. He kissed her with such passion that she was almost literally swept off her feet. He then held her away from him at arm's length and stared at her.

'Sorry,' he said. 'I shouldn't have done that.' Then he turned and walked away.

*

Polly sat on the train in shock from Ned's kiss. She could still feel the pressure of his mouth on her lips and her skin was quite sore from the roughness of his face. He probably had not shaved that day, she thought. He probably had not shaved for a week.

It was a crazy thing to have done and Ned had apologised immediately. There was no reason why it should ever be thought about or mentioned again and yet Polly could think of nothing else. Excluding that drunken snog with Den the night before her wedding, she had not been kissed so passionately since – well, yes, since Charles. She had forgotten how it felt to be wanted that badly and Ned had really wanted her, she knew that.

The scary thing was that she had wanted him too.

The train pulled into Kidbury and Polly got unsteadily to her feet. She had assumed that, as she got older and as she had been married longer, the sex thing would become less important. But, if anything, it was becoming more and more of a problem. It was really beginning to get to her.

She got off the train. Hubert would be waiting up for her, as usual, and she looked forward to seeing him. He was sweet and always full of amusing conversation and concerned to hear about her day. She enjoyed being with Hubert but she had to admit that she loved him more like a brother. Ned's kiss had reminded her that there was more she wanted from a relationship than good companionship. She still wanted passion, the passion she had only ever experienced with Charles.

Chapter Twenty-Four

Sue sat on a hard red leather sofa in the busy Harley Street drawing room, waiting for her daughter. The room was full of elegant women, mostly in their forties and fifties. They were immaculately dressed and groomed but each had at least a stripe or two of thick white anaesthetic cream painted on their faces. Some had nose to mouth stripes, some had frown marks and others had white rings around their eyes.

This was the place Adele had told her about where even the deepest wrinkles could be plumped out and made almost invisible through the injection of collagen and other filling agents. Sue had been sceptical but Adele had offered to pay for her to have her nose to mouth lines done as a late Christmas present.

'I'll come along and join you – I need to have a session myself,' said Adele.

'You!' Sue had exclaimed. Adele's skin was still as flawless as it had been when she was a baby.

'I like to do my lips,' Adele explained. 'They've always been on the thin side.'

Sue looked at her watch. The cream took half an hour to take effect and her meter expired in ten minutes. The car was only parked a block away but the idea of running down the street with her face looking as though she was about to embark on a tribal war dance did not appeal.

'Thank God you've arrived,' said Sue when Adele eventually appeared. Her daughter was wearing a long camel-coloured coat that looked and felt like it was cashmere. Sue kissed her daughter and asked Adele if she would go out and feed her meter.

Adele sighed and took the money that Sue gave her. When she returned ten minutes later she already had her lips coated with the white cream.

'I can't be long,' she said. 'I've got lunch with the CEO of MPC. I suggested we met at the Savoy so, at least, it won't take long to get down there.'

'You are always rushing,' said Sue. 'You really should slow down a bit.' Sue watched Adele as she opened her briefcase and got out a report to read. She worried about Adele. Her daughter clearly loved her job but surely working and looking after a husband and a daughter was a lot to handle.

'How's Charles?' asked Sue. She wanted to light a cigarette but no one else in the room was smoking and so she just crossed her legs and played with her wedding ring.

'Fine,' said Adele, hardly looking up from her papers.

'It was so good to spend time with you over the holidays,' said Sue. 'A pity you were so busy.' Adele and Charles had invited her to join them in the West Indies for Christmas. She knew that the principal reason for asking her had been so that she could look after Araminta while they went out in the evenings but, nonetheless, Adele had paid for everything and it had been a wonderful break.

278

'Christmas is always busy in my business. People think that if they announce a bid when the target's management are all semi-comatose from eating and drinking too much, then they will have less of a chance to mount a good defence.'

Sue said nothing. She was proud that Adele was well paid and worked for a big bank in the City but she hadn't a clue what it was that she actually did. She had listened to her daughter talk for hours on her mobile phone during the holiday about the Yellow Book, bid documents and paper alternatives. It made no sense at all.

Suddenly a mobile phone began to ring and Adele fished it out of her bag.

'What? What do you mean you're leaving me?' Adele pressed the phone hard against her ear and Sue watched her daughter put her hand to her head in despair. When she took it away again, Sue noticed that Adele had smudged her carefully pencilled brows. 'But who's going to pick up Araminta from school? And what about my trip to the States tomorrow?' Adele tore her fingers through her hair and the neat bob started to look tangled.

'What's the matter?' asked Sue. Adele waved at her mother to be quiet and pressed the phone harder to her ear.

'Well, if that's what you think, you'd better leave at once. In fact, I expect every trace of you to be removed from my house by the time I get home.'

Adele switched off the phone and put it back in her bag. Her face was red with anger and she breathed deeply.

'After I gave her paid leave for all that time we were

279

away, she's decided to leave,' she said.

'Your au pair? But why?' Adele seemed unable to keep an au pair for more than a few months at a time.

'She said she loves Araminta,' said Adele softly, 'but—'

'But?'

'But that I'm an anally retentive, neurotic, control freak.'

Adele laughed as she said this, somewhat hysterically thought Sue. 'Those were her actual words,' added Adele. 'Quite impressive really.'

'You had no option but to sack her on the spot.'

'Other than to accept her resignation on the spot, of course,' said Adele.

'Will Araminta be upset?'

'She's used to au pairs coming and going all the time. She can barely remember some of their names.'

'It's a shame,' said Sue. 'I'd offer to pick her up this afternoon but I've got Joyce coming over for the weekend with her youngest two and I haven't been shopping yet.'

'Don't worry,' said Adele.

'I could have Minty to stay if you brought her down later. She might enjoy spending the weekend with the other kids.'

'No. I'll sort it out, somehow.' She rubbed her face and it was the first time Sue had ever seen her nose look shiny.

'Can't Charles help?' she asked.

'Charles?'

Sue nodded.

'I doubt it,' said Adele.

Sue had noticed a change in Adele and Charles's relationship. It had been worrying her when they were on holiday together but she had never had the opportunity, or perhaps the courage, to discuss it with her daughter.

'Charles seems a bit preoccupied at the moment,' she said quietly. In fact, Charles had been happy to leave Adele to her work and often went out for hours on his own. He almost ignored Adele but Adele had not seemed to notice or care.

At her mother's words Adele looked up and Sue realised, at once, that she had said the wrong thing.

'He was sulking,' she said. But Sue did not dare to ask what it was that Charles was sulking about.

Half an hour later, Sue said goodbye to Adele and set off to meet her other daughter for lunch. Polly had suggested meeting in the self-service restaurant of John Lewis on the fourth floor. It was not exactly the Savoy but it was still a treat for Sue.

'You look well,' said Polly as they unloaded their trays at a table by the windows.

'Thanks,' said Sue. She had been amazed herself at how well and instantly the line-filling had worked. She was now wondering how she would afford £300 a quarter to have her face done regularly.

They sat down and ate their salads.

'How was your Christmas?' asked Sue.

'I worked most of the time,' said Polly. 'Nearly all of my colleagues have families so it's usually up to us childless people to do the Christmas shift.'

Sue nodded and took a bite of celery.

'I saw Dad though.'

Sue stopped eating and stared at Polly. 'I don't want to hear about him,' she said, unscrewing the top of a bottle of white wine.

Polly said nothing and there was silence for a few seconds while Sue sipped her drink.

'Was he with *her*?'

Polly looked at her mother, at her thin unfilled lips, and put a hand on the older woman's arm.

'Yes,' said Polly. 'Hubert and I went racing with the Goodwoods on Boxing Day. Tom knows how much Dad likes racing and invited him to join us.'

'And her?'

Polly nodded. 'Mum, they're living together now. They have been for nearly two years. I think you have to start to accept it.'

'Never.'

'As soon as he arrived, he asked after you. He still cares – he wants to be friends.'

'Cares?' Sue laughed. 'The man doesn't know the meaning of the word.' There was silence for a moment then Sue continued. 'I suppose she was all tarted up to the nines.'

'Not at all,' said Polly. 'She always looks very plain whenever I see her.'

'Trollop.'

Polly laughed. 'Hardly. She started lecturing Viola because she said she never goes to church, not even at Christmas. Viola said that she thought religion was more disgusting than masturbation and a lot less fun.'

Sue looked shocked. 'Viola Goodwood is an odd woman,' she said. 'Adele is lucky that Charles hasn't inherited any of her eccentricity.'

Polly smiled. Her mother seemed to be implying that, perhaps, Hubert had.

'Anyway, Rosie insisted that the poor woman took a little pamphlet that she just happened to have in her bag.'

'Rosie?'

'It's her name.'

'I'll never call her anything but "Trollop". No matter how many of her wretched pamphlets she chooses to bandy about – the hypocrite.'

'Dad says he'd really like to see you – to stay friends.'

'Friends,' cried Sue. 'How can I ever be friends with him now the way he's betrayed me. The way he's betrayed me right from the very start.'

Polly shook her head. Her mother had been an attractive woman in her youth but now the hatred and bitterness she bore were beginning to show in her face.

'Joyce says I should have left him years ago,' she said. 'She says I've put up with too much.'

'What does she know?'

'She's a very good friend,' said Sue. 'She understands men.'

'Does she?' laughed Polly. 'Well, she must be the only woman on the planet who does.'

Sue sniffed, drained the remains of the wine into her glass and poked idly at her salad. 'I could do with another bottle,' she said, her hand shaking slightly as she picked up her glass.

'I'm thinking of moving jobs,' said Polly, pouring some wine from her own glass into her mother's.

'Good,' said Sue. 'Some of the stuff they put in the

Globe these days is appalling. It's particularly embarrassing when it's a piece that you've done.'

'Sorry.'

'What are you thinking of doing?'

'Taking a job on a mag called *Naked Babes*.'

Sue's jaw dropped open.

'Only joking,' laughed Polly. 'No, I'm thinking of going for a job on *Mujer*.'

'Moo hair?'

'*Mujer*,' repeated Polly. 'It's Spanish for "woman". It's a new magazine – only a couple of years old – and they want a new head of Features.'

'Would it be more money?'

'Yes. And I think I'd really enjoy it. You know how much I've always loved glossy magazines.'

Sue nodded. It was true that, even as a girl, Polly had always spent her pocket money on magazines – sometimes in preference to sweets.

'You've lost a lot of weight,' said Sue. 'You must be almost as slim as Adele.'

'Don't be ridiculous.' Polly paused for a moment then added, 'How is Adele?'

'Oh, the same as ever. Doing a hundred and one things all at the same time and making a perfect job out of everything.' It was not, of course, exactly true, thought Sue, but she was so used to saying this that the words had poured out automatically.

'And Minty?'

'Oh, she's growing up fast,' said Sue. 'A beautiful child, just like her mother.' Again, Sue answered on autopilot but were the words really true?

'Adele rang me on her mobile on the way here,' said Polly. 'It's ages since I've heard from her.'

'How nice of her to call you.'

'She wanted something, of course,' continued Polly. 'She said her au pair has suddenly quit and she asked whether I would like to have Minty over to stay for the weekend.'

'I don't know why she didn't let me have her.'

'I suppose she thought you'd be overloaded with Joyce and her kids.' Polly did not like to add that Adele had said that she did not want Araminta associating with Joyce's children. She did not want Araminta coming home crawling with head lice.

'Did you say yes?'

'Well, I hate doing Adele any favours. But it is a long time since I've seen Minty and—'

'That was very kind of you, Polly.'

'Thanks,' said Polly. A compliment from her mother was a rare thing.

'Adele is going to New York to see a client and Charles is going with her. They could do with a break on their own,' said Sue.

Polly looked up. 'Adele told me that Charles is going shooting with some friends while she is away.'

'Really?' said Sue. It was true that Adele had not specifically said Charles was going with her. She had said that it would be a good break for Charles. Perhaps she had meant that it would be a good break spending time on his own.

'Do you think everything is OK between Charles and Adele?' asked Sue.

'Of course,' said Polly without a moment's hesitation. 'They're the model couple, aren't they?'

The phone was ringing when Polly got home but she

managed to get to it in time.

The voice was familiar although it took her by surprise.

'What do you want?' asked Polly.

'I need to speak to Hubert.'

'Hubert?'

'Don't forget, Pussy, I'm on politics now and Hubert will be a useful contact after he wins his seat at the next election.'

'That's still some way off, isn't it?'

'Yes. But, in the meantime, I think I have a story that your husband may find interesting.' Carslip's tone was cold, as always, and even a bit menacing.

'He's not here,' said Polly.

'Get him to call me,' said Carslip. 'I think he will find it in his interest to do so.'

Polly slammed down the phone. Carslip had always blamed her totally for the reshuffle at the *Globe* which had cost him his job on Features. He was always on the lookout for any way in his power to get his own back. Polly hoped that this would not involve Hubert.

Chapter Twenty-Five

The following day, it was pouring with rain when Polly collected Minty from her school in the Barbican. It had been raining heavily for over a week and part of Kidbury was flooded.

'Be careful on the way up,' said Hubert on the mobile as Polly helped Minty load her bags into the back of the car. 'Some of the roads are closed.'

'Shall I pick up something for supper on the way?'

'No need,' laughed Hubert. 'I've already picked something up.'

'Well done. What did you get?'

'Well, the river burst its banks at lunchtime while I was having a drink in the Crown. When I went to leave, the car park was flooded and I had to wade through water up to my knees.'

'Poor you,' said Polly as she pulled into Moorgate and headed out of the City.

'I couldn't believe it – there were all these salmon thrashing about and, well, I managed to grab one with my bare hands.'

'Hubert!'

'The publican said it was a big one and insisted on weighing it,' continued Hubert. 'It was thirteen pounds.'

'What?'

'I bought a couple of lemons and some parsley – it should be delicious.'

Polly laughed. 'You are incredible, Hubert,' she said.

The drive to Kidbury was slow and dark and Polly had been looking forward to chatting with her niece but Minty had the interior light on and was absorbed in playing on her GameBoy. Occasionally her mobile phone rang and Minty would chat with her friends.

'Hubert has hired some rollerblades for us all,' said Polly.

'Great,' said Minty without looking up.

'Hubert's never skated before. Will you help teach him?'

'Uh-hmm,' said Minty.

Polly concentrated on her driving. When they eventually pulled up outside the house, Hubert came out to meet them. He kissed Polly and Minty and ushered them inside out of the rain while he brought in the luggage.

'I have to write this feature on kids' restaurants,' said Polly. 'So, I thought tomorrow we'd go into Oxford for lunch and you could help me with my research.'

'That sounds fun,' said Minty. She had put the GameBoy away now and seemed back to her usual self.

Polly hugged her niece. 'The only problem is, Olga wants the piece for this Thursday and so I think we will have to have two lunches tomorrow – one at a pizza place and one burgers. Is that OK?'

'No problem,' smiled Minty.

They were still in the hall but Minty was already starting to unpack. She had brought lots of stuff. There was a camera and films, a CD player and a huge pile of CDs. There were books and GameBoy games and dozens of magazines.

'Are you planning to stay for a month?' laughed Polly.

'I'd like to,' said Minty. 'It's horrible at home.'

'What?' Polly sat down on the stairs and drew Minty onto her knee.

'It's just Mum – she drives me mad sometimes. You know.'

Polly knew well enough what Adele was like but she was worried to see Minty looking unhappy.

'Tell me about it,' she said.

'Well, she's just so busy all the time. You know, I think she does really care about me but she's so busy. She's never around.'

'She has a very demanding job.'

'I know. That's why she wanted me to go to school in the Barbican so that she could get to things more easily but she never does.' Minty paused and buried her head in Polly's shoulder. 'I had a leading role in the play at the end of last term and she promised to be there.'

'Sometimes things come up at work very suddenly.'

'Yes, that's exactly what she told me. But it's not as though I've got a dad either.'

'You have,' said Polly, pulling Minty away so that she could look into the girl's face.

'Charles is all right but it's not the same.'

'Did he go to the play?'

Minty nodded. 'He got there in time for the second half.'

'Both Mummy and Charles love you very much,' said Polly. 'I'm sure. Who couldn't?'

Minty said nothing. She seemed to be enjoying the comfort of just sitting in Polly's arms. Polly stroked her thick dark hair and kissed her head.

'Who was my real dad?' asked Minty.

'Your real dad?' Polly was surprised by the question. 'Has Mummy never talked about him?'

'No. She says she doesn't like to talk about him and that I must just think of Charles as my dad. But I need to know.'

'I think your Mum is right. But I understand why you are curious to know about your biological father.'

'Tell me about him.'

'Well, I never really knew him,' said Polly. 'But he was a very clever man and a good man.'

'Good?'

'Yes, I think so. You see, he fell in love with your mummy but he was already married and had children. He decided that he had to stay with his wife and family even though he loved your mummy and would have loved you too when you were born.'

'He sounds horrid.'

'He had a difficult decision,' said Polly. 'But he would have hurt the other children if he had left them.'

'I suppose,' said Minty.

There was a shout from the kitchen.

'Supper's ready,' cried Hubert.

'Did Uncle Hobbit really catch a fish in the car park?' asked Minty.

'If anyone else had told me that story,' said Polly, 'I should never have believed it. But your Uncle Hobbit is capable of almost anything.'

They laughed and went off to join Hubert.

'This film needs developing,' said Polly, as she tidied up the next morning. 'Perhaps you would drop it off at the chemist, Hubert, and get it done on your way to surgery this morning. They do a same-day service, I think.'

'OK,' said Hubert, wolfing down heaped spoonfuls of Grapenuts.

'We'll do a burger place at twelve and then go on to Pizza Presto. I presume you would rather join us at the latter?'

Hubert nodded. 'Although you might save me the toy from the Happy Meal – you know how I love toys.'

Polly smiled. 'No polluting your body with burgers – no toy,' she said. Hubert pulled a face then got to his feet.

'I must be off,' he said. 'Where's Minty?'

'Still asleep,' said Polly. 'I think she was very tired.'

Hubert kissed Polly goodbye. 'Don't forget that colleague of yours is coming round this evening to interview me.'

'The odious Arse-lick?'

'He's not that bad,' said Hubert. 'Remember, I helped him and Den out on that libel case against the *Globe* last year. I thought he was actually quite a decent bloke even if he looks rather like the fish we ate last night for supper.'

'He hates me,' said Polly.

'Impossible.'

Polly laughed.

'Well, he's due around six,' said Hubert. 'Try not to murder each other if I have to leave you alone for a few minutes.'

'OK, but be careful what you say to him,' said Polly. 'He's a slippery bastard.'

'Not as slippery as that thirteen-pound salmon,' laughed Hubert. 'He should be safe in my hands.'

'Don't you like chips?' asked Minty.

Polly had been toying with her food. She did not want to eat two lunches, particularly calorie-laden chips and then pizza.

'I'm on a diet,' said Polly.

'You've lost lots of weight,' said Minty. She pinched at the skin of her own tummy. 'Do you think I'm too fat?'

'No, of course not. Nine-year-old girls don't need to diet. You are perfect.'

'But so are you and you were just as nice before you got thinner.'

'Thank you.'

'Why is it better to be thinner?' persisted Minty.

'Oh, I don't know. I suppose grown-ups think that if they're thinner then people will like them more. It sounds silly when you put it that way.'

Minty said nothing but went on eating her chips slowly and thoughtfully.

'How's school?' said Polly, changing the subject.

'OK.'

Polly drank her Diet Coke.

'I got suspended for two days the other week,'

added Minty.

'What?'

'They said I'd been bullying someone but it was really another girl.'

'Was it? That sounds horrible.'

Polly remembered how popular Minty had been at school when she was little.

'Is Harriet still your friend?' she asked.

Minty shook her head. 'We broke up ages ago.'

It was strange to hear Minty talk about breaking up with her friends. It seemed so final and irreversible. Was it possible that even children could do things to each other that were unforgivable?

'Can't you make things up again?' she asked.

'No. Anyway, I've got another friend now.'

Hubert joined Polly and Minty at the pizza restaurant, as planned. He had eaten a sandwich at his office but still gobbled up the last two remaining slices of garlic bread before they paid the bill.

It had stopped raining at last and so there was no excuse for not going to the park and rollerblading.

'How on earth do you get these things on?' said Hubert, struggling to attach pads to his knees and elbows.

'Uncle Hobbit – you are *so* embarrassing. No one wears pads,' laughed Minty.

'They do if they want to avoid spending the rest of the weekend in Casualty,' said Hubert. 'I think you'd better let me get fully kitted out.'

Polly agreed.

They skated, most of the time with Polly on one side of Hubert and Minty on the other, pulling him along.

'I think I'm getting the hang of it,' said Hubert. 'In fact, this is really great. I think I am going to take up rollerblading regularly.' He insisted on being left alone and took off at great speed towards the children's playground.

By the time Polly and Minty caught up with him he had somersaulted into the sand pit and had a red plastic bucket stuck on his head.

'It might be time to call it a day,' said Hubert, heaving himself upright and crawling to the edge of the sand pit. Polly and Minty were crying with laughter.

'Hey, that's my bucket,' cried a boy of about six, waving a red spade at Hubert.

Hubert took off the bucket and returned it to its owner.

'You've split the sides,' said the boy.

'You've nearly split my sides,' said Polly, wiping the tears from her face. She gave the boy a five-pound note. 'Sorry. Can you get a new one?'

'I suppose. Thanks.' The boy ran off.

Hubert changed his footwear and said he would go and wait for Polly and Minty in the car. They watched him limp away still wearing all his padding. He looked an extraordinary sight.

When they arrived home, Hubert realised he had forgotten to pick up the photos from the chemist.

'Don't worry about it,' said Polly but Hubert wanted to get a few things from the deli too so he decided to go.

'I'll only be a few minutes but look after Carslip if he arrives before I get back,' he said as he went back out to the car. And that was the last Polly was to see of her husband for several hours.

'I can't think where he can be,' said Polly later as she poured her colleague another glass of wine. 'The chemist is only ten minutes' drive away and it must have closed ages ago.'

Polly chatted to Carslip but, all the time, she was wondering whether she should call the police. Perhaps Hubert had had an accident. It was pouring with rain again and windy too so the roads would be dangerous and Hubert was so accident-prone.

Carslip glanced at his watch and Polly got up and went towards the phone just as it started to ring.

'Oh, hello, darling,' she said with relief at the sound of Hubert's voice. 'Where on earth are you?' she added, allowing a trace of irritation to creep into her tone. After all, it was horrible having to entertain Carslip all this time. She would far rather have been watching TV with Minty.

'What? The pol—' Polly stopped herself from saying more as she noticed Carslip sit up in his chair. He was clearly listening intently.

She said little as Hubert told her his story. He had been met on arrival at the chemist by a policeman and taken to the station for questioning. Apparently the film he had taken in for development was of a disturbing nature, said the police officer. It contained several pictures of scantily dressed young girls.

'What?' said Polly.

'It must have been one of Minty's films,' said Hubert. 'You must have picked up the wrong roll by mistake.'

'Crikey. What were the pictures like?' She remembered now that Minty said in the car she and her friends liked to dress up in Adele's clothes and pretend they were supermodels.

'Well,' said Hubert, 'I can't say I wasn't embarrassed when I saw them. They were very innocent, I'm sure. But a couple of the poses were rather provocative.'

'What did you say?'

'I tried to explain there must have been some mix-up. But they were suspicious, to say the least.'

'Poor you.'

'They let me go and said they would take no further action, thank God. With the Kidbury by-election coming up so soon, it would only take a scandal like this to scupper my chances.'

'Yes.'

'Tell Carslip I'll be back in half an hour,' said Hubert. 'If he can wait that long.'

But Carslip could hardly wait that long, realised Polly, as she turned to look at him. She had quite forgotten that he was still there.

'What happened?' he asked, on the edge of his chair.

'Oh, nothing.' The last thing Polly wanted to do was to tell Carslip about the photos.

'Really, Pussy?' said Carslip salaciously.

Polly glared at her colleague. 'The name is Polly. Would you like another drink?'

'I'm driving,' said Carslip. 'But a cup of tea would be great. Perhaps you wouldn't mind putting the kettle on, *Polly*?'

Carslip laughed and Polly flounced out of the room. That man really needed to be taught a lesson.

Chapter Twenty-Six

Three months later Polly got the phone call she had been waiting for.

'I've got Sheila Morrissey on line one and Charles Goodwood on line three,' said her secretary.

Polly hesitated. 'I'll take Sheila and call Charles back,' she said. It was a sign of the distance she had travelled in coming to terms with her relationship with Charles that she could bear to do this. She felt quite proud of herself.

'Polly?' said a woman's voice that she recognised at once.

'Sheila?'

'Yes, it's me.' Polly looked at her watch. It was three p.m. in London and so it must be ten a.m. in New York.

'Listen,' continued Sheila. 'I've just seen Kate and the job is yours.'

'What?'

'I know this is probably not the time and place to talk about it but I had to let you know.'

'Thanks,' said Polly, sinking slowly into her chair as she registered the news.

'The formal offer letter is going out tonight but the

terms are as we discussed.' A salary double her present one, thought Polly, a bigger car and a fabulous office.

'Congratulations,' said Sheila.

'Thanks.' Polly put down the phone and looked around her. The offices of the *Daily Globe* were as scruffy and untidy as ever but she had had a good time there and learnt a lot. It was time to move on but she would be sad to say goodbye, especially to Den.

Polly called Den's secretary and made an appointment to see him at nine o'clock the following morning. She was so excited about the new job that it was only when she had left the office and was walking to the tube station that she remembered she had forgotten to return Charles's call. She took out her mobile at once.

'Polly,' cried Charles. 'Thanks for getting back to me. I only rang up for a chat.'

It was a warm spring afternoon and Polly sat on a wall to talk to her brother-in-law.

'A chat?' Polly had not seen Charles or Adele since the night she had dropped Minty home after the weekend they had spent together in January.

'Well, really, I wanted to talk about Araminta,' said Charles. 'Adele and I have been a bit worried about her and you understand her so well.'

'I used to,' said Polly.

'We wondered whether you might join us for supper tonight and have a chat about things. And, anyway, it would be really great to see you, Polly. It's ages since we got together – properly.'

'Tonight? Has something happened to Minty?'

'Oh no, It's nothing specific. But Adele doesn't like

this new friend that Araminta seems to have taken up with.'

'OK, if you really think I can add something.' The thought of having supper with Charles and Adele was not very appealing but she had been concerned about Minty and hoped she might be able to help.

'Great,' said Charles. 'How are things at the *Globe*?'

Polly could not resist telling Charles about the new job.

'That's fantastic. What magazine did you say it was?'

'*Mujer*.'

'That's one of the mags owned by MPC, isn't it?'

'Yes,' said Polly. 'You're well informed.'

'It's just that MPC is one of Adele's biggest clients,' said Charles. 'She was out visiting them that weekend you and Hobbit looked after Minty.'

'Really?' Any connection between Polly's new employer and her sister was not welcome news.

'I'll get some champagne,' said Charles. 'Come any time you like.'

'I'd been planning to meet a friend for a drink but I'll put that off. I'd like to arrive in time to see Minty before she goes to bed.'

'Thanks,' said Charles.

Polly put down the phone. The drink she had arranged was only with Ned and she was sure that he would not mind if she rescheduled.

The following morning Den was in fits of laughter when Polly arrived in his office.

'What's the joke?' asked Polly and then she noticed Carslip sitting by the window. He was red in the face and clutching his briefcase to his chest.

'I hope you're going to pay the bill for a new lock,' he said, his trout lips quivering.

'I'm sure you can work it out in time,' said Den. 'After all there are only something like a million different permutations of six numbers.'

Carslip stormed out of the office glaring at Polly as he went.

'I changed the combination code on his briefcase,' said Den. 'He went to interview some member of the Shadow Cabinet last night and couldn't get the thing undone to find his notes. He was furious.'

'I don't blame him,' said Polly. 'Your jokes are so cruel, Den, and puerile. What did he do to deserve it?'

'Oh, the usual stuff. The man can be such a pompous git sometimes. Someone has to keep him in his place.'

Polly glanced over her soulder. Den always kept the door of his office open and she could hear Carslip whingeing to Den's secretary.

'So, what's up with you?' asked Den, waving Polly to a chair.

'I'm leaving,' said Polly. There seemed no point in beating about the bush.

'Leaving? But I was just about to give you Olga's job.'

'I know. Well, at least, I thought you might and, well, the thing is I don't really want Olga's job even though it is a fabulous job—'

'Where are you going?' interrupted Den.

'*Mujer*. You know how I love glossies. It would be good to have a change.'

'You'd rather work on some poncey women's magazine than be in the front line of national tabloid journalism,' cried Den in disbelief.

Polly nodded. 'I've had a great time here, Den, and I'm really grate—'

'Forget it,' said Den. 'I only put up with you because I wanted to fuck you and don't you forget it.'

Polly went white with rage and got to her feet.

'Yes, that's right. Get out,' yelled Den. 'And have your desk cleared by tomorrow night.'

'Fine. I'll be glad to see the back of this – this shithole.'

Polly stormed out of Den's office and came face to face with Carslip, who was still with Den's secretary.

'Well done, Pussy,' he grinned. Polly glared at Carslip. Any misgivings she might have had about leaving the *Globe* were now history.

The next day Polly went through her files and chucked most things in the bin. She looked forward to making a fresh start at *Mujer*.

'Sheila Morrissey on line two,' said her secretary.

'Sheila,' said Polly brightly. 'I've just told Den—'

'Polly,' interrupted Sheila and there was something in the tone in which she said that single word that made Polly realise at once. Something was wrong.

'What is it?' she asked.

'Well, Polly, I don't quite know how to say this.'

'No,' cried Polly. 'Don't tell me you've changed your minds.' Polly's heart was pounding. Why had she not waited to tell Den until she actually had the formal offer letter in her hand?

'Something came up out of the blue,' said Sheila. 'I'm so sorry – but it meant an automatic withdrawal of the offer.'

'What is it? What happened?'

'Well, it seems there was a discrepancy on your CV.'

'What?'

'There's no point denying it, Polly. We've checked with the Board of Examiners. I'm afraid the company has a strict policy about people who lie in their CVs.'

Sheila explained how someone, she could not disclose who, had brought to MPC's attention the fact that Polly had only passed one A level – not two, as claimed.

'I can't believe this,' said Polly.

'I know it seems trivial and believe me we would like to turn a blind eye to it. But, given that it's been pointed out by an independent third party, we cannot risk any bad PR if the person was to make a thing about it. MPC is a big US company and they take these things very seriously, of course.'

'I see.'

A few minutes later Polly put down the phone and sat staring at her empty desktop. It was true that she had always claimed on her CV that she had two A levels: a B for English, which was true, and a C for French, which was not.

It had been Adele's idea years ago and had helped her get that first job on the *Dulwich Observer*.

'No one ever checks these things,' Adele had said.

Who on earth could have told *Mujer*?

She picked up her bag and put on her jacket. There was no doubt in Polly's mind, as she made her way to the lifts, that it must have been Adele.

Adele was the only person who knew. And now she thought back to the evening before. She had told Charles and Adele all about the new job, even though

Charles had told her earlier that Adele had a relationship with the magazine. Would she *ever* learn her lesson when it came to her sister? It was absolutely fucking classic Adele, thought Polly, as she pressed G and the lift juddered into action.

Adele seemed to be totally unable to cope with seeing Polly enjoy any success in her life. There was no other way to explain what she had done. She must have been jealous.

Polly remembered that Adele had been unusually quiet over supper. At first, Polly thought that Charles and Adele had had a row but then she dismissed this thought on the presumption her sister was just preoccupied with thoughts of Minty. They had spent a long time discussing Minty and had finally agreed that she just needed lots more attention and praise to lift her self-confidence. But then Adele had said nothing while Polly and Charles had discussed her new job at *Mujer*.

She must have been plotting even then, thought Polly, as she swung through the revolving glass doors for the last time.

She ran down the steps and there were hot tears of anger in her eyes. She was appalled to come suddenly face to face with Den.

'Sad to be leaving?' he said.

Polly wiped her eyes, shook her head and tried to push past him but he caught her arm.

'Look, Polly, I'm sorry about what I said yesterday. I was just disappointed and lost my temper.'

Polly said nothing. She was half choking as she swallowed back her tears.

'The fact is you're a brilliant journalist, Polly,' Den continued. 'One of the best we've ever had.'

Polly looked away as the tears flooded down her face.

'What's wrong? Is there anything I can do?' asked Den.

Polly hesitated for a few seconds then blurted out the words, 'Oh Den, I've been a complete idiot again.'

'Why? What's happened?'

Polly shook her head and sobbed. Den put an arm round her shoulder.

'Can I do anything to help?'

'Yes,' mumbled Polly. 'Will you give me my job back? Please?'

'What? You want to come back to this – what was the word you used?'

'Shithole,' said Polly.

'Ah yes, that's right. This shithole. Are you now telling me you want to come crawling back to the shithole?'

'Yes please.'

Den gave her a squeeze. 'Well, I'll have think about it.'

'Thanks.'

'For about two seconds,' said Den.

Polly looked up into her boss's face. Den was smiling broadly.

'Thanks,' said Polly and she kissed him on the cheek.

Chapter Twenty-Seven

Polly hardly slept a minute that night. She tried calling Adele over and over again but the answerphone was on. Her sister's behaviour really was unbearable, unpardonable. Although she had never forgiven Adele for stealing Charles, she had eventually come to terms with it, married Hubert and got on with her life. One of the main things that had sustained her had been her career which, although it wasn't in the same league as Adele's, had become increasingly important to her. And now, it seemed, Adele was intent on wrecking that as well.

As soon as Polly got out of bed the following morning, she started calling Adele again. First, at home and then at her office. The answer was always the same: sorry but Adele Taylor was not available. She waited until eleven o'clock and then picked up her jacket and bag and drove to the station. She would go to Stratton Walsh and see Adele face to face.

'Adele Taylor?' said the receptionist, looking Polly up and down.

Polly was wearing her best suit and it looked smart, but it was still a long way from the Cerruti and Versace that her sister wore.

'Do you have an appointment?'

'I'm her sister,' said Polly. 'It's an urgent personal matter.'

The receptionist raised one eyebrow and picked up the phone. 'Please take a seat,' she said to Polly.

Polly walked backwards and forwards across the lobby floor. She could not bear to sit down.

After a few minutes the receptionist called her over.

'I'm afraid Adele is in a meeting,' she said. 'It could go on a long time.'

It was almost déjà vu, thought Polly. It was exactly like the time she had gone to see Charles at Green Baby.

'Where? Where is this meeting?' cried Polly. 'I must see her now.'

'I'm sorry,' said the receptionist 'but—'

But, again, Polly was taking no excuses. She leant over the receptionist's desk and grabbed the huge diary of appointments.

'Give that back at once,' cried the receptionist but Polly backed away with it. It took a few seconds to find Adele's name but eventually she did.

Five – Red Room, she said to herself as she flung the diary back on the desk and bolted for the lifts.

'Stop. Help. Security!' she heard the receptionist cry but it was too late. Polly was already in the lift and going up.

When she got to the fifth floor she discovered that she was trapped. There were two sets of double swing doors but both required security codes to be opened. As luck would have it, however, someone was just coming out of one set of doors and she managed to slip through. It took a while to find the Red Room but eventually she was standing breathless outside its oak door.

306

There was a sound of hurried footsteps and Polly knew she had little time. She opened the door and about twelve white, well-groomed faces turned to stare at her. She closed the door behind her and spotted Adele at the far end of the table. She was sitting opposite a woman who looked almost her mirror image. They both had shiny black hair, flawless skin and bright white teeth. Smiles were frozen on to their faces as they waited for Polly to explain herself.

'I need to see you, Adele,' she said at last.

'Sorry, Polly dear,' said Adele coldly. 'I'm busy. I'll call you later.'

'No.' Polly made her way towards her sister. 'It has to be now.' There was an embarrassed shuffling in the room. Adele and the woman opposite her were the only women in the room. The men, all in dark grey suits, began to whisper among themselves. Adele got to her feet. She was determined to keep calm but she was clearly furious.

'I see that it's important, Polly,' she said. 'But—'

'But excuse yourself from this meeting at once,' said Polly, 'or I shall drag you out of here by – by your hair.' She advanced on Adele and Adele flinched.

'I'm sorry,' she said to the people round the table. 'I'll get Miranda to send up some coffee. Let's take five minutes' break.'

As she said this, the door burst open and two security guards appeared.

'Can we help you, Ms Taylor?' asked one.

'No, it's too late now,' said Adele. 'I'll deal with it myself.'

*

307

Adele took Polly through to a small lobby that was adjacent to the meeting room and the two women stood glaring at each other.

'What the fuck is it?' demanded Adele.

'You know exactly what the fuck it is,' said Polly. She wanted to slap Adele hard across her ice-cold face but she just managed to stop herself.

'All I know is that you have just made me look a complete idiot.'

'And you? What do you think you've done to me?' spat Polly.

'I haven't done anything to you. I don't know what you're talking about.'

'Oh no. You must think I'm stupid. Who else knew about my CV?'

Adele looked blank.

'Giving myself a C grade for French A level rather than an F?'

Adele continued to look blank.

'It's absolutely you all over, Adele,' said Polly. 'You can't stand me doing well. You've always got to put me down, haven't you?'

'I—'

'Well, let me tell you, sister dearest. This is the last time I put up with your shit. I am going to get my own back on you and soon. Do you hear that?'

Polly was yelling so there was little doubt that Adele could hear her words and probably all the people in the next room could too.

Adele said nothing. Either Polly was going to hit her or just go. Eventually she decided to just go.

'I'm sorry, I—' said Adele as Polly stormed out of

the room and immediately into the hands of the two security men.

'We'll make sure she's escorted off the premises,' said one.

'No, leave her alone. She's not a criminal.'

'She looks like a mad woman,' said the other security man as they both let go of Polly.

'She's only mad at me,' said Adele and then she turned, smoothed her hair and went back to her meeting.

Polly stood for a moment outside Stratton Walsh's offices in the sunshine and waited for her pulse to come down. As she did so, a short, plump woman trotted across the courtyard and Polly thought that she had seen her somewhere before.

The woman stumbled on her high heels as she passed Polly and fell. Polly helped her to her feet.

'Damn it,' said the woman smoothing her blond, permed hair. 'I've laddered my tights.' As she spoke Polly noticed her bright white rabbit teeth.

'Nibbles,' she said, 'of course.'

'Sorry?'

'Oh nothing, sorry,' said Polly. 'I just think we met once. Aren't you Charles Goodwood's secretary?'

The woman looked at Polly suspiciously. 'Amanda Butterworth,' she said, putting out her hand. 'Yes, I used to work for Charles Goodwood.'

'Don't you work for him any longer?'

Amanda shook her head. 'His wife got me an interview at Stratton's. The pay is much better here and I get a cheap mortgage but I miss . . .'

'You miss working for Charles?' prompted Polly. The woman nodded.

'He's so nice, so charming,' said Amanda.

'I know. I'm his sister-in-law.'

'Really?' Amanda was looking at Polly's face closely. 'Have you been crying? Your eyes are very red.'

'I've just seen my sister, Adele,' said Polly. 'She makes me very angry.'

'Charles's wife?'

'Yes.'

'She's a bitch,' said Amanda. Then she quickly corrected herself. 'Sorry. I shouldn't have said that. After all, she is your sister.'

'Don't worry,' laughed Polly. 'I've called her far worse things than that.'

There was a pause and Amanda tried twisting her tights so that the ladders didn't show.

'Are you busy for lunch?' asked Polly. She had nothing to do and she had a feeling it would be interesting to hear what Amanda might be able to tell her about Charles and Adele.

They went to a wine bar nearby and had something to eat and drink.

By the time Polly ordered a third glass of white wine for herself and her companion, Amanda had almost finished her story.

'I never got over Charles,' she said. 'And I don't suppose I ever will. Maybe one day he will realise what a mistake he has made marrying Adele and come back to me?'

Polly listened to the words and realised she could have been listening to herself speaking.

'Of course, he had other affairs at Green Baby – before and after me,' said Amanda.

'Really?'

'I think he worked his way through pretty well the whole office. The terrible thing was that everyone fell in love with him and took forever to get over him. It was dreadful.'

Polly sipped her wine. She could hardly believe what Amanda was telling her. It seemed Charles had a reputation in his office for being an appalling womaniser. Had Polly just been one of his many conquests, like these other women?

'Of course, things were special between me and Charles,' said Amanda. 'We were very compatible, if you know what I mean.' Polly thought she knew what Amanda meant and shuddered.

'Of all the women he could have married,' went on Amanda. 'He had to choose Adele and she treats him like shit.'

'Does she?'

'Absolutely. I know, for a start, that Charles is desperate to have a baby with her but she refuses.'

Polly said nothing.

'She's as hard as nails. I know he's thinking of leaving her.'

Polly smiled. It was clear that Amanda knew nothing of Adele. There was no way that she would ever let Charles out of her clutches.

'Don't kid yourself,' she said. 'They've been together for nearly four years now.'

'He called me,' said Amanda, 'and invited me out for dinner. I know something's wrong between them. Perhaps he's not getting enough sex – that's usually the problem with married men.'

'I don't believe that's the case with Charles and

Adele – they can hardly keep their hands off each other.' Polly thought back to the night she had caught them making love in the Goodwoods' kitchen. But that was over two years ago. She also thought of the night she had had supper with Charles and Adele recently and how cool they had seemed to each other then. Perhaps Amanda was right.

'I'd give that relationship another year – max,' said Amanda. 'It will be quite something to have Charles Goodwood back on the market.'

Polly drained her glass. How would she feel if Charles left Adele? Would she go running after him like Amanda and the rest of his past loves? She hoped not. She felt quite sick with panic at the thought.

She was, as she quickly told herself, married to Hubert and, although her relationship with her husband had become more platonic than ever, she still loved him. She loved him very much and would never hurt him.

'Adele will only have herself to blame,' said Amanda. 'She has neglected him.'

Polly smiled. On the other hand, the thought that something might be about to go wrong for Adele made her feel much better.

Chapter Twenty-Eight

Minty had been coming home from school on the bus since Easter. She far preferred it to staying on at Homework Club and waiting for Adele, who was always the last mother to arrive and sometimes forgot altogether. The teacher who supervised HC would sigh and call Adele on her mobile. Then Minty would have to wait in the caretaker's office until Adele arrived which was, even then, sometimes hours later.

At the beginning of the last term, Minty had persuaded her mother to give her her own key to the house and now she could come and go as she pleased. It was a big improvement and had given her a considerable amount of status among her friends. The girls in her class, who were all ten or nearly ten, liked to behave as though they were at least fifteen but Minty was the only one who was allowed to go home on the bus alone.

That afternoon, the bus was quite empty when she got on it. She had forgotten her bus pass and so she held out her money for the conductor. The conductor was a tall, loose-limbed young man with a dirty face. He sauntered up the aisle towards Minty and she noticed that he had his ticket machine slung low

313

over his hips so that it hung exactly in front of his genitals. A long white tongue of ticket dangled from the machine right in front of her nose. For one horrible moment, it seemed to Minty that the man was waving his penis in her face. It was disgusting. She gave him the money and he wagged the ticket at her.

'Do you want to take it?' he asked. She did not want to put her hand anywhere near him, particularly there.

'You do it,' she said.

The conductor tore off the ticket and pressed it into Minty's hand.

Minty scrumpled the ticket into a ball and stuffed it into her pocket. There was a time when she thought that the idea of sex with a boy might be fun, romantic. But now the thought filled her with disgust.

She had started her periods a couple of months ago. She was horrified to be the first girl in her class to start but a friend had told her that the periods would stop if she lost some weight. For the last week, she had hardly eaten a thing and no one had said a word. She had expected her parents to start complaining that she was leaving her food but they had not even noticed or, perhaps, they did not care.

Minty closed her eyes as the bus continued along the familiar route. She would lose weight, her periods would stop and she would never grow up.

Polly had never worked so hard in her life as she had over the last month. She was really grateful to Den for giving her her job back and she wanted him to realise that.

Hubert had won his seat in the Kidbury by-election

n March. Polly had been delighted of course but, with
Hubert now on only an MP's salary, she needed to help
pay the mortgage. It would have been a disaster if she
had resigned and not found another job.

'Where the fuck have you been?' bawled Den as
Carslip slunk into the steakhouse. They were having
the editors' morning conference. Polly was standing
in for Olga and Carslip was standing in for his boss.

'Sorry,' said Carslip. 'I was just listening to the
Transport Minister making that announcement about
the new regulations coming in for train operators.'

'Enthralling,' said Den.

'He didn't mention it to me when we had dinner
last week,' said Carslip.

'Of course he didn't, you twit,' said Den. 'It's price-
sensitive information. I expect all the train operator
share prices have fallen today.'

Carslip looked pale. 'Yes, they have. I had a few
myself, well, quite a few, but I sold them on Friday.'

'Impeccable timing,' laughed Den. 'But a bit suspicious.'

'I swear,' said Carslip. 'He didn't breathe a word
to me.'

Polly glanced at her watch and Den brought the
meeting to order.

'Thinking of the City,' he said. 'I liked that piece
you did on the new futures market in fine claret,
Polly.'

'Thanks,' said Polly. 'My husband has bought two
contracts of the Cheval Blanc eighty-eight for delivery
in two thousand and three. It's a long time to wait for
a drink.'

*

'Vodka and Red Bull,' said Minty as she hung her head over the lavatory.

'How many?' Adele had arrived home to find Minty lying unconscious on her bed. It had scared her dreadfully.

'I don't know. We were at Denise's house. Her brother gave us the drinks. He just kept topping up our glasses.' She retched again into the lavatory bowl. Her stomach was empty but her digestive system was still in revolt.

'I told you not to see that girl Denise again,' said Adele. 'She's a bad influence.'

Minty sat back and held her head in her hands.

'And never drink,' said her mother. 'It's bad for you. How do you think I manage to do all the things I do? If I were drinking all the time, I would be useless.'

'Aunt Polly drinks and she's not useless,' said Minty. 'Aunt Polly and Uncle Hobbit let me drink a glass of champagne when I stayed at their house.'

'Typical. Polly would be far more successful if she showed more self-control. Drinking is a bad thing to do.'

'And Aunt Polly isn't bad. I love her.'

Her mother shook her head. 'But she is not exactly the sort of person you want to grow up to be like,' she said and Minty retched again. Her mother made her so angry. It was sometimes as though she hated Aunt Polly. She was always rude about her.

'I love Aunt Polly,' said Minty defiantly. 'She's very kind – the kindest person I know.'

'Yes, OK, but you are clever, Araminta. You can do so much more with your life.'

Minty glared at her mother. 'You mean you want me to grow up and be like you?'

'Would that be so bad?'

Minty retched again.

Her mother got a cloth and wiped her face.

'I'm sorry,' she said. 'I just want you to have the best in life, Araminta.'

Minty felt exhausted.

'Can you please call me Minty?' she asked.

Her mother said nothing. She gave her daughter a clean nightdress to put on and left the room.

They met at Livebait at one. It was the first time Polly had seen Adele since the bust-up at Stratton Walsh four months ago.

When Adele came into the restaurant, late as usual, Polly did not immediately recognise her sister. The neat black hair looked straggly and in need of a good cut. Although it was a sunny spring day, Adele was not wearing her customary sunglasses and there were dark shadows under her eyes. She glanced around her nervously as she looked for Polly. There was nothing of her usual confidence as she made her way through the restaurant to Polly's table.

'Thanks,' she said as she took off her jacket and gave it to a waiter.

'Hello,' said Polly.

Adele smiled. 'Hello,' she said. 'Thanks so much for coming.'

Polly was not used to her sister being nice to her and hardly knew what to say. 'You said it was about Minty and it was important.'

Adele nodded and the smile left her face. 'Yes. It is.'

They ordered drinks, read the menu and then Adele dropped her bombshell.

'The thing is, Polly, I want to ask you a favour.'

Polly looked up. This was more like the Adele she knew and hated, she thought. She only ever got in touch when she wanted something.

'Go on,' said Polly.

'I've thought it over carefully, and come to the conclusion that it's really in Araminta's best interests.'

'What?'

'Polly, I want you to stop seeing Araminta.'

'What?' Polly put down her glass of water and stared at Adele. 'I hardly see her as it is.'

'More than that,' continued Adele. 'I want you to stop calling her, writing to her, sending her text messages or communicating with her in any way.'

There was a pause. Polly felt like getting to her feet and storming out of the room but she didn't. She wanted to hear more. She wanted to know why.

'What's happened?'

'I'm worried about her,' said Adele. 'Araminta is going through a difficult phase and is easily influenced. I think she needs time to herself.'

'Adele,' said Polly. 'I love Minty.'

'I know, that's part of the problem,' said Adele, biting her lip and picking up her menu again.

'How do you mean?'

'I had a big row with Araminta the other night. I came home and found her dead drunk.'

'What?'

'It's not the first time. And not only that but I found some photographs she had taken by her friend Denise's brother.'

318

'The ones I told you about – the ones Hubert was nearly arrested for?'

'No,' said Adele. 'These ones were much worse. I can't think why Araminta allowed herself to pose like that. She must have very low self-esteem.'

Polly hesitated. 'Why will it help not seeing me?'

The waitress arrived at Adele's elbow and asked if they were ready to order but Polly waved her away.

'She's become too dependent on you,' said Adele.

'Too dependent?'

'Yes, she never listens to what I say. It's Aunt Polly this and Aunt Polly that and I can't get her to do anything I want now.' Adele's voice was getting louder and more strained and one or two people in the restaurant glanced in the direction of Adele and Polly's table. 'Damn it all,' continued Adele. 'She loves you far more than she loves me.'

Polly said nothing but waited for Adele to compose herself.

'You're her mother,' said Polly.

'I know,' said Adele 'But she's out of control.'

'You can't control everything and everyone in your life, Adele.'

Adele glared at her sister. 'Then there's Charles.'

'What about Charles?' asked Polly, her stomach turning in knots as she thought back to her conversation with Nibbles.

'He's never around. He's taken to going off shooting or playing cricket at the weekends with his friends. I can't talk to him about Araminta. I'd like him to do more things with her, with us, but he just won't.'

Polly took a sip of water. A horrible feeling of pity

319

was beginning to flood through her but she steeled herself to fight it.

'You've got to let go a bit,' she said. 'You can't be such a control freak, Adele.'

'I've managed well enough so far. And I'm not giving up yet.'

Polly relaxed. She had been worried that Adele was starting to soften, that she might, at last, be becoming a human being but no. Adele was still the same Adele.

'I want you to promise me that you will not get in touch with Araminta in any way without my permission first,' said Adele. 'And the same goes for Charles.'

'What do you mean?'

'You know exactly what I mean.'

'I do not.'

'I know you've always been jealous of me and Charles and have just been sitting there, lying in wait for the first opportunity—'

'Don't be ridiculous, Adele. Why would I have married Hubert?'

'God knows,' said Adele, pouring more fizzy water into her glass. 'All I know is what you were up to last Thursday.'

'Last Thursday?'

'There's no point denying it. Charles told me.'

Polly looked dumbfounded. She had not seen Charles for months either.

'He told me that you had dinner together,' said Adele. 'At first, he said he was working late but then I found the restaurant bill. Dinner for two at The Avenue.'

Polly said nothing.

'He went bright red and said that he had been helping you with a feature on fashion products for kids and, because Green Baby has just launched a new kids' fashion line, you'd suggested discussing it over dinner.'

Polly stared at Adele. She wondered why Charles had lied to her and what he had really been up to. She could have told Adele the truth but she let it go. If Charles was seeing another woman why should she not let Adele presume it was her? Perhaps Adele would then have some idea how she had felt five years ago.

The waitress reappeared but neither Polly nor Adele were hungry nor did they want to spend another moment in each other's company. Adele gave the waitress twenty pounds and Polly left. She caught the tube back to her office and sat at her desk thinking through all the things that Adele had said.

There was no way, of course, that she was going to stop speaking with Minty. She would continue to e-mail her and text her on her mobile phone whenever he wanted. Adele had stolen Charles, she had messed up Polly's job opportunity at *Mujer* but she was not going to separate her from Minty too.

Chapter Twenty-Nine

Furthermore, Polly was not going to turn down a dinner invitation from Charles.

'Same place as usual?' she said.

'Sorry?'

'Didn't you buy me dinner at The Avenue the other Thursday or am I getting you mixed up with someone else?'

Charles laughed. 'Sorry about that. Thanks for not spilling the beans.'

'I think you'd better tell me what you were really up to, though,' said Polly. 'I think I deserve that.'

'My old secretary rang me up. She's quite a bore but she said she wanted advice about her job at Stratton, so I said I'd see her.' Nibbles, thought Polly. She could hardly believe that Charles was taking out Nibbles.

'She doesn't go out much,' said Charles. 'I thought I'd treat her but I knew Adele wouldn't understand.'

'Really? I thought Adele never got jealous.'

'She never used to,' said Charles. 'That was one of the things I liked most about her but she's changed.'

'Adele? Adele has changed? Never,' laughed Polly. 'You'll never convince me of that.'

'Well, what day is best for you?'

'Hubert is going out to dinner with Carslip next Tuesday. We could do it then but it has to be quite early so that I can make my last train.'

'Adele is away next Tuesday. You could always stay over at—'

'Don't,' interrupted Polly.

'Don't you trust me?' asked Charles.

Trust him? she wondered. That was hardly the point. The question was, did she trust herself? Even after all these years her heart leapt at the sound of Charles's voice. She could still remember how it felt holding him. She could still remember holding his fat penis in her hand. But no, she had to stop thinking these things. It was probably because she and Hubert had not had sex for such a long time. She really would have to make more of an effort to get Hubert interested again.

'Are you still there?' asked Charles.

'Sorry, I was thinking of something else.'

'Well, let's go to Lola's in Camden Passage.'

'OK.' They agreed a time and Polly put down the phone. It was an innocent dinner with her brother-in-law. So why did she feel so guilty?

Polly left her desk early the following Tuesday. She had got into the habit of working late and sometimes going for a drink with Den. Hubert worked long hours too and so it was becoming unusual for them to spend an evening at home together alone.

She had her hair done and then went back to the office to change. Carslip was sitting in the lobby and he waved her over to him. He seemed rather upset.

'What's the matter?' asked Polly.

'Remember that business when I sold my shares in

323

that train operator company – right after my dinner with the Minister of Transport?'

Polly nodded. She recalled Carslip saying something about it and how much money he had made before the share price plummeted.

'I got a call this morning,' he said. 'The bloke asked to speak with Mr Caslit but it was clear he was after me.'

'Who was he? What did he want?'

'He was from the Serious Fraud Office. He said he is investigating the circumstances around the sale of my shares.'

'Oh God, really?'

'Yes,' said Carslip. 'I have to give a statement next week. Do you think I should tell Den?'

Polly could not help feeling sorry for Carslip.

'Leave it a bit,' she said. 'The investigation may come to nothing. I doubt they can prove you did anything wrong.'

Carslip looked alarmed. 'That's the whole point, I swear. I had no idea the Minister was about to announce a change in the regulations.'

Polly left Carslip and hurried back to her office. She wanted to leave plenty of time to redo her make-up and get changed. She had bought a new dress which was a bit tight but looked very sexy. She wriggled into it and realised, as she leant over the wash basin to reapply her lipstick, that it was so tight she could hardly breathe. Nonetheless the dress was stunning and she stood back and admired herself. She would be thirty in a month's time but she knew that she had never looked so good, ever.

It was a warm evening and Polly walked up towards

Holborn as she looked for a cab. Eventually she saw one with its yellow light on. She waved at it and it seemed at first that the driver had not seen her. Then he suddenly slammed on the brakes and pulled up about 500 metres away. A couple of tourists were ready to pounce on the cab so Polly ran up to it as fast as she could.

She dived into the cab crying, 'Sorry, mine!' but, as she slammed the door closed and sank into her seat, she heard an ominous ripping sound. She felt behind her and realised that her dress had split up the back seam from hem to waist.

There was no way that she could go back to the office with her bum hanging out of her dress but, on the other hand, there was no way that she could turn up to dinner with Charles in that state either.

She got out her mobile phone and dialled a number. She could only think of one friend who lived remotely near and she prayed and prayed that he would be in.

'Ned?' she cried. 'Where are you?'

'I'm at Dave's, as usual.'

'Oh, thank heavens. It's Polly.'

'Polly, I haven't heard from you in ages.'

It was good to hear her old friend's voice – not only because she was hoping he might come to her aid with the dress. It was a long time since Polly had seen him, since that night he had kissed her. She had told herself at the time that the kiss had meant nothing but she had not been able to help wondering whether Ned would call her, whether he would try to take things further.

Ned had not called, however, and it was clear to Polly that he regretted the incident and she resolved to put it to the back of her mind too.

'Can you get me something urgently?' she asked. 'I'm desperate.'

'What is it? Not cannabis again, I hope.'

Polly laughed. 'No, something far more mundane but probably equally hard to come by. I need a needle and cotton.'

'A needle and cotton? Have you become so domesticated that you've taken up sewing your own clothes?'

'No, Ned, listen. It's serious. I've had an accident. I'm in this cab just round the corner from you and my skirt has ripped right up the back.'

'Can't you put a safety pin in it?'

'No,' said Polly. 'When you see it you'll understand.'

'I can't wait,' said Ned.

'Look, I'll be with you in two minutes. See if you can find the things.'

By the time Polly had arrived, Ned had dug around in his friend's wife's drawers and got what he needed.

'I'm afraid I could only find lime green cotton,' he said as Polly got out of the cab. She had her hands behind her and was holding a copy of the *Daily Globe* over her bottom. Ned paid off the cab and helped her shuffle into the house.

'Show me then,' he said as soon as they were alone in the hall. Polly dropped the paper and turned round. The skirt fell wide open revealing her slim waist, her white cotton pants and the backs of her legs.

'You see the problem,' said Polly.

'I do,' said Ned.

'OK, that's enough leering.' Polly turned to face Ned again. He looked rather red in the face and ran his fingers through his thick dark hair.

'The needle and cotton are on the table in my bedroom. You go up and get started and I'll get us both a drink.' He pointed up the stairs. 'The first door on the right – you can't miss it. It's the one with the drum kit in it and books all over the floor.'

Polly went up the stairs holding her dress together behind her but Ned still watched her go. He could see enough.

Polly found the room, took off her dress and sat down on the edge of Ned's bed to sew.

Ned came in a few minutes later with two bottles of cold beer.

'How are you getting on?' he asked, staring at her breasts. She was wearing a plain white cotton bra but Ned could see how full they were. She had a fantastic figure.

'I can't do it,' said Polly. 'My hands are shaking so much, I can't even get the needle threaded.'

'Why are you shaking?' asked Ned, putting a bottle of beer on the floor beside Polly's foot and taking a swig from the other.

'I don't know. I think it's the shock of getting myself in this state, particularly as I was feeling a bit apprehensive about the dinner I was going to as well.'

'Give it to me.' Ned took the dress out of Polly's hands. 'My Mum taught me and my brother to sew – just in case we never found a woman to take care of us, she said.'

'Thanks.' Polly suddenly felt very naked and wrapped Ned's duvet around her as she watched her friend settle himself on the floor with the sewing things.

'Who are you having dinner with?' he asked.

Polly hesitated. 'Well, Charles actually. I don't know

why on earth I should feel nervous. I mean, I've known him for years.'

Ned frowned. 'Will Hubert and Adele be there?'

Polly shook her head.

'Well, perhaps that's why you feel nervous then.'

'Don't be silly, Ned.'

'Am I being silly? Let's face it, you've never really gotten over Charles.'

Polly blushed. 'How are things with you?'

'Oh, much the same as ever.' Polly watched Ned bend over his work. His tongue stuck out half an inch or so as he concentrated. He really was the sweetest man in the world. His hands were huge and looked clumsy but he seemed to manage the needle with incredible adeptness.

'Are you still writing?' asked Polly.

'On and off,' said Ned. His hair was longer, thicker and more untidy than ever. Although it looked as though it had not been washed for a month or more, Polly had a strange urge to reach out and stroke it.

'I've got a job as a clown doctor at the moment,' he said, looking up from his work.

'A clown doctor. What is that?'

'Oh, I just dress up in funny clothes and go around the kids wards in hospitals making jokes and doing silly things.'

'That sounds fun.'

'It is most of the time. But sometimes it's hard – when a child is really unwell or sad or both.'

'It's a great thing to do.'

'Yes, I'm becoming a real Mr Niceguy in my old age.'

'You always were.'

'You were not supposed to think that,' said Ned. 'I've tried hard to be selfish, to think only about myself, but it doesn't seem to have got me very far.'

Ned licked a finger which he had just pricked and carried on sewing. Polly looked at her watch. It was just as well she had got hold of Charles on his mobile and explained she would be late.

'Are you still at the *Globe*?'

'Yes,' said Polly. 'I was offered a job at *Mujer* a little while back but Adele managed to put a spanner in the works and they changed their minds.'

'You still hate Adele as much as ever?'

'More, if anything.'

'OK, let's try it on,' said Ned, getting to his feet. He held up the dress for Polly as she wriggled into it. They were standing very close and Polly thought she could hear Ned's heart beating. He was tall and towered over her and she could smell his sweat, but it was an attractive smell.

'Turn round and I'll zip you up.' Polly sucked her tummy in and the dress zipped up quite easily.

'I need one of your Mum's girdles,' she laughed as Ned spun her round and kept his hands on her shoulders a moment longer than necessary.

'You're a beautiful woman,' said Ned as though he was seeing her for the first time again. Polly smiled. She thought back to the time that Ned had kissed her and half hoped that he would do it again but he was already stepping backwards.

'I'll come with you and help you get another cab.'

It took little time to do this as Dave lived just off St John Street. Polly kissed Ned on the cheek and got into the cab very carefully. She watched him turn and walk slowly back to his friend's house. She could not help wondering whether she would rather have cancelled her dinner with Charles at a smart restaurant in Islington and have settled for a takeway with Ned.

Ten minutes later, she arrived at Lola's and saw Charles waiting outside the restaurant. He looked as handsome as ever and immediately she stopped thinking about anything else.

Chapter Thirty

'You look stunning,' said Charles.

Polly smiled and they made their way upstairs to a table for two in the far corner of the room.

'I read that piece you wrote about politicians who grow to look like their pets. It was very funny.'

'Yes, I'm worried that Hubert is starting to turn into Bobbin.'

'Do you still have that vicious creature?'

Polly nodded. 'Minty worked out what was wrong with him. It's a condition called malocclusion or something like that. The rabbit's teeth were not lined up correctly. So they don't wear down and keep growing.'

'That explains the enormous fangs he had.'

'Yes. I just get them clipped every month or so and they're fine now. I was very impressed that Minty found out about the problem and insisted we took him to the vet. She's very clever.'

'Yes. But she's driving Adele crazy.'

'It must be a worry that she's not happy at school,' said Polly.

The waitress arrived and they ordered drinks.

'But tell me about life at the *Globe* first,' said Charles. 'The paper seems to be full of your work these days.'

'It's true I've been working really hard but I enjoy it. Not so long ago, I couldn't understand people like Ned and Adele being so absorbed in their careers.'

'You're certainly looking well on the extra work.'

'Thanks,' said Polly. She felt a little uncomfortable as Charles tried to maintain eye contact.

'How's Adele?' she asked.

Charles looked away immediately. 'She's just been promoted to the Board. The youngest woman director they've ever had.'

'That's good,' said Polly.

'Yes, it's what she has always wanted but she doesn't seem that happy.'

'Why not?'

'I don't know. She seems to have lost some of her confidence. Perhaps it's worrying about Araminta but she can be really needy sometimes.'

Polly looked up at this remark. 'Needy? Adele?' She wondered for a moment whether Charles was joking.

'She's become much more demanding. She makes a fuss if I'm back from work late but it can be such a strain being at home sometimes.'

Polly said nothing. The waitress came with their drinks and took their order for food. It was unusual for Charles to be so open about personal matters, thought Polly, but he seemed to want to talk.

'Tell me about it,' she said.

'Well, I suppose a big problem has been the question of whether we have another child.'

Polly sipped her drink.

'You see,' continued Charles, 'I suppose I'd pre-sumed Adele would want more kids. I mean, all women do, don't they? I remember you used to go on about it all the time.'

'Yes. But she doesn't?'

'No. She told me she'd come off the pill ages ago but I found a whole stash of packets in her drawer.'

'Perhaps she feels she's too busy to cope with Minty, let alone a new baby.'

'Perhaps,' said Charles.

Polly put out her hand and touched his arm. 'You should talk to her about it. Explain how important it is to you.'

'I have. But it doesn't seem to make any difference.' Charles put his hand on top of Polly's and Polly quickly withdrew her own.

'What about you and Hubert?' asked Charles. 'I always assumed you would start sprogging at once.'

'I don't know,' said Polly. She did not want to talk about Hubert. There was no way that she was going to tell Charles that they had stopped having sex so the chances of her getting pregnant were pretty remote. 'I think I've changed. I'm not sure I'm ready to have children yet. I mean, it's such a commitment.'

'Polly!' laughed Charles. 'I never would have believed you could say such a thing. When we were going out together all you could talk about was settling down and having kids.'

'Things were different then.'

And they really were, she thought to herself. She would definitely have married Charles and had his children. She would have given up her job and her life would now be the opposite of what it had become and she would have been happy about that.

'You must be pleased about Hubert winning the by-election,' said Charles.

'Yes and it already looks as though he is being lined up for a junior position in the Shadow Cabinet as soon as possible – the Tories seem so short of good people.'

'That's great. So why do you look so sad?'

'Do I? I'm not really. I'm very happy in fact.' But, in truth, Polly felt close to tears. She was not happy. Things were not right with Hubert but she had been refusing to admit it.

The more she thought about the situation, the more she realised that she had not been happy for a long time. In fact, she had not been really happy since the day Charles had disappeared upstairs with that tart of a sister of hers.

Polly looked across the table at Charles. There was a part of her, a big part of her, that still yearned for Charles to take her in his arms, to tell her how sorry he was and what a mistake he had made. But it was too late, much too late.

'Hubert's a wonderful husband,' she said.

'He's a wonderful brother too,' said Charles. 'I don't deserve him. Mum and Dad worship him.'

The waitress arrived with their first course and they ate.

'I haven't seen your parents for ages. How are they?'

'Fine,' said Charles.

'You're so lucky to have such nice, normal parents. I can never do anything right as far as mine are concerned.'

'Mum and Dad? They're far from perfect.'

334

'I'm forever grateful,' said Polly, 'that they have never once mentioned my behaviour at your wedding.'

'What?'

Polly blushed. 'You know, pouncing on you on the dance floor.'

'It was worse than that.'

'I know. I was so pissed that I don't remember a thing but Hubert told me all about it.'

'You mean that business on the bouncy castle.'

Polly nodded.

'Yes, it's just as well Hubert and Adele turned up when they did – or the whole course of history might have been altered.'

'What?'

'Well, I managed to persuade Adele that I was trying to fight you off. But another minute and I would not have been able to resist you any longer. God knows what scene they would have encountered if they'd arrived any later.'

'Don't joke about it,' said Polly. 'I behaved appallingly.'

'No,' said Charles. 'I'm serious. I really wanted to make love to you on that bouncy castle. I was just as much to blame as you were. In fact, I snogged you first.'

'What?'

'It would have been the shortest marriage ever. Adele would never have forgiven me.'

Polly could hardly believe her ears. To think she might have blown Adele's marriage apart before it had even really begun.

'You're so sexy,' said Charles.

Polly looked up and blushed. Charles was clearly

trying to come on to her. Perhaps he was even lying about what happened on the bouncy castle. But she could not help wanting to believe him.

'I've always wondered how things would have been if you and I—'

'Don't,' said Polly rather sharply. Charles was saying all the things she had ever dreamt he might say. So, why did she feel so nervous? Why couldn't she just enjoy it?

They finished their meal and Polly said it was time for her to go. But Charles insisted on coffee which the waitress brought, together with chocolates.

'I'll call a cab,' said Charles picking up a chocolate and trying to pop it into Polly's mouth. Polly took the chocolate in her fingers.

She was relieved that Charles had not suggested going back to Noel Road. If Charles had continued to come on to her, she was not sure that she would have been able to resist.

The chocolate was dark and bitter and Polly winced as the sugar hit a sensitive part of her tooth.

'Are you OK?' asked Charles.

'Death by chocolate,' said Polly. 'I really must see a dentist.'

'Open wide,' said the man in the white coat and Polly obliged. It was good to lie back on the soft black leatherette of the dentist's chair and reflect on everything that had happened in the last twenty four hours.

It was not only the conversation she had had over dinner with Charles that troubled her but also the message she had received from Adele.

Polly had returned home the night before and
ound a stream of invective waiting for her on the
nswerphone. Adele had found out that Charles was
neeting her and was livid.

'Grinding,' said the dentist.

'Sorry?' blubbered Polly, the saliva tube falling out
f her mouth and dribbling down her chin.

'Do you grind at night?' asked the dentist. 'Your
eeth, that is?' He blinded her with a flash of brilliant
vhite teeth.

'Not that I'm aware of.'

When she arrived at the office later, there was
nother message from Adele and she decided to return
ne call.

'What the hell do you think you're up to?' asked
dele.

'Jsha dunno what you're talkin about,' said Polly.
he anaesthetic still made her mouth feel like she had
football inside it.

'Are you drunk?'

'Jsha dentist.'

'Look, Polly, I know you're enjoying this but I won't
tand for it.'

Polly said nothing.

'I'll tell Hubert,' continued Adele.

'Jsha-tell him what?'

'About you and Charles.'

'Jshere is nothing about me and Charlejsh, ajsh
ou know.'

Polly waited but Adele said nothing more. She
tought she could hear something, perhaps the sound
Adele crying.

'Jsh-all right?' asked Polly.

'No,' blubbed Adele. 'I'm not all right. I'm sorry, Polly, I've just got a bit of a hangover this morning. I'll get some coffee and I'll be fine.'

'Jsha-asure?'

'Yes, sorry. It's Araminta and everything getting to me. I'm sorry, I probably over-reacted.'

Polly said goodbye and put down the phone.

She sat in stunned silence at her desk and thought for a while. Adele had burst into tears. Adele had a hangover. Why on earth was her sister drinking and crying? What was going on? And then, thought Polly, Adele had apologised. It was quite bizarre and, if she had not known Adele for the bitch she really was, she might have been quite worried.

Chapter Thirty-One

Polly continued to see Charles over the following months. They would meet for dinner or a drink and became increasingly flirtatious. Polly knew that their relationship could not develop further. There was no way that she was going to betray Hubert but ironically this made it easier to flirt and fantasise about what might have been and what might be, if circumstances were different.

Hubert was busy with his work and Polly was as fond of him as ever but she was beginning to be troubled by her increasing preoccupation with Charles. She dreamt of him most nights and in those dreams the relationship always ended in the same way: with her and Charles in bed together. She had not in reality been unfaithful to Hubert. She had not even let Charles kiss her, although he had tried to a few times, but every night in her dreams she let him do just what he wanted.

One night in early December Polly had a different dream. She and Charles had made love, as usual, but this time she awoke alone in a cold dark place. She realised, with horror, that she was in a graveyard. It was foggy and she could only just make out the shapes of the stone crosses and headstones. Polly was naked and shivering as she stumbled to find the way out. She fell and hit her head on a tombstone. As she pulled herself back on to her feet, her fingers traced the engraving on the stone. There was a single word: GOODWOOD.

Polly woke up at this moment, shivering with cold. She snuggled under the blankets and cuddled up behind Hubert. The dream had felt so real that she thought she could still feel the rough surface of the tombstone on her fingers.

'Charles should be in later today,' said his secretary when Polly phoned first thing in the morning. 'He's flying back from New York.'

Polly put down the phone. Charles was on a plane and she could not help thinking of her dream and worrying that it was a dreadful premonition.

Hubert called to say that he would be going home early and he would cook supper for them.

'Thanks,' said Polly.

'I have to open a new chocolate factory in Kidbury for one of my constituents. It's the third factory he's opened and the business is doing really well. I persuaded Adele to come along and meet him. Apparently one of her clients is looking to acquire these kind of businesses in the UK.'

Polly laughed. 'Adele is the perfect person to advise on chocolate businesses,' she said. 'I don't think I've seen her allow a piece of chocolate to pass her lips since she was about seven years old.'

'All the more for me then. I'll bring you home a big box of goodies and I'll try not to eat them all before you arrive.'

Polly said goodbye. The weather had turned cold and she looked out of her office window at the pedestrians below with their heads bent and huddled in their coats to protect themselves from the wind. She thought of Charles's plane being buffeted in crosswinds over the Atlantic and shivered.

Nonetheless, when the call came after lunch she could hardly believe her ears. It was Adele and Adele was in floods of tears.

'What do you mean – there's been a terrible accident?' she cried, her legs going numb with panic.

'It was such a shock,' sobbed Adele.

'Calm down,' said Polly. 'Just tell me what's happened.'

'They've taken him to hospital. I can't believe he survived.' Thank God, thought Polly. At least, he was still alive.

'What happened?' she asked.

'He fell into the chocolate vat.'

'Who? You mean Hubert?'

'Yes, of course.'

'Oh no, poor Hubert. I thought you were talking about Charles.'

'Charles? He's fine. In fact, he's with Hubert now.'

'Oh God,' said Polly, pulling herself together. 'Is Hubert OK? Tell me exactly what happened.'

'Yes, don't worry. It was a terrible shock and very frightening but he's going to be fine.'

'Thank God. What happened?'

'Well, a journalist turned up at the factory and we left him and Hubert on their own for a few minutes by the vat. The journalist said he wanted to discuss something in private with Hubert.'

341

'Go on.'

'I think they must have got into a bit of a scuffle. I've never known Hubert to hit anyone but that's what this hack said he did. Carslip his name was. I think he was from the *Globe*.'

'Carslip,' said Polly. 'I might have guessed.'

'Well, somehow or other Hubert managed to fall into this huge vat of chocolate.' There was a strange snorting sound and Adele continued. 'Sorry. I can't help giggling but it was very serious. He almost drowned.'

'Oh my God.'

'Yes, it was a deep mixer – about eight feet, they said. He got trapped by giant paddle blades which ripped off his clothing and spun him around. It took the ambulance crew and firemen more than an hour to get him out.'

'Where is he?' asked Polly.

Adele gave her sister details of the hospital and Polly rang straight away. Mr Goodwood was still in intensive care but his condition had stabilised. Polly grabbed her coat and made her way to the hospital as quickly as she could. There was so much she had not asked Adele that she felt quite annoyed with herself. What had Carslip been doing there in the first place? And what had they been fighting about?

She had been wondering for some time whether she had made a mistake marrying Hubert and, since she had been seeing more of Charles, she had even started to wish she was single again. But she had not wanted this. She had not wanted Hubert to be drowned in a vat of liquid chocolate.

'How is he?' Polly asked Charles, who was waiting outside the ward when she arrived.

'Well, they've cleaned him up,' said Charles, 'which is a relief. When I first saw him he looked like a giant walnut whip.'

'Don't joke,' said Polly. 'Poor Hubert. It must have been terrifying.'

'I think it may have cured his chocoholism.'

Polly went into the ward. Hubert was wired up with tubes but his face was pink and glowing as he slept. She sat by the bed and took his hand then buried her face in it and wept.

Charles sat beside her and put his hand on her shoulder.

'Don't,' she said, wriggling out of Charles's reach.

'Don't worry. They say he will make a full recovery.'

But Polly continued to cry as though her heart were breaking.

'What is it?' asked Charles.

'I don't know. I suppose I feel guilty. I've been such a terrible wife to him.'

Charles touched her hair. 'You've been a perfect wife. He's a lucky man and I'm sure he knows that.'

Polly wiped her face and Charles got to his feet.

'I'm going to get a breath of fresh air,' he said. 'I'll be back in half an hour or so.'

'Thanks,' said Polly, but she was glad to be left alone.

She sat looking at Hubert's plump, almost childlike face. Was it fair to Hubert that she had married him without truly loving him, without loving him with the passion she had felt for Charles? Perhaps that was why

Hubert found it so hard to make love to her. Perhaps it was all her fault.

She took Hubert's hand and stroked it gently. She knew that she loved Hubert. She loved him very much but she would never be in love with him. Was that enough? Hubert was a good man and deserved a wife who adored him, thought Polly. She would never be good enough for him.

As these thoughts passed through her mind, a shadow suddenly cast itself over the bed. Polly turned and came face to face with Carslip. He was holding a small bunch of flowers.

'Bernard,' said Polly. Somehow in the circumstances, despite what she knew of the fight, she could not bring herself to call him Carslip. The expression on his face was pitiful.

'I'm sorry,' he said. 'It was an accident. I didn't intend—'

'No, of course not,' said Polly. 'I'm sure you didn't.'

Carslip looked uncomfortable so Polly took the flowers and got a seat for him.

'What happened?' she asked.

'I was so angry about you and Den.'

'What do you mean?'

'You know – playing that last trick on me.'

'What trick?'

'The spoof about the insider dealing investigation. Don't tell me you didn't know.'

'What?'

'Look, I've seen you and Den going off for drinks together. He tells you everything. He must have told you – he wouldn't have been able to resist.'

'Do you mean that person who called you from the

Serious Fraud Office turned out to be Den playing another of his practical jokes?'

Carslip nodded.

'I don't believe it,' said Polly. 'He never breathed a word, I swear.'

Carslip shrugged and shook his head.

'Den knows I think his practical jokes are cruel. He probably thought I might have told you.'

Carslip stared at Polly trying to assess whether she was telling the truth or not. He decided, at last, to believe her.

'In that case, I'm even more sorry,' he said, looking down at his lap. 'I'm very sorry.' He looked so miserable that Polly was afraid he was going to start crying. 'I thought I could get back at you through Hubert,' he continued.

'By pushing him in a vat of chocolate? That's a bit extreme.'

'I didn't intend that. I hadn't expected him to react so badly.'

'React to what?'

'I showed him some photographs,' said Carslip. 'I've been seeing Hubert a bit recently. He's helped me with a few pieces I've written and we were becoming quite good friends.'

'Except you were secretly plotting against him?'

Carslip nodded. 'One night, when we were both a bit pissed I took him to a gay bar.'

'A gay bar?'

'Didn't you know I was gay?'

'No,' said Polly. 'Sorry, I never realised.'

'It doesn't matter. Why should you?'

'So. What happened at this gay bar?'

'Well, I arranged for some snapper to be there and we got this male stripper to come and sit on Hubert's lap. The photographs look very bad indeed.'

Polly stared at Carslip in horror. She could scarcely believe what she was hearing. Hubert had been lured into a gay bar. She could not help wondering how much he had enjoyed it. Perhaps Hubert just wasn't interested in women at all. Polly wondered that this thought had never crossed her mind before.

'How could you set him up like that?'

'Oh fuck it, Polly,' said Carslip. 'You've done similar shit in your time – it would have made a good story.'

'But you set it up just to get your own back on me.'

Carslip shrugged. 'I suppose I've wanted to get my own back ever since you got me shoved off Features.'

'What did Hubert say when he saw the pictures?'

'He said that he didn't give a shit about them from his own point of view – I could publish them and be damned. But he was worried about you.'

'Me?'

'He was worried you would be upset. He said, "What the hell will Polly think when she sees these?" He kept saying the same thing over and over again.'

'Poor, dear Hubert. You are a bastard.'

'I hadn't realised how much he loved you.'

Neither had I, thought Polly.

'After a minute or two,' continued Carslip, 'he flew at me in a rage and punched me in the face. There was no one around to help and I had to defend myself. I didn't, of course, intend—'

'Of course not.'

'I'm very sorry,' said Carslip. 'I wanted to tell you myself before Hubert wakes up.'

'Well, thanks for that at any rate.'

There was nothing else to say but Carslip continued to sit looking uncomfortable and Polly said nothing.

Eventually Carslip stood up. 'Will you tell Den?'

Polly looked up at the man she had despised for so long but her hatred for him had dissolved into pathos.

'No,' she said.

Carslip nodded and touched her arm. 'Thanks, Polly,' he said and left the room.

Polly shivered and looked back at her husband. Hubert's eyelids were beginning to flicker and she took his hand again.

'Hubert?' she whispered. 'Darling?' She resolved to herself that she would be a better wife to Hubert, that she would learn to love him properly and stop herself lusting after other men, after Charles.

Hubert opened his eyes and smiled warmly at her. She would never have believed then that within twenty-four hours he would ask her for a divorce.

Chapter Thirty-Two

The first person Polly wanted to call was Ned. It was
New Year's Day and she and Hubert had spent all
Christmas discussing their relationship.

'I'm so depressed,' she said.

'Poor you,' said Ned.

'The irony is that I had been wondering for some
time whether it was right to stay married to Hubert. It
took me by surprise when he said he wanted a divorce
and I feel miserable, a failure.'

'Why does he want a divorce? Is there someone
else?'

'Oh no, I don't think so. He says he's really doing
it for me. He says I need to have the chance to find a
man I really love.'

'That sounds very altruistic.'

'There may be other reasons too,' said Polly. Hubert
had sworn that he was not gay but Polly had her
doubts. She knew that homosexuality would still be
a barrier to his career progress in the Tory party. 'He
says he knows I'm not really happy being married to
him. He's sad but he's worried that if he doesn't make
a move then I'll just resign myself to things.'

'Perhaps he's right.'

'Yes. But I feel so guilty. It was so wrong to marry a man I didn't really love.'

'Yes. To be honest, I could never see it working.'

'If only I'd got hold of you the night before the wedding. I think if I'd managed to speak to you I might have had the courage to pull out of it.'

Ned laughed. 'You make me sound like some agony aunt. Is that how you think of me?'

'No,' Polly assured him. 'It's not.'

She told Ned that she was thinking about staying with Zeta for a while and they agreed to meet up the following week. Just before they said goodbye, Ned told her his own news.

'That's fantastic,' said Polly.

'Well, it's nothing yet. When my agent rang I couldn't think for a while who the hell he was – it's such a long time since we spoke.'

'When will you know?'

'Oh, I don't know. Weeks or months, these things take forever.'

'It would be so wonderful though if they accepted your script,' said Polly. 'All your dreams come true.'

'Maybe,' said Ned and they said goodbye.

The following week, Polly met Sue for lunch at a bar in the Farringdon Road. Sue had regular botox injections so her forehead was now as smooth as a board but Polly could sense the tension that lurked beneath her mother's skin.

'I'm so sorry about you and Hubert,' said Sue. But Polly knew this was unlikely to be the main cause of her mother's concern.

'Yes,' said Polly. She did not want to talk about

Hubert any more and went to the bar to buy drinks and order food.

When she returned, the two women sipped their drinks and studied each other. Sue was certainly well preserved for her age but there was a sadness, a bitterness about her that was almost overwhelming.

'How are things with you?' asked Polly.

'Your father had the nerve to invite me out to the place he's bought in Essex with that woman. They're running a pub apparently. I don't know how she squares living in sin and selling alcohol with her Jehovah's business.'

'You didn't accept the invitation?'

'Of course not. I want nothing to do with the man.' Sue paused and Polly waited.

'I drove out there though – just to have a look,' said Sue.

'You mean, you went to their house and snooped around without actually calling in?'

'I wanted to see just what the little love nest looked like. I couldn't really rest until I'd seen her sweet rose-coloured curtains at the kitchen window, the his and hers green wellies outside the back door.'

'Mum,' said Polly. 'You have to move on.'

'Why? It's what I live for, I sometimes think. I spend hours working out ways to get my own back on him. I might go mad if I didn't.'

'I think you'll go mad if you do,' laughed Polly. 'How's Minty?' she added, changing the subject. She had not seen Minty, Charles or Adele over the Christmas holidays. They had gone to stay with the Goodwoods and she and Hubert had remained at home trying to sort things out.

'Fine,' said Sue, looking away. She sipped her drink and then stared straight at Polly. 'Well, actually, no – she's not fine.'

'What's wrong? More trouble at school?'

'I don't know. Adele won't talk about it any more. She won't accept things are wrong. But Araminta has lost a lot of weight.'

'Really? She was quite skinny when I last saw her.'

'Well, she's like a pipe cleaner now.'

The waitress arrived and placed a large plate of sandwiches between them. Polly tucked in.

'I missed breakfast,' said Polly as she saw her mother register her wolfish appetite.

'They came to see me last Saturday,' continued Sue, 'and Araminta would not eat a thing and she hardly said a word to anyone.'

'I wish Adele would let me see her,' said Polly.

'She thinks you would only make things worse. She blames you for weakening the bond between her and Araminta.'

'Great. Typical Adele. You do her a favour by giving up your life to help her with her child and that is how she thanks you.'

'I can see her point,' said Sue. 'It must be very difficult for her.'

Polly continued to eat.

'Adele has taken three days off work this week and is taking Araminta to Paris to do some shopping,' said Sue.

Polly put down her sandwich. 'Really? That's a first.'

Sue glared at Polly. 'It's not a joke. We're all really worried about Araminta.'

'I wasn't joking,' said Polly, 'and I'm worried about

351

Minty too. It's just that – well, I've never known Adele
to get to one of Minty's school plays, let alone take her
away for three days.'

'You misjudge Adele,' said Sue.

Polly said nothing but no one, not even her mother,
could teach her anything about Adele. She knew her
sister through and through, inside and out.

'She has a difficult job,' repeated Sue. 'I know that
her boss gave her a hard time for taking leave at short
notice. They're working on a big deal for MPC – you
know, the big US magazine company.'

'I know,' said Polly. 'They're the people who nearly
hired me until Adele felt the need to point out some
discrepancy on my CV.'

Sue sniffed and sipped her drink. Polly knew her
mother well too. There was no way that she would
ever get Sue to think ill of Adele.

'Well,' said Polly when they eventually said goodbye,
'Please tell Adele to call me if there's anything
can do.'

Polly was surprised to find a rapid response to her
offer. When she arrived back at her desk, there was
a note asking her to call Adele's number. But it was,
of course, Charles who was trying to get hold of her
not his wife.

'Not working today?' asked Polly.

'I'm working from home,' said Charles.

'Ah yes. We all know what that means.'

'Why don't you come over and see for yourself?'

Polly's heart skipped a beat. She felt sure that if she
and Charles were alone on their own in the house, it
could only lead to one thing.

352

'I've got two thousand words to write for tomorrow's paper,' she said, wondering why she was so hesitant. She was now separated from Hubert, why should she feel any compunction about betraying Adele?

'How about dinner tomorrow night?' asked Charles. 'I'll book a table at La Granita but let's meet for a drink first at Browns.'

'OK.'

'I'll see you there at six thirty?'

'Great.'

She put down the phone and felt oddly nauseous. She realised for the first time that she was free, free again to have a relationship with another man. Free, perhaps, to win back Charles. The thought made her whole body go numb and she sat quietly until she noticed someone perched on the corner of her desk.

She looked up and came face to face with Carslip. He was carrying two cups of coffee and gave one to Polly.

'You look happy,' said Polly. Carslip was beaming from ear to ear and she realised that she could not remember the last time she had seen the man do this. For the first time the thought of fish did not leap immediately to her mind. Carslip was actually quite good-looking – when he smiled.

'I've done it,' said Carslip. 'You had to be the first person to know.'

'What?'

'I've got my own back on Den, at last. I was thinking about it and all that resentment I used to feel for you – I think it was really all about wanting to get my own back on Den for all those jokes he plays on me.'

'What have you done?'

'I called him from a phone box,' giggled Carslip, like a naughty schoolboy. 'I pretended to be one of his neighbours. I said I'd just passed his house and there was water gushing out from under the front door.'

'Christ, what did he do? Did he fall for it?'

'Yes, straight away. It was as much as I could do to stop myself from laughing on the phone. He yelled and swore and slammed the phone down. But I saw him roaring off in his car just before lunch.'

'God, he will be livid when he gets back.'

'It will be worth it.'

'Yes,' said Polly. 'Good for you.'

That evening Polly had Ned in stitches as she told Carslip's story and how Den had come back while he was still in her office and emptied a bucket of water over Carslip's head. He said he had collected it from the 'flood'.

There had been a bit of a scuffle and Polly had been about to try to pull the two men apart when they both collapsed on the floor and started laughing.

'You bastard, you bastard,' Den had repeated over and over again but he slapped Carslip on the back good-humouredly. 'I've got to hand it to you, you took me right in and I never thought I would be had like that.'

'Your office sounds a madhouse,' laughed Ned.

'It is,' said Polly. 'But I love it. I received a call from the woman who nearly got me hired by *Muje* yesterday. She wants to talk again but I don't think could bear to part from the *Globe* now.'

'Well, there's no harm hearing what she has to say I suppose.'

'Any more news from your agent?' asked Polly.

'No. It's best to forget it. The chances that they'll buy the script are very slim.'

'Zeta wants to know where you do your writing on your desk,' said Polly.

'What?'

'She believes in all this feng shui stuff,' said Polly. 'Do you write on the left or the right or in the middle?'

Ned thought for a moment. 'Well, mostly on the left, I suppose.'

'Zeta would be appalled. You must shift everything around at once and start writing in the middle.'

Ned laughed. 'That would mean moving my photo frame.'

'Whose photo do you have on your desk?'

'Yours,' said Ned. 'It reminds me of what you are always telling me – to keep on writing.'

'I'm honoured.'

'It's only a faded snap that Frankie took when you stayed with us in Scarborough. But I've got it in a red photo frame.'

'That's good. Zeta says that red is the luckiest colour.'

'So how *are* things at Zeta's?'

Polly sipped her beer. 'Just the same as ever. I feel like I've stepped back in time three years. I'm a single girl again,' she said with a grin.

'What is that supposed to mean?'

'It's a funny feeling. I was devastated when Hubert said he wanted the divorce. I suppose I'd been using him as a bit of an emotional crutch. But now I'm looking forward to getting my life sorted out – properly this time.'

'Sounds good.'

'Yes, I'm a single, available, professional woman – only just out of her twenties. What do you think my chances are?'

'You don't need to draft an ad for the personal columns yet,' laughed Ned.

'I don't want to waste too much time.'

'So, are you free tomorrow night then?'

'Sorry, I already have a date for tomorrow night.'

'A fast worker too,' said Ned. 'Can I ask who the lucky bloke is?'

Polly stopped smiling and looked down. 'Charles.'

'Charles?'

Polly nodded.

'For God's sake,' cried Ned. 'You are incredible.'

'It's just dinner,' said Polly.

'Oh yes. Give me a break, Polly.'

'Why shouldn't I have dinner with him?'

'Why shouldn't you?' yelled Ned and most of the people in the bar glanced in their direction. 'Well, it's hard to know where to begin. First, I suppose, he's a married man. Secondly, he's married to your sister. And thirdly, he doesn't love you – he's just pissing you about. Do you need me to go on?'

Polly had never seen Ned so angry. She was almost frightened.

'Why should I care about Adele after all she's done to me? And how do you know Charles doesn't love me?'

'Has he *ever* told you he loves you? Could he *ever* have treated you the way he has treated you, if he loved you?'

'That was Adele's fault.'

'Was it?' said Ned. Polly was red in the face and half rising to her feet but the peak of Ned's anger seemed to have passed. 'I met you tonight,' he went on, 'because I thought you needed comforting after splitting up with Hubert – not to hear you ranting on about his brother.'

'I wasn't ranting on,' cried Polly.

'I saw Adele the other day. She didn't notice me but she was standing outside Stratton's in the pouring rain smoking a cigarette.'

'Adele never smokes.'

'I swear it was her. The fact is, Polly, your sister is going through a rough time. Her daughter is sick and, from what I gather from you, her marriage is on the rocks. Don't you feel just a little bit sorry for her?'

'No, I don't. I'll never feel sorry for her. She's a bitch and deserves all the trouble she gets.'

The woman at the next table coughed and Polly sat down in her chair again.

'You know the trouble with you, Polly?' said Ned. 'You've turned into your fucking sister.'

Polly glared at Ned. It was the ultimate insult and she would not stand for it. She got up and flounced out of the bar.

Chapter Thirty-Three

The following morning Polly felt like shit. She had cried all the way home after leaving Ned and had been unable to get to sleep. She had finally dozed off and dreamt about drowning in hot yellow custard.

As she washed her face and examined her reflection she wondered why she felt so low, so guilty. Of course Ned had said a very hurtful thing, probably the most hurtful thing anyone could say to Polly. But how true was it? Was she becoming like Adele: cruel and selfish?

She rubbed in some pro-retinol moisturiser, followed by a thicker than usual coating of foundation, but her skin still looked pale and tired. It was getting late but she went back to her room and lay down on the bed for a while.

She glanced at the clutter on her bedside table and saw the stone. She had not brought many things with her from Kidbury to Zeta's. Hubert proposed to sell the house and then she would have some money to buy a flat. In the meantime, he was happy to store her possessions.

So, why had she brought that stone, the bloodstone as Ned called it, that she had found on Filey beach a those years ago? Her aide-memoire to get her revenge on Adele. She picked it up and held the cold hard object in her hand. Had her heart become as cold as this stone?

There was a tap on the door and Zeta appeared with a couple of letters for her. 'Time for a cup of tea before you leave?' she asked.

'That would be brilliant,' said Polly. Zeta had been so kind to her since her return, Polly was very grateful.

Zeta gave Polly the letters and went back downstairs.

One was a credit card bill which she jammed in among the debris on her bedside table. The other she studied carefully before opening it, although she had recognised the handwriting immediately. It was from Minty.

Dear Aunt Polly,
  I am going away this morning with Mummy. We are going to Paris which is fun but I feel so tired. It is nice of Mummy to take time off work to do this but it is just because she is worried I am getting too thin and thinks she can stuff me full of pain au chocolat. Of course, I am fine and eat lots. But perhaps you were right when you said that if you are thinner, people will like you more.

I did not say that, thought Polly to herself, but she continued reading.

It certainly works with Mummy. She fusses about me all the time now.

> I am very sad that I do not see you so much.
> Please keep sending letters to my friend's house
> as Mummy still does not like me to talk about
> you. She is so jealous.

Polly had to laugh. The day that Adele was jealous of
Polly would really be the day.

> Well, it's time to go. I'll give this letter to Dad to
> post as he doesn't mind me writing to you.

Polly paused. Was it right for her and Charles and
Minty to deceive Adele? She felt uncomfortable but
there seemed to be no alternative. Surely Adele
realised it was impossible for her to keep them
all apart?

> With love. Adieu! XXX Minty

Polly sat down on the bed again and felt like crying. Minty sounded cheerful enough but there was
something wrong about the letter that she could not
exactly put her finger on. It was Minty's relationship
with Adele, of course. Adele was such a control freak
that she could not accept that Minty was growing up
and needed to start making decisions and mistakes for
herself now.

Zeta arrived with Polly's tea. 'I put an extra teaspoon
of sugar in it,' she said.

'That's what they do for people who have just
narrowly missed being run over by a bus,' said Polly.
'Do I look that bad?'

*

'You look terrific,' said Sheila when Polly arrived at the small restaurant in Golden Square. Sheila had been there a few minutes and had already studied the menu.

'At the risk of being considered impossibly girlie,' she said. 'I suggest we order two starters.'

'Fine,' said Polly. The waiter came over and Sheila ordered soup and carpaccio. Polly had a Caesar salad followed by chicken and spinach risotto.

'It makes a nice change from the six-pack of Hula Hoops I usually munch at my desk. I hardly ever get time to go out for lunch.'

'Christie is still as tyrannical as ever?' said Sheila. She had once worked for Polly's boss many years earlier and would never forget it.

'He's a maniac,' laughed Polly.

'I don't know how you've put up with him for so long. I'm so sorry about the business with *Mujer* – I heard that Christie made you beg him to give you your job back.'

'He was unbelievably good about it. I was so grateful that I've worked like a slave for him ever since.'

'You've been writing some really good stuff,' said Sheila as the waiter arrived with the first round of starters. 'It was such a pity about the CV problem.'

'Don't mention it. It was a stupid thing to do.'

'Well, anyway, as I mentioned on the phone, it may not matter any more. I was in New York last week and Kate Downing asked about you. She said she'd been thinking the whole thing over, now that so much time has passed, and she was thinking of asking you to send your CV in again – perhaps with a small amendment?'

'But I thought the *Mujer* job had been filled years ago?'

'Yes. But there's an opportunity to do something similar on one of the New York titles and she thinks it might be right for you.'

'New York?'

'She says that MPC as a company cannot condone lying on a CV but she personally sees it as evidence of your early drive and determination to get a job in journalism. I think really she's quite impressed by what she knows about you.'

'She'll get a shock if she ever meets the real thing,' laughed Polly.

'Well, that brings me to the main point,' said Sheila. 'Kate wants to see you. She wants to interview you personally in New York and, if that goes well, the job will be yours for sure.'

'It sounds exciting. Tell me more.'

Sheila outlined the position and the two women talked as they ate. Polly could hardly take in everything that Sheila was saying. It appeared that her salary would be twice what she was offered by *Mujer* in London and about four times what she currently earned.

'It just remains to fix the interview,' said Sheila.

'I'll go to the airport now.'

Sheila laughed. 'Sorry. As you will appreciate, Kate is a very busy woman. She suggested the morning of February the fifteenth. MPC will pay for the flight and your expenses, of course. Do you want to check your diary?'

'No need,' said Polly. 'I don't care if it's my own funeral, I'll make sure I'm free. But can't she do something sooner? The fifteenth of February is over two weeks away.'

'That's fast for Kate, believe me. She must really want you,' said Sheila. 'I'll get my secretary to call you about the flight details – you will want to go out on the fourteenth.'

'Valentine's Day,' said Polly, studying Sheila's face carefully.

'Is that a problem? Will your partner let you go?'

'No problem there.'

'Why are you looking at me like that then?'

'I was just wondering,' said Polly. 'You're not, by any chance, related to Den Christie are you?'

'Insults will get you nowhere,' laughed Sheila. 'Why on earth do you ask?'

'It's just too good to be true. This conversation feels exactly as though it were one of Den's practical jokes.'

Sheila smiled. 'This is no joke. It's for real.'

'You cannot be serious,' said Polly as her mother explained what had happened. She glanced at her watch and thought that she should really be getting herself ready to meet Charles.

'I saw him winning all that money and just, well, flipped,' said Sue. Polly had not known that her father was appearing on a TV quiz show the night before. According to Sue, he had won £125,000.

'He's always been good at general knowledge.' Polly's nail polish was chipped and there was no time to redo it.

'I couldn't bear the thought of that woman getting her hands on all that money.'

'But what did you do exactly?' Polly rummaged in her bag for her make-up and squinted at herself in the mirror. As usual, she had a newsprint smear on her nose.

'I drove to their house. They weren't in, of course. I suppose they were out celebrating. They certainly had something to celebrate when they got home.'

'What did you do?'

'Not much. I just smashed a few windows, drove the car over a rhododendron bush and left a pair of pulverised garden gnomes on the doorstep.'

Polly couldn't help giggling and it smudged her mascara on to her cheek.

'Mum, don't you think you've gone a bit far?'

'Not far enough,' said Sue. 'I wish I'd got inside and ripped those rose-coloured curtains to shreds.' The remark made Polly remember the time she had destroyed Adele's clothes. She knew what it was to feel that angry. She had been justified in her anger and so, perhaps, was Sue but it was an ugly feeling.

'Poor you, Mum,' she said. 'I wish I could come down to Dulwich tonight but . . .' She hesitated as she sprayed Ralph Lauren perfume on her neck. 'I'm sorry, I'm doing something I can't get out of.'

It was a lie, of course, thought Polly, but why should she give up dinner with Charles to spend the evening nursing her hate-filled mother?

'Don't worry,' said Sue. 'I'll be OK. In fact, I feel much better now.' Polly put down the phone. She did not feel better for the conversation with Sue. The thought of her mother rampaging around the Essex countryside vandalising her father's property made her feel rather sick.

'What's up?' asked Carslip when Polly bumped into him on the stairs.

'Nothing,' said Polly, forcing a smile. With Adele in New York and Polly being single again, she had potentially the hottest date of her life ahead of her but the harsh tone of Sue's voice still rang in her ears. If there was anything worse than turning into Adele, thought Polly, it was the prospect of turning into her mother.

Chapter Thirty-Four

It was the first time Polly had been to Browns on Islington Green. Charles was just getting out of a taxi as she arrived.

'Christ,' he said. 'It's really freezing.' He paid off the driver and they hurried inside the restaurant.

They stood at the bar still wearing their coats and rubbing their hands.

'Very cute,' observed the barman.

Charles and Polly looked blank.

'Your coats,' said the barman. 'They match.'

Charles and Polly looked at each other. He was right – they were wearing very similar long black coats.

'Are all the clothes you're wearing identical to your partner's?' he asked Charles with a grin.

Charles and Polly laughed.

'I hope not,' said Charles but he did not correct the man's assumption that they were partners.

Later at the Granita they had warmed up and the waitress took their coats.

Polly was wearing her favourite blue dress, the one that Ned had helped her to sew up six months earlier.

But Polly was slimmer than ever now and the dress fitted beautifully.

'You look fantastic,' said Charles when they had ordered their food.

'Thanks,' said Polly.

Charles was giving her the benefit of his full-powered attention. Normally it would have made her light-headed but Polly felt oddly detached.

They talked of the usual things, their work and the latest politics. Then they drifted on to the subject of Adele. Polly listened as Charles said how Adele was forever trying to control him, that she was obsessed with Araminta and would not contemplate having another baby.

'I'm not sure I want another child now, anyway,' said Charles.

'I always thought you and Adele were the perfect couple,' said Polly.

'We were.' Charles put his fork down and looked at Polly. 'She was so self-confident and independent, so un-needy, but she's changed. The other day, I asked her to book a restaurant for us to go out with some friends and she rang me back later to say she wasn't sure where we should go. I had to choose for her.'

'Hardly an onerous task.'

'Yes, but it's so unlike Adele. She's becoming quite pathetic when she used to be, well, just the way you are now.'

'Me?'

'Yes, you used to be a timid little thing moping about in search of Mr Right. But now you are a successful self-assured young woman and you have everything you want.'

Polly laughed and shook her head. 'Hardly,' she said.

'No, really. You're just how Adele was when I first met her.'

Polly shivered.

'Perhaps that's why you turn me on so much,' added Charles, reaching across the table to touch her hand. Polly let his hand rest there but her stomach was twisting in knots. She had a curious sense that they were acting out a scene that had happened many, many times before. With her other hand, she picked up her glass and drank some more wine.

Charles insisted on Armagnac after dinner and, when they stepped back out into the cold winter air, Polly felt slightly pissed.

Charles did not ask her back to Noel Road with him but they walked in that direction and Polly did not object.

The house was in darkness when they arrived but Charles did not switch on the lights. As soon as they were inside, he took Polly in his arms and kissed her. The kiss nearly knocked her off her feet. It was full of the old passion she remembered still.

They stood together in the hall for some time together kissing, Charles running his hands all over her. Polly felt she should say something but no words came. They stumbled through to the drawing room and on to the sofa. Charles was fumbling with the back of Polly's dress and, at last, managed to pull it down to her waist.

'My God,' he said. 'I'd forgotten how magnificent your breasts are.'

Polly felt things were moving too fast. She pulled

the dress back up and sat up. 'Charles, I'm not sure we—'

'Don't be crazy, Polly,' said Charles. 'I know you want me as much as I want you.'

'Yes but what about—'

'What about what?'

'Adele.'

'Forget Adele.' Charles propped himself up on one elbow, took off his wedding ring and threw it across the room. 'Does that help?' he asked but Polly suddenly felt quite nauseous.

Charles was lying on top of her and she could feel the great rock of his penis digging into her groin. It was true that she wanted him and she could not help enjoying the thought of what Adele would say if she could see her with Charles, making out on her own sofa.

She slipped her hand inside Charles's trousers. Whatever happened, she had to feel that penis again just to check that she had not imagined it, that it really was as huge as she remembered.

Charles groaned as her fingers touched him. It was true, thought Polly. She could still not get her hand right round it. It was as big, possibly bigger, than she remembered.

'I can't,' she said, pulling out her hand and heaving Charles off her.

'Don't be crazy, Polly,' said Charles putting his hand between her thighs. 'I swear I've never had such good sex as the sex we used to have together.'

Polly wanted to believe this.

'Do you really mean that?'

'Of course,' said Charles and she let him move his hand up under her pants.

Suddenly the phone began to ring and Polly jumped away from Charles. It was a relief to be disturbed, she thought. It was maddening that she could not just relax and let this thing happen, this thing that she had dreamt about and wanted so much for so many years.

'Aren't you going to answer it?' she asked as Charles stayed motionless beside her.

'No,' he said. The answerphone was on and they listened as the caller started to leave a message. It was Adele. 'Fuck.' Charles jumped to his feet. 'I'd better take it.' He ran up the stairs and took the call on an extension.

Polly straightened her clothes. She needed to go to the loo so she went to the bathroom downstairs. As she was returning, she passed the bedroom that belonged to the au pair. Polly knew that the girl had been given time off while Minty was away and she could not resist having a peek inside the room.

What she saw made her shiver with horror. There were three framed photographs on the bedside table. Two were of Charles alone and one was of Charles with his arm around a young girl – almost certainly the au pair, thought Polly.

She went back up the stairs and switched on the drawing room lights. Charles was waiting for her. He got up, switched off the lights again and pulled her into his arms.

Outside in the dark a man stood watching the house in Noel Road. He pulled his jacket tight around him and smoked a cigarette. He had hung about outside the Granita for an hour waiting for Charles and Polly to emerge. He had followed them back to the house and waited for fifteen minutes while the house remained in total darkness.

When he saw the lights come on in the drawing room, he decided to leave. It had not taken them long, he thought to himself. After a few steps, he turned back to face the house and then yelled at the top of his voice, 'Slut. Bastard. Fucking slut.' It did not make him feel better.

'What was that?' asked Polly as she struggled to push Charles away

'Nothing. Just some old drunk,' said Charles, taking her face in his hands.

Polly pulled herself free. 'I'm sorry, Charles. But I can't.'

'Why not? Because of Adele?'

'Yes.' Then she thought again. 'Well, no actually.' Polly grabbed her coat and bag from the floor. 'Just – because I don't want to.'

She got to the front door before Charles could reach her and opened it. She could see that Charles was angry.

'I don't understand you,' he said. 'I don't understand women at all. It strikes me you don't know what you want.'

'Maybe not,' said Polly, suddenly feeling very angry herself. 'Perhaps you've kept me waiting in your harem just a little too long, that's all.'

Charles closed the door and Polly ran down the street, tears streaming down her face. Not until the following morning did she realise she had been wearing Charles's coat.

Chapter Thirty-Five

Polly stopped running when she got to Upper Street. There was no bus in sight and she wanted to keep moving so she started to walk. She ended up walking all the way home. It took forty minutes but it gave her the space she needed to think through what had just happened or not happened.

At first, she thought she must be going mad. She had had Charles simply throwing himself at her and she had rejected him. If they had gone to bed together it would have been the start of an affair. Would Charles have left Adele for her? It might have been worth a try, she thought, so why had she bottled out at the last minute?

It was not out of loyalty to Adele, she told herself as she made her way round Highbury Corner. That was absolutely clear. There was no reason why she should not treat Adele in exactly the same way her sister had treated her. So what had happened? She could hardly believe that she might have changed her mind about Charles, that she might have started to doubt whether he really was the man she wanted. It seemed ridiculous. Other than Hubert – and Hubert was different – she had scarcely looked at or thought about another man since her relationship with Charles. She had wanted to win him back so badly.

Eventually Polly arrived home.

'Don't worry,' said a voice behind her, 'I've got a key.' Polly had been fumbling in her bag and turned to see Zeta.

'You're late,' said Polly.

'I've been helping at the town hall with the Wednesday night shelter they run for the homeless.'

'God, I didn't know you did that. It must be, well, pretty challenging sometimes?'

'Yes. But most of the people I see there look in better shape than you do right now.' Zeta put an arm round Polly. 'Have you been crying?'

Polly nodded and allowed her friend to take her into the kitchen and make a cup of tea.

'Better make it two extra spoonfuls of sugar?' asked Zeta.

Polly nodded again. Zeta was so kind; she was like the sister Polly had always wanted.

'Do you want to talk about it?'

Polly shook her head and the two women sat together in silence for half an hour while they drank their tea. Zeta said nothing but she held Polly's hand and it was a great comfort.

When Polly eventually went up to bed she felt slightly better. She slept well but in the morning awoke with a single unthinkable question burning in her head. Was it possible that she had fallen out of love with Charles?

The bus was a long time coming and it was still very cold the following morning. Polly put her hands in her pockets and it was then that she realised she must be wearing Charles's coat. The pockets of her own coat had huge holes so she hardly ever used them but these ones had no holes. They contained some small change, a couple of taxi receipts and a letter.

Polly looked at the letter, which was still in its envelope. It was handwritten, marked Personal and addressed to Charles Goodwood at Green Baby. She stuffed it back inside the pocket, her heart beating madly.

It would be totally wrong to read Charles's private mail but the letter seemed to be burning a hole in her side as she put out her hand for the bus. Polly had hardly got on and sat down before she took it out again.

She studied the envelope. There was a London postmark dated a few days earlier and the handwriting was a round loopy style. It just had to be from a woman.

Dear Plump-horn, she read and her whole body froze. Dear Plump-horn. Dear Plump-horn! The name could only have been derived from one thing.

Polly shoved the letter back in her pocket but it was out again a few seconds later. She could hardly bear to read on but she could not bear to stop reading either.

It was so wonderful to see you last night. So kind of you to take me out to celebrate my engagement to Ben. Polly relaxed a little. Perhaps she was overreacting. Why shouldn't Charles have female friends? She was probably an ex-girlfriend but it was a bit silly to allow her to go on calling him Plump-horn. She read on.

Ever since, I have been wondering whether I am doing the right thing. Polly shivered. *I am sorry that you are having a difficult time with your wife. I hope the little bit of therapy I provided was some help*. Therapy, thought Polly. What the fuck does she mean by 'therapy'? But it was to become clear in the next sentence. *Is it really true that the best sex you have ever had is with me?*

'The bastard,' cried Polly out loud and a pair of middle-aged women in front of her turned to stare. She went back to the letter.

I tried calling you at the office but couldn't get you. Of course not, you poor fool, thought Polly. He'd got what he wanted from you and was on to the next target already. 'And who was that?' asked a tiny voice in Polly's head. The writer of this letter would have been trying to reach Charles just around the time he was arranging his date with Polly. She felt quite sick at the thought but read on.

I'm sorry to write – I know I promised not to – but I need to know how you are feeling. I don't want to marry Ben and regret it for the rest of my life. How many lives had this bastard wrecked, wondered Polly. How many women did he need to have pining their lives away for him? The letter was signed *Plump-bum*. There was a whole row of kisses underneath.

Polly folded up the letter and put it back in the pocket of Charles's coat. For the first time in her life, the thought of Charles disgusted her. She took off the coat. Although it was bitterly cold, she would rather freeze than wear his clothes – clothes that he had worn countless times while chasing after other women.

The bus reached her stop and Polly got off. There was a waste bin nearby and she was tempted to drop the coat in it but then she saw a young woman huddled in a blanket in a doorway and changed her mind.

'Would you like this?' asked Polly.

The young woman looked surprised. Polly could see her weighing up the coat. It was a heavy expensive-looking garment with a satin lining.

'Are you sure?' she asked.

Polly nodded and the woman got up and let her blanket fall to her feet. It was only then that Polly realised how young and thin she was.

'My boyfriend let me down. He told me to come to London and he'd take care of me but he got fed up with me and I can't bear to go home.'

Polly checked the rest of the pockets. They were empty. Then she helped the girl into the coat.

'Your boyfriend's name wasn't Charles Goodwood by any chance?' she asked.

The girl looked at Polly blankly.

'Don't worry,' said Polly. 'A private joke.' Was it a joke? Was it already a joke, she wondered: this futile obsession that had ruled her life for so many years.

The girl did up the buttons. The coat swamped her and came down to her ankles but she looked delighted.

'Thank you so much.'

'A pleasure,' said Polly, shivering slightly. She was beginning to feel very cold. She said goodbye to the girl and ran the rest of the way to her office. By the time she arrived, she felt quite exhilarated. She had given away the coat and it felt as though she had given away the burden of wanting Charles. A burden she had been carrying for far too long.

She knew that she was no longer in love with him. In fact, the more she thought about it, the more convinced she became that she had not been in love with Charles for some time. Why had she wanted him

376

back so much? Was it just the mysterious hold that Charles seemed to wield over his women or was it something else?

Polly got to her desk and smiled when she saw the message waiting for her. It was from Charles. He was probably shitting himself about losing his coat with *that* letter inside it.

Let him sweat, she thought. He'll be in such a sweat, he won't need his damned coat.

Polly worked hard all day and enjoyed refusing to take Charles's calls which came at ever closer intervals.

It was only when she got home later that evening that the high she had been on began to crash down around her. She had wasted so much of her life. Would she have married Hubert if she had not wanted to spite Charles and Adele? Why, she wondered. Why? The more she thought about it, the clearer became the answer. She would probably have got over Charles years ago, her life might have moved in a totally different direction. She might have married a man she loved and been happy. It was a hard truth to face but it was no longer possible to deny. She had *only* wanted to win Charles in order to get even with Adele.

Polly's first instinct was to call Ned. She wanted to tell him everything that had happened, what she had learnt about herself and how stupid she had been. But Ned's mobile switched straight to voicemail. She left a message and then made some coffee.

Before she went to bed, she must have tried Ned's number at least ten times. But either Ned was not around or he refused to return her calls.

Chapter Thirty-Six

'Give her a jam roll and make it a fat one,' ordered
Carslip.

Polly and Olga giggled. They were having lunch
at the counter in Sweetings, where they had been
celebrating Carslip's promotion to Political Editor.
They had drunk a lot of champagne and eaten crab
sandwiches followed by jam rolls and custard for
pudding.

Polly scraped her bowl clean and rashly stated that
the jam rolls were so good at this restaurant, she could
eat four of them.

'I'll bet you a fiver you can't even get through a
second,' Carslip had challenged.

'No problem,' Polly had said. 'But it will have to
be a tenner.'

She ate the pudding comfortably if a little slower
than she had eaten the first.

'There,' she said triumphantly and put out her hand
for the money.

'Double or quits, you can't eat another,' he said.

'Twenty?'

Carslip nodded. Olga shook her head but Polly
accepted the challenge.

The third roll was a struggle but Polly was determined. She was bright pink in the face by the time she finished and Olga gave her a glass of water.

'Fifty or quits, if you manage the fourth,' persisted Carslip.

'She'll be sick,' said Olga.

'Exactly,' said Carslip. He dug in his pocket and produced two twenty-pound notes and a tenner. 'Your eyes are bigger than your tum, Polly,' he laughed. 'You'd never eat another.'

Polly rose immediately to the bait. She put Carslip's money on the table and asked the waitress for another jam roll.

By the time Polly got back to the office she felt so hot it was like her skin was on fire. Her blood was loaded with sugar and she felt as though she could run a marathon.

'I'll take the stairs,' she said to Olga, who waited for the lift.

'Are you sure you're OK?' said Carslip.

'Well, I've gained fifty pounds,' said Polly.

'Yes, probably around the hips by tomorrow morning,' laughed Olga.

'I hope not. I'm flying to New York in the morning – I'll have to pay a surcharge for the excess weight.'

'I hope the interview goes well,' said Olga.

'Sheila says it's in the bag but she said that last time,' said Polly. 'So, don't, for heaven's sake, breathe a word to Den. As I explained to you both at Sweetings, my sister fucked me over on *Mujer* and she's quite capable of doing the same thing again.'

Olga crossed her heart and got into the lift. Carslip
said he would take the stairs with Polly.

'Er, Polly,' he said as they reached the top of the
first flight. 'There's something I've been meaning to
tell you.'

'Yes?'

'It wasn't just the Hubert set-up, you know.'

'What do you mean?'

'There was something else I did to get back
at you.'

'That's all history,' said Polly. Since Carslip's confession in the hospital, he and Polly had become quite
good friends.

'No, when I heard you blaming your sister for the
Mujer thing I knew I had to tell you—'

'Tell me what?'

'Well, it wasn't Adele.'

'What do you mean it wasn't Adele?' cried Polly.

'It wasn't Adele who told *Mujer* about your CV.'

'But she was the only person who knew!'

'No. I knew,' interrupted Carslip. 'Adele let slip to
me – ages ago – that you only passed one A level.
That time I bumped into her at Le Caprice.'

'I can't believe this,' said Polly as they continued
to pant up the stairs.

'I'd interviewed you for the *Globe* myself so I'd seen
your CV and knew what it said. I decided that De
wouldn't have given a toss if I'd drawn it to his
attention. So I decided to wait until I could use the
information to the most damaging effect.'

'You bastard.'

'I'm sorry. I hoped that you'd get this new job
with MPC and I need never admit what really

happened but when I realised you were blaming your sister—'

'Christ, and to think I went to Stratton's and nearly tore her hair out in the middle of one of her meetings.'

'Sorry.'

'Well, thanks for telling me,' said Polly as they reached the fourth floor where her office was.

Carslip continued up another flight to Politics. So it had not been Adele who had stuffed her on *Mujer* after all. Polly was pleased to know this but also horrified. She wanted – needed – every reason to hate her sister and she would fight the temptation to think any better of her. Adele was still as unforgivable as ever.

Back at her desk, Polly found that her mother had phoned and she returned the call. Sue was upset and wanted to talk but Polly felt so agitated and energised by both Carslip's confession and all those jam rolls that she could not sit still.

'I'll call you back this evening,' said Polly. 'We can have a proper chat. In the meantime, why don't you try calling Adele?'

'Oh, she has enough of her own problems,' said Sue. *And I don't?* Polly felt like saying but didn't. She let her mother go and got to her feet. She was so full of sugar that she did not know what to do with herself.

'Want a lift?' called Den as Polly left the office that evening. He was just leaving himself and his driver was waiting in a car outside.

'Thanks, Den. But I have to run.'

'It'll be quicker by car wherever you're off to.'

'Yes,' laughed Polly. 'But I have to run *literally*.'

She grinned at her boss and ran out of the door Den watched her jog all the way down the road.

Polly was still running when she got to Highbury She was dripping with sweat and exhausted but she was amazed that she had managed it. A few years ago, she would hardly have been able to run for a bus without getting totally breathless.

'Impressive,' said the man who opened the door of Zeta's house.

'Hubert,' cried Polly. 'What are you doing here?'

'I dropped off a few of your things this morning Zeta let me in and we had lunch together. She's a really nice woman.'

'Yes,' said Polly.

'Since I'd taken the day off, I thought I might a well hang around and wait until you got back.'

It was the first time Polly had seen Hubert since she had moved out. It felt strange but good to se him again.

'How have you been?' she asked.

'Struggling along.'

'No major disasters?'

'No more than usual.'

They stood looking at each other for a moment.

'You look more beautiful than ever,' said Hubert

'I must look a state,' laughed Polly. She wa nervous about what Hubert would do next. Did h regret their decision? Did he want to try to patc things up?

He took her in his arms and, childlike, Polly burie her head in his shoulder while he hugged her an kissed her on the top of her head.

'I thought we might go for a drink and something to eat, perhaps,' he said. 'I wanted to make sure you're OK.'

'I'm fine.' Polly stepped back and looked up at her husband. 'I'd love to go for a drink – but, please, promise you won't make me eat any jam rolls.'

Polly had a shower and changed and then she and Hubert walked up to an Italian restaurant on Highbury Hill called San Daniele.

Polly was a regular and the manager gave them a big table by the window.

'Where did you go for lunch with Zeta?' asked Polly.

'She took me to some New Age cafe,' said Hubert.

'That sounds exciting.'

'The menu was subdivided according to blood groups. I'm blood group AB and that means I can only eat lentils, bean sprouts and red wine.'

'Lucky you,' laughed Polly.

'As you can imagine, it was quite a liquid lunch,' said Hubert. 'But fun. A trendy young couple were sharing our table. The woman actually recognised me and asked me what I thought about that minister who has just resigned after being caught with his trousers down on Hampstead Heath.'

'What did you say?'

'Well, I said I thought it was very funny – particularly the way it happened. Imagine having to go to hospital because a kid's remote control paraglider had come down and wedged itself in your backside.'

'The sort of thing I thought could only happen to you, Hubert,' laughed Polly.

'Yes. I said to this woman that the experience must have put him off buggery for life. She said nothing and I felt terrible later when Zeta told me I'd been talking to the local vicar and her husband.'

They ordered their food and drank some wine. Polly had a green salad while Hubert tucked into a giant calzone.

'So what have you been up to, now that you are a single woman again?' asked Hubert.

'Nothing much,' said Polly. She had seen Den a couple of times but, since she had decided to put Charles out of her head, she had realised that her social life was virtually non-existent.

'I saw Ned the other night,' said Hubert.

'Ned?' Polly put down her fork. She had been trying to get hold of Ned for nearly two weeks with no success. 'I didn't know you knew Ned.'

'I don't really,' said Hubert. 'I've met him a couple of times at the odd party.'

'How did you come to see him?'

'He called me. He asked to meet.'

'Why?'

Hubert stopped eating and stared at Polly. 'You, of course. He wanted to talk about you.'

'Me?'

'You sound surprised.'

'I am,' said Polly. Why on earth would Ned want to talk about Polly with Hubert?

'He said you'd been trying to get hold of him and he really didn't want to see you or even speak to you. But he wanted to check you were OK.'

'Why won't he see me or speak to me? We've been friends for years. I know that last time w

384

met we had a bit of a row but he can't still be angry.'

'I don't think he's angry,' said Hubert. 'I think he's in love with you.'

'What?'

'I think he's in love with you.'

'What do you mean? What did he say?' Polly felt confused. How could Ned be in love with her? He wasn't interested in women – well, not seriously – and certainly not women like her. He'd always said he never wanted commitment. Had she been blind with respect to Ned as well as Charles?

'Well, he was extremely rude about you,' said Hubert. 'He said you were the most selfish stupid person he knew.'

'And you conclude he's in love with me?'

'Passionately.'

Polly gave up with her salad and sipped some wine. Hubert was being ridiculous, of course, but surely Ned must care if he went to the trouble of going to see Hubert just to talk about her.

'By the way, he left this book behind – by mistake.' Hubert passed a battered half-read paperback across the table. Marking place in the middle was the remains of a lollipop. Polly almost wept when she saw it.

'Or, perhaps he wanted to give you a good excuse to try seeing him again?'

'What?'

'To return the book.'

Polly said nothing and Hubert finished off the last mouthful of his supper. He wiped his mouth with his napkin and looked at Polly.

'Don't you want to see him?' he asked.

'Ned?' said Polly. 'Yes, I'd like to see him very much.'

'Well, he also just let slip that he is doing his last session of clown doctoring tomorrow afternoon at the Royal Free in Hampstead. I think he hoped I might pass the information on.'

'Shit,' said Polly. 'I'm flying to New York for an interview with the Chief Executive of MPC tomorrow. There's no way I can reschedule it.'

Hubert shrugged. 'Only you know what it is you want most in life.'

It was late when Polly started to pack and then she realised that she had not called her mother.

'Mum?'

'Oh Polly, is that you?' Sue's voice sounded thick and drowsy.

'Were you asleep?'

'No, it's OK.'

'I can call back in the morning.'

'No, thanks for ringing,' said Sue. 'I took a few sleeping pills an hour ago but, even after half a bottle of vodka, I can't sleep.'

'What's the matter? What's wrong?'

'It's John and that woman. They're suing me for the damage I did the other night.'

'How can they prove it was you?' asked Polly.

'I left a note. Telling them to go to hell.'

'And signed it?'

'It's my handwriting, on the back of an envelope addressed to me. It was the only thing I could find to write on.'

'Mum, that was stupid.'

'Oh, what the hell,' said Sue. 'It will be a criminal prosecution if it goes ahead. I could even go to jail.'

'I doubt it,' said Polly. 'Given the circumstances and it's a first offence.'

'That's what Joyce said. I had a drink with her tonight and told her all about it.'

'Did that cheer you up a bit?' asked Polly.

'Not really. You know, I've known Joyce a long time and she'd never told me how she and Kevin broke up. I'd always assumed that he left her for someone else the way she goes on about how dreadful men are.'

'And?'

'It was her.'

'How do you mean?'

'Well, first, she had an affair with Kev's boss which ended up costing him his job. Then she had an affair with one of the kid's teachers which ended up wrecking the teacher's career and then she had an affair with her daughter's teenage boyfriend.'

'God, you'd never believe it. I mean, Joyce.'

'Yes, it's amazing. And Kev stuck by her through it all until the last affair when he decided he'd had enough.'

'You can hardly blame him,' said Polly.

'I felt so betrayed,' said Sue.

'What do you mean?'

'By Joyce. We were such close friends. I used to worry about silly little things I didn't tell her and all the time she had kept quiet about these really big things.'

Polly said nothing.

'I drove him away,' Sue continued.

'Dad?'

'Yes. He wasn't so bad really. I could have forgiven him.'

Chapter Thirty-Seven

That night, for the first time, Polly slept with Ned. He held her in his arms and kissed her and then suddenly Charles arrived. He slipped into bed on the other side of Polly and Ned just got up quietly and disappeared.

It was only a dream but it was vivid and frightening and when Polly woke up she immediately reached for her phone.

There were three missed calls and two of them were Adele calling from her mobile.

It was a long time since Polly had spoken to her sister and she wondered what she wanted now. Perhaps she had found out about the night Polly had spent with Charles or, more accurately, the night she had not spent with Charles. Polly did not return the calls. Although it was only seven thirty in the morning, there was really no time to lose if she had any hope of doing what she wanted to do before she had to leave for the airport.

She grabbed her bag and left the house. She rushed back twice – first for her passport and then for her ticket. She was in such a panic that she did not notice the small figure in a long black coat who watched her from the other side of the road.

Polly was panting for breath by the time she got to Arsenal station. Her bag was heavy and it had been hard to walk quickly. The Piccadilly line went all the way to Heathrow but Polly changed at King's Cross. She needed to get to Blackfriars first.

The flat Polly was looking for was a five-minute walk along the river from the tube. It was in a modern ugly block in the shadow of the Tate Modern and she was so intent on locating it that she would not have noticed if someone were following her.

'Polly.' The man who opened the door was still dazed with sleep. Polly hardly recognised him. It was as though she saw him for the first time in her life. He was tall, almost head and shoulders taller than she was. His hair was thick, dark and rumpled, his eyes a penetrating blue beneath a puzzled frown. There was dark stubble around his chin which he rubbed with his hand.

'I had to see you,' said Polly. 'Sorry.'

'Sorry?'

'Yes. I'm really sorry about the last time we met.'

'It's OK, forget it,' said Ned. He glanced over his shoulder. 'I'd ask you to come in but the place is a tip and my flatmate is still asleep.'

'Who is it?' called a sleepy voice. A female voice, noticed Polly with a pang of horror. It was only then that she realised how much she wanted Ned, how much she loved him. The thought of him being with another woman was unbearable. She had taken him totally for granted, always assuming that he would be around when she needed him.

'Give me a minute and we'll go and have breakfast. There's a caff just round the corner.'

'Thanks.'

'I'll just explain to Sarita what I'm up to.'

Ned shut the door and left Polly on the doorstep.

Polly closed her eyes. She could picture Sarita lying naked in Ned's bed – the place where she should be, could have been, herself. How could she have been so stupid? If Hubert was right, Ned had been in love with her for a long time. It must have driven him crazy the way she had always been banging on about Charles. It was no wonder that he had given up on her.

No one could be expected to wait around forever. And now it seemed that Ned had a girlfriend. It was too late.

She fished in her bag for a mirror and quickly examined her face. She looked tired and pale and she had smudged her mascara.

'Give me your bag and let's go,' said Ned, re-emerging and slamming the door behind him. He was wearing the same black leather jacket that he always wore. He took Polly's bag and slung it over his shoulder and they walked off side by side.

In the cafe, they sat down at a heavily scratched pink formica table top. The room was empty except for a woman in black who sat at a table in the far corner, her back to them. Ned ordered coffee and a full English breakfast.

'But no beans,' he added.

'I'll just have coffee,' said Polly. 'A cappuccino, please.'

'That's a first,' laughed Ned.

'What?'

'The first time I've been out with you when you haven't eaten more than me.'

Polly smiled. 'You make me sound like a pig.'

'Not at all. Most women are afraid to eat a thing so it makes a pleasant change.'

The coffee arrived and they sipped it.

Polly wanted to blurt out her feelings but she kept thinking of Sarita and waited for Ned to say something that might confirm Hubert's assumption, that might encourage her to believe she had a chance with him.

But Ned talked only about work. He asked about life at the *Globe* and Polly told him about the job opportunity in New York. Then Ned told Polly that he had been asked to do another rewrite of his script, the one that the Hollywood production company was still interested in.

'We could both end up working in the States if all goes well,' said Ned. 'Same country – only two thousand miles apart.'

Polly said nothing and Ned, who had finished eating, got up and paid the bill. She glanced at her watch. It was nearly five to ten and she was running out of time.

'The Tate Modern opens in five minutes,' said Ned. 'Have you got time for a wander?'

'OK,' said Polly, 'but I have to leave for the airport by ten thirty.'

The galleries were empty. They looked at some photographs of a naked man posing with a banana protruding from various orifices. It was either funny or disgusting or both.

They laughed.

'Look at this,' said Ned. It was a large trunk overflowing with soiled underwear and labelled 'All My Fucking and Shagging'.

'I think I would only need a shoe box,' said Polly. But Ned said nothing.

They moved on.

'So, how exactly did you track me down?' he asked.

'Frankie,' said Polly.

'Frankie.'

'I had to bribe him outrageously.'

'But I made him promise not to tell you.'

'You can always count on your siblings to betray you.'

Ned walked on.

'But why?' said Polly running to catch him up. 'Why have you been avoiding me?'

Ned turned to face her. 'Oh, you know, Polly.'

'I don't.' I don't, I really don't, thought Polly. You have to tell me, Ned. You have to tell me you love me. That Hubert was right and that I've been a fool for so long—

But Ned had moved on again. He was now examining a huge metal tent in the Structures for Survival area. His shoulders were broad and strong and his hands, as he raised them and clasped the back of his neck, were beautiful. Polly wanted to reach out and touch him but didn't dare. Somehow this man, who had once been so familiar – almost like a brother – now seemed detached and unattainable. He was almost like an exhibit himself. He had been her Structure for Survival for years but she had never realised it.

'We've been friends a long time,' said Ned. 'But I suppose I started to think about you differently.'

'How do you mean?' asked Polly, her heart beating fast. A woman drifted past them and hovered outside the doorway but Polly only saw Ned.

393

'It doesn't matter.'

'It does matter. Tell me,' said Polly desperately.

'How are things getting along between you and Charles?'

'Charles? What things?' It seemed an eternity now since she had been in love with Charles.

'Really, Polly. You don't need to pretend with me.'

'I'm not pretending,' said Polly. 'There is nothing going on between me and Charles and never will be. I hate Charles. I wish I'd never set eyes on him.'

Ned laughed and walked over to the next exhibit. Polly followed.

'Listen,' she said. 'I've been stupid about Charles, really stupid. I don't love him and haven't loved him for years.'

'Oh yes. And when did you work that out? Before you got him into bed or afterwards?'

Polly winced at the harshness of the words and their delivery. 'I don't know what you mean.'

'You do.'

Polly felt hot. There was a large white igloo thing beside her and she leant on it for support. A schoolboy was sitting beside it sorting through his packed lunch.

'I know about your date with Charles while Adele and Minty were in Paris. Don't tell me nothing happened.'

'Nothing happened. I swear it. Nothing happened.'

Ned looked at her and, for a moment, Polly thought that he was going to believe her.

Then there was a tap on Polly's shoulder.

'Please. It is not for leaning – the exhibits,' said a slim East European man wearing a Tate Modern T-shirt.

Polly put her weight back on her feet and took a step closer to Ned.

'Did you go back to Noel Road with him after dinner?' he asked.

Polly felt sick in every part of her body. She wanted Ned more than anything in the world. She wanted him to take her in his arms and kiss her the way he had done that one time.

'Tell me, Polly,' insisted Ned. 'Did you go back to Noel Road with him?'

Polly knew that there was no choice. She could not avoid it. The truth was that she had not slept with Charles Goodwood and so she lied.

'No,' she said.

Ned's face froze and he glared at her in fury. 'You disgust me, Polly.'

'For Christ's sake,' said Polly. 'You don't understand. I did not sleep with Charles.'

'Don't lie to me.' Ned turned to go.

'I'm not lying,' said Polly, running after him. 'Anyway, why does it matter?' she yelled. 'I mean, even if I had slept with Charles, why does it matter?' She was desperate to prevent Ned from leaving and even arguing was better than that.

'Because he's married to your fucking sister,' shouted Ned.

Polly said nothing. She had wanted him to say because he had not wanted her to, because he loved her.

'But that doesn't matter does it?' continued Ned. 'Because you are just as bad, just as low grade as your fucking sister.'

The attack hurt but Polly fought back. 'Why is it so

important to you? You've got what you want – your oh so precious bloody career and some, some floozie in your bed.' Floozie, thought Polly to herself. Why on earth had she said floozie? Why on earth was she saying these things when all she really wanted to do was to tell Ned that she loved him?

'Floozie?'

'Oh, don't give me all that flatmate stuff again,' said Polly. She had not realised just how jealous she had been when she heard that female voice coming from inside the flat.

'Sarita is a very nice girl,' said Ned. 'And yes, she is, I'm happy to say, sleeping in my bed. But she's not my fucking sister-in-law.'

With that, he dumped Polly's bag on top of a stack of packing cases. Polly wanted to make him stay but could think of nothing to say or do.

'Excuse me, madam.' It was the smiling East European again. Polly looked round. 'Your bag – it is on the exhibit.'

Polly glanced at the bag hanging over the edge of the packing cases. The boy with the packed lunch was still close and Polly saw that he had spread his food all over the floor. There were sandwiches, crisps and – a banana.

Polly strode across the room and grabbed the banana. She waved it in the museum attendant's face.

'If you have trouble working out where to stuff this perhaps I can refer you to one of the exhibits on the ground floor?'

The young man looked surprised but obediently took the banana that was held out to him.

Polly then turned to find Ned but he had already

disappeared. She was stunned for a moment. How could he be so sure that she had lied about Noel Road? She ran to the door of the gallery but she knew it was too late. The attendant was pursuing her with her bag and the boy pursued the attendant in the hope of recovering his lunch.

Polly took the bag from the attendant and, in turn, the attendant gave the banana back to the little boy. Order was restored, thought Polly, as she limped miserably away. She had forgotten how heavy her bag was. There was no chance that she would catch Ned now.

Polly looked at her watch and saw it was nearly quarter to eleven. She would have to hurry if she was to get to the airport in time but she felt exhausted. She staggered on to the escalator almost knocking over the frail-looking woman who had been hovering in the gallery doorway but still she did not recognise her.

Polly made her way back to Blackfriars and hailed a taxi. MPC had offered to reimburse her expenses so she might as well make the most of it, she reasoned. She slumped into her seat and closed her eyes. How could she have played things so badly with Ned? But what did it matter? Even if she could get Ned to forgive her, she now knew that he already had a girlfriend and she had missed her chance.

It was too depressing. She had spent the best years of her life, all her twenties, pining for a man who turned out to be the biggest bastard that ever walked the planet. And, all the time, she might have been with Ned. Dear, beautiful, kind, gorgeous Ned – who now thought she was as much of a shit as her sister.

And was she? Polly was no longer so sure. She was glad she had become more assertive over the last few years but where was it getting her? If she was not careful, she would end up as solitary and sour as her mother.

Polly's mobile started to ring and she dug it out of her bag. It was Adele.

Chapter Thirty-Eight

A taxi drew up right behind Polly's taxi as she arrived at the airport. A woman got out of the second taxi and it was only then that Polly noticed her. She suddenly realised it was the same woman she had glimpsed several times that morning. But who was she? The woman had dark glasses and a hat and disappeared quickly into the terminal building. It seemed absurd, thought Polly, but the woman appeared to be following her.

Polly was still trying to digest the conversation she had just had with Adele as she paid off the driver.

'I'll be back on Friday,' Polly had said.

'That's too late,' said Adele. 'I need to see you now.'

'Why? What is it?'

'I can't explain on the phone.' Typical Adele, thought Polly. It was probably something trivial but she just expected Polly to drop everything and come to her aid. Well, she was not going to fall for it this time. She had worked hard and now had a brilliant job opportunity and she was not going to blow it for anyone, least of all Adele.

'Sorry, Adele,' she said. 'You'll have to sort out your problems yourself for once.' She flicked off the phone and then switched it off altogether. She was looking forward to getting on the plane, away from Adele and this strange stalker.

She went to the check-in desk glancing around her for the woman. She could not see her now and was beginning to think she was imagining the whole thing. Then suddenly she caught a glimpse of someone in a long black coat slipping out from behind a pillar and making for the Ladies.

Polly gasped. She did not recognise the woman but she recognised the coat. It was Charles's the one she had given away. The stalker must be that young beggar she had met.

'Aisle or window?' asked the woman behind the desk.

'What?'

'Aisle or window?' repeated the woman in a bored tone.

'Aisle,' said Polly.

A few minutes later she took her boarding pass and headed towards the departures gate. She had never felt so eager to get on a plane and escape.

Terminal Four was busy and a group of medical students dressed in surgical gowns were collecting for charity. They wore big pink hearts on their sleeves and had a banner that said HEARTS ARE NOT JUST FOR VALENTINE'S DAY. A few people were stopping to give money, but most seemed more interested in last-minute shopping in the smart shops that lined every walkway. There were branches of Hamley's, Harrods, the Sunglass Hut, the Caviar House, the Disney Store – the travellers who shopped here had plenty of money, thought Polly, as she put a pound coin in the tin, but they were not too keen to give it away.

Polly checked through Security and breathed a sigh of relief. She was just picking up her bag as it emerged from the scanner when she heard shouting. She turned and saw the woman in black running towards her at top speed, hurdling over obstacles and pushing passengers aside. Security men were in pursuit but the large group of medical students seemed to be in the way and had tripped them up.

Polly was alarmed. Who was this woman and what did she want from her? Was she going to attack her? Polly backed away as the woman approached and then gasped.

'Adele,' she said.

'I had to see you. I've been following you all morning but couldn't find the courage to speak to you – you've been so preoccupied.'

'What? Can't it wait? Have you gone mad?' Polly could see the security guards struggling with the students; one had a stethoscope caught up round his legs.

'I'm begging you,' said Adele. 'Please don't go. It's Minty.'

'Minty?' It was the first time Polly had ever heard Adele refer to her daughter as Minty.

Adele glanced behind her. The security men were free now and heading towards her. She did not have much time. Just as they were almost upon her, she threw off the coat and stood before Polly completely naked.

Everyone gasped and the security men stopped dead in their tracks.

'Gotta gotta,' said Adele. 'You've got to help me Polly.'

'Put this coat on and come with me,' said one of the security men picking up the coat and holding it at arm's length to Adele.

'It's not my coat,' said Adele.

'Whose is it then?' asked the man.

'Hers,' said Adele, nodding towards Polly.

'Is this your coat, madam?' asked the man.

Polly looked at the coat. 'Yes, I believe it is,' she said and took it from the man.

'Last call for all passengers for the 13.45 British Airways flight to New York – please make your way immediately to Gate Twelve.' Polly had only a few minutes before she would miss her flight.

'Can't it wait until I get back?' said Polly. 'This job is so important to me. I really want it and I won't get another chance.'

'Get something to put on this woman,' yelled the security man to his colleagues.

Adele stood there, white and frail. She had always been skinny but she seemed to have lost more weight than ever. Someone gave her a surgical gown and she wrapped it round herself. At last, the security guards felt comfortable about getting to grips with her.

Polly had seconds to make up her mind. She owed Adele nothing. In fact, it was her opportunity to teach her sister a lesson. Adele had behaved selfishly all her life, expecting her friends and family to drop everything and come running to her aid at a moment's notice.

'Final call for flight BA009 to New York. The flight is now boarding.'

The guards were starting to pull Adele away.

Polly would be back in London on Saturday morning. It was only three days and why should she sacrifice her job for Adele? Was there any way that Adele would do the same for her? And what had Adele meant about Minty? Was something wrong with Minty and, if so, how could Polly help? More likely, thought Polly, Adele was just using Minty to get her to stay. She knew that Polly would do anything for her niece.

It was classic Adele, absolutely fucking classic Adele. She had stolen Polly's boyfriend, she had totally messed up Polly's life and now she expected Polly to drop everything and help her.

Polly picked up her bag and shook her head at Adele. 'Sorry,' she said. 'Remember Beaumonts. Remember what you said when I said I really needed something.'

Adele started to cry. The tears flooded down her face and she fell to her knees. The security men half lifted her as they struggled to drag her away. A sticker fell from the gown she was wearing and Polly picked it up. It said 'Hearts are not just for Valentine's Day'.

Polly stuffed the sticker into her pocket and frowned as she watched Adele disappear. She had to get her own back on her sister, didn't she? After all, what was the alternative?

Chapter Thirty-Nine

The alternative, of course, was to forgive her. Not just to help her or to make another sacrifice for her but really to forgive her.

The thought surfaced slowly in Polly's mind as she trudged behind Adele and the security men back into the Departures lounge. She realised that she had been fighting her impulse to feel sorry for Adele for some time. It was obvious that Adele was in trouble, that she was deeply unhappy and needed help.

Her sister had done some terrible things, that was undeniable, thought Polly. They were terrible but were they *unforgivable*? Was anything really unforgivable?

She thought of the things Ned had said to her recently, that she was turning into Adele, that she was becoming selfish and uncaring. She thought of her mother and how she had been unable to forgive her father for the things he had done and how bitter and lonely Sue had become.

The idea of forgiving Adele seemed to take on a fresh perspective. It was no longer a defeat, a surrender. It was a chance to get on with her own life, at last. It was an opportunity to put down the burden of hate and vengeance she had carried with her for so long.

'She says you're her sister,' said one of the security men who walked beside Polly.

'Yes.'

'Some kind of mental breakdown, do you think?'

Polly nodded.

'Will you be taking her home?'

'Yes,' said Polly.

'Well, I don't think there's any point in keeping her here or pressing charges. But, if she comes back to the airport within the next twenty-four hours, we will arrest her on sight. Do you understand?'

'Yes.'

'I'll get one of my men to see you off the premises. How are you leaving?'

'We'll get a cab,' said Polly, glancing at Adele who sat on a bench shivering and still weeping in the thin green surgical gown, a security guard on either side of her.

'Doesn't she have any other clothes?' asked the man.

'I'll sort her out but we'll need to go the Ladies.'

'I'll get a female member of staff to go with you.'

They went to the Ladies that Polly had seen Adele disappear to while she had been checking in.

'I left my clothes in here,' said Adele and they were still there, folded neatly on a chair.

'We were wondering who they belong to,' said the lavatory attendant. 'I was just saying, "Who would just leave a Donna Karan T-shirt and a pair of Joseph trousers, like that?" Sadly they're much too small for me or I might have been tempted.'

'Thanks,' said Polly as she took the clothes from the

405

chair. The neat pile reminded her of the way Adele had folded her clothes the night after that dreadful day when she had stolen Charles. Polly had been so angry that she had cut them into shreds. Now she took the clothes gently and passed them to her sister.

'Do you need any help?' she asked but Adele shook her head and went into a cubicle to get dressed.

It was not until they were in the taxi and alone that Adele said thank you.

'I'm sorry, Polly. I really need you and no one else can help.'

'Tell me about it.'

'I hadn't realised how critical things were until last night.' Adele's fingers were trembling.

'Would you like a cigarette?' asked Polly.

'I don't smoke,' said Adele. 'Well, not often.'

'Neither do I. But I'm going to ask the driver to stop at the next newsagent.'

They bought cigarettes and a large box of tissues and got back in the cab. The driver insisted that they opened both windows but it was worth it.

'Thanks,' said Adele, taking a long drag on her cigarette. 'I feel like a naughty schoolgirl doing this.'

'Tell me what happened,' said Polly.

'They took Minty into hospital. Just for monitoring, they said, but I knew they were worried. She has lost so much weight and hardly eats a thing.'

Polly took Adele's hand. It was a long time since she had touched her sister and it felt strange but Adele held Polly's hand tightly.

'The nurse suggested that I should try feeding her She said sometimes it helps to spoon-feed yoghurt

"Do it just the way you used to feed her when she was a baby," she said. But Minty wouldn't open her mouth.'

'What did you do?'

'The nurse kept telling me to make a game of it – the way I'd fed her when she was little. Eventually I just cracked and told the woman that I hardly ever did feed her when she was a baby. I was too busy working and my sister brought my daughter up virtually night and day.'

Polly gave Adele another tissue from the box.

'The nurse looked a bit shocked. Then she said that I should get you to come in as soon as possible. I told her that we did not get on too well but she said it was our only real hope. They could force-feed Minty but that approach rarely works. Afterwards, the girls go back to starving themselves. Someone has to persuade Minty to stop what she's doing to herself or she will die.'

'She won't die,' said Polly. 'I'll help in any way I can.'

Adele squeezed Polly's hand tighter than ever. 'Thank you. You've been so kind and I, well, I know I don't deserve it.'

Polly said nothing.

'I never thought you'd forgive me,' said Adele. 'It's been eating me up for years.'

'Me too,' said Polly and she put her arm round Adele and kissed her. As she did so, a great weight seemed to lift from her mind and she felt suddenly almost deliriously happy.

But by the time Polly got to Minty's ward, she was

sick with apprehension. Poor Minty. She only hoped that there was something she could do to help.

Minty was asleep and Polly put down her bag by the bed. It was extremely heavy but it was as well she had packed everything into her carry-on luggage or her bags would still be at Heathrow.

The little girl's breathing was so light that it was almost undiscernable. Her face was thin and very pale and even her hair seemed to have lost its colour. She looked like a ten-year-old girl going on eighty.

The ward was decorated with very amateur paintings and the words from the nursery rhyme 'Monday's Child is fair of face.' Above Minty's bed was Thursday's Child – with far to go.

'Best to let her sleep for a bit,' said the nurse and Polly sat down and surveyed the piles of cards, soft toys, toiletries and letters that littered her niece's bedside table. It was clear that Minty still had a lot of friends.

Adele was in the lobby making a call from the phone box since mobiles were strictly forbidden in the hospital. She said she needed to cancel the rest of her meetings for the week.

There was a little boy of about eight or nine in the bed next to Minty. He had a leg plastered and in traction but he was smiling.

Polly smiled back.

'You missed Boz,' said the boy.

'Sorry?'

'Boz. He's the funny man. He comes round at lunchtime sometimes and tells us jokes and makes things with balloons.'

'Really?'

408

'He's brilliant. The nurses say he does a better job of making us better than the doctors do. But he doesn't give us any medicine. Do you think that can be right?'

'I'm sure it's right.' Polly thought of Ned and the clown-doctoring work he was doing. How could she ever have been so blind about him?

'What does he look like?' she asked.

'Who, Boz?'

Polly nodded.

'Well, he has a big red nose and enormous feet and his trousers are too short for him.'

Polly smiled. She wanted to ask if he was the most gorgeous, most handsome man in the world but managed to restrain herself.

'Hello,' said a voice behind her. Polly turned and came face to face with her mother.

'Hi, Mum, sit down,' said Polly, getting to her feet and kissing Sue.

'How is she?' asked Sue.

'We've just arrived,' said Polly as Adele joined them.

'Why don't you two go downstairs and get some lunch?' said Adele. 'I'll stay here.'

'I'm happy to wait,' said Polly.

'No, I'd like to be here when she wakes. I want to tell her what a wonderful surprise I have for her,' said Adele.

'What's that?' asked Sue.

'Polly, of course,' said Adele.

Sue stared at Polly and then at Adele.

'Come on, Mum,' said Polly. 'We won't be long,' she added to Adele.

*

Polly ate a tuna and mayo baguette in the cafe but her mother only had coffee.

'I'm so worried about Araminta,' said Sue. 'I can't think what is wrong with her, why on earth she won't eat.'

Polly sipped her Diet Coke. 'They say anorexia is all about problems with your mother. It's a wonder I'm not in the same condition myself.'

'I don't know what you've got to complain about,' said Sue. 'You had a good childhood. You never wanted for anything.'

Except love, Polly wanted to say, but it was not the right time. It would never be the right time.

'And the same goes for Araminta,' continued Sue. 'Adele has given her everything. She has that new Play-Station thing and one of those trendy little scooters.'

'It's not about things,' said Polly.

'What is it about then?'

'It's care and attention and just being there. I know Adele loves Minty but she's been so busy.'

'She's got an important job,' said Sue. 'She's just been promoted to the main board.'

'Exactly,' said Polly. 'But Minty doesn't understand all that. All she knows is that she doesn't get enough of her mum. I suppose she's angry with Adele.'

'Angry? What right has she to be angry?'

Polly looked at her mother, whose face had gone rigid with tension. Polly knew she was thinking about John.

'Can't you forgive him, Mum?'

Sue shook her head. 'Never.'

'Relationships do break up sometimes,' said Polly

410

'This woman Rosie turned up and it was clearly something special. I suppose he felt he had to go for it.'

Sue sniffed. 'It's not just that woman.'

'What is it then?' Polly wanted to unwrap her chocolate muffin but decided to wait.

'There were other things, years ago,' said Sue. She took a sip of coffee.

'What?'

'I've never told either you or Adele but I think it's time to do so.' Sue put down her cup. 'Just so that you know what a bastard your father really is.'

Polly felt sick. She was not sure she wanted Sue to go on but her mother needed to speak.

'Do you remember your Aunt Julia?' she asked.

'Yes, of course. She left me some money when she died.'

'Exactly. Your father had an affair with her.'

'When?'

'Years ago – before we were married. I thought it was all over or I never would have married him, of course, but afterwards I found out that he was still seeing her.'

Polly felt cold and shivered.

'He got her pregnant – at exactly the same time I was pregnant. Amazing, don't you think?' Sue gave a hard little laugh.

Polly said nothing.

'Mum was a midwife and so we both had our babies at home. Two daughters, two granddaughters, born within twenty-four hours of each other.'

Polly could hardly believe her ears. 'You mean—'

'My father had the idea. He just said, "Wouldn't it

have been better if our Susan had had twins and Julia's poor little bastard had died?" John told me that later.'

'What?'

'It's true, I swear it.'

Polly stared at her mother – or was Sue really her stepmother, her aunt? It was too much to take in.

'Why did you agree?' she asked.

'There was a lot of pressure and then as soon as Julia was well enough she just disappeared. She didn't come home for years and so I suppose I was stuck with you.'

'Thanks,' said Polly.

'Sorry,' said Sue. 'I didn't mean it like that. You were a lovely baby and I did love you – I still do. But it was hard.'

'I can imagine.'

'I only got through it by swearing that I'd never forgive him, that one day I'd get even with him. I wanted him to have a miserable marriage. It makes me sick to see him happy with that woman.'

'Aunt Julia was my mother,' said Polly, trying to register the information.

Sue nodded. 'Only biologically,' she added, reaching out for Polly's hand. But Polly put both hands to her head.

All her life she had seen her mother – she would *never* stop thinking of Sue as her mother – as the nagging wife, the 'baddie', and her father as the good guy, the stoical, long-suffering husband. Now it was clear that Sue had been horribly wronged by John. It was no wonder that her mother had found it hard to forgive him. Polly only wished she had known all this earlier; it would have explained so much.

Sue put her arm round Polly. No one in the hospita

cafe seemed to think it unusual for two women to be hugging and crying. These things happen in hospitals, thought Polly, as her brain grappled with the shocking information she had received.

'John insisted on choosing your name and I chose Adele's,' said Sue.

'So you had no part in the Pamela decision?' said Polly, looking up.

Sue shook her head.

'Well,' smiled Polly. 'At least that's one thing I can't blame you for.'

She squeezed Sue's hand. She felt suddenly angry with her father, betrayed. She realised that she had almost worshipped him all her life but he too had behaved appallingly. She would speak to him, she would get to the bottom of the whole story, but she knew now that she would not, could not, hold it against him forever. After all, if she could forgive Adele, surely she could forgive anyone?

When they got back to the ward Minty was awake. She was propped up in bed and was smiling. It was still the same smile Polly remembered from her niece's earliest days.

They all talked for a short while but Minty tired easily so Adele suggested that she might like some time on her own with Aunt Polly.

'Oh yes, please,' said the little girl.

Sue and Adele left and then Polly sat on the bed beside Minty and cradled her in her arms.

'Dear, dear Minty,' she said. 'We all love you so.'

'It's wonderful to see you,' said Minty. 'I was worried that Mummy wouldn't let you come.'

Polly laughed. 'You wouldn't believe the effort your mother made to get me here.'

They talked for a while and then a nurse appeared.

'Would you like a yoghurt, Minty?' she asked. 'You can have one too, if you like,' she added to Polly.

Minty started to shake her head but Polly got up and went over to the nurse's trolley.

'Let's see what they've got. Hmmm, two banana yoghurts, one apricot and, er, one strawberry.'

'Strawberry's best,' said Minty.

'It's my favourite too,' said Polly. 'But I'll let you have it if you're going to be very nice to me.'

Minty smiled. It was exactly what Polly used to say when she was little.

'OK,' she said.

'Come on,' said Polly, picking up a spoon. 'You're still my little baby. Let me feed you.'

Minty started to retreat into her pillows.

'Your mummy says you won't eat. And yet you used to be the only girlfriend I had who could eat more than me. You could eat a whole portion of fish and chips and then force down chocolate chip ice cream too. What on earth am I going to do now?'

Minty smiled but looked hesitant. 'Mummy's wrong.'

'How do you mean?' Polly sat down on the bed again and peeled the top off the yoghurt.

'She said I didn't eat a thing on the holiday in Paris but that's not true. I licked a stamp for the postcard I sent to you and stamps are 5.9 calories each, you know.'

'Sweetheart,' said Polly. 'You don't need to worry about calories, let alone count them in decimals. Do you remember you used to say you wanted to grow up and look exactly like me? And that was when I was at my fattest.'

'I still do,' said Minty.

'Then you've got a long way to go. We'd better get started now.' Polly dipped her spoon in the yoghurt.

'I can't,' said Minty.

'Why not?'

'Mummy,' said Minty, tears forming in her eyes. 'Mummy only cares about me when she's worried about me. If I get better, she'll forget all about me again.'

'Your mummy loves you very much.'

Minty shook her head. 'She doesn't. She doesn't love anyone and that's why no one loves her back.'

'Don't they?'

'Even Da— I mean Charles – has got fed up with her.'

Charles? Polly had hardly thought about Charles for days. He had stopped calling and she presumed he preferred to forfeit his coat rather than tackle the subject of Plump-bum's letter.

'He's gone off to stay with Uncle Hobbit. He went last night. I suppose Mummy will blame me.'

'No, I'm sure she won't,' said Polly. There was a time when she would have felt triumphant that Charles had left Adele but all she felt was sadness, sadness that she and Adele had both wasted so much time on him.

'Even you don't love Mummy,' said Minty. 'Don't say you do because I know how angry she makes you.'

'She does make me angry,' said Polly. 'And I really thought once that I didn't love her, that I might even

415

hate her, but hating people is no fun. I realised that she'd made mistakes, lots of them and big ones, but we all make mistakes and it's not nice if someone won't forgive you. Particularly if you're really sorry.'

'Is Mummy sorry?'

'Yes,' said Polly. 'I think she really is.' She held the spoon up to Minty's lips. 'Remember the game we used to play? One for you and one for Mr Bogeyman?'

Minty nodded.

'One for you,' said Polly. Minty opened her mouth and took the spoonful.

'One for Mr Bogeyman,' said Minty. Polly took a spoonful.

'One for Miss Poo-face,' said Polly. Minty laughed and took the next spoonful.

'One for Mrs Jelly Pants.'

'Master Dog Breath.'

'Sir Sausage Nose.'

'And the last one is for Mummy,' said Polly. Minty took the spoon from Polly's hand and licked it clean. The yoghurt was finished.

'For Mummy,' repeated Minty.

Chapter Forty

When Sue and Adele returned, Adele looked paler than ever and Polly guessed that Sue had told her the same story that she had also just heard.

Adele squeezed Polly's arm and the two sisters shared a glance of mutual astonishment at the news they had just received. But there was no time to talk about it yet.

Adele went over to Minty and kissed her.

'I've eaten two whole yoghurts and had some Coke,' said Minty.

'That's fantastic,' said Adele, looking up at Polly.

'I was going to have the apricot one too but Aunt Polly beat me to it.'

'It's true,' laughed Polly.

Minty smiled. 'I think I'll sleep for a bit now – until supper.'

The three women took the opportunity to go for a short walk. As soon as they stepped outside, Polly checked for messages on her mobile phone. She was hoping that Ned might have called but there was nothing.

'I can't believe you kept things secret for so long,' said Adele to Sue.

'It seemed for the best – until I knew he'd left me for good.' It was drizzling with rain and so they did a couple of circuits of the car park and then sheltered by the hospital entrance.

'I can't believe Dad asked you to do that,' said Polly.

'Well, I suppose it was my choice too. Since Julia had disappeared, it really was the only thing to do.'

'Poor you.'

'No, not really,' said Sue. 'After I'd got over the initial shock of it all, I enjoyed looking after you, bringing the two of you up like twins.'

'But I can hardly blame you for not forgiving Dad,' said Adele.

Polly leapt as her phone started to ring. The number that came up was familiar but it was not Ned's.

'It's Hubert,' she said, putting the phone to her ear. 'Hello?'

A man's voice answered. But it was not Hubert. 'Polly? It's Charles.'

Polly gasped and pressed the phone close against her ear. It was raining harder now but she walked back towards the car park so that Adele and Sue could not hear.

'What do you want?'

'You know exactly why I'm calling,' said Charles in a tone that sounded as though he was just managing to hold back from adding, 'You bitch.'

'Your coat?'

'No, not my fucking coat. Although I suppose it's connected.'

'To what?'

'To the crazy little stunt you pulled this morning.'

'What stunt?'

'Come off it, Polly. It could only have been you.'

'I don't understand,' said Polly. She pulled her jacket tight around her chest.

'I was doing a live interview with the BBC outside our offices when they arrived.'

'Who arrived?'

'It was so embarrassing. Obscene, in fact, and it blew our chances of having the interview broadcast on the Children's Channel – when we had really wanted to promote Orgie Porgies.'

'Orgie Porgies? What the hell are you talking about?'

'Green Baby's new organic sweets. My boss is livid.'

Polly laughed. 'I'm sorry, I don't know what you're going on about but it serves you right. You should be here with Minty not having Orgie Porgies with anyone.'

'Umbrella?' Polly spun round and came face to face with Adele, who was holding an umbrella above the two of them. 'I've got to go,' she said and flicked off the phone.

'Is Hubert OK?' asked Adele.

'It wasn't Hubert.'

'Charles?'

'No. Well, yes.'

'He didn't ask to speak with me?'

Polly shook her head.

'He left last night,' said Adele.

'I know. Minty told me.'

'I suppose, on top of everything else, I should be distraught about it. But I just feel relieved.'

'Relieved?'

'He's a compulsive womaniser. I know he's been unfaithful with—'

'Not with me.'

'No, not with you,' said Adele. 'But there were others – he was totally unscrupulous.'

'Are you sure?'

'I came home once and found him fucking the nanny – on my desk. He's always enjoyed making love in dangerous places, where he might just get caught out.'

'They were doing it in your study? The room where Oliver Johns—'

'Yes,' said Adele. 'There were some sharp scissors on the desk and I was tempted to stab him in the back with them but then I remembered what you had said.'

'What?'

'About that room,' smiled Adele. 'And how I had said you were superstitious and that lightning never strikes twice in the same place.'

Polly said nothing.

'Those words may have saved Charles's life,' laughed Adele. 'I couldn't bear the thought of you being proved right.'

Polly put her arm round her sister, who had now started to cry.

'I forgave him the first time he cheated on me,' said Adele. 'But he couldn't stay faithful. That's why I refused to have another baby. I didn't want him to leave me like Bunk did and then I would be a single mum with two children and each with a different father.'

'And to think how Charles made it seem that you were being cruel by not having a baby.'

Adele wiped her eyes as she saw her mother hurrying over to them in the pouring rain.

'Come on you two,' called Sue. 'I just got a message from the ward. Araminta is awake and – wait for it – she's hungry again.'

Around nine o'clock, the nurse turned out Minty's lights. She had eaten a small bowl of soup, half a bread roll and a mini Magnum ice cream. It didn't seem much to Polly but the nurse assured them it was an enormous meal.

'If she eats any more she will almost certainly sick it up,' said the nurse. 'Her stomach has shrunk so much.'

They kissed Minty and said goodnight.

'Do you want me to make the camp bed up for you again?' the nurse asked Adele.

'You go home, Mummy,' said Minty. 'I'm fine now – really. And you look exhausted.'

'I'll stay with her,' offered Sue.

'That would be great, Granny,' said Minty and Polly smiled at the amazing transformation in the child. She really seemed back to her old self.

'Are you sure, darling?' said Adele.

Minty nodded.

'I'll be back first thing in the morning,' said Adele, hugging her little girl. 'I love you.'

'I love you too,' said Minty.

Polly and Adele drove down Archway, under Suicide Bridge, and back towards Islington.

'Let's go for a drink,' said Adele. 'I'll dump the car in Noel Road and we'll walk somewhere.'

'OK,' said Polly. 'But aren't you exhausted? It's been

an incredible day – what with Mum's revelations and everything.'

'Exactly,' said Adele. 'Which is just why I think we both need a drink – or several.'

It was unlike Adele but Polly had had so many surprises that day that she was no longer sure of anything.

They wandered along Upper Street. There were couples everywhere, arm in arm and kissing.

'It's Valentine's Day,' said Adele. 'I'd completely forgotten.'

'Yes,' said Polly. 'We must look a right pair of sad old bags.'

'I feel happier than I've felt for a long time.'

'Me too.'

'Thank you so much, Polly, for everything. I really never thought you'd forgive me – I've treated you so badly. I don't deserve you to be so kind.'

'No. It's been an unhappy time for both of us.'

'I'm really sorry,' said Adele, starting to cry again. 'Particularly what I did to you when I stole Charles. It was unbelievably cruel and selfish. I've felt so bad about it for years. I'm very sorry, Polly.'

'I know you are,' said Polly. 'I should have forgiven you ages ago.'

Adele wiped her eyes.

'Come on,' said Polly. 'Let's eat – I'm starving.'

All the restaurants were packed but they eventually got a table for two in Pizza Express. As Polly sat down, her phone began to ring. She went to the door to answer it.

'Hello, Sheila,' she said. 'You must have heard about me missing the flight? I'm so sorry.'

There was a lot of noise as people pushed past Polly into the restaurant. They were talking loudly and laughing and she could hardly hear what Sheila was saying.

'What? Are you sure?' she yelled into her phone.

When she got back to the table, Adele had ordered a bottle of champagne.

'Are we celebrating?' asked Polly.

'Absolutely.'

'Minty? Us?'

'Yes, of course. But something else as well?'

'Yes,' said Polly. 'Somehow or other I seem to have got that job in New York.'

'Brilliant. I could tell from your face as you came in.'

Polly stared at Adele. 'You had something to do with it, didn't you?'

Adele shrugged.

'Sheila told me,' said Polly, 'that a good friend of Kate's – someone she trusted completely – had called to explain that something very important and personal had come up that meant I had to stay in London for a few days. You know the Chief Executive of MPC, don't you?'

'She's been an active client for a few years,' said Adele.

'This person said that I was the most promising journalist in London and Kate would be mad not to hire me at once.'

Adele poured Polly a glass of champagne. 'Congratulations. I didn't lie.'

'Thanks, Adele.'

They ordered their food and talked about the news

they had received from their mother. It had been a great shock for both of them but they agreed that it did not really matter.

'You'll always be my twin,' said Adele.

Then their food arrived and they ate hungrily without speaking. It reminded Polly of the times she had spent with Zeta when there had been no need to talk. It had just been a comfort to be with someone who cared, who understood.

'If it hadn't been for those medical students,' said Polly as she put down her knife and fork, 'the security men would have had you at once – before you even had a chance to get to me.'

'I know,' said Adele.

'What do you mean? You sound as though you planned it?'

Adele laughed. 'Let's just say I gave them a sizeable donation.'

'How much?'

'I signed a covenant for a thousand pounds a year.'

'They must have been amazed.'

'I explained my problem to them and I told them I only needed them to hold the security guys off for five minutes.'

'You are amazing,' said Polly. 'You never cease to impress me.'

'Thanks.'

The waitress cleared their plates and brought coffee.

They talked about Minty and how encouraging it was that Polly had managed to get her to eat something.

Polly felt wonderful to be talking to her sister

again, really talking to her, without a wall of hate between them. Nonetheless, throughout their conversation, Polly was constantly thinking of Ned. She felt miserable as she told Adele exactly what had happened that morning at the Tate Modern and how she now realised that she had loved Ned for a long time.

'I can't believe I've been such a fool.'

'And you've never realised that Ned is in love with you?'

'No. Is he?'

'Madly. You must be crazy not to have noticed.'

'I think I am,' said Polly. 'Hubert said the same thing but I suppose I was just too obsessed with Ch—'

'Don't worry. You can say it.'

'I've been so stupid.'

'No,' said Adele. 'It was all my fault. I did a really dreadful thing when I stole Charles from you that day but I paid dearly in the end. He's the sort of man who will only ever be in love with himself. You know, in all the years we were married, he never said that he loved me.'

'Really? I thought you were crazy for each other.'

'It was just sex. Charles was only ever interested in sex. He had no idea about love.'

'I've been such an idiot,' said Polly. 'I was so jealous of you, so desperate to get my own back on you, that I've ended up ruining my own life in the process.'

'There's no need to be quite so despondent,' said Adele. 'Perhaps you can make things up with Ned yet?'

Polly shook her head. 'He thinks I slept with Charles a couple of weeks ago – when you were in Paris.'

'How ridiculous.'

Polly looked up. 'How can you be so sure I didn't?'

'Well, I'm sure that Charles would have tried it on but,' Adele paused and took Polly's hand, 'I know you, Polly. I know that, when it really came to it, you would not do be able to do it.'

'You're right. That's exactly what happened.'

'The thing is that you're too nice,' said Adele. 'I've always been so jealous of you for that.'

'Really?'

'Yes. Sometimes I've felt quite hopeless when I see how popular you are and, no matter what I achieve, I shall never be like you.'

Polly laughed. 'I could never imagine you wanting to be like me.'

'Shall I call Ned?' asked Adele.

'What are you going to say?'

But before Adele could answer, Polly's phone started to ring.

'I'll pop outside and try to get Ned,' said Adele, getting up.

Polly answered her phone.

'Hello, darling. It's Hubert. Happy Valentine's Day.'

'Thanks,' said Polly. 'It's not been a particularly romantic one so far but it's certainly been eventful. What have you been up to?'

'Well, I went to Zeta's this evening,' said Hubert, 'and she gave me this most amazing aromatic Indian head massage. I felt almost stoned by the time I left.'

Polly laughed.

'Bernard and I have taken Zeta out for a drink in the West End. Do you want to join us?'

'Bernard?'

'Yes. We've become, well, rather good friends lately.'
Polly thought she knew what Hubert meant but she also knew that he would not say more.

'I'm with Adele in Islington. Why don't you both come over here?'

'OK,' said Hubert. They spoke for a few minutes about Minty and then Polly told Hubert where exactly she and Adele were and switched off the phone.

Seconds later it rang again.

'And to think you were always moaning about how unpopular you were,' said Adele, who had returned to her seat.

This time it was Den.

'I couldn't resist ringing,' he said.

'Why?' asked Polly. 'Are you a sad old man in search of a Valentine?'

'Well, certainly that. But I meant about Charles – has he called you yet?'

Polly's face froze. 'I told you Den, last time I saw you. Charles is an absolute bastard—' She suddenly remembered Adele and stopped.

'Don't worry,' said her sister. 'Feel free to slag him off as much as you like.'

'Yes, yes, of course,' said Den. 'And I remember the letter you showed me too.'

'So?'

'Hasn't he called you? Isn't he hopping mad?'

'What?'

'Didn't he think it was you?'

Suddenly the penny dropped and Polly burst out laughing.

'Christ, it was you, wasn't it? What exactly did you do to him?'

But Den insisted on coming over and telling her and Adele in detail what he had done.

By the time he arrived, Hubert, Bernard and Zeta were already there too.

'I can't believe it,' laughed Polly. 'You had a special six-foot helium balloon made in the shape of a giant willy?'

Den nodded. 'I hope he keeps the damn thing. It was pretty bloody spectacular.'

'I can imagine,' said Hubert. 'And you say it had *Plump-Horn* written along it.'

They all fell about laughing.

'I would love to have seen his face,' said Adele, pushing away her champagne glass and pouring some fizzy water.

'Aren't you drinking any more?' asked Polly.

'I've had enough,' said Adele as her own phone started to ring. 'If this is who I think it is we may have some driving to do.'

They all stayed quiet while Adele screwed up her face and tried to hear the caller.

'Frankie?' she said. 'Is that you, Frankie?'

Polly's stomach contracted. It had to be Ned's brother.

'Could you put Frankie on, please?' She covered the mouthpiece with her hand and looked at Polly. 'It's his girlfriend – Sarita.'

'Ned's?' whispered Polly, hardly able to speak.

'No, silly, Frankie's,' said Adele, putting the phone back to her lips. Polly could hardly believe her ears. What did Adele mean? Was Sarita Frankie's girlfriend or Ned's?

'Damn,' said Adele, still talking on the phone.

428

'What do you mean Sarita is Frankie's girlfriend?' persisted Polly. Adele signalled for her to be quiet but drew a heart crossed with an arrow on the paper tablecloth – with Frankie and Sarita at opposite ends of the arrow – and wrote '100% certain' underneath.

'When do you say he left?' she said into the phone.

There was a pause while Adele nodded, frowned and scribbled some more on to the tablecloth. It looked like directions. 'And you're sure he'll be there?'

Adele thanked Frankie and said goodbye.

'What was all that about?'

Adele smiled. 'Come on. If we get going now, you might just get a Valentine tonight after all.'

She got up, ripped half the tablecloth away and picked up her car keys.

'Polly and I are off to Scarborough,' she announced.

'Adele, are you mad?' said Polly.

'No, are you?' Adele sat down again next to Polly. 'Look,' she said. 'Ned goes off to LA tomorrow night and Frankie says he has no idea when he will be back. He's just gone home to say goodbye to his parents. It's your only chance.'

'But, Adele, you must be exhausted – and it will be a nine-or ten-hour drive there and back.'

'It's the least I can do after all the things you've done for me.'

'Hang on,' said Den. 'I've got my driver parked round the corner. He'll take us.'

'What?' said Polly.

'That's very kind,' said Adele. 'Are you sure?'

'Absolutely fucking certain,' said Den. 'I realised a long time ago that Polly was never going to succumb to my charms but I'm very fond of her. I never thought I could be friends with a woman without wanting to get my leg over the whole time.'

Polly laughed.

'No, really, Polly,' said Den. 'You're a great girl and you deserve some happiness – so let's get going.'

'Well, OK, if you're sure,' said Adele. 'It's really kind of you, Den.'

Den beamed at Adele. 'Glad to be of service,' he said and Polly could see the old goat's brain begin to assess his chances with Adele.

'And to think that Polly always described you as though you were some kind of monster.'

Den laughed. 'You should hear the way she described you.' He took Adele by the arm and Polly followed almost as if in a trance. She could still hardly believe the news that Sarita was Frankie's girlfriend. Perhaps she did still have a chance with Ned?

'Come on. Let's go,' said Adele.

'Go on,' said Hubert. 'I'll sort out the bill.'

Polly looked at Zeta and Bernard who were both smiling and nodding their heads. Everyone was being so nice, she felt quite overwhelmed.

'Yes. Come on, Polly,' said Adele. 'Remember, I have to get back to London by tomorrow morning for Minty.'

They left the restaurant. Den bundled Polly and Adele into the back of the new Jag he had just bought and his driver got a blanket to put over them.

'Now, no tricks tonight, Den, OK?' said Polly. 'If I fall asleep I don't want to wake up in Timbuktu.'

Den laughed. 'Don't worry. Real life with you is enough of a joke anyway.'

The driver started the car and, like kids snuggled up together on the back seat, Polly and Adele were soon fast asleep and hurtling northwards along the M1.

Chapter Forty-One

The roads were empty and so they travelled fast and were approaching Scarborough at around three in the morning.

Den woke Polly and Adele for instructions to Ned's house.

'I can't get them all up in the middle of the night,' said Polly.

'You'll have to,' said Adele, struggling to unfold the paper tablecloth and decipher her scribbles. 'After all, it's an emergency.'

Polly's heart was beating fast. What if Ned told her to go away? What if he refused to see her? They would have come all this way on a total wild goose chase.

Adele seemed to read her mind. 'Don't worry,' she said. 'He can hardly turn you out on the streets in the middle of the night.'

Polly was not so sure. Why had Ned let her think that Sarita was his girlfriend? Surely, only so that she would think he was committed to someone else. He obviously did not want her any more.

There was a full moon and it was quite bright as Den's car slunk through the streets of small moder houses. It took a while to find the Butlers' house but they got there eventually.

'We'll wait until you're safely inside,' said Adele.

'Oh, Adele, don't leave me,' said Polly.

'Good God, you don't want a chaperone at your age, do you?'

'Just come with me to the door.'

Adele and Den got out of the car and all three made their way across the small drive.

Den rang on the bell at once. Polly was so nervous she thought her heart had stopped beating.

'No point in hanging about,' said Den. 'It's bloody cold out here.'

There was no response until Den had rung the bell several times and started shouting at the upstairs windows.

Eventually a light came on and footsteps sounded on the stairs inside.

'Who is it?' called a female voice. It had to be Ned's mother.

'It's Polly Taylor, Mrs Butler, er, Margaret,' stammered Polly. This was dreadful, she thought. The poor woman would not even remember who she was. 'I'm a friend of Ned's,' she added through the letter box. 'Remember, I borrowed your girdle once.'

'For God's sake,' boomed Den. 'Out of the way.' He pushed Polly to one side.

'Mrs Butler,' he said. 'This is Den Christie – Editor of the *Daily Globe*.'

'Oh no – it's the papers again,' they heard Margaret say. Then, more loudly, she added, 'He's not here. I'm sorry my son's not here.'

Den, Adele and Polly all looked at each other.

'But Frankie said he would definitely be here,' said Adele.

'He's not here,' repeated Margaret from behind the closed front door. 'So go away, go away at once or I'll call the police.'

Den and Adele started to back away but Polly stayed. She heard someone else moving inside the house and then she heard that wonderful, familiar voice.

'What is it, Mum? What's going on?'

'It's the papers. Frankie must have done something indecent again in Trafalgar Square.'

'Are you sure?'

'He's there, he is there,' cried Polly.

'He's not, he's not,' yelled Margaret.

Then suddenly the door swung open and Ned stood there. He was wearing striped pyjama bottoms and no top. His shoulders were broad and muscular and his face, though heavy with sleep, was as handsome as ever.

'Polly,' he said.

'Ned.'

'What is it?' said Margaret. 'What do these people want? I tell you, Frankie isn't here.'

'They're not looking for Frankie,' said Ned.

'Can I come in?' asked Polly.

'Of course,' said Ned. 'What about them?' He looked across at Den and Adele who had retreated as far the gate.

'Oh, no thanks very much,' said Adele. 'We have to go.'

Polly glanced back and saw Den take Adele by the arm and help her into the car. She smiled as she saw

434

him get in beside her and pull the blanket over the two of them. Good old Den, he would give it his best shot, she thought.

Then she turned back to Ned. Neither of them knew quite what to say or do, so Margaret bustled them towards the kitchen.

'I'll put the kettle on,' she said.

When Margaret had placed a mug of hot sweet tea in front of both of them she left them to it.

'This is a surprise,' said Ned.

'I heard you were leaving and had to see you before you went.'

'Thanks.'

'You must be delighted about the script being accepted. It's very exciting.'

'Yes. It's been a long wait.'

Polly made him tell her about the contract and how the film was going to be produced and when.

But soon they had finished their tea and fell silent.

Eventually Ned stood up. 'Shall we take a walk down to the beach?'

It was still the middle of the night but Polly got to her feet at once.

A short while later, they were walking side by side on the cold wet sand, being careful not to touch each other.

'I'm sorry I upset you,' said Polly.

'I'm sorry I got so angry,' said Ned.

They walked on. It was just getting light and a little colour was beginning to filter back into the scene. Polly stopped and picked up a stone.

'Look,' she said. 'This stone is almost identical to the one I found when I was here last, all those years ago. The bloodstone.'

'The stone you kept to remind yourself how much you wanted to murder Adele.'

'I don't want to murder her any more.' Polly slipped the new stone into her pocket. 'I'll take this one back for Minty – she always loved the one I kept on my bedside table.'

'Do you mean you've forgiven Adele, at last?'

'Yes. In fact, I'm very grateful to her really. I know now that if I'd stayed with Charles I would have been very unhappy.'

Ned stopped and Polly turned to face him.

'I don't love Charles and I don't think I've loved him for a long time,' said Polly. 'I saw it that night when he wanted me to go to bed with him and Adele was away. I went back to Noel Road with him but I couldn't do it.'

'I'm sorry I didn't believe you this morning.'

'How did you know I was lying about not going back to his house?'

'I followed you,' said Ned. 'It sounds really shabby but I had to know. I stood outside and saw you go in. It was agony waiting for the lights to go on and when they didn't for over fifteen minutes, I had to assume the worst.'

'It took some time to convince him I wasn't going to.'

'I can imagine.'

'I thought I wanted to, at first, but then I realised that I only wanted to sleep with him to hurt Adele and that was pathetic.'

436

'I'd been trying to tell you that for so long.'

'I know. I've been so stubborn and stupid.'

Ned put his hands on Polly's shoulders. 'Adele told me you might be getting a job in New York.'

'I've got it.'

Ned's hands tensed and he forced a smile. 'Well done.'

Polly put her hands on Ned's face and she felt him shiver. 'Ned,' she said. 'I've loved you for so long and never known it. Will you ever forgive me?'

Ned took her close in his arms and kissed her. It was just as good as the kiss he had given her before but this time there were real waves crashing on the shore behind them.

'I couldn't live if I didn't,' he said.

They kissed more and then walked on, Polly wrapped up against Ned's side.

'George's will just be opening,' said Ned, looking at his watch. 'Let's get some hot chocolate there.'

They sat at the same table they had before and the picture of Kevin Stanick was still on the wall above it.

'It won't be long until you have your picture on this wall with George,' said Polly.

'And with you? Do you remember he said he wanted you in it too?'

'He said "with your wife".'

'Exactly.'

'Oh, Ned – you can't mean that. I thought you never wanted anything to do with the C-word and all that?'

'I changed my mind. You don't have exclusive rights to getting things wrong, you know.'

Polly laughed.

'I love you,' said Ned.

'I love you too.'

They kissed again. There was no one in the cafe apart from George and he was being careful not to watch.

'Do you think we can make it work with you living on one side of the continent and me on the other?'

'No,' said Polly. There were tears running down her face. 'It's impossible.'

'You mean, you won't marry me?' said Ned.

'Of course I will. But I won't go to New York.'

'You mean you'll give up the job?'

'Yes.'

'But Adele said you really wanted it. You had been working all your life for an opportunity like this one. It was your dream come true.'

Polly smiled. 'You have a short memory. My number one dream has always been to find the right man and settle down.'

Ned took her hands and stared into her eyes. 'To think I laughed at that dream.'

'And to think I nearly gave up on it.'

They kissed some more and then went back to the beach. Some children were out there already. They were building a sandcastle right down at the water's edge even though it was bitterly cold.

'Do you remember Frankie's sand sculptures?' asked Polly.

'Of course, they were great.'

'He said then that he didn't mind them being washed away because he didn't like to hang on to thing. He liked to start again.'

'Quite a philosopher, our Frank,' laughed Ned.

Polly smiled. 'Thanks for waiting,' she said. 'But I think, at last, I'm ready to start again.'

Would I Lie to You?
Francesca Clementis

Lauren Connor doesn't usually tell lies. She's really only trying to make conversation when she meets Chris Fallon at her best-friend Stella's party. But somewhere between running out of small talk and agreeing to a date, she ends up telling a few inconsequential lies to make herself seem more likeable. Now Lauren's going to have to deal with the fall-out from her fabrications...

If that wasn't enough, she's about to get caught in the crossfire from her well-intentioned friends and relatives. But could it be that Lauren isn't the only one telling lies...?

From the bestselling author of *Big Girls Don't Cry* and *Mad About The Girls, Would I Lie To You?* is a warm, witty and intelligent comedy of errors about love, life and deception.

The Girl Can't Help It
Melissa de la Cruz

Cat McAllister is about to celebrate her 25th birthday for the fourth time. A child-actress turned fading It-girl, she's well aware that her fame is starting to lose its shine. She really should have tragically overdosed by now. Or else succumbed to some harrowing disease brought on by a steady diet of vodka-tonics and TicTacs. She's currently in danger of being consigned to that seventh circle of celebrity hell where she's just recognisable enough for people to think she's someone else. Worse still, her trust fund is running dry...

What's a girl to do? With few assets (aside from a temperature-controlled closet) and fewer talents (shopping and an encyclopaedic knowledge of *Best-Dressed Lists*) there's only one way out of B-list obscurity: to marry and marry well. Her quarry: not just Mr Right but Prince Right – New York's most eligible bachelor, Stefan of Westonia...

'Grab de la Cruz's debut and get caught up in Cat's whirlwind quest for fame, fortune and designer outlet stores'

Glamour

A SELECTION OF NOVELS AVAILABLE
FROM JUDY PIATKUS (PUBLISHERS) LIMITED

THE PRICES BELOW WERE CORRECT AT THE TIME OF GOING TO PRESS.
HOWEVER JUDY PIATKUS (PUBLISHERS) LIMITED RESERVE THE RIGHT TO
SHOW NEW RETAIL PRICES ON COVERS WHICH MAY DIFFER FROM THOSE
PREVIOUSLY ADVERTISED IN THE TEXT OR ELSEWHERE.

0 7499 3275 9	**Would I Lie To You?**	*Francesca Clementis*	£5.99
0 7499 3281 3	**The Girl Can't Help It**	*Melissa de la Cruz*	£6.99
0 7499 3252 X	**Angel**	*Kirstie Speke*	£6.99
0 7499 3248 1	**Redeeming Eve**	*Nicole Bokat*	£6.99
0 7499 3270 8	**The Urge to Jump**	*Trisha Ashley*	£5.99
0 7499 3274 0	**Nothing Ventured**	*Ann Taylor*	£6.99

All Piatkus titles are available from:

www.piatkus.co.uk

or by contacting our sales department on

0800 454816

Free postage and packing in the UK

(on orders of two books or more)